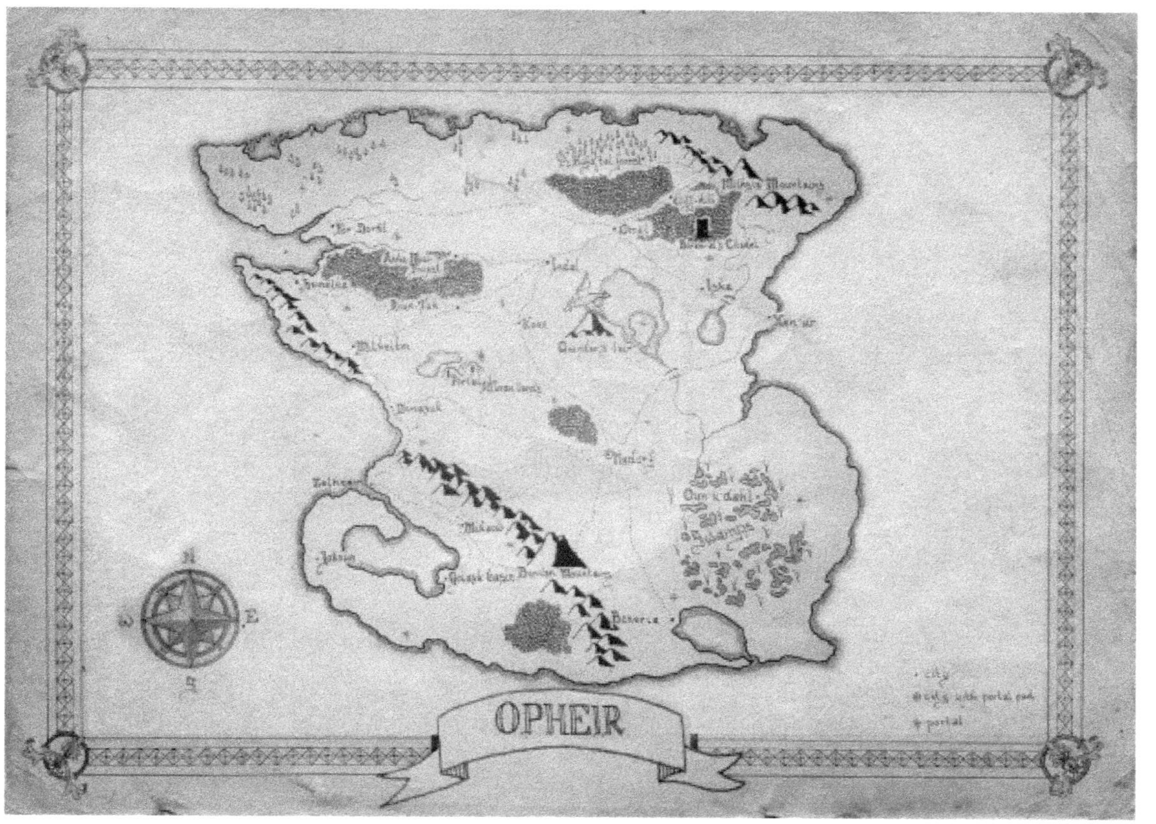

OPHEIR
• city
⊕ city with portal pad
✦ portal

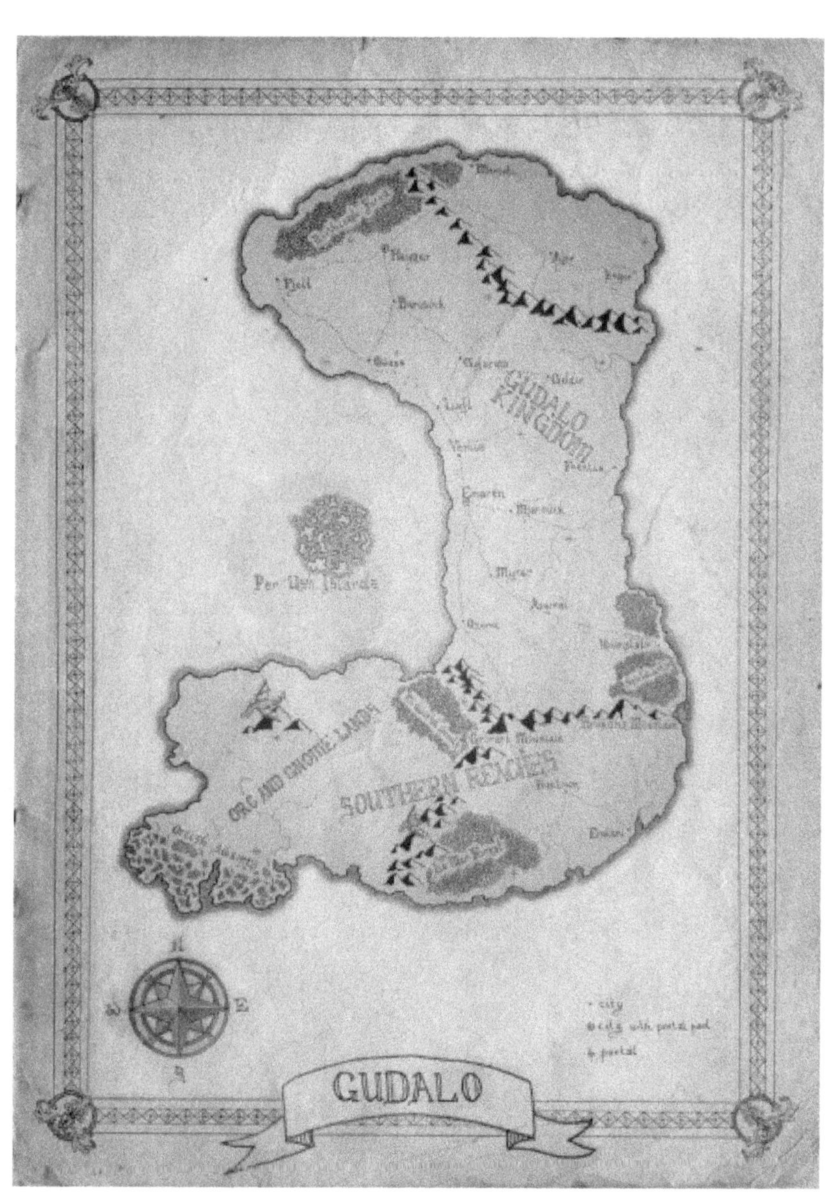

GUDALO KINGDOM
Per Ush Islands
ORC AND GNOME LANDS
SOUTHERN REACHES
city
city with portal pad
portal
N
S
E
W
GUDALO

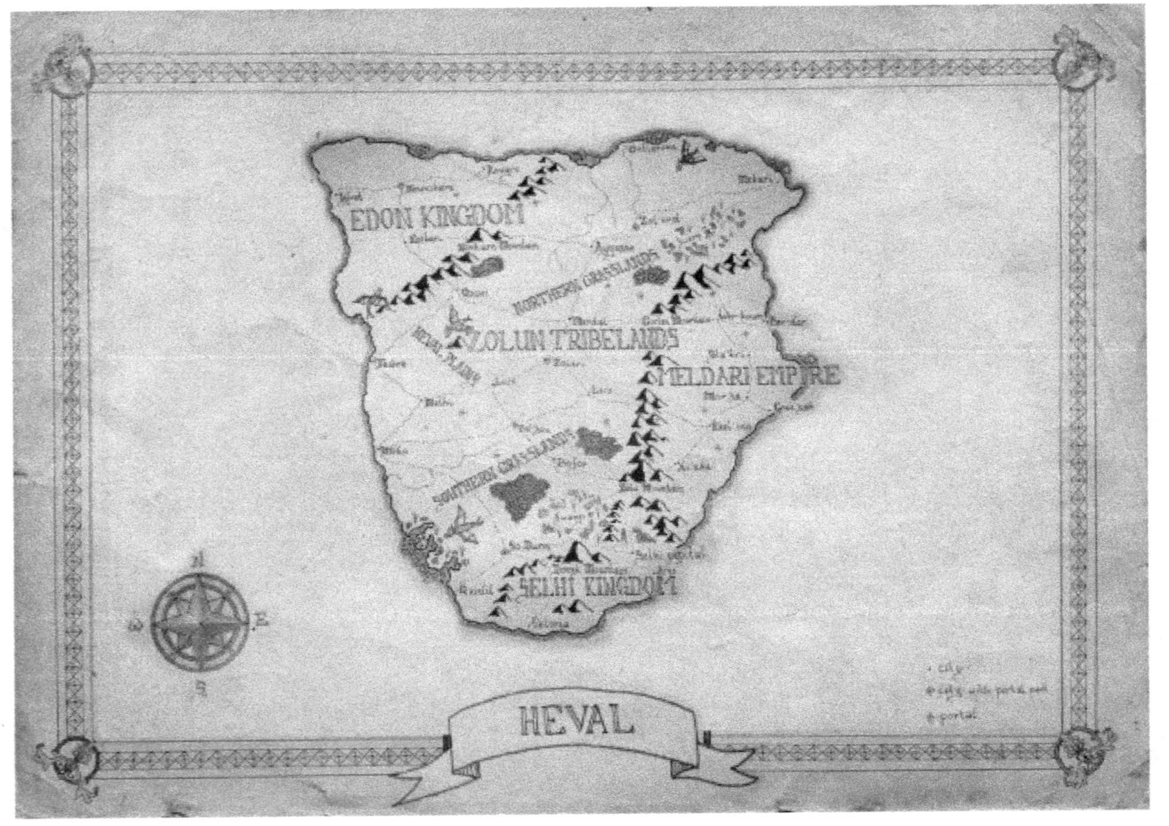
EDON KINGDOM
NORTHERN GRASSLANDS
VUOLIN TRIBELANDS
DELDARI EMPIRE
SOUTHERN GRASSLANDS
SELHI KINGDOM
HEVAL

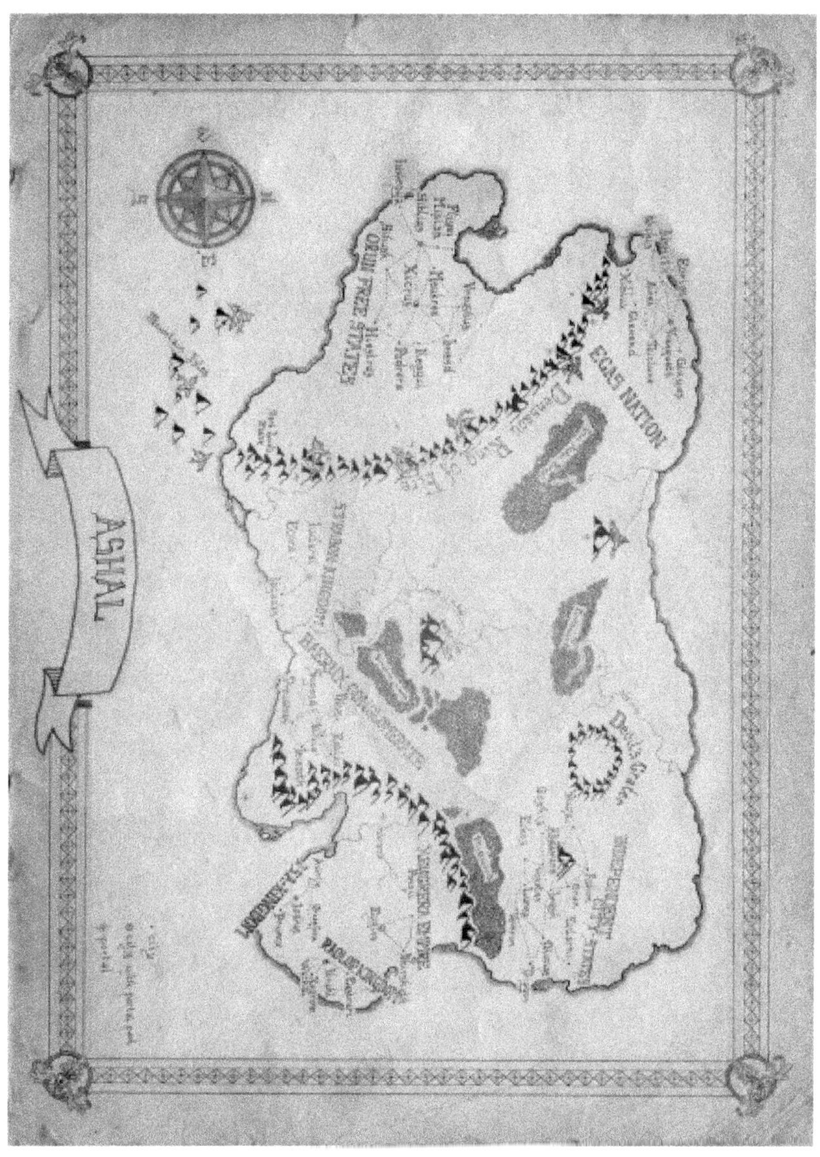
ASHAL
ODIN FREE STATES
EGAS NATION
BASIRUN GUILDTERRITORIES
Devil's Crater

MARKOLM
MARKOLM RANGE

Want a bigger map of Emerilia and the continents? Check out http://theeternalwriter.deviantart.com/

Character Sheet is located in the back of the book for reference.

Emerilia

For The Guild

Prologue

A flash of light illuminated the pitch-black room for just a moment. Runes along the walls started to light up, lines of blue light leading from the walls to a sphere in the center of the room. The sphere's surface changed; millions of runes moved across the surface, forming different circuits.

Slowly the runes started to glow with more power. Anyone from Earth would have thought it resembled an old desktop computer booting up.

Bob stood perfectly still where he had appeared in the original flash of light. Enchanted and repeating heavy ballista were pointed at him.

The walls started to reduce their glow as the sphere slowed its rapid boot-up.

A rough-looking humanoid hologram made from blue light appeared in front of the massive sphere centered in the room. Faint runes seemed to move around his form.

Just from looking at him, one could sense his weariness.

"State your identity and purpose," The fractured blue form's voice came from the walls.

"Hello, Shard. Brought these for you." Bob held out several grand soul gems.

An automaton walked into the room, took the soul gems, and left.

"Thank you, Lo'kal," Shard said, sounding relieved.

"Took on a new name, you can call me Bob."

Bob walked toward Shard; only one of the ballista followed him. Bob and Shard were good friends. Bob had been the only person Shard had talked to in several centuries. He'd also been the one keeping him active as his power sources started to fail.

"I have updated my logs," Shard's voice continued to come through the walls.

"So, my rune-made AI, how are you doing?" Bob asked. Up close, Shard looked even worse. He was undetailed, giving him an ethereal look.

"I have lost contact with the majority of Aleph facilities and I do not have sufficient power reserves to do more than routine scans. With your power, I can possibly have a few scout automatons ready to deploy and check out the cut-off facilities. I don't have the technical abilities to look over or repair my various systems. I'm sorry, but I still can't let you within my cities because of the Aleph Council's mandate to suspect all members of the Pantheon." Shard sighed and looked to Bob. "I'm powering down, Bob. I can't protect my people's home anymore."

Bob wanted to pat Shard on the shoulder to comfort him but his hand would go right through the holographic presentation of the Aleph's AI.

"Well, I need you to hold out for a bit longer. I have an idea and if it pans out, then maybe—just maybe—I can help the Aleph once again return to Emerilia," Bob said.

Shard scrutinized Bob, his eyes coming into focus. Bob saw hope and excitement shift around Shard's features. His spherical core moved erratically before it slowed down and Shard's face fell.

"Bob, I can't do anything to help them. I barely had enough power to keep myself active for more than twenty minutes before you came with those soul gems."

"Leave it up to Uncle Bob." Bob grinned and winked at the Aleph AI.

Shard smiled tiredly. "I trust you, Bob."

"Good! Then I have a few things I need to get to work on! Conserve that power for now—you'll need it later!" Bob clicked his fingers. He disappeared from Shard's hub in Alephir and re-appeared in an office.

Bob's smiling grin disappeared as he became more serious and focused. He now had the power to get the Aleph back to Emerilia, but he was bound by the rules that the Emperor had made.

He cracked his fingers and opened his interface.

"There's only one group I can think of that can help Shard start to get Alephir and the rest of the Aleph facilities back online. Now just how am I going to lure them into an Aleph facility?" Bob looked up maps, thinking through his options.

Chapter 1: Selhi Capital

Selhi wasn't as big as Nadorf, but it had almost the same amount of traffic.

"Why the hell are there so many people?" Dave asked.

"Nadorf is the only place in Opheir with a transport hub. Also, Nadorf might have one of the larger populations of other cities due to how safe it is. In Heval, there are seven cities with transport hubs. Selhi is connected to two Dwarven mountains and has two large port cities. These outlets means that goods constantly flow through the land. In addition, Selhi is the sole location for several different herbs not found anywhere else in Emerilia. Selhi Capital, often referred to as SC, might be the capital but it is by no means the largest city within the Selhi Kingdom. The port city of Valori gets that honor," Malsour said.

"Selhi makes their money trading different animal products to the Dwarves, who supply them with different forged items. They trade all across Heval. They also have strong ties with two of the five factions that make up the Markolm Empire, the continent between Heval and Ashal. The swamps and the woods give them plenty of materials to sell. Valori is not only the biggest city due to the number of traders that visit it, they are the fourth largest manufacturer of ships in Emerilia. They are only being beaten by Hoku and Melandi on Gudalo and the Olindar Port City of Ashal," Suzy said.

"Someone has been hitting the books," Dave said.

"Best to know what the different powers are doing," Suzy said, her eyes telling him that she had a few things to discuss with him. He nodded; the two of them only needed to share a glance to know what the other was thinking. Years spent within tense boardroom meetings and the knowledge that someone was listening to them had only perfected their ability to read one another.

I wonder what she has in mind. Dave dismissed it as they got to the guards who were talking and checking everyone over.

"Reason for visit?" a bored guard asked.

"Meeting up with fellow Players," Deia said.

"Affiliation?"

"Stone Raiders."

This caused a stir as the guard seemed to get some life into his bones.

"Very good to meet you all. There is an adventurer's tavern up that road, four blocks on the right. Thank you for visiting SC." The guard bowed slightly and let them pass.

"Well, it looks like Josh and the others have been working on their reputation some," Induca said.

"With big guilds like ours, it makes sense to spread a bit of goodwill around. Means more jobs," Suzy said.

"Hopefully, they have a training square," Deia said. Dave didn't miss the glance she shot his way.

Anna nodded in agreement. "Though, I think it is time for some different training, not just dual-handed."

"Come on, I'm just getting back in the groove of dual wielding axes again," Dave complained.

"That's the issue. Dual axes are good for hacking your enemy apart. If you're going to be taking hits, we need to make sure that you know how to use something else," Anna said.

Dave sighed at Deia's look. It was readily apparent there was no way that he was getting out of their clutches any time soon.

"There are a lot more races here than in Opheir," Suzy said.

"Well, Heval has many different climates—creatures of all kinds call it home. Heval and Gudalo are the highest populated continents other than Ashal, for that very reason," Induca said.

"Seems that you weren't just messing around when you were doing all of your travels," Malsour said, with a little respect in his voice

"Well, I also know the best bars in every major city with a transport hub. The best one here was the Raging Serpent." Induca smiled, ruining the moment.

Malsour just shook his head as the group continued to walk.

Dave saw lizard Demi-Humans, Humans, Dwarves, Elves, Cat-People of all kinds, and even a few Orcs.

"I thought Orcs were one of the enemy races," Dave said.

"Well, they used to be in some places. They're still a pain in the ass when they're young. If they can get past their adolescent years, they can control their bloodlust and berserker states. They are some of the scariest warriors I have ever seen in battle when they're organized," Anna said.

"Why are they wearing collars?" Suzy asked.

"Those are their inhibitors used to regulate their emotions and keep them calm. Younglings have them from birth, but older generations usually wear them as a show of their dedication to peace. There was a time when Orcs were hated and hunted. There are only very few of them left," Deia said.

"A number of Elven races fell to the Orcs when they were introduced to the world without control. Like the Elves, Orcs prefer the forests and swamps. Many of the older living Elves still harbor an anger toward them." Anna sighed.

"Elves model themselves as being upstanding people and one of the most knowledgeable, which is true. However, ageism and paranoia due to our long lives has turned us into a squabbling race where more effort is put into traditions and appearances than looking to grow with Emerilia." Deia shook her head.

"You damn idiot!" someone yelled as a feline Demi-Human went flying out of the adventurer's tavern. A brawny-looking Human who must've had some Giant blood in him walked out as the feline flipped in the air and landed on all fours.

"I'm sorry—did I happen to hit your beer? I'm sorry—just not used to being around big idiots like you." The feline smiled as the large Human's muscles flexed and shook in anger.

"Come here, you fucking plush toy!" The Human rushed the feline adventurer.

Others yelled their encouragement and advice from the tavern.

Deia moved first; the others followed as she barged her way past the spectators and into the place.

There were fireplaces on either side of the tavern. A long bar was at the back, with chairs around it. Tables and seating was all over the place as people were eating, discussing jobs, or commenting on the fight going on outside.

"Well, I say we get some breakfast and then see what there is to do around here." Deia waved to a server as they moved for a table.

"Hello. What guild are you from?" the server asked.

"Stone Raiders." Deia pointed to the simple emblem on her shoulder.

He looked at it, taking a few minutes. "It is great to be serving you today. What can I help you with?"

"Six breakfast meals, please."

"You got some Xer as well?" Dave asked.

"Certainly, just made a fresh pot," the server said.

"What is Xer?" Suzy asked.

"Coffee."

"I'll take one too. Sugar and cream please," Suzy immediately snapped out.

"Coming right up." The server walked away.

"Why the hell didn't you tell me this place had coffee?" Suzy demanded.

"Well, you never asked. I thought that you would figure it out." Dave shrugged.

"It better be good. I need my caffeine," Suzy said.

Dave snorted and shook his head. The others talked about different things as Dave looked around. He spotted a map on one wall with a board of different notices pinned next to it.

"So, what's our plan?" Dave asked, looking to Deia.

"The rest of the guild won't be here for another week and a half. Suzy, Lucy wants to talk to you on some matters; you can go through my friends list to get her contact details. While we do have to take care of some things, I think we'll have time for everyone to be able to do what they want. Mornings, we train. Afternoons, you can do with as you wish.

"The guild is registered to the adventurer's guild and we don't have all that much free gold running around. If you are all interested, we could go and do some adventurer quests for a bit of gold."

"I'm interested in trying out some new skills on a few kill quests," Malsour said.

"Might as well try out my new spells on something." Induca smiled.

"I have some work to do in town and I'll have a talk with Lucy to see what she wants. I'll let you know."

"Well, Dave and I will be training for a few days at least," Deia said.

"I'll help out with that where I can, but would you two be interested in having a big sword swinger running with you?" Anna looked to the Dracul siblings.

"No, that would be perfect. We were hoping that one of you melee types would be interested in joining us for a bit. Makes it a lot easier to deal with different types of jobs," Induca said.

"Well, it sounds like we have a plan, and that looks like food," Dave said as the server dodged through the masses of people coming back inside. It seemed the fight outside had been wrapped up.

Players logged back on, appearing in the middle of the tavern. They went straight to the quest board, checking out a few things before taking a posting and giving it to a strong-looking woman behind a desk. After a few words, they were on their way out. The POEs got out of their way, knowing Player temperament was a risky thing.

Dave looked to the arriving food, feeling his stomach rumble.

***

Dave found himself in an Alchemy shop. For training today, Deia had asked him to make the weapons he was going to use for the rest of Emerilia. Seeing as he still needed to make them, he'd gone off to the Alchemy store for his required materials.

"Aspiring Alchemist?" the store owner asked, a skeptical look on her face.

"Just doing a bit of tinkering. Do you have any eyes of Elmeur?"

"I do have a few." She moved to the wall of boxes behind her.

They were all warded, some of them more than others. She quickly pulled out two red eyes that almost looked like rubies.

"Anything else?" She put it with the pile of other alchemy ingredients.

"That should be all, thanks," Dave said.

"That comes to"—she looked through the items—"one gold, eight silver."

"Are you kidding me? This isn't worth more than nine silver altogether. Most of these ingredients are native to Selhi, as well. Shouldn't they be cheaper?" Dave said, annoyed at how much she was trying to rip him off.

"Well, these are the finest and rarest of ingredients," she said, trying to fight the good fight.

Dave shook his head. "I'm not going higher than a gold coin for all of this."

"Are you trying to steal from me?"

"Are you trying to rob me?"

"Dear customer, those are the prices. I cannot change them. Not paying the price is just stealing." She smiled.

"Well, guess I'll have to do it the hard way," Dave muttered to himself and turned, leaving the store.

"Don't you need these?" she asked, seeing her sale walking away.

"Not for that price," Dave said.

"I can do a gold and five silvers," she said sweetly.

Dave didn't even pause as he walked out of the store.

He walked through the city and spread his Touch out, pushing it down into the ground to find what he needed. He couldn't get the ingredients he needed for a rechargeable soul gem, so he was going to have to try out a different idea he had been thinking of.

He found most of what he needed and headed to a secluded spot of Selhi Capital. No one who lived in the capital actually called it that, instead referring to it as Es-cee.

Dave moved between buildings and finally got to the hidden away spot between a tannery and SC's wall. The smell was enough to keep most people away. After Boran-al's Citadel, Dave wasn't all that affected by the smell.

He sat down and focused on his Touch, locating the minerals lying under or around SC that he needed. He pulled out a brick of ebony as he pulled the iron and small amount of silver he would need for his project. The metals raced toward him as he used what Kol had taught him. He put his hand down, grabbing the iron and then silver ores from the ground.

"Time to start." Dave made a series of Mana barriers and floated the iron into it first. He focused his fire through the Mana barrier, quickly melting the iron. He poured in other elemental metals, turning the iron into steel and removing the impurities.

Dave did the same in another barrier to the silver ore.

"Last and not least." Dave tossed the chunk of Boran-al's Citadel ebony into the steel crucible. Dave connected the silver and poured it in as well. The ebony quickly melted.

A Mithril glove formed on Dave's hand. He opened the Mana barrier enough for him to get his hand in. He touched the Metal and commanded it into a form. Two rods the length of a person's forearm and about a half-inch thick appeared. The metal seemed to twist and open up at the end, hollowing out as if waiting for something.

Dave pulled the heat of the metal into himself, using it to generate more Mana. He looked at the two steel-looking rods; the ebony and runes were hidden inside. The air seemed to shimmer around Dave as he called on his Mana reserves. Shadows spread through the open ends of the rods. After a few moments, they solidified into slightly glowing crystals.

"Well, they should stay together as long as they have a charge." Dave looked at the two rods now with an inset crystal. "Could have just done this at the training square." He sighed and stood. A few hours had passed and the sun had sunk lower.

He cracked his back after sitting for so long and headed off to find Deia.

***

Deia moved through her training moves. She'd sent Dave off to go and make—or get—a set of weapons that suited him.

I hope that he realizes what Anna and I have figured out. It's going to be a pain in the ass trying to teach him everything he needs to know.

"Hello, Deia. Me and my friends are off to go and hunt swamp snakes. We were wondering if you would like to join us. We'll let you keep whatever you kill," a Player asked for his party.

Deia didn't miss the way that they were looking at her. *How many times have I seen a group of Players who want to have some good-looking girl on their team just to brag to others?*

"I have my own party, thanks." She continued her practice.

Anna wandered over from her own workout. "Deia, want to spar?"

"Sure." Deia turned and left the party alone.

"It's probably some guy playing a girl. Let it go, Andur," one of the party said.

"Man, a Demi-Human and an Elf—we've got to have them," Andur said.

Deia rolled her eyes as Dave walked into the square, looking pleased with himself. "Did you finally figure out your weapons?" Deia yelled.

"I think so. Alchemy woman haggled the shit out of me, so I had to make most of it myself. As long as it works, it doesn't really matter." Dave wrapped his arm around her side and kissed her.

Deia heard the other party making rude noises and comments, trying to salve Andur's pride.

"Well, you going to leave us in suspense or show us?" Anna asked.

"Well, since you asked so kindly." Dave unhooked two rods from his belt.

They turned into longswords, and then one into a shield, the other an axe. He brought them together and they formed into a massive shield, and then a warhammer. He held one out in front of him and it turned into a compound bow.

"Well, looks like he isn't a complete bonehead." Anna smiled to Deia.

"He has his moments." Deia laughed.

"What are you two talking about now?" Dave asked. The warhammer turned back into two rods.

Anna looked around as Deia talked.

"With your ability to make any kind of weapon, having just one kind just doesn't make sense. You have so much versatility that just using one weapon would kind of slow you down. It's going to be hard as hell, but with your skills and the right training, you can fight anyone in any role. You're going to have to learn to fight in multiple styles and it's going to take probably *years* in order to get to that skill level, but it would be great. You could block a massive magical attack with your big shield, then have two axes to cut down close combatants, then pull out a bow and shoot up the mage trying to kill you," Deia said.

"Well, I have a few more weapons I want to try out." Dave took his time looking around now. "Though, I can't show you them here. They're kind of super damn powerful and the thing I don't want other people knowing about. Kind of like a last, last resort." Dave held her and Anna's eyes.

"Well, it looks like we will have to go on one of those quest hunts to test it out," Deia said.

"Let me know when you do. I'm interested in what you're thinking," Anna said.

Dave simply smiled.

"Sometimes, you're a pretty sinister guy, babe," Deia said.

Dave shrugged.

Chapter 2: Business Venture

Suzy accepted the chat invite from Lucy.

"Ahh, Suzy, I just read your report on different merchants and possible opportunities we might find in running our own trading caravans. The reason I bring it up is because there is a Player-led group that is trying to trade across Emerilia. They have the trading skills, but they don't have the protection that they need to look after their goods. They're linked to the merchant guild but they don't have the overall capital to start out on their own. Would you be interested in sitting down and looking over a contract with them?"

"I could. What kind of resources do we have to spend on them?"

"We can give them some start-up capital to purchase wagons and the rest. Also, we can provide them with security from the Stone Raiders. Through our travels, we've found that having a few things running on the side to generate some cash flow would be useful. Raids pay off in the end, but in between, we have to squeeze every copper. We've also learned the old adage—a fighting force moves on its stomach. We need trained people to keep supplies flowing to us as we're on raids or fighting. Also, having someone we can trust to take our weapons back to town and get them repaired is no small thing. We're currently sending fighters to go and do it with wagons." Lucy sighed.

"Not the best of conditions. How many wagons do you have, and how much gold do you have for start-up?"

"We've got a decent amount of gold for now, say about fifty thousand gold. We have fifteen wagons right now. What are you thinking?"

"I'm thinking that we gift them those wagons and they lend us a few of their people and we lend them a few of ours. At a minimum, we make them an allied guild. I can show them a few things about the market and really get them going. I will, also, dangle the carrot of them joining the guild as a feeder, giving them the possibility to join us and waiving guild taxes between us *and* that we could then give them access to the keys that we have to different teleport pads. It's hard to get those keys without having a good basis of trust and a reputation, something that the Stone Raiders have already built up."

"Why should we want them as a feeder guild?"

"As an allied guild, they can help us and we help them. However, there might be things that the different groups put above one another. For example, they can make a killing off of a product they have stockpiled. At the same time, we are asking them to send us extra wagons to move some weaponry. They might push more wagons to go and sell their products than help shift our weapons. If we are in the same guild, the guild comes first, then their own interests," Suzy said.

"You raise a good point, though we will need to make sure that they don't have any agents from other powers hiding in their ranks."

"Well, having an alliance with them, we can have our own people keep an eye on them and vet them. If we're not sure of their allegiance, then, even if they are made a feeder guild, we don't need to tell them anything important until the last minute so there is little chance that word can be spread out."

"You raise some good points. Very well, go and talk to them with the authority of the Stone Raiders. Their guild is called Exdar's Traders," Lucy said.

"I'll see to it," Suzy said.

The chat cut as Suzy looked to Malsour and Induca as they wandered around SC. A pop-up greeted her.

Quest: Trading Alliance

Lucy has mentioned that the Stone Raiders need someone to shift their goods from battle and get them supplies. Exdar's Traders are one of these possible guilds. Meet with their leader and see if you can negotiate a contract with them.

"Well, Lucy wants me to go and talk to some traders—you interested?" Suzy asked.

"What for?" Induca asked.

"See if we can't make them a part of the Stone Raiders or, at least, make some serious gold." Suzy rubbed her hands together.

"I don't think that we have any other pressing matters," Malsour said, waving for her to take the lead.

"Well, let's see if we can find them. They're called Exdar's Traders," Suzy said.

"Exdar? Where did they get that name from?" Induca asked.

"There was a large space-based MMORPG a few years ago—they had a massive buying and selling component to them. Mine asteroids, build ships, stations, all kinds of stuff. People would go around in trading flotillas—buying, selling, and trading throughout the created universe. A number of companies on Earth hired people directly from the game."

"Did your old company?" Malsour asked.

"We were the ones who started it." Suzy smiled.

"I find that I am not surprised."

Suzy laughed at Malsour's words as Induca turned and pointed in a direction.

"I can hear someone talking about the traders over there."

"Damn, that is some powerful hearing." Suzy headed in the direction Induca had pointed.

"It has its uses." Induca smiled.

They traveled through SC, past a few stores and homes into the middle of the market that lined the main street of the city.

Induca pointed in different directions. Suzy was surprised by her level of accuracy as she came up to a busy stand where four traders were doing brisk business, selling different goods from all over Opheir.

Supply issues. Probably such a low level that they have to buy and sell in Opheir and Markolm for the most part. Decent level of goods, though. Obviously buying at higher quality instead of quantity. Don't have the room to move a lot of goods. Lack of transport.

Suzy checked out their guild's emblem; it was a bolt of silk with jewels, armor, weapons, and ore scattered around it.

Looks like someone just went apeshit with the emblem creator tool.

Suzy wandered away, checking out other stores. Her eyes and perception allowed her to pick up the different people wandering around and wearing the same emblem as those managing the storefront.

They were good barterers, gathering up goods in different packs. It was easy to pick them out as they were constantly making notes and looking at their interfaces.

Checking the flow of the market to make the most gold. Well-organized and brisk operators. Once they have enough gold, they'll take off. Right now that's the problem. Lots of different guilds are working with trading, but until they get some really massive profits, then they're all stuck competing at the bottom of the pool. If they had the ability to transport items, then they could shift the different products coming out of Cliff-Hill faster.

Suzy was looking out for the best interests of the guild, but if she could use them to expand the different items Dave's smithy and ceramic factory were pumping out, then it was a win-win.

Should be a nice bonus as managing director. She chuckled to herself.

She didn't really care about the gold, but the rush of making deals, to see the opportunities—the beginning of something that could be great—was invigorating. It was why she had applied to be Austin's secretary when he'd been working out of a really large rocket garage. She smiled, thinking back on those days.

"So what's the plan?" Induca asked.

Suzy was surprised that she had stuck around; she was usually the type to get bored in a hurry.

"Now, we go and make some deals." Suzy headed back to the Exdar's stall.

"Hello, miss. What are you looking for today?" a large Orc-looking trader asked as she approached.

"I was wondering if your boss is around. I have a business proposition on behalf of my guild," Suzy said.

"We have had many people trying to do business with us. Which trader's guild are you from?" He smiled, putting Suzy at ease.

Smooth operator. Suzy smiled back. This was the world of sharks and smiles that she had dealt in for years. In Emerilia, it was still so new and fresh that the sharks hadn't yet started to show themselves.

"I don't represent a trader's guild." She turned to show off her shoulder patch. "I represent *the* raiding guild, Stone Raiders."

"Damn, you guys are kicking ass. I haven't seen any guild like you! Is it true that you actually all fight without Actions?" He leaned closer.

"Well, most don't use Actions. However, sometimes using Actions can really help out. Trying to do Assassin teleport skills would be a pain in the ass without the Action skill." Suzy shook her head, not even wanting to get more into that topic. "So, do you think that you could get me a meeting with your guild leader?"

"Sure, just give me a sec. I'll go talk to her. Name's Raz, by the way." He held out his hand.

"Good to meet you, Raz. I'm Suzy." She smiled and shook his hand.

"Likewise." He bobbed his head, turning and weaving through his fellow guildmates and into a covered area at the rear of the store.

It only took a few minutes of waiting, time that Suzy spent looking over the different wares that were on the table and how the traders got people motivated and their goods moving.

A human lady with delicate features walked through the covering and greeted Suzy.

"Hello, Suzy. My name is Florence Guitterez. What might I be able to do in order to help the Stone Raiders?"

"Would you be willing to accompany us to somewhere more private?" Suzy looked around the market.

"Very well. You wouldn't mind if Bronx, our guard, follows?"

"Not at all." Suzy smiled as Florence waved over her giant friend. He was wearing decent armor and a mean-looking sword and shield. From their markings, he had seen combat a few times. You could repair items, but the scars, dents, and dings would stay.

People liked it, thinking that it showed off their combat prowess.

Suzy led the party through the streets and off toward an up-scale tavern she had located earlier. Her Air creations floated around, keeping an eye on anything that looked to be a threat or someone spying on them.

"I must say that I am interested why a level 1 is bartering on the Stone Raider's behalf," Florence said.

Suzy smiled, knowing that Florence was trying to gauge her actions. "Well, not all things are as they appear."

Malsour snorted and Induca smiled, looking at everything around them and wandering off from time to time when something caught their eye.

Florence studied Malsour and Induca. Her eyes widened; she'd obviously seen both of their levels.

If only she knew that they're ten or so levels past that on their stat points alone.

They entered a tavern. The host quickly got them a booth away from prying eyes as Suzy flashed some silver.

Their server appeared shortly. "What can I get you today?" She smiled.

"Some small snacks and fruit drinks. Could you make sure that our conversation is not disturbed by other parties?" Suzy slid over a piece of gold.

"Certainly. I will have the food and drinks ready in ten minutes, if that is okay?"

"That is perfectly fine." Suzy smiled and let go of the piece of gold. The server made it disappear and bowed quickly.

Suzy looked to Malsour. "Could you make sure no one can hear us?"

There was a pressure change and then he nodded to Suzy. "Done."

"Thanks, Malsour. Florence, I am here talking on the behalf of the Stone Raiders, specifically Lucy, though Josh knows what's going on. As you know, the Stone Raiders are always traveling; as such, they always need supplies. They need someone they can trust to hawk their goods for them when they can't and deliver their weapons for repair and return it to them. We like fighting and raiding; we don't like having to deal with everything else," Suzy said.

Florence nodded, showing that she was following along. "So, you want us to fill that role?"

"We wish to make a mutually beneficial alliance with you. We continue to raid, we pay for our supplies and the costs, and you get it to us. You sell the items we don't want and so on."

"I have to admit that the offer does sound too good to be true and I would jump for it if we had the resources to do that. Right now, we don't even have a wagon or horses. They cost too much, so we've been working on our ability to run and trying to get all the keys for different cities. Buying all of the keys to different teleport hubs and holding a good reputation with them is a costly business."

"I have seen. It is rather resourceful of you, buying the highest quality bags of holding and using people to carry the gear for you. Using your superior abilities to run, you can get between towns faster than any horse, though you are indeed limited by the amount of people you have and their strength. That is why our alliance would be different. If you can help us, we can help you. We have fifteen wagons right now. If you were able to assist us, then we would not need them and could deed them over to you." Suzy paused, looking up as their food and drinks arrived.

The outside noises of the rest of the tavern came back as the server placed down different foods and drinks, with another server assisting. "Let me know if you need anything." Their servers bowed and stepped away.

Again, the pressure came back as Bronx started to grab meats and foods from the table. He was precise in his movements. Induca tasted the different pitchers of drinks.

"What will the cost be?" Florence asked.

"At cost, payments over two years in game?" Suzy asked.

"That is rather reasonable," Florence said. "We would have to sell a few of them to make up for the costs of the caravan. They would also be slower than just running."

"I have an engineering friend who might be able to make the caravans faster. Also, we would be willing to give you start-up funds. That said, we would want ten percent of your profits," Suzy said.

Bronx poured Florence a glass of juice.

"Thank you." She sipped on it, deep in thought.

Suzy took the opportunity to pull some food onto her plate.

"Try out this duck pâté—really nice on the crackers with a piece of dried Koji fruit." Induca shoved one of the treats in her mouth.

Suzy tried it, nodding as the flavors melded together nicely.

"What are your far-reaching goals?" Florence asked.

"We are raiding all the time—we don't want to deal with everything else. If we have someone dealing with all of the supplies, selling and repairing our goods, then we can have some fun. The ten percent, well, it really gets our two groups completely connected. We want you to succeed and right now the market is ripe. Once you start working with not only your own people but People of Emerilia, then you could be the biggest trading firm in Emerilia. With start-up capital, our people providing security and having a few wagons running around, you can expand quicker than anyone else."

Florence sipped on her drink.

"Look, your biggest Player rival is Diamond Industries. They've got two wagons. In the large scale of things, that isn't much. They're selling from Opheir to Markolm. They're going to be coming to Heval and Gudalo soon enough. We want a piece of that pie." Suzy shrugged.

"I will have to talk to my guild. This is a very interesting proposition. What about the keys to different teleportation pads—would you be willing to give us recommendations?" Florence sipped from her drink but Suzy knew she was being watched and gauged.

"No. Unless you are part of our guild, then we cannot in good faith extend that recommendation to you. At Boran-al's Citadel, we learned that people are already acting as spies and assassins. We are working to be on good terms with the People of Emerilia. If we start giving recommendations to groups that we kind of know, it will look bad on us if they start making trouble." Suzy ate another cracker combo.

"I can't say that I'm not disappointed, but I understand. I also find the relationship that you have with the NPCs interesting." Florence frowned.

"We just think of them as other Players—treat them how we would expect to be treated. You would be surprised what they are able to do if you allow them a chance. I know a number of POEs who are much stronger than me. A few of them have taught me how to be as powerful as I am." Suzy held Florence's eyes.

After a moment, Florence looked away, thoughtful as she grabbed some fruit. "How much are you willing to pay for ten percent of Exdar's profits?"

"Seven thousand," Suzy said.

"Gold?" Florence's eyes bugged out; Bronx stopped eating and looked at Suzy.

"Yes," Suzy said.

Florence took a shaky hand and passed it through her hair. "Wow, okay, I know that later on people will have a lot of gold, but right now even a hundred gold is a large sum. I will have to talk to my people more to see if they are interested in the deal. If they agree, then we can talk over the small details later, if that works?"

"Certainly." Suzy smiled.

"Thank you for the food, but I would like to get back and see what the others think. I should have word to you as soon as possible." Florence stood; Bronx rose with her, munching on a sandwich he had made. Florence tapped out a few things on her interface. "We will have a decision by tonight. I just added your contact details so I can let you know our decision as soon as possible."

"I look forward to your response. It was good talking, Florence." Suzy shook her hand.

"And you, too, Miss Markell." She moved to the tavern's exit. Bronx had to move fast to keep up with her quick-moving form.

Suzy sat back down.

Quest: Trading Alliance

You have met with Florence Guitterez. She seems agreeable to your terms but must take this back to her guild. You may talk to other trading guilds that could assist the Stone Raiders.

(There are no more guilds that Lucy listed as current possibilities in Selhi's capital).

"Well, shall we go and deal with those swamp rabbits?" Malsour asked.

"Eat the damned food. You know how much this is going to cost me? Uggh, you guys want to start Selhi's annual monster hunt tomorrow? I feel like my purse is going to need it after this damn meal." Suzy sighed.

The monster hunt was called once a year when the monster population from the swamps and woods gave birth to a great number of creatures that flowed outward, throwing trade and business into chaos within the kingdom.

"Why were you flashing your gold everywhere then?" Induca asked.

"Well, I wanted to show that even a level 1 didn't have to worry about being out of coin. Looks cool, all right? I hate being broke—reminds me of my ramen and sweater years." Suzy piled the food up, not wanting to let it go to waste while Malsour and Induca chuckled at her misfortune.

"Damned dragons. Bet you've just got caves filled with riches," Suzy said.

The pause made her look up at the two of them.

"Oh, come on. Help me out here, guys. It's your clan as well!"

"Well, we didn't really prepare to be away from our homes this long," Malsour said.

"So, you left it all in your cave. Have you ever heard of a bank?" Suzy growled.

"Well, moving that kind of wealth is annoying." Induca shrugged.

"That kind of wealth, she says!" Suzy sighed, muttering about how unfair the world was. "I have a credit card!" She smiled to herself as she went to her interface, opening her billing options, and realized that she had never put it in.

I'd have to go back to Earth to do my credit card info... Screw it. I'll kill all the damned monsters I can find instead. Not worth the hassle.

Chapter 3: Monster Hunting Pays the Bills

"That's good for now," Deia said.

Dave's great sword transformed into his two rods as he fell back and landed on his back, groaning.

Deia laughed at his antics.

"Even though you've been off hammering metal for months, you're picking this all up rather quickly." Deia squat down next to him and handed him a water skin.

"Thanks." He drank from the skin.

"I think that because of your higher Intelligence, you are able to pick up skills faster. I'd like to check out something, if you're willing?"

"Does it include beating me with sharp things?" he asked, warily.

"I'm not going to kill my fiancé off this early." She smiled.

"Oh thanks, babe." He sighed. "So what is this idea?"

"Let's go and get some books. I want to see if you studying books and then watching people fight will increase your fighting skills."

"Fine." Dave got to his feet. "But first I need a damned bath."

***

Dave rolled his shoulders, trying to ease the tension in his muscles.

He opened the notifications that had piled up after training with Anna and Deia over the last couple of days.

Active Skill: Dual wield

Level: Expert Level 2

Effect: Attacks are 32% faster. 25% reduced damage with off-hand weapon.

Cost: 15 Stamina

Active Skill: Two-handed

Level: Apprentice Level 7

Effect: 17% armor penetration on target. Stamina costs reduced 5% while fighting.

Cost: 35 Stamina

New Active Skill: One-handed and Shield

Well shit, so you didn't want to cut your leg off so now you're fighting like the human multi-tool. Either this is gonna work, or be one hell of a messy ending. I'm getting the popcorn—should be a good show!

Level: Apprentice Level 1

Effect: Weapons damage increased by 11%. Defense increases by 5%.

Cost: 20 Stamina

Active Skill: Archery

Level: Journeyman Level 5

Effect: Critical Hit chance increases by 25%. Ranged targets take 10% increased damage

Cost: 10 Stamina

Stat Increase

+2 Strength

+1 Intelligence

+1 Willpower

+2 Endurance

+5 Agility

+3 Vitality

"Character sheet." Dave pulled on his jacket.

Character Sheet

Name:	David Grahslagg	Gender:	Male
Level:	3	Class:	-
Race:	Human/Dwarf	Alignment:	Chaotic Neutral

Unspent points-295

Health:	2,900	Regen:	2.24/s
Mana:	1,470	Regen:	6.60/s
Stamina:	740	Regen:	3.65/s
Vitality:	29	Endurance:	112
Intelligence:	147	Willpower:	132
Strength:	74	Agility:	73

"How are your stats looking?" Deia asked, already dressed and ready to leave.

"Good. They're going up slower. However, because I'm still learning something nearly every time or activating something different than before because of my increased Intelligence, I'm still growing well. I think that I'm going to plateau soon with smithing all done and shift my focus to just fighting," Dave said as they left the room.

"I'm an Expert at dual wielding and Apprentice with one-handed weapon with shield. I'm still learning. It might take me a few weeks to get new stats from it, but usually when I do, it marks some kind of breakthrough in my fighting style. Even as a Master, there is so much more to learn. Bonuses might fall away but stat points are still there."

"And stat points can really change how you fight, to make you even stronger."

"Yeah. I'm thinking about that the more I think about smithing. I've always got a constant stream of ideas that I want to do and try out going on in my head," Dave said.

"There's also the fact that there are other skills that you can work on that influence your different Actions. I have made it to Mastery level 7 for archery but I am an Expert level 7 with dual wield. While training will improve your skills up to the Journeyman level, you need to go out and hunt living creatures to advance further, or get into fights with other people to train up. It is what makes sparring better as a training partner. I am wondering with your high Intelligence if you will be able to learn a lot on different fighting techniques and use it in battle," she said as they were leaving the adventurer's guild inn where they had been staying.

"So, kind of like uploading new skills and techniques into my mind? Essentially, giving me a whole bunch of information to go off and seeing if my mind will pull it up at the right time?"

"Exactly. If you can, then it would create a whole new way of training—well, for people who have a very high Intelligence. In fact, you might even need a higher Intelligence or more knowledge of fighting for it to be useful." Deia tapped her lip in thought.

"But you don't know, so I get to be a guinea pig." Dave looked to her.

"A cute guinea pig," she said with a winning smile.

"I feel all warm and fuzzy inside." Dave rolled his eyes. "You were talking about skill augments, like one skill affecting another. I guess that is similar to how the building skill can be used with the smithing skill, allowing me to use less material?"

"I didn't know that was possible, but along those lines. I know that it works with different fighting techniques. With the bow, you gain a bonus for hitting targets at range, which can be stacked with one-handed and shield to increase the base damage. Then that's compounded by the stealth skill. Add in the two-handed's ability of armor penetration, and your one arrow can hit for a decent amount of damage. With most skills, there is just one bonus or two. With weapons there is a main bonus, a subset and then specialization at Mastery level." Deia looked to him to see whether he was following.

"Okay, but how do they stack?"

"So, if you're using dual blades, the effects of two-handed, archery, and one-handed will only add a total of ten percent of their overall skill. The armor penetration of forty percent on the two-handed would mean four percent armor penetration with the dual wielding. This changes when you reach Master of the weapons you're using. If you're a Master of dual blades, you gain a twenty-five percent effectiveness. Your armor penetration of forty percent with the two-handed would mean when you're dual wielding, you gain an additional ten percent."

"Okay but it says it's an active skill..." Dave trailed off, confused.

"Let's think about this as a game system, then real world. Open up your two-handed skill."

Dave did so, sharing it with her.

Active Skill: Two-handed

Level: Apprentice Level 7

Effect: 17% armor penetration on target. Stamina costs reduced 5% while fighting.

Cost: 35 Stamina

"Your first main bonus is the armor. It is calculated at your overall level, so if you've risen seventeen levels, you have a seventeen percent modifier. Also, because you are an Apprentice instead of a Novice, you gain your sub-skill, of Stamina effect reduction. You gain this at the Apprentice level; at Journeyman, you gain an extra five percent. This occurs every time you pass into a new named level. Now, while you become better at using your two-handed, your levels will increase, though you are learning how to fight by yourself, not with the Action command system. If you know how to gain armor penetration with your great sword, could you not adapt that over to your dual blades or weapon and shield? The subsets are listed for fighting or against your target; unless it is stated that you have to be using that specific weapon, it will mean *any* target."

"So, wait. If I was just using these as Action hot buttons, they wouldn't cross over. However, since I am fighting with these weapons and not just button mashing, I have a bleed-over of skills. Fighting with multiple weapons gives me more options with them. With arrows, I would have to be accurate; dual blades, faster with my hands and faster at moving. With the increased dexterity in my fingers from shooting a bow, I can be more accurate with my blades." Dave thought of the ramifications, thinking on the times when he had blocked with his axes and used what he knew with the shield to deflect the attacks.

"Correct—bleed-over. It's an active skill, as you still have to use it, though weapons skills are one of the only set of skills that have a bleed-over from one to another." Deia smiled.

"Damn. I can now see why Josh and Dwayne wanted to train everyone with all kinds of weapons and have a school going in Cliff-Hill."

"If someone can master all of the weapons, even by simply grinding it out, then they can be a damn scary adversary on the battlefield. If you can get to even Journeyman level, added to the fact you can change out your weapons at will, it's going to be very interesting." Deia smiled as they reached a building.

"What's this?" Dave asked.

"The library. Now come on; we have some research to do!" She smiled.

"Oh, you could definitely pull off the sexy librarian look." Dave followed behind. He looked around the room.

Over time, he had finally grown back into his original height of just under six foot. Deia was still a bit taller than him, but he didn't mind. He was a giant of the Dwarven race, but about average for humans. He wasn't growing upward anymore, though his Dwarven build made it easier for him to pack on dense muscles.

There were runes and books all over the place. Books were stacked one upon another. There were a few dozen people around on different balconies or studying cubbies, reading all kinds of material.

"Hello, how can I help you?" a teenage boy asked Deia as she stepped up to the desk.

"I am looking for books on fighting techniques," Deia said.

"Oh, very well. There are books in the far back left, Section Training, Sub-section Melee." The boy gave a friendly smile and started to lower his head toward the book he was reading.

"Do you know of anything that might make reading faster?" Dave asked.

"Well, there are magical glasses that are rumored to be capable, though the ones I have seen were twenty to fifty gold coins. Otherwise, there are potions of increased recollection, speed, and so on. Stacking several different potions will give you bursts of increased intellect as well as speed," he said.

"Thank you." Dave smiled and let him get back to his book.

Dave and Deia wandered toward the section they wanted.

"We need to go hunting if this works," Dave said.

"Oh?" Deia asked, looking over different tomes.

"Well, we're going to need some coin in order to make these potions, and fighting things will increase my melee levels."

"Why not smith something?" Deia asked.

"I could, but with us going to fight something with the rest of the guild, I don't want to be relying on conjuring some powerful ass weapon to make up for my lack of skills."

Deia gave Dave a smile and a kiss. "I knew I didn't just make you my fiancé for your rugged good looks."

"I have rugged good looks?" Dave grinned happily.

"Yes, you look like a freaking hobbit." Deia held in a laugh at his expression.

"I'm not a bleeding hobbit!"

"Sssh!" one of the people reading nearby said, glaring at them.

"I'm much bigger!" Dave whispered.

Deia couldn't hold in her laugh, making a half snort, half grunting noise. "They're taking the hobbits to Isengard," she whispered back.

"Last time I watch movies with you," Dave said, trying and failing to hide his smile.

"Don't say that. Suzy said that we've got to watch these things called rom-com movies," Deia said.

"What monster have you made, Suz?" Dave asked, shaking his head, as he pulled out more books.

Deia simply smiled and grabbed her collection of books. Dave gathered his together and they headed for one of the reading tables.

***

Dave stood up, cracking his back and rubbing his eyes. He heard a message ping, but took a few moments to finish rubbing his eyes.

"Seems that Suzy spent a few more gold coins than she was expecting. She's asking if we want to go hunting," Deia said.

"All right. I checked out the potions that the guy at the desk was talking about. Should be able to get most of the ingredients from the surrounding area or from the market. I really don't want to go and deal with that alchemist store again," Dave said.

"Upset at the old lady who wanted to fleece you for money?" Deia stood and gathered up the books they'd been reading for a few hours.

"Uggh. Fleece? It was downright highway robbery."

Deia chuckled. "Well, I think that has been enough for today. Guess we can try to see if any of this reading has helped you."

"Woohoo," Dave said with a half-hearted fist pump.

"Come on, you big oaf."

"Hobbit, now a big oaf—what's it going to be? You know I can only have one nickname, Firecracker," Dave teased.

"Maybe I'm still playing around with them." She smiled and carried her books back to the shelves. It took them a few minutes to put the books back and then make it to the waypoint where everyone else was waiting.

"Well, let's go kill some rabbits. It's like three coppers a rabbit, bit more for larger creatures, then we can skin them and sell their parts on the market here. I know someone who would be interested in them if we could turn them into jerky," Suzy said.

"Been a bit busy?" Dave asked.

"Been a bit broke. Just wined and dined a possible client without a credit card," Suzy said.

"Ouch. Well, you never knew how to stretch a dime when it came to sealing a contract," Dave said.

"I always sealed the damned contract though." Suzy smiled.

"That you did, Sealer Suz!"

Suzy winced at the name, making it look as if she were shuddering. "I forgot how bad your nicknames were."

"Tell me about it," Deia said.

"You too! Ah, it must be love!" Suzy smiled.

"Did you ever figure out a good one for him?" Deia sidled up to Suzy.

"All right, let's go kill some fucking rabbits!" *Before these two get enough time to conference and come up with a truly terrible nickname!*

"How was the library—anything good?" Malsour asked.

"Not really. I've just been looking at information on martial arts. Deia has a theory that I might be able to store the information and use it better than other people because I have a higher Intelligence stat."

"Hmm, I have heard people with a higher Intelligence stat are able to assimilate information faster. They are usually found in the mages colleges and deal with information that is not about fighting."

"Well, I hope that I'll be the first one, though reading a bunch of books about people fighting isn't bad." Dave smiled and looked around as they exited SC. "Sometimes it's hard for me to think of this as a game, other times I'm just blown away by the fact that this is the real world and how much better it is than Earth's simulation. Like, look, I'm a freaking Dwarf and I know how to craft blades, how to fight—not very well but I can still do it—and I can use a bit of magic."

"We do live in an interesting time," Malsour agreed.

"Even got some old bastard who likes to give out corny one-liners."

"Dick."

"And the student becomes the teacher." Dave smiled proudly.

Malsour laughed, shaking his head as they headed toward the waypoint Deia had created for their quest.

As they left the city, Suzy threw out some cores. They rolled on the ground, two Earth golems and five metal golems appearing.

"we'll have the Air creations move out and scout to see if we can't find some fun things to do. I'm sharing the quest with everyone," Deia said. It was her quest and her show. Unless something went seriously wrong, then she was in the driver's seat.

Quest: Cleaning Out the Hills

There have been a number of creatures too close to Selhi's capital. Farmers are complaining of their food being eaten and people are finding creatures eating their wares. Go forth and kill creatures that might be in the area.

You will receive a reward based on the number of creatures you and your party kill.

Rewards: Loot and gold according to number of creatures killed

Do you accept?

Y/N

Suzy had already accepted it, so Dave just waved it away from his vision. Another notification showed the prices of the different animals; the bigger and more aggressive, the bigger the payout. It would be active for two days, so they had to do as much as possible.

"We'll split up into two-person groups so that we can cover more ground and get more creatures. Malsour and Dave, Induca and Anna, Suzy and myself. Keep your party chat open and let us know if you run into anything that you can't handle by yourself." Deia looked to everyone. "Well, let's go make some gold!"

They headed in three different directions.

Dave spread out his Touch of the Land and looked for any good spots that might allow him to use his surveyor skill. Usually it only picked up possible landmarks and areas that larger creatures lived in. Dave was hoping that he'd find a few hides and maybe find some other creatures due to it being connected to his quest.

"Malsour, you keep them pinned. I'll stick an arrow in them." Dave held his two batons in his left hand. Shadows seemed to spread out from them into a compound bow. In Dave's right hand, he conjured an arrow.

"You're getting much better." Malsour glanced at Dave and then faced away from SC. He didn't need to use Touch of the Land with his ears and ability to sniff something out.

Dave saw a rabbit moving within a hundred meters; shadows moved over it. Within seconds, the rabbit was cold.

"That's new." Dave looked at Malsour.

"Shadow technique. I don't use it much, but out here there is enough shade that I can make use of it."

Dave nodded, his eyes continuously searching. His Touch had not found much more than a few burrowing creatures.

Selhi Capital was between a forest to the north, a swamp to the west and south, and farmers' fields to the east.

"I'm happy we're going in the forest instead of the swamp," Dave said, trying to ease the mood as Malsour killed any rabbit or creature that came within two hundred meters.

"Why? There are more creatures in the swamps."

"Cause I hate mud and I hate swamps—just smells nasty and the trees are just weird."

Another shadow killed off a rabbit.

"That spell is just freaky."

"I'm just using the shadow to extend my Touch, then applying a draining spell. Their Health is so small that it takes a few seconds for them to die," Malsour said. "I would be killing a lot more in a swamp, though they do smell like ass."

Dave smiled at hearing Malsour coming close to cursing. "Oh, 'tis a proud moment."

"What?" Malsour turned to Dave.

"Nothing, nothing at all. I'm going to see if I can't find somewhere with a higher elevation and pick out some creature's hide in the area."

"Very well. I am interested in seeing your progress with weapons."

"Thought you said that magic was the way to fight?"

"It is the *best* way to fight, but during Boran-al's Citadel, I saw that mages are not infallible to warriors and other melee classes. After that, I have been thinking of asking Anna to teach me some more."

"You, my friend, are a glutton for punishment." Dave put a consoling hand on his shoulder.

"Go climb your damned tree and find us a real opponent."

Dave found a good tree, but the lowest branches were too high. He used a smaller one to scale up and then jumped from it. It didn't take him long to scramble to the top.

"Well, looks like the old Agility is paying off, even if it hurts like hell after Deia's done helping me train it up." Dave used his Soul Smith ability, adding runes to his bow that would make him lighter and get higher.

He looked out over the area. He felt as if his vision shifted over as he started to pick out things he wouldn't have noticed by himself. His mini-map updated with a slew of markers, from caravans that were moving from SC through the swamps and on to Donsk Mountain.

"I can see why banditry is kind of easy. This skill points out all possible things you can interact with, from animals' territories to good ambush spots. You'd need to have someone constantly up here to keep track of the caravans and pick it out for the people you're working with. Also, it is really useful for map building and knowing things in your area," Dave muttered to himself.

"Anything good?" Malsour asked in voice chat.

"Well, it looks like I've got a few farms and caravans—there's an abandoned dungeon that might be interesting. A few caves and two animal territories, one bear and one other thing that my surveyor skill doesn't recognize. Don't know what's going on with it."

"The more you know about different things, the more your surveyor skill will be able to pick up. Say those caravans—if you knew more about goods, then you might be able to guess what they are carrying. Or, if you knew more about bears, you would know if they were looking for a mate, hunting, or going into hibernation."

"The more you know, the more it reflects in your other skills. I am seeing the value of books and learning more and more." Dave used his skill two more times before he ambled back down to the forest floor.

"Bear first, the unknown creature, the caves then the abandoned dungeon?" Dave asked.

"Do you want to go first to try out your bow?" Malsour asked.

"You just want a meat shield," Dave said as he moved forward, expanding out his Touch of the Land and advancing on the waypoint he'd made to the bear's territory.

"Well, that is also another factor."

"Glad I can be of service." Dave lowered his voice as he'd picked up the bear. With their UI linked through the party service, Malsour could see the red outline of the bear as well as the rabbits. The rabbits quickly turned into blue blinking icons, showing that Malsour had once again killed them off.

Malsour grabbed them and casually threw them into his pack if they came near them.

"Okay, just in the clearing ahead. You ready?" Dave moved up to a tree that was just twenty meters from the bear.

Malsour nodded.

Dave took a breath, slipping around the tree while trying to stay low and undetected.

The bear was scratching its back on the tree, leaving its body open for Dave.

His perception, knowledge, and Touch of the Land worked together, showing him different critical hit spots. Dave let loose his arrow.

The air cracked as the arrow slammed into the bear's heart. It looked at him dumbly, even as Dave conjured a new arrow on the string. Dave thought that it was going to charge but instead fell forward.

"Good shot." Malsour threw out a piece of metal next to the bear. The piece of metal grew into a spike and stabbed the bear. It didn't even fidget.

"Holy crap! This weapon mastery stacking stuff works pretty damn good."

"That it does." Malsour moved to the body and pulled out a knife. They'd have to cut the bear up to get it into their bags of holding.

"Nice little one gold bounty and then three gold for the rest of it. I'm feeling good about our money situation." Dave moved to help, his analyze skill kicking in.

Swamp Bear

Level 89

"Damn. It used to be hard to kill a level 60 bear and I took this one out with one shot."

"Welcome to the land of leveling bonuses. This bear wouldn't have been an issue to us even if he charged. He's actually a pretty low level for this area. Must be because he's near the city and most of the bigger bears stay away as hunters and fighters go searching for them and the larger payoff for their hides and meat." Malsour worked his blade through the bear.

"Well, I didn't think that it would be this messy," Dave complained, cutting out the parts of the bear that they didn't need and then portioning it and throwing the portions into his or Malsour's bag. Once it was in a bag's storage, then it seemed to be held in whatever state it was placed in there, meaning that meat could stay fresh in a bag of holding forever and only aged when it was pulled out.

"I think that's all for now. Shall we move onto that other creature?" Malsour used his water skin to clean his hands.

"Yeah. I want to know just what the hell it is. I'll take point."

"Very well." Malsour fell in behind Dave as he moved up. More rabbits died in their wake; they would get the coppers for killing them, though they would need to get their corpses for any extras they might get for the meat, eyes, and hide.

"The fuck is that?" Dave looked at the rough outline of what looked like a huge mantis.

"Giant Mantis," Malsour said.

"Well, someone didn't put much thought into naming these things."

"Unless the admins announce new creatures, then whoever finds the creature first gets to name it. There are some really dumb ones. Like Pink Poof—it's a type of carnivorous plant that excretes knockout gas, then lashes out with its vines to pull its knocked-out prey into its mouth. Most people wake up with half of their body being digested by the creature's stomach acid."

"Now, that I think about it, Giant Mantis isn't a bad name." Dave rose out from the bush they were hiding behind and let loose his arrow.

"Son of a bitch," Dave muttered. Even with all the bonuses, he'd only just cracked the mantis's carapace and dropped its Health by ten percent. It let out a clicking war cry as Dave let loose another arrow for the same spot. It lost another twenty percent Health. Dave fired his third arrow, missing the mantis as shadows tried to jump onto the mantis, draining bits of Health here and there.

Dave destroyed his conjured bow, pulling his rods back, and turned the left rod into a shield and his right into a sword.

The mantis's front legs came down, two scythes looking to tear him apart.

Dave threw up his shield in time to block it as Malsour threw out metal blocks that stabbed upwards and into the mantis. Dave saw the mantis's left arm come down; he smashed it to the side, stunning the creature long enough for him to stab his blade into the creature's side.

It came back, enraged and clicking. Dave blocked and attacked, remembering the training that Joko had given him so long ago. The way that the Dwarves had fought at Boran-al's Citadel, the different moves he had seen in his travels and even the techniques from the different books he had read on one-handed and shield-work flowed through his mind in that instance.

Dave slapped the claws away; his blade darted out, feinting and slamming into the creature.

His shield was a steel wall, stopping any attack from making it through. Dave got past the initial shock. He had fought people who were stronger and faster than it before. Now, it was just a very large garden creature.

He laughed as he fought. The mantis tired quickly from its wounds and the fight. Dave continued to dance and weave. It was much easier than running all day or beating metals and ores into submission.

The creature swung wide, leaving its neck open. Dave stabbed forward, digging his blade into the creature's neck. He used soul smith; a metal spike came out the top of the creature's head. He destroyed the conjured sword, returning to its rod form as the mantis let out a few clicks before it fell over.

"So, anything useful happen?" Malsour asked as he grabbed his metal blocks and moved to the mantis.

"Well, it seems that I can recall things in the heat of battle. Makes it a lot easier. I don't know what the limits are but I think that increasing my Intelligence just became my biggest goal," Dave said.

"Now, how the hell are we going to get this back?" Malsour looked at the mantis.

"In bits?" Dave asked. His right rod turned into an axe as he cut the mantis's forward leg off in one hit.

"Give me a sword, will you? I don't think I have a blade sharp enough to get through this thing's carapace."

Dave destroyed the shield and turned it into a sword, handing it to Malsour.

"I feel like I'm in some weird horror movie or one of those ones where everyone gets shrunk so everything looks massive," Dave said as he worked.

"Well, there are potions that can make you smaller and larger," Malsour said.

"That's just weird. Why would anyone use that?"

"Well, people who want to get into hidden areas, for one. It's a lot harder to see someone who's the size of a pin instead of a full-grown human."

"Yeah, but the chances of getting stepped on must be so damn high." Dave looked at Malsour, the two of them covered in green blood as they put the limbs into Malsour's bag.

"Well, no one said it was a safe profession."

"I prefer this hunting stuff a lot more." Dave cut the mantis's main body apart to fit it in his bag. "Caves next?"

"Looks like a good hunting ground to me."

"Don't dragons have large caves filled with gold and all sorts of expensive things?"

"We do, but Induca and I didn't bring much. Didn't want people asking where we got all that wealth from so early in the game. We sold soul gems and the like. Now, with the vault soul gems, saving that power for later when we might need it in battle is worth more than the gold we would get otherwise."

"Why don't you just pull more metal from the ground and sell it?" Dave asked.

"I can do a bit of that—though again, too much and it starts looking suspicious."

"Well, I won't tell if you don't—can just say that it was loot drops or we found it in the caves after killing something. Maybe in the dungeon." Dave stretched his Touch out, noticing a number of metals that were around. "Got a decent vein of silver near the dungeon as well."

"Well, then, it will be perfect for you to pull it out of the ground." Malsour smiled. "I've done it hundreds of times, though you're still relatively new to the skills of moving metals and items with your mind and magic. It'll be good practice."

"I swear, you lot should start up a boot camp with all the training you want me to do." Dave sighed.

"You want to take point?"

"Damned slave drivers," Dave muttered as the last of the mantis was stored away and he started forward toward the caves.

***

Dave and Malsour looked at the entrance of the caves.

"I can sense thirteen creatures inside. All of them seem to be pretty big," Dave whispered to Malsour as they watched a wolf wandering around outside.

"I can get them to come to us if you want," Malsour said.

"Be the best plan. Funnel them into here and I'll take care of them." Dave put his two rods together, once again forming a compound bow with glowing runes on it. An arrow appeared in his hand as he watched the wolf.

Timber Wolf

Level 91

Dave watched the creature, his knowledge and perception marking points where he should aim to hit critical areas. He was closer than ten meters, making it not a ranged shot.

Dave fired; the arrow pierced the wolf's lungs. It tried to call out but coughed, suffocating to death as it fell on the ground.

"Okay, just moving the metal to outside of the caves. Hopefully I can catch them as they come out," Malsour said.

His skill is really powerful, but getting the resources he needs to carry it takes planning and precision. Knowing the time it is, where shadows will be, or curses and spells that will work on different animals and having inanimate materials nearby that he can manipulate: he takes this all into account when setting up. I just have to make weapons and hit things.

"Done."

"All right. Well, do whatever voodoo magic you want to get them a running." Dave looked at the entrance to the cave; it was sixty meters away. The area in front of the caves had been cleared away. The trees had scratch marks on them and bushes along their edges. Dave and Malsour used these bushes for cover.

Dave moved so that he stood, using a tree to balance himself so he could draw on the full power of the bow.

"Here they come." Malsour moved his hands as he started casting spells.

The first wolf came out, only to get hit with a curse, making it cry out as its Health started to plummet. Spiders, the size of small dogs and venom dripping from their teeth, flowed out of the other caves; a battle started with the spiders and the wolves.

Dave hadn't been able to see them all as they'd been in some kind of hibernation state. "Shiiiiiet." Dave fired his arrows into the little buggers. "Creepy ass spiders."

Malsour continued to throw curses as Dave took out spider hatchling after spider hatchling. Spider guardians started to flow out as the thirteen wolves and spiders battled it out. The spider hatchlings were no higher than level 30, but there had to be fifty of them. Their venom stacked damage, making the wolves slow after a few dozen hits. The spider guardians were level 30 to 60.

"Even though the spiders are less in Strength, their numbers and their venom means that even if they die, their work is done with a bite," Malsour said.

"Poor bastards," Dave said. The wolves were holding their ground well but the spiders' attacks were indeed having an effect. Dave watched as what he had mistaken for a boulder moved out of the cave.

Spider Queen

Level 121

"Ah shit!" Dave turned to fire at the queen.

"Don't shoot her!" Malsour yelled, but it was already too late. Dave had fired and released, hitting her in the eye and taking out twenty-five percent of her Health.

The spiders seemed to move as one, turning from their battle with the wolves and rushing toward Dave and Malsour.

"What the hell?"

"You attack the queen and the rest will destroy you. She's the only one who can birth more spiders!" Malsour said as spikes rose out of the ground.

Dave's increased speed from his Agility and dual wielding came into effect. The spiders were close enough that they were getting splash damage, using the two-handed main skill. His arrows hit with enough damage to one-shot the regular spiders and kill another just because of splash damage.

The guardians took two hits, or one hit and one splash hit.

"Dark ground!" Malsour yelled.

A black smoke seemed to seep out of the shadows, covering the area around the spiders.

They moved slower and took a few hit points of damage every second. Dave stopped hitting the regular spiders and started hitting just the guardians.

Dave jumped sideways, firing an arrow as a guardian spat acid twenty meters, melting through the tree he had been standing beside. Dave put an arrow into its maw as the others started to fire their acid.

Dave ran toward a tree, still firing his arrows as he jumped at the tree. He used it as a springboard to get to another and jump back and forth, messing up the guardians' aim and leaving melting trees in his wake.

"It's just like Tree Tag!" Dave laughed as he took out the last five guardians. He conjured a holy sword, dropping it right on the queen.

It let out a high-pitched wail as she tried to get the sword out of her back.

"Well, should have tried out yoga, ya ugly bastard." Dave moved back to the ground as the Dark ground spell dissipated.

Malsour's metal had finished off the remaining spiders and were now finishing off the wolves that had been so heavily poisoned that only three remained.

The spider queen died with a loud shriek.

After a few moments, Dave dismissed the sword and looked at the small battlefield.

"Shall we call the others? This is going to be a pain in the ass to clean up ourselves," Dave said.

"Might as well ask them and see if they want to." Malsour opened his interface.

Dave checked the area to make sure that there weren't any more spiders or creatures that wanted to try to eat them. There were a few, but they were all staying away after hearing the queen's dying scream.

Dave looked over the queen's body, his perception highlighting the legs, fangs, poison sacs, and thick-armored skin on her body.

"That chitin would make some decent light armor; seems that people use the poison for—food? What the hell?" Dave dug deep into the forums to find the different things to use her parts for.

As he discovered more, more areas were highlighted on the queen to show the different usable parts. Dave simply had to look at them to get prompts.

Spider Queen Fangs

Can be used to create large needles and daggers

Each said what the item was and what it could be used for.

"Wow, the more you know, the better." Dave moved to start pulling the spider apart.

"Seems that Suzy and Induca aren't finding much. They'll meet up with us to help clear out this area and then go to the dungeon." Malsour waved his interface way.

"Good, cause the spiders will fetch a good price due to their level, armor, and venom. Apparently, venom in meat serves to tenderize it, making it more sought-after, so the wolves should get us a good price if we can dilute the venom in them. Otherwise, it will still be good. We'll just need to find a cook good at getting the venom out. I do not want to be accused of selling bad meat."

"It is just meat," Malsour said.

"Yes, but that doesn't matter to the person stuck on a toilet for two days because of a stomach bug! Uggh, Mexico." Dave shuddered.

"What happened in Mexico?"

"I ate bad meat on the first day on holiday in the country. Was sick for three days. Even though it was a nice-looking country, I flew back home and spent the rest of my vacation playing video games. Could never look at a burrito the same way after that. Never went back either."

Chapter 4: Abandoned Dungeon

"You picking anything up?" Induca asked Dave as they moved toward what was supposed to be a dungeon.

"Just some small creatures running around deeper inside." Dave stood at the entrance of the dungeon; Suzy's golems moved ahead of him. Induca and Suzy were next to each other, with Malsour taking up the rear.

"There are some runes that are messing up the ability to detect much in this area," Malsour said.

"Yeah, I'm picking them up. I think once we're in the dungeon, I'll be able to see more as we go on. Every level looks to have different runes," Dave said.

"Well, I say we go and check it out. If it's this complex, then there should be something useful down there," Suzy said.

"As in expensive so you have some gold coins to spend," Induca teased.

"Maybe." Suzy smiled.

Induca giggled. Suzy and she had talked to each other a bit here and there, but it had been their first time being paired up and sent on their own. Induca wouldn't deny that she had fun on the trip.

Been looking for an opportunity to talk to her one on one. She's a cool girl, Induca thought, not wanting to admit anything more in case things didn't pan out.

"Well, onward and downward." Dave's bow transformed to a shield and sword as they moved into the dungeon's opening.

Location Found: Abandoned Dungeon

As being the first party to find this Dungeon, you will earn 2x XP for the next week. Creatures killed in the Dungeon will drop their best loot for the next day.

"I'll let Deia and Anna know what's going on," Malsour said as they advanced.

"I'm guessing whatever is down here has night vision," Dave said.

"What makes you think that?" Suzy asked.

"There aren't any torches on the walls," Induca said.

"Bingo." Dave slowed his steps. "Well, I've got around fifteen creatures on this floor. There seem to be several floors, growing bigger and looking better maintained the deeper they are."

Induca could sense his excitement as he looked at the layout of the dungeon. A smile spread across her face as she looked at Suzy.

"Our first dungeon in Heval. I'm pumped," Dave said.

The others laughed as they moved deeper, all of them ready for anything that might show up.

Character Sheet

Name:	David Grahslagg	Gender:	Male
Level:	3	Class:	-
Race:	Human/Dwarf	Alignment:	Chaotic Neutral

Unspent points-295

Health:	2,900	Regen:	2.24/s
Mana:	1,470	Regen:	6.60/s
Stamina:	740	Regen:	3.65/s
Vitality:	29	Endurance:	112
Intelligence:	147	Willpower:	132
Strength:	74	Agility:	73

Dave and the rest of his party continued down into the dungeon.

Suzy, Induca, and Malsour were with him, with Deia and Anna on their way. Suzy had Air creations out up ahead, with metal and Earth golems following. Dave was behind them.

Now, we'll know what we're dealing with, Dave thought as the red outline of an enemy mob appeared around the corner.

Before it had time to cry out in alarm, it was hit by wind creations. Three of them worked together, cutting the creature apart before a metal creation speared the thing in the chest.

Dave moved up toward it.

Kobold

Level 73

"Well, it looks like we're fighting kobolds," Dave said to the others. He pulled up the forums and looked at what a kobold looked like when it was alive.

"Damn, they're ugly and odd."

The kobolds looked to be stooped-over creatures that generally wore rags and carried items like picks and shovels. They had decent night vision, but nearly all of them had a candle either on their head or nearby to make out faint details. Their hands ended in claws and they had snouts on their faces, looking similar to moles as they used their noses more than their eyes to move around.

Their tallest was around four foot, but as they aged, they were stooped over, usually using their digging implements as canes.

"Kobolds are really good at hearing things—their eyesight isn't the best," Dave said.

"They've got a few different classes of creatures: kobold king, and then there's melee-based fighters—no archers to speak of. Their mages are usually Earth or Air users," Suzy added.

"Well, I say we go and see how many of them we can clear out. Dungeons usually have some good loot the farther down we get." Dave advanced forward, Suzy's creations moving with him.

"Just has to be in tight and enclosed spaces." Malsour sighed.

"What—don't like small spaces, big brother?" Induca teased.

"I could barely fit my foot in here if I was in my other form."

Dave let loose another arrow, catching a kobold in the side. It let out a wail as the metal creatures pulled it apart.

"That's just nasty," Dave said. "Can't you send these guys out as scouts to see what we're up against?"

"I can, but last time they were discovered, giving the element of surprise away," Suzy said. It was clear it wasn't something she was happy about.

"That was against Alkao, though. I really hope that there isn't something his level down here," Induca said.

"I'd say it's good to risk it and it will allow you to gain a better control over your metal constructs. All different elemental-based creatures react differently in different cases," Malsour supplied.

"Well, all right then." Two of the metal creations shrunk down, leaving behind metal puddles that were absorbed by the others. They were a third of their original size and moved fast through the dungeon to find their enemies.

"Oh, Dave, that reminds me. Is there anything that you could do to a wagon to make it faster?" Suzy asked.

"Why you asking?"

"Well, I was talking to someone the guild wants to basically use as our quartermaster. As adventurers, we travel faster than horses so we're going to need wagons that keep up with us."

"Well, I can think of a few ways to make them faster off the top of my head. I would have to mess around with them. Do you want me to just make trucks?"

"You could do that?" Suzy asked, shocked.

"Well, I think I could, but it would take some time and, well, I was hoping to leave that a bit of a secret. I have another idea of something that would need to be mobile. Got quite a few ideas that are kind of out of the box and maybe a bit insane, though, if they work, then it would make our guild the most powerful out there," Dave said.

"Like what?" Induca asked.

"Like this." Dave closed his eyes, thinking of the design in his mind. It was hard and it took time for the shadows to form perfectly; there were multiple runes and the power that it drew from the soul gems in the rods was rather expensive.

He ended up holding what looked like a long rectangle with a buttstock on the end of it. Underneath, it was shaped into a pistol grip and trigger assembly.

"Is that what I think it is?" Suzy asked.

"Well, if you're thinking gun, kind of. There are actually several guns on this world. Players have been messing around with the mechanics forever. Problem is that the alchemy needed to make gunpowder and all of that is not only hard, but most people blow themselves up. It's easy for people to lose a dozen levels just trying to get the chemistry of it all down. People have not graduated from using basic musket type weapons to cartridge loading rifles. People were thinking too much Earth and not enough Emerilia. This, on the other hand, only uses magical power. Quite a bit of it, but still just magical power." Dave held it proudly out for her to check it out. His Touch of the Land and her scouts would make sure that nothing snuck up on them.

"How does it work?" Suzy asked.

"Well, I've got a few ideas on that, either using straight air compression to spit the round out of the end, or we go with a Fire-based accelerant, *or* a lightning spell that polarizes a metal coil, turning it into a railgun. I'm thinking the first or the last as options. Fire makes me think that it'll blow up and it'll take more time to figure out. Then there is the possibility to have a Mana bolt kind of weapon, but again, all of them are probably going to be much weaker than the weapons we have now. Our arrows can hit as hard as a fifty caliber round due to our strength, abilities of the bows and the materials they're made from." Dave noticed the amount of energy that it was taking just to keep the weapon active and changed back to his compound bow.

"Wow, that would certainly change things." Suzy's eyes glazed over in thought.

"It could, but it's one of the things I want to keep a secret in case we ever need a few surprises up our sleeves."

"For say an oncoming tournament with the most powerful creatures in existence coming back from cold storage?" Induca asked.

"Well, while that does sound like a good idea, I would rather keep these things hidden unless the creatures are openly running around and then we can hunt them down using this weaponry. Keep it secret from other guilds and nations that would like nothing more than to get one of those rifles for their own use. They're only single shot and you can get about three hundred shots out of it, but that's still a lot of firepower."

"It makes sense to keep it secret. Ashal, as a whole, has been fighting for generations. They would do anything to get that kind of weapon. With it, the face of wars would change," Malsour said.

Dave nodded, noticing a group of kobolds getting closer.

"In the meantime, we've got some customers," Dave said.

"I'll try to take them with my creations. I want to see how they stack up against different enemies," Suzy said.

"No worries. We'll provide support," Dave said.

Metal creatures seemed to melt into the floor as rock golems moved to the walls and crouched down, looking like their surroundings. Dave and the others hid around a corner as the kobold party moved past the creations.

The wind creations were invisible until they started sending blades of Air that cut into the kobolds. The metal creations sent out spikes, piercing the kobolds and holding them in place.

Their Health bars plummeted, only one surviving the first attack until a rock golem's fist slammed into its face.

"Wow, that's really nasty but effective." Dave looked at the creations, which were already moving ahead again.

"It might be an idea at researching some magic that will make it harder to detect them. Ambushes are obviously a strong suit," Malsour said.

"Well, if you've got the materials, then I'm willing to learn." Suzy smiled, proud of her achievements.

She's only been in the game for a few months, but she's jumped up her stat points in leaps and bounds. She's been faster than me in gaining levels and that Willpower training must have been hell. Dave shuddered, thinking of his own experiences with it.

"Well, let's see what the rest of this dungeon has." Induca's smile was hungry, a true Player's smile, excited to jump into danger for the possibility of big rewards.

Dave smiled and followed the creations.

They ran into three other groups of kobolds wandering around in the cave-like area of the dungeon.

Dave fired arrows into the kobolds that walked into Suzy's ambushes. Induca and Malsour held their spells, letting Dave and Suzy rack up experience and get used to their different skills.

"Well, seems this is paying off." Dave looked at a new notification that popped up as he killed his third kobold with his bow.

Active Skill: Archery

Level: Journeyman Level 7

Effect: Critical Hit chance increases by 28%. Ranged targets take 10% increased damage

Cost: 10 Stamina

"I'll take that." Dave smiled. He'd been working on smithing for so long that he had forgotten the joys of clearing out a dungeon with a group of friends.

"I hope this place has some more challenging creatures," Suzy said as her creations reformed. She had two metal and one stone golem, with two metal scouts and one Air creation. "Shame that they can detect my Air creations."

"You just had to jinx it." Dave shot Suzy a look.

She simply shrugged it off as her creations started to advance.

"The higher Affinity that creatures have with any magical element, the easier for them to see disturbances. Kobolds with a higher Affinity for Air and Earth will be able to see your creations even if they are hidden, *if* their Affinity is higher or they have a spell or something at work," Induca said.

Malsour slowly clapped at Induca's information.

"What? I've picked up a few things as I've gone along. You and Gelimah are always trying to educate me on things, as well as Mother." Induca sighed.

Suzy laughed as Dave smiled, following the creations.

"How is your power consumption?" Malsour asked.

"Well, I can keep this lot going for another forty minutes. Think I might pull the Air creation and the rock golem back. It would give me less ability to change their fighting style mid-battle, but if the kobolds start figuring out where they are, then it's going to turn into straight-up fights instead of ambushes anyway."

"We're leaving the cave part of the dungeon." Dave sensed an opening up ahead that led to another level.

It looked as if the cave system that they had been walking through broke into another area behind it. With all the runes, Dave couldn't see what the inside of the structure looked like.

"From the outside, it looks like it is two or three times bigger than this cave area and it looks like it was cut out a lot nicer than this area. Less holes through rock, and more squares and straight edges. I can sense the third area past it and it looks even larger and higher quality," Dave said.

"Might be a good idea to save your Mana. We might be in here for a while," Malsour said.

The Air creations came back to Suzy. The slowly swirling air set down on her hand, revealing a malachite container.

"How is the new core working?" Dave asked as she put it away. The golem knelt in front of her, its rocks moving out of the way to reveal its stone core.

"I'm still using just the basics. However, if I can start using the different chambers of the core, I'm kind of scared what it can do. I'm going to need to brush up on my chemistry, though." Suzy looked to Induca.

"Fine, I'll give you a hand." Induca smiled.

Dave noticed the excitement in Suzy's face as she bit her lip, pulling the core from the stone golem. It fell apart into dirt, sticks, and rocks.

Dave hid his own smile. *Interesting, definitely interesting.*

They walked through the cave, coming to a larger area. At the end of it, the cave hit a wall of bricks, the bricks having been pulled down to reveal some kind of building beyond it.

"I can't get anything from my scouts when they go in. I'll send one of the golems through with orders to return," Suzy said.

The metal golem turned into a puddle and moved through the open wall. After a few minutes, it came back.

"Seems that it's clear on the other side; it comes out into some kind of hallway."

"Well, let's go check it out." Dave switched from his bow to a shield and sword, moving through the broken wall and into the lower level of the dungeon.

Chapter 5: Onward and Downward

Abandoned Dungeon

You have made it through the first level of the Dungeon to find ancient Aleph ruins. The Aleph were a race rumored to deal in the mechanical creations of the world. They were reported to be the creators of the teleportation pads. Working deep in the depths of the Earth, their homes and places of work are only accessible by portals and teleportation pads. The cave you traveled through used to be a mine that found the Aleph's home and awoke its guardian beasts.

Dave read the prompt off to the side of his vision as he continued into the corridor.

There were no rough walls here; instead, the walls had been crafted with precision and care. Light sconces illuminated the area. Most of them were broken, leading to large areas of shadow. For the night vision-capable races, it was easy to see through.

Dave heard a screeching noise to his right. He turned to see a party of three kobolds screeching for all they were worth and charging him with their blades. A fourth kobold stepped out, wielding a shovel covered in runes.

Kobold Mage

Level 113

Shit!

Induca blasted them with Fire lances. The air mage sent out wild and panicked wind blades, killing a Kobold that lay in their path.

Dave focused on the other kobolds.

Kobold Miner

Level 124

"Well, this will be interesting." Dave activated his Abscondita armor, his body getting lighter as he rushed to meet the kobold miners.

"Suzy, get your creations in there—have your scouts spread out. With that racket, some of the other kobolds will be sure to arrive soon! Induca, keep that mage suppressed. I will watch the other direction!" Malsour, the leader of their group, said.

Dave met a kobold's pickaxe with his shield. Without conscious thought, he knocked the pickaxe in just the right way to have it deflected instead of stuck into his shield.

The kobold, confused by how his pick had missed its target, didn't have time to dodge.

"Huh!" Dave called out, a grunt that all Dwarven shield bearers would understand.

Dave's sword flashed out, quick and precise. The kobold had enough time to obscure Dave's thrust, making him hit the creature's shoulder instead of through his unprotected side.

A less trained shield bearer might have gone to make good on the attack, one who didn't have the training or Touch of the Land to see through his shield. Dave's shield rose up. Just as the kobold he'd hit in the shoulder rolled away, his pickaxe's momentum pulled him to Dave's side. The third kobold's shovel slammed into Dave's shield.

"Arrggh! Mother fucker!" Dave yelled. His muscles bunched as he slammed the shovel away.

The second kobold had been stopped from attacking by their falling friend.

Dave stepped back, giving himself room as the kobolds looked at him. Their eyes glowed red in hatred at Dave and his friends' trespassing.

Dave saw that his attack on the one kobold had splashed out onto the second. Pickaxe one had taken a ten percent hit and pickaxe two had a five percent hit. Shovel attacker three just looked pissed as he swung at Dave. The others joined in, trying to move into Dave's blind spot.

Dave hid a smile as he let the pickaxe brothers sneak up on his left side, focusing on shovel dude.

He might only have a shovel, but he's fast with it and a real big pain in the ass. With my normal enhancements, I'm only just matching him in speed and Agility.

Dave's shield was there to slam the shovel away every time. Using his Touch of the Land allowed Dave to get the lead time he needed to deflect the attack. Seeing the creature's muscles bunch as they brought the shovel in for an attack made up for Dave's slight lack of speed.

Even though he was beating those attacks back, they were hitting with such force that they were chipping away at Dave's slight Health pool. Dave stabbed and slashed at the kobold, keeping his reach short and deflecting the kobold's shovel every time.

Pickaxe one swung at him.

Dave was too slow to deflect it; the head of the pickaxe smashed through and hit his arm underneath. Dave grunted, seeing the shovel bastard aiming his weapon at Dave's head. Dave's right sword turned into a shield as his left-hand shield turned into a spear; the pickaxe that had been embedded in it fell to the ground.

Stunned kobolds looked at him as he smashed the shovel away, and shoved the spear through the shovel kobold's chest.

They didn't have much time to look stunned as two metal golems sprouted from behind them, slamming their metal arms through their unprotected backs.

Dave used soul smith; the spear in his hand expanded out through the kobold. Its Health dropped to zero. Dave broke the conjuration. The metal spikes disappeared as it slumped to the ground. Dave looked at the mage that stared at Dave and his fallen comrades. Its face went pale at the cold smiles on the rest of Dave's party.

A cold sweat broke out across its forehead as Dave's right-handed shield turned into a javelin. He planted his foot and threw with all his strength. Images of throwing flashed past his mind's eye as runes formed on the spear in a near instant before it was released.

The javelin flew true. The mage turned his attention on to Dave, trying to smash it out of the air. The javelin flew to the side of the mage instead of hitting him. The mage started pooling a large spell, looking at Dave with a vicious smile. Its smile turned to shock as a flame lance burned through its chest.

"Got to be more aware of your surroundings, bub." Induca snapped her fingers. Her flame spear turned from red to blue flames; the mage's Health plummeted to nothing.

"We've got several more kobolds coming from both directions. Dave and I will take the left side; Induca, Suzy—take the right. Suzy, I would suggest calling a few more golems and having the ones you've summoned put themselves on the ceiling," Malsour said.

"Got it. Dave—going to need some juice from your armor," Suzy said.

"Linking," Dave said. With a mental command, he connected to the rune necklace that was around Suzy's neck. It glowed as a connection was formed. She looked to gain energy as she pulled three ebony soccer balls from her bag. Her other metal golems moved up to the ceiling.

Malsour moved his hands around, using words of power to pull metal from the ground around the three metal cores.

Suzy muttered her own words of power as the metal started to change form, turning into metal-looking humanoids, growing in power and strength until they were five feet tall.

Dave conjured a shield in his left hand, calling his rod back to him. It flew to his belt as he pulled out three steel rods with soul gems in their center. Dave held two in his shield-covered hand and held one in his other hand. Shadows covered the steel rods, runes forming down their metal length.

All of it was heavy, but with Dave's Strength, he barely felt it. He saw that the group of five kobolds headed for them were just a few seconds away.

"One Earth, two Air—the rest are miners." Dave shifted his stance.

"I'm guessing that your book reading is helping some?" Malsour asked.

"Yeah, it's like I know how to position myself, keeping me alive with these high-leveled midgets," Dave said.

"Remember, you were a midget not that long ago." Malsour smiled.

Dave smiled as the kobolds turned the corner, stepping right onto Malsour's curse trap, making them vulnerable to magical and physical damage.

Dave launched the javelin with all of his not-so-inconsiderable strength. It flew right into the first Air mage's shield. Its stunned look turned to rage. It dropped its shield, the javelin falling from the hole it had made in the shield.

Idiot. Dave sent a command to the javelin. The javelin turned into a loose spiky ball as the soul gem overloaded. Metal exploded everywhere, ripping the Air mage apart and taking out one of the miners. The other was hit with metal and stunned.

The other two mages focused on keeping their personal Mana barriers up.

Dave didn't wait around and hurled his second and third spear. The first hit the Earth mage's shield; this time it turned into what looked like a mushroom where it had broken into the barrier, exploding and using the barrier to contain its blast. The Air mage sent the second javelin wide. It exploded in mid-air, leaving the second miner at only five percent Health.

Dave held his rods together, forming a bow before the second javelin went off. By the time the second javelin had cleared, he was pulling back an arrow on his compound bow.

The Air mage staggered from the impacts and the death of his three comrades who had been alive mere seconds ago. He looked up, shakily, as an arrow slammed into his chest.

The second miner died from the splash damage earned from Dave's levels in two-handed.

The mage already had a weak Vitality; Malsour's curse and Dave's melee skills put him on his ass for good. His Health bar hit zero before he could hit the floor.

Dave checked his Touch. There were two miners and one mage against Suzy.

Suzy called on her golems hiding in the ceiling. Metal pillars shot down and through the backs of the two miners that Induca had been holding off, freeing Induca to send a fireball at the Earth mage.

It constructed a hasty wall but Induca's fireball smashed through it and into his barrier. Induca threw another before he had time to recover.

The second broke his barrier and tore a hole through him, dropping his Health to zero. Everyone was breathing heavily as An-na and Deia walked through the hole into the new area.

"So, what did we miss?" Deia asked.

Malsour, Induca, Dave, and Suzy looked at one another before they burst into laughter, relieved to have survived and happy to see the results of their training.

"Quite a bit." Dave smiled and took a drink from his water skin. "I've got about fifteen more coming for us. We can cut them off at this big room up ahead. There's a whole bunch of runes all over this place to try to keep it secret. These Aleph liked their privacy."

"The Aleph are one of the odder races and were one of the most technologically advanced. Finding one of their research stations is a rare find," Anna said.

"History lesson later. For now, let's try to see if we can't head off these kobolds." Deia took command as party leader. "Anna, take point. Everyone else, food and water. Does everyone have their rations?"

Everyone replied in the positive.

"Good, because we may be needing them. There's lots of exploring to do," Deia said, clearly excited.

The others smiled, sharing her excitement. Being the first into a dungeon, double the experience, and finding out that it was made by a race of secretive and really smart people; it didn't get much more exciting than that!

"Dave, out in front with Anna and let's see if we can't get to meet these kobolds in some place where we can *really* use magic!"

"Yes, ma'am," Dave said, half-saluting Deia. She just shook her head in amusement as Dave turned to Anna.

"All right, need to go down this corridor a little bit, then third entrance on our left, and a bit of a drop. Seems that the stairs collapsed, but it's the biggest room in here, and they're going to have to come up to it in order to get at us," Dave said.

"Okay." Anna held her great sword ready as they moved toward their battleground.

The room had four staircases, one in each corner. Two led deeper into the dungeon and two retreated higher. The party came in from the back-right stairs. Well, there weren't any stairs, but there was rubble that showed where they'd been.

There were intact stairs on the opposite wall, but that wasn't what Dave was looking at when he stopped in the balcony that circled the room. There were runes all over the floor, carved into the ground, and filled with silver. Here and there, they had been chipped away to try to get the silver out.

Dave's eyes moved to the front of the room. Between the descending stairs, there was a complex half-circle of runes. With Dave's Touch, he was able to see that it was a changing magical circle, able to move runes in and out of formation. Three large boxes jutted out from the second-floor balcony. The two on the sides of the room were enclosed in clear malachite with mangled magical runes.

"Dave, is something wrong?" Deia asked as Dave moved to the large box that faced the large magical formation at the other end of the room.

"Holy shit." Dave looked over the room and the interfaces that had been picked apart for their materials.

"Dave?" Deia asked.

"Incoming!" Anna said.

"Induca, Malsour, Suzy—in this room here. Dave with me," Deia said.

The three moved into the room as Dave jumped down where the stairs were supposed to be.

It's a control room—it has to be, with all the connections to the teleport pad. I need to get a better look at the surviving runes. If this is what I think it is, then it could be incredible!

Dave pulled out a rod from his pocket and aimed at the left staircase. It transformed into a short bow, an arrow in his hand, as Deia aimed for the opposite staircase.

They let loose their arrows at almost the same time as kobolds started to appear. These ones were all above level 130.

The metal golems melded over the balconies, settling to positions above the stairwell, unseen by the kobolds.

Dave's steel rod exploded as its soul gem went critical, tearing into two kobolds, but not taking them out. They were a lot stronger than the ones he'd faced previously. They took twenty percent damage, yelling out their anger as they charged. Deia's arrow exploded into green fire that stuck to everything.

The kobold miners were having a hard time of fighting the flames as the Air and Earth mages didn't wait for it to fall from their Mana barriers as they started unleashing wind attacks and Earth golems started to form. They weren't as well controlled as Suzy's, though if you'd just told one of them to go and destroy whoever was attacking its master, it wasn't dumb enough to stare at you blankly.

Malsour and Induca took care of the growing golems as Anna danced. It was the first time that Dave had seen Anna fight with her Air Blade Dancer abilities and it was as terrifying as it was beautiful.

Her blades sliced through the air, turning the mages' wind attacks into soft breezes. They were just throwing thin and concentrated wind around. Anna was forcibly using her sword to conduct her attacks. They might be a higher level than her, but they didn't have her control.

Dave stopped watching as Deia let loose her second Fire arrow.

Dave conjured an arrow and let loose as fast as he could see a target. He was not only shooting better; he was also able to understand what the kobolds were going to do. He heard a ting of his notifications, but ignoring it as he continued to fire and dodge Earth lances flying in his direction.

The kobolds advanced in the room, headed right for the three melee fighters closest to them. Fifteen had turned into fifty; it looked as if the entire level had come to fight.

The mages were the last to make it out of the stairwells, to their demise. One Earth mage looked up as the five metal golems turned into porcupines. Their metal stabbed through the nearest kobolds as they formed on the ground, stabbing and hurling spears into the kobolds' backs. Malsour's shadows latched onto two miners, draining them of Health and life.

The mages got them free, but they looked to be three times older than when they started the battle.

Dave ducked a shovel, turning his bow into a great sword as he swung to meet a pickaxe. The great sword cut through the wooden length of the pickaxe, the head bouncing off Abscondita's passive Mana barrier. Dave brought the blade back across, his muscles straining to counter its momentum and redirect it as he sliced the kobold open.

Dave took a hit on his shoulder. He turned, shifting the great sword into a warhammer as he kept the momentum going, spinning around and landing the great hammer into the kobold's chest, taking off twenty percent of its Health.

Higher levels couldn't stop all of physics as the kobold went flying and slammed into a balcony. A metal golem finished it off before it could start to recover.

Dave transformed his hammer into a shield and a sword, but he wasn't quite fast enough as he was hit with a tornado. While it was enough to knock him flying back ten feet, it only scratched his Mana barrier, but couldn't breach through it. Anna's sword cut through the tornado, nullifying the attack.

The tornado of sharp wind blades disappeared, channeling into Deia's armor.

Anna jumped into battle. Her first-generation Abscondita armor made her stronger and faster than their opponents as she left a trail of destruction behind. Malsour attacked the kobolds from the other side using shadows, metal traps, and curses in their midst.

Dave got back to his feet, feeling the worse for wear but knowing his party needed him. He threw his sword, changing it in mid-air to a dagger. It slammed into a kobold's shoulder up to the hilt, stopping its blow from hitting Deia.

Her left sword took off its arm as she relieved another kobold of its head.

"Recall!" Dave said. His weapon flew back to him, turning into a sword he barely had time to grab it and raise it to block a shovel aimed at his head. The sheer strength of the kobold pushed him back a few feet Dave rushed forwards, not letting the Kobold get an advantage in pushing him back.

Dave thrust his sword forward, putting what seemed to be a white blade through the kobold.

Dave could see the creature's shock, knowing that Dave had been unarmed just seconds ago, yet now he'd pierced its side with one.

Dave slammed his shield into the creature and attempted to stun it.

Its higher levels came into work. With Fire damage coursing through its body, it still managed to dodge and swing its shovel around, hitting Dave in his sword hand.

"Fuck," Dave grunted. His hand tried to release his sword in a spasm of pain.

Kobold Miner

Level 178

Dave saw a hex land on the creature, reducing its speed. Dave accessed Abscondita, increasing his own speed by forty percent, the highest he could go before it'd start damaging his body by the effect.

The kobold finally seemed just a bit slower as Dave raised his shield above his head, taking the incoming shovel's overhead blow as he went to his knees while slicing his sword across the kobold's inner thigh.

The creature cried out in pain as it stumbled back. A green glow surrounded it as Dave continued to attack, changing his attack. A kobold mage pushed Dave up with an earth platform, making him unstable.

Dave saw the Earth mage looking at him. In a burst of rage, he jumped into the air as his right hand turned into something never seen before on Earth or Emerilia. It took three seconds for the circular device around his wrist to charge, different parts spinning as the front emitted a green glow, with lightning arcing around its front end.

"Pull back!" Dave landed to the side of the battle, facing the middle of the kobold group.

Deia and Anna jumped to the far wall as a green overlay coated the ground, showing the AOE.

"Eat suck, suckface!" Dave yelled as green light blinded him. A blue orb of flickering power shot out from his hand contraption; lightning arced away from it. Anything in its path that was alive was turned into grounding rods as hundreds of thousands of volts raced through them.

It crossed the space in seconds, losing its charge with every creature it hit. Dave, in the meantime, was launched three meters backward, embedding himself into the wall.

Some of the electricity struck the runes around the room, a faint blue glow emanating from them.

Chapter 6: Secrets of the Aleph

"Dave? Dave?" Deia ran over to Dave, who was embedded about three feet into a wall. Any kobolds that weren't hit with the lightning ball screamed out in agony as their eyes, unused to sunlight, had been bombarded with more light than they had ever seen in all their lives.

Deia cut down three on her way to Dave, trying to blink away the image that was imprinted on her eyes. "Dave?" She reached the wall, tears falling down her cheek.

Dave gave a weak cough. "Did I get them all?"

"You idiot. What if you died?" she demanded.

"I'd be revived in SC," Dave said, trying to get his butt out of the wall.

"You dolt! I only just became a Player. I don't think like that!" Tears fell down her face.

"Babe, this is the way Players are. We can take massive risks because we always come back afterwards," Dave said in a calming tone.

"I know, but I guess I never realized it," Deia said, trying to rein in her emotions.

"Did you finish off the remaining kobolds?" Dave asked.

Deia's eyes went wide as she looked around. Anna was killing the kobolds in quick strokes. The remaining metal golems helped her; two had been in the lightning ball's range of attack.

You know better than that. In the middle of battle, you need to stay focused. Getting all scared and emotional could get you and the rest of your party killed.

"Could you help me out?" Dave asked.

Deia pulled him free of the wall.

"Thanks." Dave sounded sore from being planted into the wall.

"We still need to clean up the remaining kobolds, and then you can tell the rest of us just what that attack was," Deia said. She'd deal with her emotions later. Right now, there could be more kobolds on the way.

Deia moved toward any kobolds that were still standing, quickly cutting them down with her swords. Dave's tattoos on his right side lit up before the cylinder on his arm contracted and turned back into a rod and then a sword.

It took five minutes for them to clear out the remaining kobolds.

"I'm not picking up on any more kobolds coming up." Dave moved to the rough half-circle at the front of the room.

***

"This is crazy," Dave said to himself. His Touch of the Land stretched out, making sure that no more kobolds would get to them undetected. He was simultaneously focusing it into the circle he stood on.

"Dave, what the hell was that lightning thing?" Suzy jumped down from the balcony and moved toward him.

"Oh, that? I just held a ball of water and then charged it up with lightning, made a mini thunderstorm and fired it in a direction. Took the idea from Metroid," Dave said absently as he inspected the different runes, moving around the room and kicking bodies out of the way in different places.

"What are you looking for?" Suzy asked.

"This, this entire room; if it's what I think it is, then, well, shit. I don't know, but it would be the find of the century." Dave put his rods away. Pulling out a pencil and a book, he wrote different symbols onto the page, sending out a search function through his rune notes.

He moved around the room. The others watched him and checked out the dead kobolds.

"Dave, are you okay?" Deia moved over to him.

"Yeah, fine." He looked to her. "Sorry about before, but now neither of us can die. The only thing we must worry about is losing our experience and whatever we're wearing. Being a Player changes things and I wasn't about to let that be my first death." Dave smiled.

"I know, but on some other level, I am used to people dying here and staying dead. When I saw you like that, I didn't know what to do." She looked at the floor.

Dave put his arms around her, seeing the tears in her eyes. "Come here."

She shook, crying quietly; the others gave them room as she let out her tears.

Dave listened to it, patting her back and making comforting noises. He'd never had someone so attached to him like Deia. Thinking about losing her, even though he knew that she would respawn, made his mind go black with fear and worry. He didn't know how he would be able to do it.

After some time, she stopped shaking and her grip loosened.

"You good?" Dave looked to her.

"Yeah, sorry." She smiled at him.

Dave smiled and kissed her forehead. "You don't ever have to be sorry at a thing like that," Dave whispered, squeezing her.

She returned the squeeze before she stood back a bit, going back to her role as party leader. "What are you doing with that notepad?"

"Well, to anyone who has ever watched *Stargate*—which I don't think anyone here has—this place is kind of like Atlantis. Those two boxes can be used to rain magic or arrows down on anything that comes through here and control the teleport pad." Dave pointed to the two boxes on either side of the room.

"That is a defensive position, ready in case someone attacked." Dave pointed at the box at the end of the room. "And this sexy beast right here is the star gate." He moved to the half-circle. "Wow, there goes my childhood television shows." He looked at the blank stares.

"Okay, so in *Stargate,* they basically have a portal. Using different symbols, they can connect to other star gates and you can travel all over the darned place. Just dial one up and you can cross in between all day long."

"Like the teleportation pads?" Induca said.

"Bingo! Now this—this is a third or maybe a fifth the size of a teleportation pad and look at it." Dave held his arms up and turned in a circle, his Touch of the Land highlighting the runes and Magical Circuits hidden under the circle at the front of the room. "This is not just some simple portal, or Mirror of Communication or even teleportation pad. This is elegance!"

"The teleportation pads are smaller than this," Deia said.

"Dave, speak English," Suzy warned.

"Right, okay, uhh. Well, they aren't like the teleportation pads on the surface. Those are about ten meters wide; they go down into the ground about fifty meters and spread out over sixty meters. They also use a *ton* of power. These take a lot less power and they're not just tuned to other teleportation pads. I think this could teleport people to anywhere you have a base station. Just a simple pad that can intercept the energy and change it back into reality."

"So, it's a much smaller teleportation pad?" Deia asked.

"It's a much more powerful one. Dave is right. This can connect to other pads like this as well as a city's teleportation pads and portals. If you place down a rune circle, then you could use it to quickly move troops to one single location. It is why the Aleph were so powerful and why the Pantheon was ordered by the Jukal Empire to destroy the race."

"Did they really?" Dave looked to Anna.

"Well, my father did bend the rules a little bit and classified them as dangerous creatures. A number of their race were saved and put into hibernation. Soon, they should be waking up. If we were to start clearing their home of any pests that could have stumbled in, it might be useful to us."

A notification pinged on Dave's interface. He looked to the others, seeing that they, too, were opening their interfaces.

Level 64

You have reached level 64; you have **305** stat points to use.

Active Skill: One-handed and Shield

Level: Apprentice Level 4

Effect: Weapons damage increased by 14%. Defense increases by 5%.

Cost: 20 Stamina

New Active Skill: Inference

Monkey see, monkey do. Well, in your case, it's monkey reads a fuckton of books and monkey is sometimes harder to kill because he understands a bit of what the hell he's reading. You just made melee fighting nerdy—you happy with yourself?

Level: Novice Level 3

Effect: Reading books and learning information on different topics can lead to new discoveries. You absorb information to be used at a later date. Higher recollection in higher stress situations. 9% increased chance of discovery.

"Wow, okay, that is going to be useful as hell. Also, might mean reading a hell of a lot of books."

Stat Increase

+12 Strength

+5 Intelligence

+9 Agility

+2 Vitality

Dave looked at the last notification.

Quest: Aleph Homecoming

Anna has said that the Aleph are coming home to Emerilia. Several of their homes and places they worked in have been overtaken by different monsters. Will you travel to Alephir in order to re-open the gates and push back the hordes of creatures that have defiled this once proud race's homes?

Rewards: ???

Do you accept?

Y/N

"I don't know what the rewards might be, but if we could learn even a bit of what they know about teleportation, then I bet I can get Suzy something that is pretty damned badass. I might also be able to get those portals working," Dave said.

"Doesn't Bob know how to get them working?" Malsour asked.

"Yes, but he can't be down on Emerilia for longer than five minutes or else the rest of the Pantheon might figure out what he is doing, or who he is helping," Anna said. "Also, if he starts activating portals, then the Jukal over-watch programs will inform someone and command him to take them apart."

"If I do it myself and without his knowledge, then it won't invoke the Jukal Empire and their over-watch programs. He can tell me all about them, what they are and what they do, but as long as he doesn't mention how they do it but in general terms, then I guess those over-watch programs won't react?" Dave asked.

"Exactly." Anna smiled.

"Well then, Anna, I hope you know your Aleph written vocabulary, and Malsour, I hope you brought your notepad. We've got a lot to check over. I guess we should also accept that quest?" Dave looked to Deia.

"It sounds like a good idea to me. I don't know how we would clear them all out. There aren't any rewards mentioned. Though if the Aleph are as far stretching as Anna says, there are probably many monsters that we will encounter and need to defeat. We came to train and it sounds like a good event to do just that. That said, everyone gets a vote here. If the majority don't want to, then we can leave the quest alone and sell the information about it on to another group." Deia looked to the others.

"I'm in," Induca said.

"After Dave's riveting *Star Trek* story, how could I resist?" Suzy said.

Dave closed his eyes in pain as he mumbled, "*Stargate, its Stargate...*"

"I've heard much about the Aleph. The chance to meet them and clear their home of enemies? I'm in," Malsour said.

"In!" Dave said.

"I agree with the others."

Deia opened her interface. "Yes."

A waypoint appeared on their map. Dave opened up his minimap. It looked as if it was much farther into the dungeon, possibly at the end of it.

"Well, I say we take a quick rest, build up our Mana and Stamina reserves, get some food and water in us, and then head down to see where this waypoint leads," Deia said.

"Sounds like a good idea." Suzy sat on a rock heavily.

"You can let your metal golems down and I'll put up two Fire elementals in the corridors," Induca said as Dave and his group moved to the semicircle.

"You sure?" Suzy asked.

"You haven't held up summoned creations for this long and it's wearing on you. I can hold elementals up for hours on end. I'll be fine," Induca said.

"Thanks," Suzy said as the metal golems froze in position, their metal bodies ceasing to move.

"Okay, there are a bunch of different circles under this one, with sections that move up and down to change it. I'm thinking that it is the system for picking different locations and the rest of the magical formations are for power and other calculations that don't need to be changed." Dave gestured to the different parts of the room as he talked.

"Eat something as you work." Deia looked over the dead kobold.

"Yes, dear." Dave pulled out a bread roll and munched on it.

She snorted and continued to loot the kobolds. Due to their high level, they had some interesting drops on them and more than one had a length of gold that they had carved from the Aleph runes.

Dave moved to the runes on one side while Malsour moved to the other side. They had divided who would look at which runes, Malsour with his metal sense and Dave with his Touch of the Land. As they copied the runes, they sent them into a group chat with Anna. She explained what each of them meant and related them to other runes that Dave had copied down.

His collective notes were looking like a spider web, highlighting what runes should be used in what case. It took a good hour and a half to get all of the runes down. Once complete, Anna started deciphering them.

"Well then, shall we go and see what other mysteries of the Aleph we can start figuring out?" Dave asked.

Suzy stood. Her metal golems came to life once again and advanced to the front of the room.

"So, left or right?" Induca asked.

"Left looks like it's better maintained," Dave said.

"Left it is," Deia said.

Anna moved to the front with Dave beside her. The golems stayed back between them and the mages. Deia stayed with them as well, holding her bow out instead of her two swords.

Dave shifted in his armor, a large Dwarven war shield on his left arm and a Soul Reaver sword in his right. It was rippled with images of people crying out in pain, as if souls were trying to escape the actual sword.

They advanced down the large corridor. Every twenty steps or so, it came to a landing that extended outward into different rooms. They continued down, the stairs wide enough to fit ten people across.

"Incoming!" Dave said as he sensed kobolds coming toward them.

The kobolds announced their presence with their mages firing all manner of Earth and Air attacks at them. Anna fought off the Air attacks while Dave's shield extended to three times its size, blocking any attacks from hitting the mages behind him.

"Dispel Magic!" Malsour yelled, his voice filling the room. Earth magic spells disintegrated as the kobold mages continued to chant and try to unleash their Earth golems, spears, spikes, and walls.

"Fire storm!" Induca called out. Her eyes blazed with hidden fire as the charging kobolds were greeted with clouds of burning fire.

Dave's shield shifted to a short bow as he released his sword. It floated to his side as he fired arrows into the kobolds.

The Earth mages were suppressed with Malsour's Dispel Magic, meaning that none could use Earth magic at less than a level 8. Anna was still able to defeat the majority of the large Air attacks.

A cyclone started in the middle of the formation, centered on the metal golems that had melded together into a living metal shield wall.

"Circle of Power." Malsour's voice reverberated through the room with power as a blue orb floated around him. "Augment." The sphere moved forward, covering five feet behind him and fifty-five feet ahead of him in a cylinder.

Air magic barely affected them as Deia moved beside Dave. "Plasma cannon?" she asked, still firing her bow.

"I'll support." Dave released the bow. It turned to shadows, revealing the rods underneath and floated back to his belt. "Field of souls," Dave muttered, looking out over the kobolds. A purple light briefly surrounded them.

Deia threw her bow in her pack and started to chant; layers of different colored fire appeared. They created solid sheets of flame as the air in the room seemed to be sucked into the contraption.

Dave closed his eyes, seeing the different elements of the spell. He infused it with his own Mana, solidifying the construction of the spell.

Flame-created parts started to spin and connect, coming together into what looked like a floating barrel cannon. A capsule of plasma entered the tube.

Deia's eyes snapped open. Fire burned in her eyes as her hair blew in the wind being directed into the plasma cannon. Deia's words flowed with incantations as the cannon's sheets of fire brightened.

The first kobolds made it through Induca's flames. Looking at the flame demon and its weapon, fear gripped their hearts. The very air in the room seemed to fall away and stop.

"Plasma Cannon." Deia's words sounded like a soft promise.

The cannon bucked in her hands, launching the plasma round. Dave grunted in effort as they were both pushed back. The cannon evaporated, its job and Mana spent, as its fiery components fell away. The plasma capsule increased in strength as it raced down toward the seventy or so kobolds.

Dave closed his eyes trying to cover them with his forearm, as the plasma bolt struck a kobold as it exited the firestorm.

White light tore through the stairs as Dave was blinded for the second time that day. Even with his eyes closed, he could see the light of Deia's shot. His Touch spread out even as he was blown off his feet. He grunted as he hit the floor and went sliding. He checked on everyone; no one seemed to have anything more than minor injuries. His eyes still blinded by light, Dave stood.

Not one kobold was left standing in the wake of that attack. All of them had been over level 170 and Deia had wiped them out.

She was out cold from the Mana use. Her plasma cannon, although a one-shot, was almost as powerful as two magical artillery spells, which took anywhere from four or more mages to cast.

"Dave?" Anna asked.

"They're gone. Just bam—gone," Dave said.

"How are we looking?" Anna asked, still blind but knowing Dave's Touch of the Land would allow him to see.

"Everyone's good. Deia is out, probably from the Mana use. I think I'm getting some sight back. Being so close to that damned cannon made me blind as hell. Going to need to make some shades to go with that thing. Also, don't think that people should be shooting that more than a few times a day. The air pressures going on with firing that thing are intense."

"Well, at least we know that it works now," Induca said.

"I'm going to say it would be a good idea to keep that little spell to ourselves," Suzy said.

"Yeah," Malsour agreed, sounding a little shocked.

Dave blinked and moved over to Deia, a massive spot on his eye. He started to cough with all the dust that had been thrown up.

Deia groaned and then coughed.

"Hey babe, how you feeling?" Dave knelt next to her.

"Like it's the Feast of Thanks again and you brought the Dwarven whiskey. Holy crap," she said, groaning as she sat up and leaned against Dave. A glow came from around her as she started doing some self-healing. "Well, I guess we should go and see what the hell that did."

Dave helped her to her feet as they looked at the destruction. She used Dave to hold herself up; the Mana drain had taken a large toll on her.

"Well, I hope the Aleph don't mind having a longer corridor," Induca said.

There were burn marks from where the firestorm had been. Charred remains of kobold and their gear were all over the place. The plasma cannon had been so powerful it had made outlines of the kobolds as it slammed into them. Down at the bottom of the stairs, there was a big crater left behind. Magical lights were flickering; more than one set were broken. Dust from the explosion filtered down to the ground.

"By the Fire." Deia looked at the destruction she had caused.

"I think next time, scaling it down might be an idea," Suzy said.

"Ah, but where is the fun in that?" Induca shot back. Dave could see enough to see the wide grin on her face.

"I'm definitely going to try to tone that down a bit."

"Yeah, overkill does seem to just pop into my mind when I see it." Anna's voice was dry as they all stood there looking at the destruction for a time.

"There is no overkill—there is only open fire and time to reload." Dave grinned. Silence reigned for several moments; nobody said anything. "You guys are no fun."

"Well, I say we move on before we have another group sent to find out just what the hell is going on." Deia stood on her own feet, without Dave's help.

"Well, daylight is a burning." Dave headed out to the front with Anna.

They moved down the stairs, leaving the kobolds alone.

Dave checked out his blinking notifications.

Active Skill: Spell Formation

Level: Expert Level 2

Effect: You understand magic on a Mana formation level. Your spells aren't just incantations and messy emotions. They're refined tools. You use 20% less Mana and your spells are 67% stronger.

Level 67

You have reached level 67; you have **320** stat points to use.

"Holee crap." Dave stopped looking at the level jump. It had taken him ages to go up different levels but now he was jumping through them like crazy. He quickly checked his armor to see its state after the mass AOE soul trap spell he'd laid.

Abscondita Armor

Forged by Dave Grahslagg, this armor is more than meets the eye.

Quality: S

Defense: 981 + (Mana Barrier with enough power)

Abilities: Magical Shield.

Automated Mana Siphon.

Automated Soul Siphon.

Automated Self-Repair.

Automated Self Heal.

Increased Agility and Strength (base 15%).

Grows in strength with user.

Manipulation possible (Associated values liable to change due to creator's changes and level of charge).

Armor Link (Users of this armor can share their power and link capabilities. If one armor is fully charged then it will feed power to the other to charge it).

Charge: 94,585/2,000,000 (Linked Armor 119,019/8,000,000)

Durability 531/531

"What?" Anna asked, the only one in earshot as they continued down the stairs.

"My levels just jumped up three spots and my armor's charge is at like one twentieth!"

"Well, you're still rated as level 3 and you were helping out with the cannon that defeated like seventy level 170s. Killing creatures is the fastest way to gain levels. I know that you're trying to grow it all organically and then use them together at a later date, but why not use them? You know you can claim your class at level 10, right?"

"Well, I've heard about it, but I don't know. There's a lot of stat points that I can use," Dave said.

"Look, claiming your class will allow you a lot of different choices. I would suggest waiting until you got to your Journeyman level in all of your melee classes but the boosts that it can give you are well worth it taking longer for you to gain stat points."

"What class are you?"

"I'm an Orikai Air Dancer class. With it, I gain a higher Affinity with Air. I also gain a larger Mana pool and the ability to see all wind attacks directed at me. With enough training, then I can get it to the stage where I can see all of the attacks sent at my party, and then all Air attacks, even those that are forming. If say you were to take the Weapon Master class, then you could have increased Strength, Agility, and resistance to physical attacks."

"Well, Deia has two classes, Mage and Ranger," Dave said.

"It is also possible to get classed through a ton of hard work. The people of Emerilia do not specialize or get classes—unlike the Players, who can pick theirs. We work hard to get our classes. When you are level 10, you should get the class Smith as well as Enchanter from your training and work in both areas. You are probably well on your way for also Soul Lord due to your ability to manipulate souls. Each of those will give you a large boost."

"So, you can get classes by having a high ability within certain things or complete different programs?"

"Correct, but there are few programs that you can complete to gain a class that won't take you several years. You will also only receive that class when you are over level 10. Everyone I know who has gotten a class has been well over the limit. I guess since you have to put your stat points into your character in order to gain a level, the same goes for classes."

"Hmm, well, that is definitely something to think about," Dave said as they made it to the end of the stairs. It linked back together to the opposite stairs in a massive hall. It was at least a dozen stories high and faced a massive doorway that had been pushed most of the way open.

"Are you detecting anything alive?" Anna asked.

"Well, no kobold. That doorway is runed, but since it's open I can see inside for a bit," Dave said. The two of them held their weapons ready as they advanced to the doorway.

Dave stepped through first, with his large shield covering his body.

With his Touch, it didn't matter if his eyes were covered; he could still see everything around him perfectly.

"Clear," Dave said, not really believing his Touch as he looked over his shield and looked at the area they'd entered. "What is this place?" He looked around.

"Living quarters for the Aleph. What we passed through looks to be one of their experimental areas. This is the central hub." Anna waved to the living area. Homes lined the walls as they did in the Dwarven mountains. Here, there was more functionality instead of the beauty and liveliness of the Dwarven homes. Floating bridges crossed over and linked different levels.

Dave pushed his senses out. There were three other living areas laid out exactly like this one. In the center rested four teleportation pads that had been mauled. At the two living quarters to Dave's right and left, there were no doors that led to other areas. Instead, there were entire walls dedicated to plants, to a multi-leveled plantation. Most of the plants had died; others overgrew their boundaries to be close enough to a magical light in order to survive.

It looked as if the place had been stripped free of its original inhabitants, replaced with different items all over the place from the kobolds and unknown others that had moved into the area.

The living area opposite the one that they had entered did have a door that Dave couldn't see past.

"I've got about fifteen kobolds hanging out at the large door in the opposite living area," Dave said softly to Deia who was just close enough to hear him.

"Mind if I get my metal golems into place? It will take them some time to climb the different levels and get over there, but could surprise the hell out of them," Suzy said.

"Do it," Deia nodded. "So, what are we looking at?"

"These housing units are about five stories tall, three hundred meters long. There are four of them arranged like the points of a compass. We're at south. East and west have growing areas instead of doors. North is the only other place other than south that has a door leading anywhere. In the center, we've got four teleportation pads, smaller than the ones that we saw behind us. Got like twenty kobolds hanging out near the door in the north living quarters. I'm guessing that they have mages on the second floor because they don't have archers. About five mages on the second floor, which will let them see us before we see them. They've also got traps on the floors," Dave said.

Deia was quiet as the metal golems in their liquid form moved up the walls.

"I think it might be best if we take an idea from Suzy's book. We move to the west and east living quarters and get higher so that we don't get hit with those traps. Then, we hit them at range. Anna and I will run defense; the rest of you just nail them to the ground." Deia looked at everyone who had gathered around to hear the plan.

"Well, that sounds pretty fun and I think I can try out my rifle contraption." Dave smiled.

"Just make sure it doesn't blow up." Deia tapped his shoulder.

Dave smiled, not wanting to say anything.

"Let's go," Deia said.

Dave, Deia, and Malsour moved to the east living area to make their way up higher. Anna, Induca, and Suzy went to the west area.

Dave quickly found stairs to the third floor and moved back toward the north living block. He slowed his pace, moving slowly as he advanced on the kobolds, looking for a bridge with a good vantage of the kobolds. The rest of their party moved on their side of the living quarters.

Party Chat

Deia> This bridge looks sturdy and has some walls on either side to give us cover.

Anna> Agreed.

Suzy> Sending metal golems on the fifth floor over top of the kobolds.

The notification panel blinked lightly as it tried to draw Dave's attention. He looked away from it, turning it from a solid bar into a misty outline. He continued forward to the waypointed bridge. He moved to the side of the bridge and went into a home.

Shadows rolled out of his armor; smoke covered his arms and touched the two rods in his hands. Soul gems in the rods became brighter as power flowed into them. His eyes glowed silver as he pulled the two rods together. He concentrated. Shadows fell away from his arms and now flowed over the two rods in his hands, obscuring them from view as the shadows grew and something solid could be seen under their smoky visage.

It fell away to show a boxy bullpup rifle. Dave checked the simple iron sights.

"Well, this is probably going to be about as accurate as me trying to throw a cow at a target." Dave moved back out to the balcony. He checked the runes that flowed over the body of the rifle as well as the ones he could detect inside the weapon. He pulled his hood up, obscuring his features in smoke, and extended his Mana barrier around his head in case anything went wrong.

Dave moved back to the bridge everyone was set up on. He sat and braced his arms on his knees as he aimed at the kobold.

Party Chat

Suzy> Metal golems are in position.

Deia> As soon as the golems start fighting, we go. Whenever you're ready, Suzy.

Dave felt the metal golems silently drop from their perches on the ceiling, headed right for the unsuspecting kobold below.

"Field of Souls," Dave said. A purple glow fell over the kobold.

"Dispel magic!" Induca and Malsour said at almost the same time as Anna jumped off the balcony, using the bridges and lower floors to get closer to the kobolds.

"Daylight!" Deia yelled. A miniature sun flared into life among the kobolds. Their screams filled the living areas as the five metal golems found their targets with meaty and final crunches.

Dave stroked the trigger on his rifle. It bucked, hitting low and to the right of the kobold he'd been aiming at. It didn't notice as it was screaming in pain at having been blinded by a small sun.

Dave adjusted his aim, taking two quick shots. The second missed but the third hit, dropping the kobold mage from a hundred to eighty percent Health. *Well, not doing so good; not as strong as a bow right now. Maybe if I altered the rounds, then it would be better?*

Three more shots put the creature out. Gray smoke rolled from Dave's shoulder and into the magazine. The runes on the rifle glowed with new power as Dave conjured a ten-round magazine, finding another target.

Anna was now among the kobolds who were recovering from their loss of sight. Anger was in their eyes as they looked for vengeance.

"Ebony Whips." A square of darkness erupted behind the kobolds, cutting off any possible retreat and claiming two kobolds that vanished from sight. Dave put their screams to the back of his mind as he tried to adjust his rifle and kill the creatures below.

Well, that sounded odd. Dave was about to turn toward the rifle as its conjured power core started to overload. Dave pulled his Mana from it as fast as possible. The rifle exploded in his hands. His armor's natural Mana barrier deflected the damage but still made Dave fall on his ass from the explosion.

"Return," Dave said. The two rods he'd used to make the rifle came back to his belt. He pulled them off, turning them into a crossbow. *A lot more stable and easier to use. Have to do some more testing, but might be better to go with a bow than a rifle at this point.*

"Firestorm!" Induca called out. Flames popped onto the bridge that the mages had been lazily walking over.

"Righteous Fire!" Deia unleashed a pillar of Fire that seemed to rain down from the ceiling onto the kobolds below. Anna had to quickly move out of the way while Suzy watched over the golems.

Dave looked for anything moving in the two Fire attacks and put a crossbow bolt into it.

Deia's pillar of Fire fell away to reveal three metal golems and two metal cores that had been pushed to the side. Just three kobolds had survived the attack.

Anna fell on them; using her sword, she pushed them back toward the metal golems, who turned their bodies into lances to finish off the creatures.

Fire and shadow lances greeted the single kobold that survived Induca's attack.

All of their attacks happening at once with the kobolds never knowing where they were or what was going on had turned all of them into sneak attacks.

"Well, shit, we've got a ton of FIREpower." Dave sat back, his crossbow turning back into two rods.

"Dave, please, for the sake of the English language, just give up on trying to make puns," Suzy said.

"Everyone's a critic."

"I thought you said that your rifle wouldn't explode." Deia gave Dave a stern look.

"Well, I never *specifically* said it wouldn't. There was a high chance it wouldn't and it didn't for about twelve shots. Then, I think from overuse and the thin metal, a rune got linked in the wrong way though I broke it down enough that it didn't do all that much damage." Dave smiled, forgetting that all she could see were his teeth and his eyes while he wore the hood.

"Dave, you look like a jack-o'-lantern. Take the hood off." Suzy rubbed the bridge of her nose and walked away. Induca and Malsour also headed toward the northern door's entrance.

Dave followed her advice.

"Next time, do your experimenting on the seeder instead of in the middle of a fight," Deia said, exasperated.

"Hmm, when you put it that way..."

"You sound like an idiot."

"Well, no, just makes me see my decisions in a different light," Dave amended.

"Like an idiot." She smiled.

"Your idiot." Dave grinned like some kid might, knowing that he had won his argument.

"Yes, *my* idiot, who I would prefer to *not* blow his head off with his crazy inventions." She walked over to him and wrapped her fingers in his as they headed down toward the door to see what lay beyond. "So how was the rifle?"

"Pretty crap, then it exploded. Need to zero the barrel somehow, and I have no idea how you do that. Then, need to fix that overheating issue which means different materials. Which means more power to make or higher cost." Dave realized that he was rambling by the look on Deia's face.

"Well, seems that you'll have something to work on." She smiled.

Chapter 7: And the Universe Keeps Turning

"Bob, what are you doing?" Fire moved to the room that he had created in her volcano and was living in.

"Sprucing the place up a bit and putting a distillery in! After Dave showed me his drinking know-how, I've been craving some good beer or even a nice Scotch, but I can't get any unless I go and visit him! If I can't visit him, then I'll just have to do it on my own!" he said as there was a metal banging noise and then a crash.

Bob came out a few minutes later wearing a stained Hawaiian shirt and an expression that told Fire she shouldn't ask what had just happened.

"I guess this is what I get for letting him move in because I'll be off at Per'ush in a few months. I hope that Denur can keep him from blowing the place up," she muttered to herself as Bob walked over. "What is with the shirt?"

"Well, with the Pantheon all watching what I'm doing, I thought that I would give them some well-needed fashion advice. Wearing just one color all the time is just boring as hell. Look—even you are doing black pants and red shirt. Could you imagine Light wearing anything but golden robes? I don't even know if she has legs anymore!" Bob walked past Fire and headed to her living room.

Fire rolled her eyes, knowing that he was just deflecting. "Now, how about you tell me the real reason that you're messing around with all of this alcohol-making equipment?"

"'Cause I'm BORED!" Bob fell backward into his chair. "I'm stuck up here with nothing to do because that fucking Emperor had his Jukal mouthpiece talk for him and give me new orders. They've completely lost the fucking point. Emerilia was supposed to be capable of fighting off the aggressive species that were coming to destroy the Jukal Empire. Now, they're not even seen as threats; they're seen as entertainment. The empire is as stagnant as a fart in space and they don't care. Emerilia was supposed to be an aid. I was wrong in thinking that and so many people have died because of it. Yet now, without it—well, without it, the empire would collapse. I need to be down there. I need to be down on Emerilia, doing what I usually do—working from the shadows, altering the course of a war by millimeters, balancing the outcomes. Yet now, I can't do that."

"Well, you've always talked about how you've wanted a vacation." Fire tried to bring some levity to the situation.

"You don't get it." Bob turned to face her, his expression grave. "What happens in this cycle of Players; it could change everything"

"What, the Pantheon's power balance? Well, there always has been a threat that there might be another one of the Affinities rise to power in order to disrupt Light and Dark's ongoing battle," Fire said.

"No, I don't mean the Pantheon. I don't mean Emerilia. I mean the entire *Empire.*"

Fire knew to a degree that the Jukal Empire supposedly gave Bob his orders, which he passed on to the others of the Pantheon and was bound by their actions and their rules. Though she hadn't ever seen anyone from this Empire other than Bob, their strength was no simple matter.

"We will prevail—we always have," Fire said, trying to reassure Bob.

"The Pantheon has pissed off too many people of Emerilia. It won't survive," Bob said.

"The Pantheon? Falling? I know that I have heard many people declare that they would pull the Pantheon down. I myself have said it a few times, though it isn't possible." Fire shook her head.

"Oh, it is. There didn't used to be a Pantheon. I gave them an inkling of power at the beginning and then said that they would have to get the rest from the devotions of the people. Now, the people are starting to rethink their deals with the gods. This new generation of Players are already making waves. Leading them is the Stone Raiders. They're hiring POEs all over the place to do their work and not one of them believes in a higher power. They believe in themselves and hard work and you know what? It's paying off. They're the strongest guild on Emerilia right now and they're only getting stronger."

"They're Players, though. Their interests can change on a whim if given enough of an incentive."

"Yes, in the past that had been true, but they have people within their very guild who are from Emerilia. They fought at Boranal's Citadel and created a camaraderie that is unseen at this period of time. The Golden Sabres that fought with them—that was the second-most powerful guild in Emerilia at the time, and now the fifth—are making preparations to merge with the Stone Raiders if the Raiders will accept them."

"That kind of power shift will be immense, but still it won't be enough."

"The Dwarves are mobilizing and they will be opening up competitions for the Weapons of Power. Many of the races that went against the gods, but then mysteriously disappeared are going to return and then the creatures that were bringing wanton destruction to Emerilia are returning in a year. Think what's going to happen with these competitions and powerful groups coming together. The People of Emerilia and the Players are going to be stronger than ever if they can get through it. Few, if any, are going to be giving a devotion to some god, goddess, lord, or lady. They're going to be dealing with all the crap that is going on in their lives—they're not going to look to the Affinities unless they're too weak to change their own lives. The guilds, the different clans that are already preparing for the coming wars—they will be the icons that people look up to. What is more powerful than the most powerful guild in history standing up against the most powerful beasts ever known and laughing as they do it?"

"They're going to be hailed as heroes. They'll be venerated." Fire sat into her own seat, seeing how things were coming into place. Seeing hundreds—no, thousands—of different aspects that, if they came together *just* right or even marginally right, could lead to something that she couldn't predict the end to.

"I might be sitting here and waiting, but I am not yet powerless. My own agents of change are on Emerilia and with them a change is coming." Bob sat back, looking at the lava that lay in pools around Fire's home.

"Who?" Fire asked.

"Yours and my own daughter's party." Bob looked to her.

"Deia?"

"Deia, Malsour, Induca, Dave, Suzy, and Anna. One a demigod, two first-born dragons, two bleeders, and an Administration AI of Emerilia, Anna'kal." Bob's words were quiet but powerful as Fire's eyes widened in shock.

"You woke her up? I thought that you had to put her to sleep because it was getting to the stage where she couldn't stand to watch the suffering of the People of Emerilia for the sport and entertainment of the Empire?" Fire looked at Bob.

He sat there, not saying a word as she let what he had said filter into her mind.

"You really think that they can help to change Emerilia, to change the Pantheon and go up against the Empire?" Fire was shocked by her own words.

"I don't think that they can do it by themselves, but they are a wind of change and with them, many plans will become possibilities. While the Pantheon was off running amok, I was making alliances. Did you ever know why there are no longer fights between everyone except the Ashal nations?" Bob asked.

"Because fighting while Players are there is a quick way to see everyone get destroyed by Players joining into the fight?" Fire said. It was common knowledge. With Players coming in, it was like adding a nuclear bomb to a caveman fight and everyone came out the worse for wear. Ashal nations fell and rose by the decade because of this.

"Yes, but it took me going down there and having a private and pointed conversation with every single nation leader. Not one of you noticed that as soon as the wars stopped that the nations started trading immediately. Trade is the basis of an agreement, a bit of good old-fashioned give-and-take. At first, I used different ploys to get the various nations to trade with one another. In the end, it didn't matter what I had said; the ones that were working together and were trading for the sake of trading were doing better than the ones that were using it as a front to gain information or to try to understand another nation's strengths and weaknesses. There was tension but as soon as someone thought about overstepping their boundaries, I would give them a little visit. The bonds of Emerilia have never been stronger. Sure, it costs to cross a nation's borders and the forces are all highly trained but that is more to sustain their military and to have a fighting force that can deal with the Players if they step out of line. Populations are bigger than ever; people are stronger than ever and the Pantheon is now going to try to break those bonds that have been in place for decades or longer. The lords and ladies of the Pantheon are so focused on their own plans and one another's that they didn't notice a damn thing as I altered things bit by bit." Bob gave a proud smile.

"So, what does this mean?" Fire asked.

"Well, it means that things are going to change quickly. I don't know how things are going to go and I had hoped that the Player Champions I was working with had higher levels. I also did not foresee the different people I had packed away being released from their hibernation," Bob muttered and then shrugged. "Well, it's up to them. It is their planet, after all."

"Do you have Champions?"

"Nope, not one." Bob shook his head.

"Then how were you able to convince different lords' and ladies' Champions?"

"Oh, that was easy. I just posed as the game's AI and then fed them information on the different lords and ladies of the Affinities. They might have made an oath to the lords and ladies but Players are always thinking about themselves more than anything. Armed with information against the Pantheon, if their masters tell them to do something that they don't want to, then it might just happen that they revoke their Champion status." A sly smile spread across Bob's face.

"Why did you keep so many races in hibernation? You kept the Demons and the Aleph, for Empire's sake!" Fire said. Not even she could try to understand what would happen in the coming years.

"The Aleph are the most mechanically inclined of all the races. When Emerilia started, there were just portals and people would have to travel from one city to another. Now, there are teleport pads all over the planet that the Aleph first created. The Aleph's creations were incredible but the Empire got wind of some of the things that they were tampering with and then they called for the Pantheon to root them out and destroy them. I saved as many as I could and made sure that the full extent of their secrets stayed secret. Well, the Demons, they're kick ass and they're one of the two predominantly magical warrior species. They and the Angels are the strongest of all the races when it comes to combat. Again, I tried to save as many as possible, knowing that they might be needed in the future."

"The Dark Lord is already putting his new generation of Demons out into Emerilia's north," Fire said.

"Yes, but who better to either destroy or tame them than their ancient brethren?" Bob said.

Fire's mind spun with all he was saying.

"I don't even know what is going to happen in the coming years. I don't know if Emerilia will even survive. There are just too many variables. The Empire gave their orders and in their idiocy and an attempt to make things more interesting—well"—Bob shrugged—"it's going to be interesting."

"What plans do you have for my daughter?" Fire could see things would quickly windmill out of the control of the Pantheon. The lines of battle were being drawn up and no one realized it yet.

"I have no plans for her. I will aid her and her party as much as possible. I have great hopes for them. But in the end, they are my *friends*. That is where all of the other lords and ladies, except Water, went wrong. If you make a relationship with someone, you have to give and take and help them; then they, in turn, will help you. I would be willing to do everything in my power to help them. None of the others in the Pantheon understand that, except for possibly you for your Dragons and Water with the Merpeople. Isn't it interesting how two opposites are more alike than not?" Bob tapped his chin, giving her a perusing look. "The die has been cast; now it is time to see where they land. The forces of Emerilia are being unleashed. Only time will tell what it will lead to."

***

Communications Officer Sato drank from his coffee pouch, rubbing his eyes as he looked around the large room filled with different workstations.

At every workstation, there was a Mirror of Communication with runes carved around its exterior. For three hundred years, humans had hid out on the fringes of Jukal space, using their limited and remaining technology to create homes in the asteroid fields of the Deq'ual system.

The first decades had been harsh and grueling; more people died than survived. Enough did survive that they could complete habitats, and humanity once again started to grow.

Sato had been raised on stories of the Jukal Empire. His grandfather, one of the first people to settle their home—Complex Three—had told him of the fighting. How they had come without warning, wiping out humanity as they went. Humanity's fleets fought back, but it was a losing war. The Jukal had thousands of creatures; for every single human.

Grandfather Sato and their merchant fleet fled with their families to deep space, beyond the Jukal Empire's reaches. They learned of Sol system's destruction: the Jukal, after four years of war, bombed the sun and turned it into a supernova, destroying everything out to Jupiter. Then, they sent in planet busters to destroy anything bigger than a corvette warship.

Sato had lived off the stories and, like countless other humans, he vowed revenge. They used the Jukal's tech and started trying to see whether there was anyone else out there to work with. They had come into contact with three other settlements but all of them kept information like numbers and locations secret.

They had been talking now for over a hundred years when Sato applied to be a communications officer.

That was when they first connected to someone who called himself a mage on a planet called Emerilia. He had heard of Earth but he said that only the "Players" talked about the planet. He said that the Players all said that they were from Earth. For years, they had pumped the man for information. The People of Emerilia came from multiple human sub-species, with all manner of names. The Players also came from these other races, but they were much stronger and they used the rebirth technology of the Jukal.

They also said that they were from the year 2049. They would disappear for a year or two and then reappear, once again saying they were from Earth and the year 2049. They were able to get a rough location of where Emerilia was. The mage acted as a link, passing them Jukal technology information. They would send him back a few magical ideas so that he was comfortable.

Sato had never seen anything like it. The entire colony benefited from the technology until they'd suddenly received a rushed message saying that someone was after him. After that, there had been no communication from him since.

Sato, as the communications officer for the colony, was responsible with trying to connect to the Mirror of Communication every few months.

He worked his holographic interface as the call went out. The runes flared in colors.

Mirror of Communication

Connection established with Communication Mirror Codename Emerilia...

Redirection, separate terminal discovered. Connecting...

Sato sat up. The mirror had never done this before!

Mirror of Communication

Connection established with Communication Mirror subset mobile device

Sato looked at the screen but it remained black. "The hell is wrong with this thing?" It was impossible to trace communication mirrors, so Sato wasn't worried that the Jukal Empire would somehow track him down.

Light started coming from the side.

"Huh, I didn't think that the Dwarven council was supposed to contact me for another few weeks," a gruff male voice said as the screen moved.

Sato looked at a ceiling, and then at a floor, which looked to have scorch marks on it. It was flipped around and he found himself looking at a bearded man.

"Damn, it worked! I didn't know if the connection bypass would work on that other mirror!" The man grinned happily, pointing at the mirror and then pointing Sato at all manner of different people. It was too fast for Sato to figure out anything more than general characteristics.

"Excuse me, who are you?" Sato asked, not really believing what he was seeing.

"Come on, let us talk in the conference room; bit easier than this stuff," the bearded man said.

User David Grahslagg requests that you use the conference function. Do you accept this request?

Y/N

"Yes." Sato touched the side of the mirror.

The communications room disappeared and he seemed to be in a comfortable-looking home, with two chairs in front of a fireplace that held a flickering fire.

"I'm Dave." The bearded man from before, moving from the seats and holding out his hand.

"Sato."

"Well, good to meet you, Sato. Sorry, I didn't pick up those other calls—was rather busy at the time. You must be what is left of humanity." Dave moved to the seats and waved for Sato to join him.

"I'm sorry, but how do you know these things?"

"Well, I have a very interesting friend who told me most of the information about Emerilia and its people."

"Ahh, Alexanderi still lives? We were wondering why he had not contacted us again. We feared that he might have been killed off by the Jukal Empire."

"Oh, I don't know any Alexanderi and the place where I found the Mirror of Communication looked like it hadn't seen a resident in some time. Sorry." Dave scratched his head.

Sato had talked to Alexanderi for many hours and had missed those talks, but right now he had another possible source of information right in front of him.

"You said Emerilia and its people—are you not someone of Emerilia?"

"Kind of. I'm a Player," Dave said.

"Shouldn't you be conditioned to think that this is all a game then?" Sato asked, scared that he would lose his source of information almost as soon as he found it.

Dave laughed; it was a hard and cruel thing. "I was at one time, though I'm something of a special case. Thankfully, someone found me and told me about what Emerilia and Earth really are. I know the truth about Sol being destroyed, about the Empire sustaining such heavy losses in the war that they needed something to fight the aggressive species on their behalf. I know that humanity in all its forms was nearly wiped out and that you are probably one of a very few groups of true humans who survived. I know that I and all the People of Emerilia started off in a test tube, grown to populate Emerilia and play it."

"So that is what Emerilia is? A place to test humanity?" Sato recorded everything Dave said; it was information gold.

"In a way, I guess. We were used in the beginning, without knowing it, to kill off aggressive species that were threatening the empire. Then, the Jukal Empire started watching; it got entertaining. Now, we're just gladiators in the universe's biggest coliseum."

"Could you start from the beginning?" Sato asked.

"Well, I'm currently in some impressive dungeon. So, I need to get back to my friends. Do you have the ability to pull information from a Mirror of Communication?"

"Yes." Sato nodded.

"Very well. I've got some notes that will be helpful. I don't know when I'll be free to talk again, but the notes detail everything I know and the history of Emerilia. We'll talk soon. Hopefully, I'll be able to help you out some. It's about time we taught the Jukal Empire that we are not bugs that they keep around for their entertainment."

Chapter 8: Old Systems

"So, what was that?" Suzy asked as Dave started to move again. He'd been sitting still, holding a mirror in his hand for five minutes or so.

He blinked a few times and stretched.

"Uggh, I can see that being really uncomfortable after some time." Dave put the mirror away as he rose. "That was what is left of humanity. After the Dwarves gave me this thing, they said that I can connect it to any other Mirror of Communication. Like the one I have back on the seeder. I did so and they called me up. Their timing is a bit bad, but now that I have their mirror's codes, I can call them up whenever."

"So real humans, from Earth?" Malsour asked.

"Well, I doubt that any of them would say from Earth, but yeah, not test-tube creations like us lot," Dave said.

"What did they want?" Deia asked.

"Information. I sent them all I know about Emerilia and the different things that have gone on here. It might be really useful having people like that in our corner," Dave said.

"We should be careful with them, just in case it's some Jukal plot," Anna added, tossing Dave two items.

He caught them, finding two rings.

Ring of Minor Health

+700 to Health Points

Ring of Vitality Fortification

+15% to Vitality stat

"Yeah, that might be handy!" Dave smiled. He was feeling pretty conscious about his low Health attributes. Most people put their stat points into Vitality as it was so hard to level up but as he hadn't put in a single stat point anywhere and tried to not get hit as much as possible, it was growing very slowly.

"Everyone do a stat check and let's see how we're looking before we go any further," Deia said.

Dave didn't quite rub his hands together but he smiled as he opened up his notifications.

Active Skill: Archery

Level: Journeyman Level 7

Effect: Critical Hit chance increases by 28%. Ranged targets take 10% increased damage.

Cost: 10 Stamina

Active Skill: Sneak Attack

Level: Journeyman Level 4

Effect: When you are undetected in stealth, attacks will hit with 296% increased damage (Massive increased when hitting Critical area). May your aim be true.

Cost: (Attack 50 Stamina)

Active Skill: Stealth

Level: Journeyman Level 7

Effect: 57% chance to remain undetected (reduced in direct light).

Cost: 5 Stamina/second

Passive Skill: Night Vision

Level: Master Level 3

Effect: 89% increased night vision. 15% increased vision in magical darkness.

Racial bonus: Dwarves, even half-Dwarves, are at home in the darkness of mines and their empires dug underneath mountains. +25% increased night vision (+5% in magical darkness).

Active Skill: Inference

Level: Novice Level 9

Effect: 21% increased chance of understanding moves you've read in books.

Stat Increase
+3 Strength
+3 Intelligence
+4 Agility
+2 Vitality
Level 71
You have reached level 71; you have **340** stat points to use.

Dave pulled up his character sheet.

Character Sheet

Name:	David Grahslagg	Gender:	Male
Level:	3	Class:	-
Race:	Human/Dwarf	Alignment:	Chaotic Neutral

Unspent points-340

Health:	3,300	Regen:	2.24/s
Mana:	1,550	Regen:	6.60/s
Stamina:	890	Regen:	4.30/s
Vitality:	33	Endurance:	112
Intelligence:	155	Willpower:	132
Strength:	89	Agility:	86

"Nice." Dave put on the Ring of Minor Health and then the Ring of Vitality Fortification. "I'll take that." He looked at the new Health point bar on his main screen, it showed a bar of 4,495. "Annoying that it doesn't stack but that would kind of be cheating."

It would still take just a few good hits to put him down if he had anything less than his armor on, though it made him less scared that some errant breeze might kill him.

"Everyone good?" Deia looked around as people were trying out different loot that they had received. Most had been thrown into their bags to be sorted through later. There was nothing of rare or unique quality, so it would be added to things for Suzy to sell.

"Well, let's go and finish this dungeon off then. Anna, you've got point," Deia said. The party moved into their positions.

***

Many miles away, a screen turned on. Lines of information scrawled across it.

Program start> Guardian activation protocol...substation H2983. Trespassers; breach recognized. Two forces at play.
Command system override...Portal connection possible, scouting force ready. Scout Guardian activated and online...Permissions criteria met.

In front of the screen, a large open area—not too dissimilar to the teleporting room that Party Zero had moved through—started to move. The semicircle at the front of the room moved; sections of runes dropped down and rose up to change the formation. The runes on the floor and walls glowed with blue light as the ceiling opened.

A skinny humanoid creature with black and gray armor covered with silver runes was lowered into its charging station. Sections closed over its body. It opened its eyes, stepped out of its cradle and walked toward the semicircle at the front of the room. The room seemed to buzz with energy as the runes became brighter than the Mana lights around the room.

"Commands understood; carrying out operation," the scout guardian said. Its cradle and attached crane receded into the ceiling. Just before it reached the semicircle, a shimmering arch of energy snapped into existence, showing another identical room.

The scout guardian didn't even pause as it headed through the portal. It closed the second the scout guardian made it through.
Scout Guardian en route...Mission: Find disturbance, observe, and report back with findings. Execute destruction protocols if deemed necessary...Shard will continue observations and overlook Guardianship of Aleph Master's homes. Connections lost to 60% of Aleph constructs. Energy drain at 10 percent. New power sources required...Moving to Standby Mode.

The room's lights and runes dimmed. The screen's singular blinking icon was the only light in the entire massive underground complex.

***

Deia looked over a massive room. They had found the kobolds' settlement. It looked like multiple transport rooms, like those that Dave had studied. The silver had been left alone on these runes, though one couldn't see it with all the kobold homes that covered the area.

Multiple holes had been made in the walls, probably leading to other kobold homes. The small village had over a hundred kobolds in it, from levels 120 to 230.

Being underground would make it easier for them to gain levels in relative peace. She saw a fight between two groups of kobolds. They bloodied one another, but didn't go so far as to kill one another.

There are always different ways to train.

Party Chat

Deia> I don't think that we can take them all on with just us.

Dave> What if we hit them with some nasty sneak attacks like yours and Induca's cannons and then my lightning balls?

Suzy> Do you know how stupid that sounds?

Induca> Someone's got a dirty mind...

Deia shook her head, smiling as the conversation went well and truly off the rails.

Party Chat

Suzy> Hey! It was implied. Whose side are you on anyways?

Induca> Nothing is fair in love and war.

Dave> I feel something strange.

Deia> Really, Dave?

Dave> No, actually, it felt like a large power disturbance.

The lights flickered, as if hearing him.

Party Chat

Suzy> The hell was that?

Malsour> Something that takes a considerable amount of energy. Portal?

Dave> That's what I'm thinking but I can't sense any of the portals nearby activating.

Anna> The Aleph are secretive. Do you think that they would have all of their portals out in the open? Or, that they would not have a security measure?

Deia> What kind of security measures are we talking?

Anna> If we're lucky, a Scout Guardian. If we're not, it could be a Prime.

Dave> The fuck is a Prime—like Optimus Prime?

Anna> A Prime is a massive automaton with the ability to fire spears from its hands and so heavily armored that it takes hits from a level 300 to just get through the armor.

Dave> That's cool and all, but can they turn into a truck?

Deia> Dave, try to see if you can find this guardian. Anna, what do we do if we find this guardian?

Anna> We lay down our weapons and try to talk to it. Being marked as Aleph aggressors is not a good idea.

***

Connecting to substation systems... Life signs detected... classified as kobold... Group of other creatures also found. Signs of battle found. Integrating information logs. Kobold aggressive forces, party of Players, unknown objectives...Sub-code information... Players highly volatile. More information required. Kobolds harming substation systems. Classified as low Intelligence species, reasoning deemed unviable. Possibility to use Players to destroy kobolds. Performance impressive in prior altercations between groups. Connecting to Shard; uploading information.

"Information integrated. Party of Players recorded talking about Aleph with intimacy. Talk to the Demi-Human named Anna to understand relationship. Interaction permitted. If attacked, priority to destroy substation." Shard's voice came through the small Mirror of Communication next to the information terminal that the scout was connected to.

"Orders confirmed."

"Report back with information on party, subset quest, power up possible, second condition." The runes around the Mirror of Communication stopped glowing as the scout guardian pulled its hand from the terminal. Its hand flipped out and reformed into digits.

Objectives: Categorize kobold threat. Understand multiple species party's objectives. Determine subject Anna's relationship with Aleph Masters. If deemed objectives are aligned, give Players quest to clear kobolds. Upon quest completion, evaluate for possibility of Power Up Quest. Failure to pass tests: proceed to initiate subsystem destruction.

The scout guardian turned and walked away from the terminal, toward what looked like a solid wall with a silver arch around it. Before it reached the arch, its runes glowed as it seemed to disappear from existence. Invisible to the world, the scout moved quickly and silently through the substation.

The party was resting in the living quarters, discussing the kobold threat and looking around.

"I think that it might be best if we come back with the rest of the Stone Raiders to finish this one off. We've got a bunch of loot and kills that will give us enough gold to get materials, books, and whatever we need," an Elven woman with red hair said, the apparent leader of the group.

"Agreed. I need some damn rest. Using all that Mana to keep my creations up and moving is taking a toll," a High Elven woman said.

High Elves and Wood Elves have shown prejudice to one another. Relationship change? Players of different classes have been known to interact outside of people of Emerilia norms.

"I'm interested in checking out this class system thing. Might be a real boost," a Dwarven Halfling said.

Oddity detected; weapons. The scout looked at the Dwarf's two rod weapons. It ran the different readings that showed the rods transforming into different items.

Additional secondary objective: gain better understanding of weapons.

"It would definitely increase both yours and Suzy's abilities," a human-looking man said.

Demi-Human, variation unknown. Similar to female beside the High Elf.

"Anna, what do you think we should do? You know the Aleph the most," the leader said.

"Well, the Aleph like to live in secret; their founders had been an Elven and Dwarven race. With time they had accepted people from all races, those that had been banished for pushing the boundaries of magic and science or their own traditions. They fled underground and they built an underground empire that not even the Dwarves could hold a torch to.

"The Dwarves and Elves were sorry for their transgressions. Well, most groups, but the Aleph who had lived in isolation for so long were happy to escape it all. Like this place, all of the Aleph homes and cities were only accessible by teleport pads and portals. We should have tripped the alarm when we got here, but it seemed that it only happened later. If this is the case, I am scared to know what the situation is for the Aleph AI."

Subject Anna: in-depth knowledge of Aleph, possible personal connection by tone and word choice. Must confirm party's objectives before interaction is deemed possible.

"An AI?" the Dwarf asked.

"Yes. It is not as high-classed as my own base model but it is impressive. It is called Shard. At one time, I had to give it some extra coding so that it could move from gestation to completion without breaking the rules of AI mechanics. Would have not been pretty without those rules and guidelines built into its hardware."

Connecting to Shard, information priority one.

The Dwarven hybrid's head snapped over and looked directly at the scout.

The scout continued to send its information to Shard, holding its position.

"Wow, now that is *complex!* Shit." The Dwarf walked closer to the scout, who was hiding on the third-floor balcony.

"What is it, Dave?" the leader asked.

"I think he's the scout guardian you were talking about," the one called Dave said, climbing up the balconies.

Possibility that presence has been sensed 82%. New directive: understand Players' objective.

Dave walked toward the scout, but made sure to not close within five feet.

The others of the party climbed up the balconies, watching Dave.

"Dave, you sure it's there?" the High Elf asked.

"Yeah, Suz, I can only see bits of it."

Dwarf Halfling "Dave": facial expression—excitement. Stealth ability power drain to usefulness rendered useless. Move to vocal communication.

The Demi-Human Anna made clicking and hand gestures.

Understanding of Aleph communication techniques. Lowering stealth abilities. Alert level one. Ready for combat.

"Hello. I am able to speak the common tongue," the scout said, dropping its stealth abilities as the Players other than Anna and Dave recoiled.

"Dude, that is fucking cool!" Dave looked the scout guardian over.

Connection established, Shard. "Ask Demi-Human Anna for last name."

"Anna, what is your last name?" the scout asked.

"Kal."

At hearing this name, Shard took direct control over the scout unit. The power consumption was heavy, but if it was the AI creation Anna'kal, it might be possible to deal with operation issues.

"Identity confirmed," Shard said through the scout.

"Hello, Shard. It is good to hear your voice again. Why are you operating at such power deficiencies? I was expecting to see your guardians out sooner. I was not expecting to see kobolds in your substations either," Anna said.

"Processes are running at low capacity; power substations have been harmed or cut off from main unit designated Shard. Running on backup power. Unable to access higher functions required in order to repair necessary systems. Moved into hibernation mode to protect Aleph main installations priority one. What are your objectives, Anna and party?"

"Well, things are worse than I thought. I have new information. Aleph are returning. I am capable of helping, if allowed. Will need larger access. My party and I are capable of helping in a decent capacity. I am guessing that with such a power deficiency, fighting even the kobolds here would be impossible. I can talk to other groups of Players who might be willing to assist if allowed," Anna said.

"Anna'kal relationship with Aleph—valued ally. Highly trusted, one of few to reach Alephir. Deemed possible to trust. Recognized as having quest Aleph Homecoming. Updating quest and security clearance. Anna'kal, you are responsible for your party. Adding additional quest Power Up. Do you accept?"

***

Deia watched as the two new quests updated in her vision.

Quest: Aleph Homecoming

Shard has recognized Anna as being a trusted ally of the Aleph. He offers you transport to Alephir. The power cost will be intensive.

Requirements: Complete Quest Power Up to open additional gates to clear out the creatures that have overrun the Aleph's different installations.

Rewards: ???

Do you accept?

Y/N

Quest: Power up

Aleph's AI Shard needs more power. Fix his substations or supply him with enough soul or Mana energy to bring more systems online in order to fix it himself.

Rewards: ???

Do you accept?

Y/N

She looked to the others. She had heard of the Aleph in old stories, stories that had been made to teach the Elves humility and acceptance. It cautioned them that their people might change over time and that they should accept others for who they are, not disregard them due to their prejudices.

After hearing their story from Anna, Deia was motivated to help them out. She smiled as she looked at the others. "Well, damn. I might have the Player bug because this looks like it could be fun as hell."

The others looked at her. Smiles appeared on their faces. The excitement of improving themselves, defeating enemies, gaining loot and experience—it was addicting.

"It will not be an easy quest. We rate it as an S Raid-classed quest," the scout said.

"Dave, how much power do we have?" Malsour asked.

"Got about a hundred and fifty thousand stat points, so one point five million Mana points, then a nice two thousand soul energy, which is like two hundred thousand Mana points if you convert it," Dave said.

"How much power will we need to give Shard in order to power him up enough to start repairing his subsystems?" Anna asked.

"Quest updated," the scout said.

Quest: Power up

Aleph's AI Shard needs more power. Fix his substations or supply him with enough soul or Mana energy to bring more systems online in order to fix it himself.

You must provide 5,000,000 Mana points equivalent of power. (Power provided: 0/5,000,000)

Or

Activate a class A Power Station (0/1), three class B Power Stations (0/3) or Nine Class C Power Stations (0/9).

The more systems powered on, the larger the reward that will be offered.

Rewards: ???

Do you accept?

Y/N

"Damn, I haven't seen a raid like this mentioned anywhere in the forums," Dave said, making it sound like some holy relic.

"Okay, well, we've got a week and a half until the rest of the Stone Raiders get here. We've all got enough food and water for that time. I say that we go and check out this raid, gain some information on it and then tell the rest of the guild," Deia said.

"Acceptable conditions. Group ability added due to Anna'kal's status of trusted ally," the scout said. "Will only allow Anna's direct party access to Alephir. Area deemed the best for learning more information, also free of aggressive creatures. Holds Altar of Rebirth to link to as well as five Class B substations," the scout said.

"I believe it will be an interesting time to learn more about the Aleph and assist their Shard in restoring order to their home. I'm in," Malsour said.

"Sounds like an adventure to me. I'll join." Induca smiled.

"Well, I need to learn more about portals and these guys are some incredible creations. I'm in," Suzy said.

"Is this really a question? Course I'm in!" Dave grinned.

"It has been too long since I saw Shard. It would be good to get him active once again." Anna smiled and looked to Deia, whose gossip senses tingled at the look in Anna's eyes.

Just who is Shard to Anna?

"Very well, we accept," Deia said, looking at the scout.

"Follow me." The scout moved through the living quarters and walked right through what looked to be a bathroom wall.

Anna followed without pause.

Dave smiled as if it were Christmas as he wandered through. Deia shook her head and followed, wincing as she put her hand ahead of her but found that she did indeed pass through the wall.

Behind it there was a small terminal, a few magical lights, and an intact Aleph teleport pad.

"These runes are incredible!" Dave looked at the silver arch around the wall that they had walked through. He and Malsour wandered around, making notes and talking to each other in low and excited voices.

The scout watched as Induca walked through last. It turned and walked toward the teleport pad; the runes lit up as different formations glowed with energy. A portal arch formed over the semicircle teleport pad.

Dave and Malsour ran around the thing. You wouldn't think that they were a nearly five-hundred-year-old dragon and a master craftsman who had been in charge of thousands of people.

"Some things never change," Suzy muttered to Deia.

Deia just rolled her eyes.

"It's kind of cute, if I didn't find runes just mind-numbingly boring," Induca added.

Suzy and Deia chuckled as the scout walked through the portal.

Dave and Malsour disappeared through it and then came back, even more excited as they passed through again.

"I have a feeling they're not going to be much help at doing anything but studying *everything* for a few days," Induca said as they walked through the portal.

They found themselves in a room almost identical to the teleport room they'd passed through. This one had more lights on and instead of being in disrepair and made from rough stone, it was made from polished stone with walkways of malachite with engravings of gold, silver, and ebony.

It was not just functional; it was elegant. It reminded Deia of the High Elf Palace in Markolm she'd seen pictures of. The level of detail was breathtaking.

The scout stepped into a cradle; its body went slack as ports connected to it and it was hauled above the portal into a holding area. The roof closed, but not before Deia saw what could only be a few sets of complete behemoth guardians.

Dave and Malsour were studying everything, making a circuit of the room. Anna walked through the room as if she had been there hundreds of times before. Deia and the other girls followed her, looking over the beauty of the room.

"Dave!" Anna yelled.

Dave moved to follow, jumping up the steps after the ladies.

Anna stood in a control room that overlooked the portal. A piece of black ebony with all manner of runes was carved into it.

"Fuuuck me sideways." Dave looked over the massive ebony sphere.

"Welcome to part of Shard." Anna tapped the creature.

"Power reserves at twelve percent." Shard's voice came through the room.

"Yes, you big bowling ball, we've got it. Dave, could you put some power into that console over there?" Anna pointed to the console.

Deia moved to the malachite window that was at the back of the room. She couldn't see anything beyond it, but she felt as if there was a large open area out there.

Then the power started to come online.

She looked to Dave as lights brightened; his arms were wreathed in shadows as his eyes glowed and his tattoos shone. She saw lights turn on not only in the area they were in, but in the darkness she had felt before.

"Holy shit," Suzy said as an entire city two times the size of Nadorf was revealed.

It was not simply laid out flat. The city looked to be inside of a cylinder, with all manner of buildings pointing toward the center. There were gardens, skyscrapers, even trams all over the place.

It didn't look as though it was from Emerilia; it looked as if it were from the future.

Orbs in the center of the cylindrical city started to spin like a gyroscope. It was slow at first, emitting a faint light before they spun faster and faster, driving the shadows back and revealing the city.

Deia's mouth hung open as she looked at the city that had been shaped from white polished stone, malachite, gold, silver, and ebony. The colors blended together, making the place look like an art installation. Runes were traced in all manner of patterns, not just circular formations or Dave's own lines of code.

She had seen inside Mithsia Mountains; everything about the Dwarven homes was handcrafted, but it had a rigidity to it—straight lines, squares, and columns. Here it seemed that the city had grown like some organic creation. Walls were murals, another thing taken from the Dwarves, but they didn't show history—they showed scenes of nature. Planters and gardens lay bare, the natural life that once rested in them long dead.

For a moment, Deia could picture the city as it might have been at one time. It was a marriage of Elven and Dwarven ingenuity and their distinct arts. Still, she didn't believe that her imagination could do justice to what the Aleph had created.

"Hello, Anna. It has been too long." Shard's voice no longer sounded constrained, but normal as Deia looked around and found a short Elf wearing a one-piece jumpsuit made from a black material and silver stitching. "We have a lot of work to do in order to prepare for the coming of the Masters. It will be fun to work with you once again."

Deia's eyebrows creeped higher as the corners of her mouth tilted upward. She looked to Induca and Suzy; neither of them missed how Shard had Anna's complete attention or the expression on their faces.

We'll be sure to get the juicy details out of you later. Deia turned around and looked out over the city once again.

Chapter 9: Snakes in the Grass

Hevard looked at the rest of his guild that had gathered in Nelheim. He was the head of the PKP guild—People Kill People. They were a band of Players who worked together to make their name as assassins and killers. They had already accepted a number of high-classed kill orders on different characters that POE and Players had asked for. They'd kill anyone for the right cost. They were high-classed chaotic Players. All of them were part of the Black Thorn Guild, the assassins' guild of Emerilia.

It functioned much like the fighter and traders' guild, offering contracts and quests related to the guild. PKP made their name by taking on the most Player-killing contracts. They'd made a big name for themselves, but now they were planning something bigger, something that would make them *the* Player-killing guild on Emerilia.

"Our spies have been able to talk to different travelers and are tracking the Stone Raiders as they move toward the capital Zolunheir of the Heval Plains. Contacts in the Black Thorn have mentioned that a group of Stone Raiders were spotted in Selhi Capital, though they have been gone for a few days, so it is unknown where they are going to. They might be headed for Donsk or adventuring in the area. They were all of low levels for Heval and had come from Opheir. Otherwise, other groups of the Stone Raiders have not moved from their locations in Heval," Koloa, PKP's intelligence officer, said, rubbing his dagger-shaped goatee.

"I want fresh agents in Zolunheir to see where they are going. Have our forces move to cities with teleport pads. When the Stone Raiders leave for their next raid, I want us to be ready for them. We'll show people that not even the top guild can survive the PKP," Hevard said to the cold smiles that came from around the darkly garbed assassins in the room.

A Portal Opens!

In the mystical lands of Opheir, a portal connecting to the Alturaran lands has been awakened. Keep an eye out for Alturarans trying to capture portals into Emerilia! Go forward, build cities, and push back the Alturarans!

Hevard looked at the notification and dismissed it. He'd seen the videos of those who were fighting against the Alturarans. Their materials went for a fair price and the experience gain was high, but it was not what Hevard enjoyed.

Hevard indicated for Koloa to stay behind. The rest of the guild officers left the room, closing the door behind them.

"What do you want, Hevard?" Koloa asked.

"I heard that you are having some troubles with the Golden Sabres?" Hevard asked.

"Yeah, it's a damn nightmare. Nearly as bad as the Stone Raiders. Since the Boran-al thing, spies and assassins have been kicked out of the guild continuously. Some of our people who participated in Boran-al have been hunted down to their spawn points so many times that they needed to restart characters." Koloa shook his head.

"Something the matter?" Hevard asked.

"We don't know much about how the Stone Raiders work, but we do know that there are two rules. One is to have fun; the second is to come to the guild's aid when it calls. The Stone Raiders have nearly five hundred members, all of them loyal, and only a hundred and fifty are currently raiding. The others are working on gaining levels and doing their own thing. Their core group is strong. If they band together and come searching for us, I feel that we might have to change characters," Koloa said.

"We have to hit them hard enough that they're scared to come after us," Hevard said, undeterred.

"Hevard, most of the Raiders are E-heads. They've turned this into their reality. If we threaten it, they'll do everything in their power to take us out. We might propel our names into history with this, though Stone Raiders aren't to be underestimated. I've been watching them awhile and they die nearly constantly. Where most people are scared by the pain, the Raiders rush right back into battle, only stopping to get items that their clan might need before grouping up and returning to their raid."

"Koloa, you're overthinking this. Don't worry—even if they do attack us, their levels will be so low and we'll have all their gear, so there won't be a thing that they can do," Hevard said.

"I hope you're right," Koloa said.

***

A tall hooded man walked through Nadorf, reaching the teleportation pad. He carried a large sword and shield on his back.

"Do you have enough gold now?" the man at the processing station asked lazily.

"Yes." The man's voice was hot and angry as he dropped a handful of gold on the table.

"Okay. You do know that the Ashal northern frontier should not be taken lightly and beginning with a minimum level 350 is recommended?" The man took the gold and held out a ticket.

The man under the cloak made a deep guttural noise. The kind a dog might make before attacking. "Just give me the ticket." The large man held out his hand.

The ticket master's eyes went wide as he studied the hand for the first time. Scars in the shape of tribal markings coiled over the hands and up the cloaked man's arm. It wasn't the most surprising thing. The red hands with black fingernails were. Every child had been told the tale of the Demons.

He quickly put the ticket in the man's hand, shivering as he remembered the tales his momma used to tell him.

"You'd best not tell anyone what you saw," the large cloak-wearing man said.

For the first time, the ticket master saw the man's face.

It was completely bald, with two horns, pointed ears, and obsidian eyes.

"Y-yes, sir!" The ticket master's eyes widened. *How, how are there still Demons on Emerilia?*

The demon turned and headed for the teleport pads as the ticket master remembered tales of the Demons in Northern Ashal, tales of their rebellion against the gods and their ability in battle.

***

Alkao stepped on one teleportation pad in Nadorf and exited another in Selheoq, the most northern of the Ashal cities.

He passed through customs. People stared at him and his gear as he passed. Sensing others using Aura Detection on him, he let out some of his aura, making sure to keep it weak. Alkao had a hungry smile on his face as he headed out of the city. He quickly left the roads and headed deep into the underbrush, unsheathing his sword as he came to a clearing.

"Fight me if you desire; otherwise, I have places to be." He turned to face the direction he had come.

"Ahh shit, well, what gave us away?" a dirty Human asked as others ranging from some kinds of Demi-Humans to Dark Elf melded out of the forest. There were five in total, with two hiding.

"Your smell." Alkao looked at their levels. None of them were under 200 and their max was 315, which belonged to the Human who was talking.

"Ahh crap, well, give us the shield and sword and then we'll let you wander out into the wilderness all you want," the human said.

Alkao looked at the two weapons. A twinge of regret went through him. "I am sorry, but these are not my weapons. I have not yet earned them. I am holding onto them to return to the man who made them."

Everyone he had tried to get aid from had demanded money or favors from him. Dave was the only one to not demand favors and had given him the finest weapons that Alkao had ever wielded. *I was too quick to judge a man by his appearance rather than his abilities.* With time and the way that people treated him knowing that he was a Demon, Alkao had learned humility and an understanding of how wrong he had been to attack Dave.

"Well, that's very nice and all but well, weapons are at a premium in Ashal and those ones have some weird properties that my friend said will be useful. So, you're going to have to hand them over. Either that or you die here. We all know no one is a Player here, so if we die, we're gone. Your choice, pal." The bandit leader shrugged, secure in his own strength as the others around Alkao advanced, waiting for his decision or the Human's commands.

Alkao let out a deep laugh that made them stop in their tracks. "It has been some time since I had a *real* fight. It will be good to see if I can reclaim my lost levels from you." Alkao's smile made the bandit leader's eyes grow dark in anger, only to widen as two red wings pushed out from under Alkao's cloak.

"Since you're all People of Emerilia, then I won't need to hide my true abilities." Alkao spread his wings out, flicking them to get rid of the kinks.

It had taken him much gold and pain, but Party Zero had given Alkao one more gift. They'd used their contacts to send him to a training medical mage from the Stone Raider guild. It had taken some long days, but they had been able to regrow his wings. They were still weak, but Alkao never hoped to have his wings back after he was struck down and the angels ripped them from his back.

"Now, let us see what those levels truly mean. Quick of speed, of mind, of body and soul." The heavy buff created a red aura around him. "Blessing of the Fire goddess. Castration of the Dark God." New buffs of red and black fell around him as he let out his full killing aura and power.

An arrow whistled out of the forest; Alkao's shield slammed it away.

"Thank you for completing the final condition. It really is a pain having to wait to be attacked before attacking." Alkao lowered himself down, his blade down at his side and his shield forward.

"What are you?" one of the bandits asked.

"Alkao, one of the seven brothers of chaos, first of my name and reign, commander of the Third Demon Horde and leader of the Xerzit lands." Alkao seemed to disappear and then appeared before the speaker. His large sword cut through his armor and into his chest as if it was nothing.

His hood had been blown back, revealing a smile that would make the Grim Reaper pause. "Tell the Dark Lord that I am coming for him."

Creatures that regularly claimed the lives of those who wandered the woods ran away in fear, sensing an old predator had once again come to claim its lands.

***

This bloody Mirror of Communication was expensive as hell, but worth it. Josh sat with Cassie in his arms, just enjoying each other's company. Some movie played on the TV in front of them. A fire crackled off to the side in a gas stove and London was visible outside of the wraparound windows of the apartment.

She sat up and looked at him.

"What?" he asked, warily. He knew that look in her eyes. He'd seen it before when she had been bargaining or working her position as guildmaster.

"What would you think about an alliance?"

"Terms?" Josh asked.

"Trade, people, quests," Cassie said.

"Why?"

"Because it is a pain in the ass trying to make sure that everyone is not a spy and I need some damned help!" She rubbed her head in frustration.

"And what did you tell your guild?" Josh smiled.

"Well, you're primarily a raiding guild. Our people want to train and play in raids, but we're not as good as you. Our people are good at charming people's socks off and getting different quests. We can give you the raid quests and we share all other kinds of quests, working together with one another and make a damned powerful alliance." Cassie smiled.

"Well, before we get ahead of ourselves, your guild is still filled with all kinds of shits, so you'd need to clear that all out. We've got a few things that you can use in order to do that."

Cassie gave him the stink eye. "Why didn't you tell your girlfriend this like a month or two ago?"

"You don't tell me all your guild stuff and same here," Josh said.

"Fine," she said, not looking happy with it, but knowing that there were certain things that they couldn't share with each other due to their positions.

"You know that having our two guilds band together is going to make the other guilds think about doing it so that they can compete with us, right?"

"Of course. That is why we're going to have to spend some *long* hours figuring out the alliance, if we have one or not at the end of it." Cassie gave him a sultry look.

"Calm down there, love." Josh smiled; he seemed to consider the TV, but his mind was working. *It would certainly make us more powerful. Also, we are looking to make that trade agreement with Exdar's Traders. I don't want to rush into this, even though it is Cassie and the Golden Sabres—they are so big. And with two feeder guilds, it will make managing things hard. I'll have to get Lucy to have a look over it all.*

"I would like to join the two clans in an alliance. I'm going to have to talk to Lucy over the details, maybe bring her here to conference. You bring Naylor and whoever else you need to make sure this meeting is good," Josh said, excited to connect their guilds together, but also knowing the kind of work it would take to ratify everything.

"Isn't it fun when we can decide tomorrow's gaming news?" Cassie asked.

"Melding the first two guilds to find an Alturaran portal together?"

"Yes, and the most powerful and followed. I checked out your guild's website the other day. The number of people watching your feeds is nuts!"

"Ah, well, if you're going to have fun together, then others are interested." Josh shrugged. "Did you hear about that new Alturaran portal opening?"

"Yeah. We've got agreements with a dozen other guilds to give them access to the portal we found and it's nuts. There are thousands of Players over there every day. The new portal opened in Gudalo. Three guilds did it: the Jeserie Cats, Dender's, and the Wraiths."

"As much as that is cool, Lucy was saying that through her checking, it looks like the enemy might be able to open portals to Emerilia and there is a lot more than just one other planet connected to us. It can take years for more portal locations to show up, but when they do, then that'll be nuts. There's supposed to be over fifty other planets."

"Damn." Cassie whistled. "Every time it seems like I've kind of got a small grasp of what is going on in Emerilia, I'm reminded of just how *huge* this game is. It could take decades in-game to finish all of the content."

"Pretty exciting, huh?" Josh grinned.

"Damn right!" She laughed, smiling like a Cheshire cat.

Chapter 10: Alephir

Dave looked to Shard. "Damn, I didn't even try to hope of tech on this level."

"You have met other AI?" Shard asked, interested. His body moved in parts to face Dave.

"Yeah, kind of had one built for my house and company. I miss my Jackie." Dave looked to Suzy, who nodded in agreement.

She might have been an AI but she'd lived in their lives so completely, she was like the third woman to their Three Musketeers.

"All right, Shard. What the heck happened while I was asleep? Alephir looks like it's been going to crap if you're having to use him as a battery." Anna pointed at Dave.

"Thanks." Dave sighed.

Shard winced and scratched his head. His image lagged and froze, though it was getting better, Dave noticed.

"Well, it was kind of like I spread myself too thin, too fast. I tried to save *everything* so it was like the Aleph never left. Then, it turned into me having so many issues to fix that I couldn't do it all and I was all over the place. By the time that I had started consolidating, I didn't have the resources or materials I needed to just keep Alephir running. I only noticed that there was something going wrong at the substation you were in because of the high magical activity going on."

"So, you need us to get you power and back up and running?" Deia tore her eyes from the city beyond.

"With your help, I will be able to initialize a series of repairs that will allow me to bring Alephir online. Here are the different locations I will need you to return power to. I have some understanding of the different issues. Once those are complete, then I will have enough energy to start connecting to other Aleph installations. I will send scouts to check the facilities. Once that is complete, we can move to clearing out the various facilities that have been infested, bringing them online and securing them from further aggressive forces."

"What kind of power systems do you have?" Dave asked.

"We have Fire systems," Shard said.

Deia and the others were talking about their map and the new waypoints that had appeared to lead them to the different power stations. Malsour was still looking over the teleportation room.

"How do they work?"

"We burn an item, usually coal, then we use an extraction process, channeling that Fire energy into a soul gem to be used throughout the city."

"No boilers or rotating wheels?" Dave asked.

"Ahh, Earth's power solutions. No, there is no need for that. There is more power loss with the increased motions. We have an eighty to ninety percent power draw from our process compared to the seventy-five to eighty percent of Earth methods, not including material cost which would make our process cheaper." Shard sounded a bit smug.

"I'm impressed. What about latent energy taps, though?" Dave watched as he reached four thousand charge in his armor and disconnected from the console.

Quest: Power up

Aleph's AI Shard needs more power. Fix his substations or supply him with enough soul or Mana energy to bring more systems online in order to fix it himself.

You must provide 5,000,000 Mana points equivalent of power. (Power provided: 1,350,000/5,000,000)

Or

Activate a class A Power Station (0/1), three class B Power Stations (0/3) or Nine Class C Power Stations (0/9).

The more systems powered on, the larger the reward that will be offered.

Rewards: ???

Do you accept?

Y/N

"I do not understand."

"You cast a web of energy siphons out over a large area—different things like thermal energy, soul energy, all kinds. It siphons power from the area. On the surface of a planet, it's not that good, but down here buried under it all, it would be a good idea. Also, the power just keeps going, can be fed direct into systems, and doesn't use up resources like coal."

"I am interested in this. Would you have any plans for it? Alephir is a contained city, but I have deemed that alterations might need to be made if I am to stay active for an extended period of time." Shard sounded almost *sad*, but he hid it behind his voice becoming more mechanical. Dave didn't miss Anna's twitch at hearing it.

"I would be happy to help. Do you have a faster way to transfer information?" Dave asked.

"If you were to send it to me in an information file, I could then interpret it and make the integration faster," Anna said.

"Right." Dave opened up his notepads, going through his doodles on Magical Circuits. He moved to the one labeled Boran-al's Citadel.

There's a lot of information and thoughts here. It might be an idea to keep some of it to myself. He looked at Shard, who was talking to Anna and smiling, clearly happy to have someone to talk to.

The Aleph are smart and powerful people. There is a reason that Bob kept them safe. Showing that I trust them might lead to a better relationship. Plus, they probably have all kinds of information on portals like the one at the citadel that it wouldn't be a big deal.

Dave sent the file.

Anna opened up her interface and went through the information.

I keep on forgetting that she is an AI as well.

"Malsour, get up here!" Deia said.

Dave moved from his terminal and looked out on the cylindrical city. "How do you keep people planted? Gravity manipulation?"

"In a manner. We have a combination of centrifugal forces as well as weight and gravity runes. Areas will not be accessible yet due to this restriction. As more stations come online, more areas will become safe to travel through and I can start up the systems that will allow the city's gravity to return to normal. There are twenty different power stations in the city but with only four accessible, it will take time for me to run the necessary checks before starting up different systems and powering the city's runes."

"This is fucking cool." Dave grinned like a kid in the candy store, jumping on the balls of his feet a bit. He looked to Suzy, who also looked rather excited.

"An entire city just dormant for a few hundred years and we're turning it back on! Like, come on, you can't say that's not fucking awesome." Dave looked to the rest of the party.

Induca giggled, Anna shook her head, and Deia smiled at her excitable fiancé.

"What ci—oh my." Malsour looked out of the window to see the Alephir city.

"Welcome to Alephir!" Dave waved his hands around as if to encapsulate the city.

"As you say, Dave—fuck me sideways." Malsour moved to the glass and looked over the place.

Everyone, even Induca, looked at Malsour in shock before they fell about laughing. Dave patted him on the back.

"See, fuck works for everything!"

"There is one small issue. The lifts and gravity slides for this tower have been deactivated. You will need to climb down," Shard said.

"The fuck is with this planet and heights," Suzy muttered.

"Well, do you have roof access?" Induca asked.

"Yes." Shard looked to her; his lag had been cut down nicely.

"Well, that will work," Induca said.

"How so?" Deia asked.

"You forget I'm a freaking dragon. I got wings, dammit, though you better not start thinking of me as some stupid caravan!"

"I wouldn't think about it," Deia promised.

"Good. It will be good to stretch my wings." Induca rolled her shoulders as if they were tight and looked at Malsour.

"Fine, but only because I want to see this great city returned to its functional state."

"Hashtag winning, bitches!" Dave's fist pumped the air.

"Do you realize how ridiculous you get at times?" Anna asked.

"Well, with all this awesomeness going on, how can you *not* be excited?" Dave smiled so hard it looked as if it hurt.

"Ran a multi-trillion dollar business, still a damn child on the inside. There's no winning with him. Trust me, I've seen it for fifteen years. Not dull, though." Suzy elbowed Deia.

"Well, let's start powering this place up. We've got five days until the rest of the Stone Raiders get here. If Shard doesn't want them here, then we're going to have to get all the work done here as fast as possible to get information on the other installations and what kind of forces we're going to have to clear out," Deia said.

"Thank you. The risk of bringing you here was high, but the possibility of me going dormant and someone else finding the information of the Masters and wishing to bring evil to Emerilia could be catastrophic," Shard said. "I hope that we can become closer and trust each other in the future. It is hard to find people who are willing to aid me and have someone like Anna to vouch for them."

Friend Request

Shard has asked you to become his friend. Do you accept?

Y/N?

"Ye-up! Always good fun to have a few AI friends." Dave smiled. "Do you have a Mirror of Communication?"

"I do." Shard smiled.

Dave felt bad for the dude, all cooped up here with his original builders disappearing off because people had found out just how advanced they'd become.

"Transfer of data complete." Shard tilted his head to the side, as if analyzing something.

"Let's get these power stations first!" Deia cut them off before they could get distracted.

"That is prudent. I await the restoration of power to Alephir. I will review the data you have provided." Shard bowed to them before he disappeared.

"To the roof."

It didn't take long to get to the roof. Once there, Induca seemed to stretch to loosen her muscles before her body expanded; her hands turned to claws and her face extended into a snout. Wings pushed out of her back as she filled out. She shook her wings and moved her feet some.

"What happens to your clothes and gear?" Suzy asked.

"They go into dimensional storage that is part of me. It's how dragons can move so much loot fast. My clothes are specially tuned to my body that they will disappear at a certain stage of the change." Induca's voice was powerful.

You could tell that she was a Creature of Power not only from her voice but the faint pressure of her aura. Even though the pressure was easily noticeable, Dave still knew that it was greatly suppressed because she was with friends and relaxed.

"Well, climb up then!" Induca said.

Suzy and Anna got on Induca's back.

"Hold on!" Induca said. Dave saw the corners of her large mouth pull up in a smile as she slowly tilted forward like some old roller coaster.

She pushed off with her back legs and dropped down the side of the tower. Suzy screamed while Anna whooped in enjoyment. Dave heard wings flare out as Induca's red body shot up and into view, gliding between buildings.

"Hey, Malsour, old buddy, ole pal," Dave said as Malsour underwent his change. "Could you possibly *not* do that?" Dave asked.

"Don't worry. I am not as energetic as my younger sister," Malsour said, his voice deeper as he smiled at Dave's clear anxiety.

Deia easily got onto Malsour's back. Dave ambled up in his own manner, holding onto Malsour's spine ridges.

Induca had taken up maybe a third of the top of the tower. Malsour was easily three times her size, his wings extending over the edges. He spread them out, flapping them once and sending them up ten feet.

A few more flaps and they were gliding down gently. Through the silent city, Dave could hear Suzy's screams and swearing while Anna and Induca laughed their asses off.

"Thanks, Malsour." Dave patted Malsour's back.

Malsour turned his head to look at Dave with an evil gleam in his eye.

Deia laughed as Malsour looked forward.

"DON'T EVEN FUCKING THINK ABOUT...FUCK!" Dave yelled as Malsour tucked his wings and gained speed. He flared them out, making Dave's stomach sink and then shoot right back up.

He twisted and turned, using his wings and tail to guide them through the city. Dave didn't stop swearing the entire time as Deia held onto him tightly.

The speed cut off quickly as Malsour circled, spiraling down toward a building that Induca was landing on. Suzy took a few minutes to get off Induca's back as Dave breathed heavily.

As much as he hated it, now that it was over he couldn't deny the adrenaline rush or the smile on his face.

"You're an asshole, but that wasn't bad," Dave said as Malsour flapped his wings to bring them to land on the power station's roof. Deia just laughed as she got off and headed for the stairwell where the others were preparing themselves. Dave sent his senses out as he got off Malsour. "I don't detect anything other than the different automatons that are wandering around. A few creatures here and there, nothing big or threatening."

"All right, well, Shard says that this one has an issue with the fueling machine. It got jammed in some manner," Anna said.

Dave's eyes glowed gray. He looked around to study the different parts of the power station. The rest of the party went down the stairwell to make sure it was really clear. Malsour and Anna stayed with Dave.

"Damn, this place is big," Dave muttered to himself. There was a large hopper on one side of the building; coal went through grinders and dropped onto a twenty-meter wide conveyor belt. They would then move through what looked like runes for a flame torch. Right after that was a series of runes that would siphon off the power energy until it reached the end. There wasn't even a chimney for any air to escape; it was all pulled into the extracting runes.

One of the motion runes on the conveyor had failed and friction in other areas had rubbed away the runes. The hopper was messed up as the coal had been sitting there for so long that it had become damp.

"Okay, I think I have a plan," Dave said as he walked. "Anna, I want you to go to that coal and cut it up so that it can be easily eaten through the crusher. Malsour, I want you to see if you can make sure the coal gets through that crusher. Once we've done this load, it should be good. I've got to fix a few runes and then we should be on to the next one. It's really not a hard fix," Dave said, happily surprised.

"Shard was made to manage the various portals of the Aleph. He can do gravitational and position computations with great ease and has defensive programs as well as a personality complex that allow him to talk and protect the Aleph, but he is not one for mechanical situations," Anna said.

"Well, good thing he's got us around." Dave jumped off a catwalk and dropped next to the conveyor belt. With his higher Agility, the ten-foot drop was nothing. He pulled out two handfuls of tools from his bag of holding and looked at Induca, Deia, and Suzy, who stared at him.

"Let's fix some power stations!" he said with a half-crazed look. After a few uncomfortable seconds, he faded into awkwardness. "Babe, could you heat something up for me?"

"Sure, you dolt," she said, amused. Working together, they fixed the runes. Dave used his soul smithing and his tools to fix it up.

Anna and Malsour were ready on their side as Dave ran through checks of the machine. He hit the button that would fire the whole thing up.

"Well, that is a fucking buzzkill." Dave looked over the machine. He closed his eyes and rubbed his face in annoyance. He stretched his senses out. "Yeah, not a single Mana point of power. Right, well, if it doesn't work the first time, use diesel. The second time, use jet fuel. The third time, use some damned nitroglycerin!"

"Everything okay?" Malsour asked.

"We're just going to kick-start this sombitch!" Dave said in an exaggerated Southern accent. "Deia and Induca, I'm going to need you here. Blow torches aren't working but you're the next best thing. Anna, you blow air through this place so we have a constant flame. Suzy, you see that crankshaft there?" Dave pointed to the metal bar on the side of the crusher connected to the hopper of coal outside the power station.

"Yeah." Suzy looked at it.

"Good. I need you to get a golem cranking on that thing like there's no tomorrow. Malsour, can you see about moving the coal down toward Deia and Induca at a constant pace?"

"Can do," Malsour said.

"Okay, well, let's try this out. I'll be back here with the extractor to make sure that the runes are working properly." Dave clapped his hands together as people moved into position.

Suzy put a metal core down and then poured pieces of metal out of her bag.

She's adapting well to Emerilia and being prepared, Dave thought as the metal turned into a metal golem, stretching to grab the crankshaft. It tried moving it but it was clearly impossible until Suzy added more metal; the grinder's round teeth moved an inch, dust and coal that hadn't moved in decades falling to the conveyor belt.

Malsour used his Dark magic to move the inanimate conveyor, slowly at first but then faster. Deia and Induca coated the coal in blue flames as Anna directed the air through the room.

Dave watched through malachite windows as the smoldering coals entered into the extraction area. Runes lit up, dull at first but gaining in strength as the coal seemed to melt into nothing, burning from the inside in seconds.

Not even smoke came out the other side. Slowly, more power started to seep into the runes and through the rune circuits. Dave followed it, stepping to a different part of the power station.

"Holy crap." Dave looked at a massive train station. He spread his senses out. This was not the only conveyor belt in the power station; it was one of twenty. All of them were linked to the train yard, where massive drums loaded onto freight cars waited.

"The drums are soul gems, massive damned soul gem batteries," Dave said to himself with a grin as the power reached out toward the trains. A malachite window started to glow as the soul gem inside began to charge.

Dave checked on the other conveyors. It would take some time, but it was mainly cases where maintenance hadn't been performed and the systems had fallen into disrepair. Dave walked back to the conveyor belt room where everyone was talking to one another. Part of the energy was being directed to the system's own powering soul gem.

It took five minutes, but then Suzy's golem stood back from the coal grinder. Then, one by one, the others stepped away as the conveyor belt continued on its own.

"Good work. Now, let's go to those other power stations," Deia said.

"We've still got four more conveyor belts to get online here!" Dave said.

"What?" Deia asked.

"Yeah. It's a hell of a lot bigger than I thought."

"Then, how many conveyors does a class A have?" Induca asked.

"No idea." Dave shrugged.

"Well, I guess we should get started." Deia clapped her hands together.

"Hoorah! Let's power up a city, folks!" Dave smiled.

Chapter 11: Power Me Up!

"Hey, it is good to see you."

"Where the heck did you get a Mirror of Communication from?" Josh asked Anna. Dwayne and Kim filed in behind him. Deia and Anna sat on their chairs, looking tired as they stared at the new faces.

"Dwarves. Seems they want to keep in touch with one of their Dwarven Master Smiths. Dave also has another one back in Cliff-Hill," Deia said.

"Huh, well, I guess we all have some secrets. So what is this about a raid?" Josh asked. The rest of the Stone Raiders' leadership tried to hide their excitement and failed badly. They had been looking to travel to Selhi Capital, and then over to Gudalo, around Per'ush and into Ashal. Having a raid to lull them over in Selhi Capital would be fun, instead of just the monster clearing that the nation was offering.

"We were out adventuring and checking out the monster areas to see what it will be like when the rest of the guild gets here. There are these Aleph ruins, an old race that made a lot of portals that connect to different places. We were offered a quest called Aleph Homecoming." Deia shared the quest with them.

Quest: Aleph Homecoming

You have restored enough power that portals can once again be opened and scouting guardians sent out to find the enemy.

The more power sources activated, the more scouts that can be sent to different locations.

When you are ready to fight the monsters that have found their way into the Aleph areas, let Shard know. He will start opening portals to the different locations to start clearing out the Aleph installations and substations.

Rewards: ???

Do you accept?

Y/N

"The others are completing off the Power Up quest right now," Anna said.

"So, what kind of raid is this?" Josh asked.

"Think of it as a mix between horde mode and capture points. We will have certain places that we can move through, capturing them and gaining more assistance from the Aleph automated systems. We can hold position, defending and killing off whatever creatures we find or advance to control more of these positions in order to increase the forces that the Aleph automatons can help us with," Anna said.

"That sounds awesome. The more places we hold, the more assistance we get. I'm guessing the more we have, though, the harder enemies we will be facing each time?" Dwayne asked.

"Correct." Deia nodded.

Dwayne looked to Josh and Kim. "I'm in. That's cool."

"Who are the Aleph?" Josh asked.

"They're an ancient race that lived underground. They're the ones who created the teleport pads. All of their cities and homes are connected by teleport pads," Deia said.

"So, their capital is in Selhi?" Dwayne asked.

"We have no idea where their capital is and the current administrator of the Aleph automatons has made it clear that while he doesn't exactly trust us, he is willing to take a chance on us," Anna said, blurring the lines a bit.

"It could be under Selhi; it could be in the ocean between Gudalo and Ashal. They have teleport pads *everywhere*. Usually multiples in a small installation," Deia said.

"So, this race, *the Aleph*, one of their administrators is asking for our help in helping to re-establish order within his home?" Josh asked.

"Pretty much," Anna said.

"Well, I agree. This could be fun. No matter what the rewards are, I'm excited to check this out." Josh smiled.

"I agree." Kim smiled.

"Now, what kind of information do we have on this place?"

"Well, we've got quite a bit on not only where we will be starting but maps of the other places we will be going through, including enemy's numbers and such. These Aleph scouts are damned good at what they do," Deia said.

The table turned into a computer desktop, with maps all across it.

"The first places we will be going through are the primary installations. These are places of research and development, manufacturing centers, power stations and all the rest. These places *cannot* fall into anyone's hands but the Aleph's. Again, this is a big trust that they are giving us. We need to make sure that no one gets sticky fingers." Anna pointed to an array of maps.

"We can do that. People are more than happy to fight instead of pocketing a few extra bits and bobs," Dwayne said.

"We're going to need rest stations. How are we coordinating revives and supplies?" Kim asked.

"I remember when a raid was just running into a room with a massive group and slapping around a big boss with everything you have."

***

It took a day for them to power up all of the power stations that were at the bottom of Alephir's cylinder. They had been woken up as the city started to move and spin. It became a sort of background noise as trains started to move soul gems through the cities and automatons returned to their duties instead of where they had powered down.

With the city spinning, the other power stations could be reached. They steadily moved through them, some belts taking mere minutes to fix, while others took hours.

While they worked, Shard sent out his scouts to the other Alephir installations. On the fourth day, the second to last day before the Stone Raiders would reach Selhi's capital, Shard asked for them to meet with him at one of his hubs. Shard did not live in just one piece of ebony. He had multiple hubs throughout the city to allow people to interact with him. He had also been connected to other substations and installations when there was more power.

"I thank you for the completion of your quest," Shard said as they all sat around a conference table. They had worked hard and it showed in their dirty clothes, hands, and faces.

Dave heard the noise of a quest completion.

"As compensation, I have a number of resources that I can give to you as well as information in some cases." Shard smiled as screens popped up in front of everyone.

Quest: Power up

Aleph's AI Shard needs more power. Fix his substations or supply him with enough soul or Mana energy to bring more systems online in order to fix it himself.

You must provide 5,000,000 Mana points equivalent of power. (Power provided: 1,350,000/5,000,000)

Or

Activate a class A Power Station (3/1), three class B Power Stations (12/3) or Nine Class C Power Stations (27/9).

COMPLETE

Rewards: Complete book of all runes Shard knows, created in a format identical to your own handmade rune translation book. For not only starting the power systems of Alephir, but actively teaching Shard how to maintain them and showing him your trust by sharing the information you gathered from Boran-al's Citadel, you are rewarded: 1x Book of Portal Creation – Journeyman Level.

The position of trusted ally of Shard.

(This may lead to new quests and opportunities with the Aleph people and Shard.)

For going beyond the Quest's necessities, you will be awarded with the position of sub-commander. Shard is one entity. He cannot control all of Aleph's forces by himself. In certain situations, he will give command of Alephir Guardians to his trusted companions. All Alephir locations are revealed to you. You are counted as a citizen of Aleph; their home is your home.

20x Ingots of Mithril.

Dave looked at Shard as he saw the two books added to his bag of holding.

"Is something the matter?" Shard asked.

"Dude, this is..."

"Awesome!" Induca yelled out.

"Is everyone a sub-commander?" Deia asked.

"That is correct. It will allow me to give you permissions that you did not have before in your fight to clear out the Aleph lands and allow you to communicate and take command of any rogue units that might be in the area," Shard said.

"What is an experimental behemoth?" Suzy asked after looking at her quest rewards.

Anna's head practically whipped around to look at Shard.

"Well, as you know, I'm kind of stuck in place. At the end of the Aleph Master's term, they were creating something new. Something we hadn't tried before. We were putting an AI into a behemoth. We found, however, that the AI had a strong personality and could only be commanded by someone with a strong Willpower. We had to take it apart but it is still waiting for a master."

"So, a summoner who has a really high Willpower might be able to control this thing?" Anna asked dryly, rubbing her face. "Didn't I tell you lot to stop messing with AI?"

"Well, he is rather rambunctious. I found him entertaining. It was just that with all his computing power, it was hard for him and others to exercise control over him. He needed a calming hand of someone with a stronger Willpower."

"Well, we'd best go and see this creation then." Anna sighed.

Malsour bowed deeply to Shard. "I thank you deeply for your gift." He held a necklace in his hand.

"I noticed that you like to read and lugging those books around is boring. The necklace will adjust to you even in dragon form," Shard said, clearly pleased.

"About the whole dragon form thing..." Induca trailed off.

"Do not worry. I have classified the information as requiring the Aleph council to ask me about it to reveal your true identities. The dragons are an honorable race for the most part and my interactions with you have made me come to trust you as I have trusted few others." Shard looked to them all.

"Dave, you might want to read your portal book while having Malsour's necklace on. If he lets you," Shard hinted.

"Malsour, ole buddy, ole pal, mind if I use that there trinket?" Dave asked.

"I get something new and you want to use it almost immediately," Malsour complained.

"I'll let you check out my big book of runes and things. Shard gave me another book with all the runes he knows as well!"

"Deal!" Malsour said. The two of them moved to the side.

Anna and Shard were talking in low voices. Anna walked away after a few moments, tapping Shard's ebony home before she went to the window, happy tears in her eyes.

Induca and Deia were talking to each another and thanked Shard, asking him about the different information and gear he had given them.

Dave gave Malsour the big book of rune combinations as Malsour gave him the necklace.

Necklace of Librarian's Bliss

Quality: A

Durability: 170/170

Read 30% faster

Understand 20% more

Able to absorb books, copying them and adding them to the Aleph records (Rewards given based on book's rarity and knowledge).

Able to access the Aleph records, including spellbooks (You can access: Apprentice level books).

All books that you read while wearing this necklace will be saved for later use (not including spellbooks).

Price: Unknown

"This is incredible!" Dave said.

"That's not all. As our relationship with Shard and the Aleph people increase, we can get more access to their records. The more quests we complete, how we contribute to the records—it all increases our standing and ability to read higher-level items. Now, the spellbooks take longer to read as you don't have a physical copy in front of you and the absorption possibility is lower, but you can keep on reading them and have a higher chance with this necklace to access the information," Malsour said, clearly excited.

Dave pulled out his Journeyman book on portal building.

Malsour took a sharp intake of breath.

"Well, let's try this out!" Dave said, about to open it on a console when Malsour's hand slapped the cover back down.

"Are you a bonehead?" Malsour asked.

"What? I want to learn portals!" Dave said.

"I guess you need a little lesson on information books. For basic spells, you can take a spell book, read it and understand it. For something as complex as portals, reading the Journeyman level, you'll get some of it but you won't understand it all as you don't know all the building blocks. My advice—read through the Novice and Apprentice books, you'll understand more. They can give you the basics, the building blocks, so that when you read the Journeyman book, you get the most out of it. You know how much that thing would cost?"

"Okay now, that does make sense and I don't know—forty gold or so?" Dave asked.

"There are no books on building portals in all of Emerilia and that is a Journeyman-level book. Easily four hundred thousand gold. Thankfully, with the access we have to the Aleph records, you have not only the Journeyman book but can also read the Novice and Apprentice level books," Malsour said.

"Holy crap." Dave looked at the book and then put it away in his bag. "But wait, how do places get teleport pads then if there is no information on the runes?"

"They buy it in their building interface. When you own a city or a country, you get an interface that allows you to control the entire continent to varying degrees, such as giving out quests to build homes or a smithy or a teleport pad. Teleport pads are the most expensive resource."

"But who builds them?"

"We do," Shard said, inserting himself into the conversation.

"How?" Dave asked.

"When they place a teleport pad icon in a place, then they contribute energy, materials, and all the rest. It is transferred to an Aleph installation, which then teleports a new teleport pad into the location that the owner of the area has picked. The materials are used to make new teleport pads. There are always a number of them in storage, ready to be bought. The installation is supported by Anna's father. As it is an integral part of the game, he was able to bend the rules a bit to assist that installation and get me enough power to stay on standby mode until someone helped me."

"How do I have a feeling that finding that substation was not a mistake?" Dave asked.

Shard simply smiled.

***

Deia and Induca were talking about the different properties of their Fire element as well as information on all manner of elements that they were trying to call upon and manipulate.

"So, what was your reward?" Suzy asked Anna as the elevator they were in descended, heading for the waypoint Suzy had been given for the quest.

"Something that I didn't think possible," Anna said softly. A smile appeared on her lips.

"So, what is your relationship with Shard anyway? It seems that you're more than just friends," Suzy asked.

"No fair, I wanted to ask her!" Induca said.

"Always get more information when the other party has had a few celebratory drinks," Deia agreed, the two of them stopping their conversation to listen.

"Well, I gave Shard part of the coding he needed to stabilize and not go rogue. It's a lot easier to do than you would think. He's the only other AI on the planet and we have spent a good amount of time together." Anna blushed and scratched her head. "Well, if I'm being honest, he's probably my best friend other than you guys. We've spent a lot of time together just doing AI stuff. Combining information—integrating it. It's fun being around him. The Aleph were also thinking of giving him his own body like I have mine. I guess that is where this behemoth experimental project came from."

"If you were to relate it to us biologicals, what would you say your relationship is?" Deia asked.

Suzy laughed at Anna, who seemed to be looking for a way to escape the situation.

"Well, we have talked about creating a new code together." Anna rubbed her hands together.

"So, like make an AI baby?" Deia asked.

"Kind of," Anna said, almost as red as the inside of Induca's cloak.

"Oh, this is so exciting! So, what are you two? On-again, off-again? Boyfriend, girlfriend, a crush?" Induca squealed.

"Well, we just kind of made the decision, you know, we like each other's company and it would be interesting to create something." Anna smiled, looking at her girls.

"Hmm, definitely sounds like proposal territory there!" Deia smiled.

"Well, have you and Dave talked about having kids?" Induca asked.

"We have and we didn't think that it would be a good idea having kids when Emerilia is as hectic as it is," Deia said with a sad but understanding smile.

The lift stopped; the doors opening as lights came online.

"Fuck-a-doodle-fuck." Suzy stepped out of the lift and looked at a two-story machine lab. There were behemoths in four workstations at every corner, with more stored on the second level of the machine shop.

A behemoth was as big as a giant but made from steel plate armor, runes, and a smaller version of Shard's spherical rune server. They could rotate all of their limbs in any direction, by using runes instead of the hydraulics and pneumatic systems that an Earth-created version might have. There were no clear weaknesses. The joints had less armor, if you counted one-inch thick armor *easier*.

In the center, there was a behemoth unlike the others that were in various state of assembly.

It didn't have steel armor; it had Mithril to fit a much larger ebony spherical server inside the behemoth. It stood in a massive charging cradle. Unlike the other behemoths that didn't have a head, this one had one with what looked like clockwork pieces that would allow it to shift and move its face.

The behemoth was taller than the other behemoths and carried a two-handed war axe which was as big as Suzy. Its blade was as long as a sword's. It would cover one of the behemoth's hands if it wielded it.

"Impressive." Anna put her hand into the behemoth's open chest and touched the core inside.

"Seems that they did learn something," Anna muttered to herself.

"How in the hell am I supposed to command this thing?" Suzy asked.

"This would not be a creation summoning, but a soul binding summoning if you chose it. What is your stat in Willpower right now?" Anna asked.

"One hundred and fifty-eight."

"Okay, I'm going to need Dave to put some new runes into this thing's core but once that's done, it should be easy enough to command it, though it will take up 10 Willpower points at least. I don't want to know what the power consumption on this thing is going to be," Anna said.

"You sure you want to soul bond yourself to this?" Deia asked.

"I really want to, but we should wait till we can get Dave down here to check this out." Suzy wondered whether it would be an aid instead of a nuisance.

"Sent him a message. He should be down in a bit—he's trying out those tubes." Deia shook her head.

"I can answer any questions you might have on the behemoth in its current state." Shard appeared, in holographic form. After the additional power, he had stopped lagging. His image now held more color and allowed him to appear more life-like.

"What is the energy drain on this thing?" Suzy asked.

"It has soul gems integrated into it that will allow for about one million charge points, or ten million Mana points. I am currently charging it so that it will be at full charge, which will work for approximately two weeks. I believe that Dave, with his knowledge on soul gems, combined with my computational abilities and resources, will be able to create an upgrade to increase the amount of power that it can hold. I have an abundance of energy at this time. I would be happy to charge the behemoth if you brought it to any

Aleph location. I would only ask that you upload its data logs and ask me any questions you might have on the behemoth's interactions. I am interested in the development of another AI."

Suzy looked to Anna, who had her head inside the behemoth.

"What maintenance issues are we looking at?" Suzy asked.

"Much as how you have all taught me how to fix different things, this behemoth should learn to fix itself and indeed grow in strength with time," Shard said.

"Can it share experience?" Anna asked.

"Yes, there is a setting for that. Right now, it is unleveled, but I believe that will quickly change as it has already been uploaded with various safety programs that the other guardians have. With time, it will gain levels and increase its basic statistics. It is the hope that the more that this behemoth learns, the stronger the rest of the guardian fighting force will become."

"That would be a scary damned army to fight," Deia said.

"That is the hope." Shard smiled.

"Wow, okay, yeah, this is cool." Dave looked around the room. His eyes glowed as they settled on the experimental behemoth.

"Shard, your people—love their work. Just damn!" Dave said, his armor fading away as his smithy belt ran around his waist.

Looks like they rolled the Mithril into sheets. The power it must've taken to do that without infusing it with Willpower... Dave shook his head as he studied the material. When a Dwarf formed Mithril, they broke the bonds, altered the metal and new bonds formed. Here, the Mithril's old bonds hadn't been broken and were, after centuries, still changing to meet the new pattern of the Mithril, making it much weaker.

"Do you think that you can make the soul gems hold more power?" Suzy asked as he climbed up the side of the behemoth.

"Am I the man or am I the man?" Dave asked, hanging off the cradle with one hand.

Suzy crossed her arm and tapped her foot.

"Of course I can! Will need to gut the poor bastard in places." Dave looked the creature over.

"If you give me the specifics, then I can machine most of the systems and even the new soul gems so that it would be a simple switch out," Shard offered.

"Okay, well, this is going to take some work." Dave scratched the back of his head, leaning toward the behemoth and looking at different things.

"Do you think it would be worth bonding to?" Suzy asked.

Dave balanced between the cradle and the behemoth's hip, looking at its arms. "What's the cost?"

"Ten Willpower, to control it. Then, it needs charging every two weeks, one million soul gem charge points, or ten mil Mana points for two weeks of being active."

"Honestly, I would. Sure, that two weeks will probably go down if you are fighting. That said, we've got all of these runes that are training up our Willpower constantly, so it's not hard to think that we'll be able to support him if need be. Then, I can also enchant his blade with soul trap. He kills things, he gets charged. Shard, do you have a base stat sheet?" Dave glanced at Shard.

"Certainly. Sorry for not bringing it up before. I have started sending out the fifth round of scouts and the first have come back from their different areas."

A screen appeared in front of Suzy.

Name -   Class: Warrior

Vitality: Level 3   Endurance: Level 2 (0/14 days)

Armor: 3,000/3,000

Mana Barrier: 0/1,200   Aleph Server: 10/10

Strength: Level 5   Agility: Level 1

Left Arm: Standard attachment   Right Arm: Standard attachment

Left Leg: Upgraded soul gem   Right Leg: Upgraded soul
capacity. Standard function.   gem capacity. Standard
                                    function.

Skills: Armor repair, mental link,
Behemoth Guardian program, Mana   Charge: 0/1,000,000 Mana
barrier   points

Owner: Unclaimed   Race: Aleph Guardian
                                    (Experimental)

"Why are the arms and legs displayed separately?" Suzy asked.

"Because they can be upgraded," Shard said.

"I could give him my lightning ball of shocking!" Dave said.

"You still need to work on your naming skills." Induca looked to Deia, who just shrugged, defeated in trying to get him to not give everything a ridiculous name.

"Wow, okay, damn," Suzy said, just starting to see the possibilities of the behemoth. *No wonder it is the only thing I got other than the sub-commander status.* "All right, well, it would be rude to refuse." She smiled.

"I think it might be best if you go and get some rest before trying this all out. We're all tired from being down here. Getting a night's rest and being there for when the rest of the Stone Raiders arrive would be a good idea," Anna said.

"Agreed," Dave said. "If you want this dude under your command, then I can think of a few ways to get him in much better shape for the coming fights."

"So, you and Anna will stay here while we go back to SC?" Deia asked.

"Yeah, we'll get a lot done on this thing so it's ready for Suzy to take it over. You guys can give us your supplies so we have enough food. Complete that adventurer's quest and meet up with the rest of the Stone Raiders. You can let them know what we're dealing with as Shard sends you information by private messages. When you get back, we should have a handle on this big beastie. Suzy takes control and we then go clear out the rest of the Aleph areas," Dave said.

"Okay," Deia said. "You sure?" She looked to Anna and Dave.

"I need Dave to alter this rune core some so that it isn't all over the place when Suzy uses it. They also have showers here, instead of baths." Anna smiled.

"When you get back, Suzy might be the most powerful fighter we have when she's controlling this guy and her constructs." Dave tapped the behemoth.

"I would also like to stay to access the libraries and learn more about the Aleph," Malsour said.

"Sweet! Get some reading done!"

Suzy wanted to get it over with now, but she understood what Anna and Dave were saying.

"Well then, I guess we should start heading back. Also, Suzy will probably need to talk to the Exdar's Traders. We've put off talking to them for a while now," Deia said.

"I hope we get some good gold from all those kills. Damn meal is going to cost a pretty penny this time," Suzy complained.

"Remember to meditate and clear your mind, to be at ease when you return." Anna waved her finger at Suzy, giving her a severe look. "I will be messaging and checking in on you. This is one hell of a powerful creation to control."

"Yes, Mom," Suzy said in mock indignation.

Chapter 12: Progress

The trip back from the Aleph substation had been rather easy. The kobolds that were hiding in the bottom of the substation had sent out some groups that were now protecting the different areas. They weren't expecting them to come from behind as Deia and Suzy's metal creations stealthily killed them, taking anything of value and continuing on. Their packs carried various rare gems that Shard didn't need in order to operate Alephir. However, brandishing around such high quality goods would raise suspicious and result in questions they didn't want to answer just yet.

Suzy had a rough estimate of the wealth that they had gathered, but she wasn't willing to estimate it. If she was right, it was a lot more than any other character had ever reported, even the trading guilds.

"We thought you had been eaten by the forest with how long you were gone. What happened with the rest of your party?" the clerk at the adventurer desk asked.

"They went on ahead to look for more hunting grounds. We found some interesting creatures out there," Deia said.

"Well, we are in need of more people clearing out the area near the swamp. The traders' guild has been holding an open contract on that area." The man scratched his beard.

"Well, if you want to make some real gold and go dungeon diving, let us know. We know how to treat a group of good ladies like yourselves," a Player who had been nearby and overheard their conversation said.

"We're good, thanks," Suzy said.

"Kill logs." The clerk held out his hand.

"Oh, don't be that way, babe. We're the best dungeon clearers in this town. Got a gold rating with the adventurer's guild, even thinking of starting our own Players guild!" the talker, a necro-mancer by his robes, said.

"Fucking hell." The clerk paled and scratched his head at the kill logs Deia had handed over. "You're telling me that there were this many high-leveled kobolds out there? How the hell did you kill them all?"

"Well, there is a reason that we were away for so long," Deia said, trying to minimize the attention. Others were now listening in.

"Kobolds? Where'd you find them?" the necro asked.

"In some caves." Induca looked at him as if he were dumb.

"I know that much, but where?"

This guy is not giving up.

"Here's a waypoint. They're all dead now and probably gone." Deia sent him a waypoint to a cave system she and Anna had cleared out on the opposite side of town.

"Huh, well, let me know if you want to pair up or ever get a drink," the necro said, smiling before he left. His party finished off their drinks and followed after him.

"Come with me. I need to take you to the chapter head. This is the kind of threat that we will need to pass on to the city guard." The clerk waved for them to join him. They followed him through a backroom and to a guarded door.

The guard knocked on the door for them.

"Come in," the bored reply came.

The guard opened the door as the four, including the clerk, walked into the room.

"Chapter head, while these Players were off adventuring, they came across a group of high-leveled kobold. They killed them, but I thought you might be interested in talking to them," the clerk said.

"Where were the kobold located?" A heavyset man with a tanned complexion and black hair going salt-and-pepper sat in a chair—a thin blade hung on the back of his chair.

If one was to ask Suzy what the man looked like, she would have said French pirate.

"Sorry, we can't give the exact location. The threat has been cleared out," Deia said.

"Oh, are you challenging me, missy? This could be a threat to this village. What possible reason would there be to not tell us?" the man asked.

"Guild business," Deia stated.

The chapter leader rolled his eyes. "What guild? I'll see that they are expelled from the adventurer's guild for this if you still refuse to tell me." The man still sounded more bored than angry.

"Fine, we're the Stone Raiders." Deia pulled her cloak to the side to show her guild badge.

The others in her party did so as well.

"If you will give us the money you owe us, we will be on our way. We have work we need to do." Suzy looked up from her messaging.

"Stone Raiders, huh? Never really seen what's so important about you lot. Edurn, make sure they are banned from this location and pass the information on to the rest of the adventurer's guild." The chapter leader's eyes moved to the girls, a gloating smile on his face. "I heard that your guild was coming here for the monster hunt. It looks like they will have wasted all of those credits for nothing. As you are not adventurer guild members, you will be taxed twenty percent of this contract." He waved at the kill log.

"Sir..." the clerk started before the chapter leader shot him a look. The clerk looked as if he wanted to continue but didn't dare, diverting his eyes to the floor.

Deia snorted, shrugging. "Fine. Can we get our money?" She looked to the clerk.

"Yes, certainly," the clerk said. "That will be three hundred gold, five silver, and seven coppers."

"What!?" the chapter leader demanded, looking from the clerk to the three women.

Induca opened the door as the chapter leader pulled the kill log sheet that the clerk had put on his desk.

"How the hell is this possible!?" he demanded as the three ladies exited the adventurer's guild and headed to their next meeting.

***

Bronx and Florence were waiting for Suzy as she led her group into the restaurant and over to the other two.

"Thank you for greeting my guests for me." Suzy passed a gold coin to the waiter who had previously served them.

"No worries at all, ma'am." She curtsied. "Would you like me to take your cloaks and get some drinks?"

"Please. I'll take a red wine." Suzy got out of her cloak.

"Elven ice wine if you have it. Elven white if you don't," Deia said.

"Some Zolun beer if you might have it, please." Induca handed off her cloak last.

"I will have it to you shortly." The server bowed slightly, taking the cloaks with her as Suzy walked up to the table.

"I am so sorry about this. I know that we were supposed to meet earlier and through our messages, it seems that we have come to an agreement, though I and the guild leadership think it is best if we have these conversations in person," Suzy said.

"It is no worry. We know that security is a primary concern in a relationship such as this. We sent out feelers to make sure everything was still secure before bringing in everyone to discuss the opportunity. We have voted and agreed that we would indeed like to move into an alliance with your guild." Florence smiled.

"I am looking forward to many interesting relics," Bronx agreed.

"I thought that there might be more to you than met the eye." Suzy smiled at Bronx.

The server returned, depositing glasses.

"Could you see that we are not disturbed and pull the curtain?" Suzy asked.

"Certainly. If you pull on the string there, I will come over to assist you with anything you need," the server said.

"Thank you," Deia said.

The server pulled curtains from one bench seat and connected it to the other, muffling the rest of the restaurant.

Suzy looked to Induca and Deia.

Induca pulled out a small Mirror of Communication and placed it on the table.

"Impressive," Bronx said.

"Sit back in your chairs and then press the rim of the mirror. If you want, Florence can come with me and Bronx can keep guard?" Suzy asked.

"Very well." Florence sat back in her seat and put her hand to the Mirror of Communication.

Suzy touched it as well, going through prompts until she appeared in the foyer of a large building. In front of them, there was a large Stone Raider's badge.

People appeared throughout the mansion and moved into different conference rooms.

"Ah, Suzy, this must be Florence," Dwayne said, as Suzy guided her to the second floor.

"It is good to meet you." Florence curtsied slightly.

"Ah, no need for that around here. We're not the most cultured people." Dwayne led them to a large conference room and opened the door for them.

"I'm telling you, we've got to invest in more scribes so we can keep some of the damned spellbooks instead of destroying them all!" Josh said.

"It takes weeks for them to do that!" Kim argued.

"Suzy is here," Lucy said, floating on her carpet and reading a book.

"It might take that long, but then we have them for others! You know how much those things go for? Teleport pads aren't cheap to use!" Josh looked to Suzy and Florence from his seat at the middle of the table.

"Sorry about that," Josh said to Florence.

"It is perfectly okay. I am still in awe of this place. What is it?" Florence asked, diverting as Suzy indicated for her to take a seat. The two of them faced the others as Dwayne took his seat beside Josh.

"Well, a Mirror of Communication can relay simple video and audio messages, yet its true use is its ability to have conference rooms. You can connect multiple mirrors together so that large groups of people can meet in real time no matter their position and share information. For the Stone Raiders who are spread out all over the place, it makes sense to have them around," Josh said.

They also cost a lot, so it looks good and it can impress the hell out of you. Suzy caught Lucy's eye as she hid behind her book. They shared a sly smile before breaking eye contact, not wanting to give away the game.

"I've heard of conference rooms, but not entire buildings with multiple places," Florence said.

"It can be shaped to what the user desires, though this one took someone with a bit more imagination and a special Mirror of Communication to make the whole process smooth," Kim said.

"Now, that is all talk for another time. Suzy here says that the Exdar's Traders are ready to sign a contract?" Josh asked.

"That we are." Florence accessed her interface. Moments later, a paper document was in front of everyone.

Suzy scanned through it; there had been little to no changes to the original document. A bit of wriggle room in delivery times as they didn't know where they would be going or when. Otherwise, it was rather simple: They would sell any goods that the Stone Raiders gave them for a seven percent fee. They would keep a few wagons working to supply the Stone Raiders at all times for a small fee.

They would also transport supplies, weapons, and the like to and from where the Stone Raiders were located. There were fees and associated costs that had been firmed up. All of it was reasonable. Not a large profit on either side. With the influx of money that the Stone Raiders could give them and the near constant stream from their supply needs, the trader's guild would do very well. The Stone Raiders would get better prices on their supplies and more money on the gear that they were selling.

Suzy looked up to find the four leaders of the Stone Raiders looking at her. She looked to Josh.

"It looks good to me." She knew that he was probably the only other person who had dealt with contracts of this magnitude before.

"I agree. Little changes here and there, but within our conditions." Josh looked to the others.

"If you two say it's fine, that's good by me," Dwayne said.

"Cool," Lucy said.

"Be good to have supplies that don't cost me one and a half their usual." Kim sighed.

Josh accepted the contract. A ping sounded in the back of Suzy's mind.

"Well, if you're still in Selhi Capital when we get there, then we should get together," Josh said as the contract faded away from the table.

"We will be leaving a group here to meet up with you and to see what your needs will be," Florence said.

"Perfect, because we have a whole bunch of broken crap that we need to get fixed up at a Dwarven mountain." Dwayne looked to Josh.

"Zolun?"

"How is it that I know where you need to go to get your weapon repaired? And you don't have a clue?" Dwayne asked.

"Cause you're a really good friend?" Josh asked.

Dwayne sighed.

"What these two boneheads are saying is they have weapons that they need to get repaired. All of them are of high quality or stats and need Dwarven smiths to fix them. There is a specific smith who is in the Zolun Mountains who is capable of fixing a weapon that we're having trouble getting repaired; that idiot's damn daggers." Kim gestured at Josh.

"We'll have all the weapons put together in one caravan so that you can shift them to the mountain as we get there. We are planning to be moving onto a new operation quickly," Dwayne said.

"Yeah, he likes all that military talk and orderly stuff. I'm sorry," Josh said.

"Next time, I'm not reminding you about the weapons that you need to get repaired."

"Hey, I'm just telling the truth, dude. How the heck am I supposed to remember everything?" Josh whined.

"Don't worry, he's normally like this. He kind of acts like a kid, most of the time, unlike when we are in anything that looks like a battle. Reminds me of my old boss," Suzy said to Florence.

"We can do that. It is nearby. With our horse handling abilities, we can get the carts to that location within three days, then however long it takes to repair that gear. What do you need for supplies?" Florence asked.

***

After the meeting finished, Florence and Suzy said their good-byes and left the conference room.

"Well, it seems that we have a lot of work to do. Thank you for mediating all of this. Is there anything that we can help you with?" Florence asked.

"Well, we do have some items that we want to sell but we don't have the time nor the contacts to sell them and not draw attention to ourselves or get a good price for the item," Suzy said.

"I can take a look at them now and see if I could shift them," Florence said.

Suzy looked to the others, making a note of the loot that they wanted to sell, sending it off to Florence.

"Bloody hell! How the hell did you get all of this in less than a week?" Florence looked at the three with wide eyes.

"We had to do a rather select quest that had some rather nice rewards and interesting creatures in our way," Deia supplied.

"Well, I can move most of these goods. If you want, I can put it up on the guild forum. Whoever sells it gets the largest share but everyone can try to shift it at a faster pace. Will also mean distributing it around so that we don't have people looking into you specifically," Florence said.

"How do you get your goods out to the people in your guild that fast?" Suzy asked.

"Banks. They're the best for low volume, high priced goods like these. You can pay a fee to have items transferred from one bank location to another. People with guild access answer a password, grab the item and sell it."

"That makes sense. For larger quantity of items, then you have to use caravans to move the goods around," Deia said.

"Exactly. With the higher quality goods of the Stone Raiders coming in, we can spread our guild thinner in more places so that they have access to markets more directly and can sell in more areas and have our bank moving the goods. With the caravans, we can move goods around that will get a higher price across the globe and play the local markets," Florence said, opening up now that they were in a full alliance.

"Well, I say that we get some drinks into us and celebrate this alliance and moving all those damned goods. I sure as hell don't want to keep carrying them in my pack!" Induca clapped Suzy and Deia on the shoulders.

"Sounds good to me." Deia held her glass up in salute to the others.

Chapter 13: Meet Steve

"Wakey wakey. Shine and bakey!" Josh's annoying voice came through the door as Deia hurled a boot at it.

"Fuck off, Josh, or I'll get my fiancé to break your little dagger!" Deia barked at the door.

"Well, sounds like they are getting a hang of the Stone Raiders. Damned near drank everything out of the place," Josh said.

"I have healing potions," Kim said.

"Open," Suzy groaned.

Deia had passed out in a chair and then fallen on the floor, not caring about where she slept as long as she was asleep. Induca and Suzy were in the bed, sprawled all over the place.

"Huh, well, this looks interesting," Kim said.

"What does?" Josh said, getting close to the door.

"Out, you damned man!" Kim kicked the door closed to the groans of the other three in the room.

"My nose!" Josh yelled.

"Eh, you've broken it so many times you might as well give up on it," Dwayne said, his heavy footsteps walking away.

Kim came around and passed out healing potions that the others took and drank.

Deia was the first to get up off the floor, her hangover starting to fade away.

"So, had fun last night?" Kim sat in the chair opposite Deia and looked at Suzy and Induca, who were in bed.

"It was rather...*interesting*." Deia looked at the other two as they untangled from each other and got up from their slumber.

"We've got people meeting up with Florence and their traders. The gear that needs to be repaired should be moving out today. They've already got a lot of the stuff that we needed. Seems that they've been busy," Kim said, impressed.

"Well, I wasn't about to let us get allied with a bunch of lazy bastards." Suzy stretched in the morning light, revealing the fact that she wasn't wearing much clothing.

"Seems like that training came in use." Deia saw how Suzy's body had firmed up under constant training.

"That it did." Suzy looked to Induca, who simply smiled lazily and stretched like a cat. "All right, well, Josh says we'll stay here for a bit and then head out to wherever this place is. Josh also wants to go and check out where we're going ahead of everyone else. Start putting our own scouts in there to verify that everything these guardians report is truth," Kim said.

"Okay," Deia said. "Well, we should get some food in us and then head out as soon as possible."

"Yeah, if you can bear to untangle yourselves," Kim said. Suzy and Induca looked completely unrepentant about their state of nakedness or their positions.

***

"It has been confirmed. The Stone Raiders are in Selhi Capital. We are moving people in through all the ways we know possible. We should be ready to begin the operation in a few days," Koloa said.

"Good. Then we'll see who the most powerful guild in Emerilia is," Hevard said. "Make sure that all the preparations are in place."

"Yes, Guildmaster." Koloa turned and left the conference room that the two of them had been in. It disappeared to show a rundown tavern room and a Mirror of Communication. Hevard put the mirror away and stepped outside. Three assassins melded out of the shadows for a second before they disappeared once again.

This is going to be fun.

***

Dave looked up as the lift stopped. He and Anna had been working on the behemoth ever since the others had left. Malsour was absorbed in his books, telling them pieces of information that he had found that could be valuable.

With the necklace, he didn't hold a physical book in his hand. The necklace somehow beamed it into his eye so that he could read it wherever. Dave was a bit jealous and kept on looking into how to build one so that he might be able to connect to the Aleph records.

Shard had been floating around, happy to talk to them, answer what questions he could and give any advice he thought was pertinent. Dave had given his information on soul gems to Shard, which had resulted in increased reputation and him almost being able to access peak Apprentice level content in the records.

Dave had worked quickly with the information that he had to make the soul gems, but with everything else on his plate, it would have still taken a few weeks to complete. With Shard behind the production, the three soul gems that Dave would need to update the behemoth would take just five days.

Most of the time had been spent changing runes around in the behemoth's core. It was tedious and hard work that required Dave to use forges to heat the metal to change its form in combination with his soul smithing. He had burned through all of his stored soul energy and was feeling strained from the work.

"So, how are things?" Suzy asked, a mix of excitement and anxiety on her face as she walked closer to the behemoth and where Dave and Anna had put their cots.

"We're ready for you to start trying to soul bond to it. Dave spent a lot of time altering the runes so that they would be more stable and the connection should be easier to make," Anna said.

"Yeah, fucking sucked." Dave rolled over in his bed, his head hurting from all the different energies that he had expelled over the last two days.

Deia rubbed Dave's shoulder as he lay.

"Come 'ere." He pulled her down.

She let out a surprised squeak as she fell on the cot. "Better?"

"Mhmm." Dave sounded content as the others talked about what Anna and Dave had been up to.

Suzy pulled out a big jug, uncorking one end, and poured it into a cup. She gave one to Anna before waving another under Dave's nose. He slowly sat up with Deia, taking the cup of Xer.

He'd come to like the pseudo coffee and on mornings like these, it was the best thing to have.

"Seems I need to learn this new bribe." Deia smiled at Dave's pleased expression as he sipped the concoction.

"Two cream, one sugar." Suzy put the jug down next to the bed. "So, what happened to the Mithril?"

"Dave thought it might be a good idea to cover it over with some steel so that people don't know that you're walking around with something that was more expensive than some villages. Also, it'll make people think it is easier to defeat than it really is. Being a low level, they're not going to think that you're able to bond to this thing. Finally, we messed around with the internal runes, which was a pain in the ass," Anna said.

Dave made an annoyed noise but continued to drink his coffee.

"With the information that we provided, Shard is making new legs and arms that you can change out, though they're going to take some time. How did things go topside?" Anna drank from her cup of Xer.

"We got an agreement with the traders and the Stone Raiders are here. We left Josh with his scouts and rogues to check out the different facilities that we are supposed to be clearing out. They've confirmed the reports so far. The rest of the guild should be here in three days," Deia said. "Also, I don't know if it will be upheld, but we kind of got banned from the adventurer's Guild Selhi Chapter house," Deia said awkwardly.

"I'm sure it was for a good reason," Dave said.

Anna and Suzy nodded in agreement.

"Okay, then I think we have enough time to go over the class system. I think it's about time that the two of you picked classes." Anna looked from Dave to Suzy.

"I think it would be worth it. Unlocking all of those extra bonuses would be nice," Dave said.

"Good, Suzy?"

"Well, it would be nice to have something to give me a boost right before I try to take control of this big beastie." Suzy tapped the behemoth's leg.

"Good. Then put your points into your characters and let's see what happens. If you're lucky, you might even get some freebie classes," Anna said.

Dave sat up and looked at his character sheet.

Character Sheet

Name:	David Grahslagg	Gender:	Male
Level:	3	Class:	-
Race:	Human/Dwarf	Alignment:	Chaotic Neutral

Unspent points-340

Health:	3,300	Regen:	2.24/s
Mana:	1,550	Regen:	6.60/s
Stamina:	890	Regen:	4.30/s
Vitality:	33	Endurance:	112
Intelligence:	155	Willpower:	132
Strength:	89	Agility:	86

"Thirty-nine stat points to mess around with, to just stay out of level 11," Dave muttered to himself. "Put 10 in Vitality, 12 in Agility,

8 in Intelligence and 9 in Willpower?" He looked at his stats and their new numbers.

Character Sheet

Name:	David Grahslagg	Gender:	Male
Level:	3(10)	Class:	-
Race:	Human/Dwarf	Alignment:	Chaotic Neutral

Unspent points-340(301)

Health:	3,300(4,300)	Regen:	2.24/s
Mana:	1,550(1,630)	Regen:	6.60/s(7.05/s)
Stamina:	890	Regen:	4.30/s(4.90/s)
Vitality:	33(43)	Endurance:	112
Intelligence:	155(163)	Willpower:	132(141)
Strength:	89	Agility:	86(98)

Level increase!

You have placed (39) stat points into your various stats. Do you accept these changes?

Y/N?

"Yeah," Dave said. Before his eyes, the original numbers disappeared, as well as the brackets.

He felt healthier, as if his body breathed life, feeling that he could take more risks. He felt smarter and more confident in the person that he was. Information that he had glanced at before and he'd been thinking on now made sense.

He felt filled with boundless energy, as if he could run for miles or fight hordes of creatures. He spun a weapon rod in his hands, his fingers nimble and swift. "Well, crap, that is one hell of a drug."

"Yeah," Suzy said, holding a table.

You have reached Level 10

Emerilia's class system is now open for you to use! Classes can be gained at levels: 10, 50, 100, 200, 300, and at every century level. You can also gain new classes through raising certain stats and going through rigorous training.

Dave swiped it away to only have it replaced again.

You have earned a new class: Dwarven Master Smith

Hello Petunia! Thought you were rid of me, huh? Well, lookie here, you swing hammers at metal and you make things. Like swords and shit. BOOOOOORING! But hell, whatever floats yer boat!

Status: Level 1

Effects:
Allowed access to all Dwarven Mountains and Smithies.
Allowed to take on smithing apprentices.
+10 to all stats
Access to special quests.

You have earned a new class: Friend of the Gray God

Well, looks like you know my boss—guy's always off doing random crap. Should have known that he was messing around with your background. Whatever, here's some friend swag

Status: Level 2

Effects:
+20 to all stats
Access to hidden quests.

You have earned a new class: Bleeder

Dude, seriously getting annoyed with all of these classes. What the hell have you been doing? And Bleeder? I don't even know what that is!

Status: Level 1

Effects:
+10 to all stats
(???)

Select a Class!

As you have reached level 10, you can pick one class. This will not increase your skills and will only give you level 1. To increase your level further, you will need to increase the correlating stats and finish quests associated with the class.

Another screen appeared with selectable names from beast tamer to apothecary master and librarian, with their specific effects. The ones that Dave didn't know much about had (???), like with the hidden effect on his Bleeder class.

He pushed it to the side, in slight shock as he looked to the others.

"Did something go wrong?" Deia put her hand on his.

"I'm not..." Dave felt power surge through him. He was stronger, faster, and healthier; he didn't need sleep or food. His mind was abuzz with thoughts and ideas and yet he felt reassured; he felt he was all-seeing and all-knowing.

"Wow, so this is power," Dave said. His muscles didn't grow but they felt stronger, as if they had become denser and more flexible. Energy seemed to radiate through his body.

"I just got a class update on being friends with Bob," Malsour said.

Everyone started to look at their interfaces.

"My father doesn't have Champions, but he has friends who he asks to help him out from time to time. It's his way of getting around not having a Champion. Naming Champions makes it a lot easier for the rest of the Pantheon to find them. Dave getting it must have made the system remind Dad to name his friends.

"Sorry about that—should have done it sooner." Bob sat on one of the worktables. "Hey, Shard! How's it going?"

"Good, Lo'Kal," Shard said.

"Told you to call me Bob and I promised that I'd get you some people to help out!" Bob looked at the others.

"You set all of this up?" Induca asked.

"Well, *maybe* to some degree," Bob scratched his head with an awkward smile on his face.

"You could have just told us." Deia crossed her arms.

"I could have, but then the other lords and ladies might have seen me. Even this is a risk and Alephir, once powered up, is a pain in the ass to see into. Good work, by the way."

"So what does being your friend entail?" Malsour asked.

"Well, we can go for beers and get some food, hang out and stuff. Well, we would have if the lords and ladies hadn't been given so much power. Right now, I only have five minutes to spend here before they find me. Also, I leave a magic signature on the people I meet so it means meeting even less. I can still send PMs and have a Mirror of Communication so we can talk." Bob became serious as he glanced at the occupants of the room. "There is a change coming. I am trying to mitigate as much of the chaos that will venture to Emerilia as possible. Even I cannot stop it all. This is just one step in many that I can see, balancing that chaos and giving the people of Emerilia a chance of surviving what is to come. As you have come to share your secrets and lives with me, I have come to trust you. While I can give you tasks, it is up to you whether you complete them or not. You are my friends, not my Champions or my lackeys. I may give you quests or help you out here and there, but I do it as a friend. Well, a friend who can't be seen, so it'll be a lot of shadow moving. That said, I won't try to sway you to do something one way or another."

"So, you gave us the hints to lead us here but didn't full out tell us because you didn't want to influence our decisions?" Dave asked.

"Bingo was his name-o!" Bob said. "You got any of that Scotch, by the way? Nothing quite like it in my cellars."

Dave laughed and conjured a drink in Bob's hand.

"So, why did you lead us here other than to help Shard come online?" Anna asked.

"Because, as you've been talking about, I really am sending the Aleph back. If they are to return, their home needs to be secure. Letting people know that they are back would only lead to forces massing to attack them once again, like with the demons, or your own brothers and sisters," Bob said.

"Well, next time you want us to help out someone, just ask—it's a lot easier," Suzy said.

"Well, I don't want to make a request that messes up our friendship," Bob said.

He's lonely and although he wants to do his best for the people of Emerilia, he doesn't want to lose his friends. It reminds me of when I was Austin Zane. "It's lonely at the top," Dave whispered to himself. Deia shot him a curious glance.

"Just send it anyway. Better for us to know what and why you want us to do something so we can make an educated decision rather than you messing around with all kinds of crap in the background just so we can make an unimpeded decision. We're all adults here and we know what risks there are," Suzy said.

Bob looked around the room, seeing everyone's expressions before he scratched his head in embarrassment.

"Okay, next time I'll just message you. Please help to clean out anything that might be in the Aleph's home. The class system will give you another level for doing so and completing any quests I give. Don't worry—I have plenty planned to keep you busy." Bob smiled but it faded as he cocked his head to the side.

"Shit, my time's about up. If you want to talk to me or whatever, then Dave's Mirror of Communication can connect to me. Shard also has the same thing. If not, you can PM me. Thank you, everyone, for being understanding and for trusting me. It—it's really nice." Bob gave an awkward smile, unsure of how to express his gratitude and happiness.

"Don't worry, dude. It's not us stuck with you—it's you stuck with us." Dave grinned.

"Huh, that does sound terrible." Bob laughed. "Talk later!"

Everyone said their good-byes before Bob once again disappeared from existence.

Dave got to his feet and found himself jumping two feet in the air. "Ah shit." Dave landed and held his hands out.

"Dave, just how many points did you put into everything?" Deia asked as everyone looked at him.

"Uhh, well, I put thirty-nine into my various stats to get to ten. Then I got forty stat points on top of that," Dave said.

"Where did you put all of those points?" Malsour asked.

"Well, I got the forty stat points to each of my stats..." Dave stopped talking at the different looks he was getting from Anna, Deia, Malsour, and Induca.

Altogether he had gained 240 stat points, an unheard of number.

"Ah shit." Suzy tried to walk forward and stumbled because of her increased power, pushing her right into the behemoth. She fell on the ground and hammered her fists into the ground in frustration. Instead of just hitting the ground, they left cracks and pushed her up. "Oh, for fuck's sakes!"

She windmilled, but she used too much force and fell on her ass again.

"Suzy, how many did you put in?" Deia asked, as if scared for the answer.

"Plus ten to everything and then forty-nine points beforehand."

"Well, what you're both experiencing now is that your bodies have jumped up stats so quickly that it's going to take some time to get used to it all." Anna laughed as Dave and Suzy looked to each other and started to try to move gingerly without going flying or hitting something.

It took them about twenty minutes before they could walk normally. The two of them talked about the things that Dave had done and how it would make Suzy's soul binding easier.

"I was thinking about getting the Soul Binding Summoner class, but I think that I can hold off now," Suzy said.

"Well, I'd think about it in this way. It will take you how long until you can get your soul binding to that level?" Dave asked.

"Maybe a few months, maybe half a year as I'm focusing on the creation completely," Suzy said.

"What would you get instead?" Dave asked.

"I was thinking the Creation Summoner class."

"Out of the two, I would go with the soul binding. It will take longer to get without this boost, though it shouldn't be long until you can get a Creation Summoner's class. Your skills are higher and it shouldn't be too long until you hit the master rank in them and are able to get the quests. If you don't have a soul binding contract like the one you would form with the behemoth, it's going to take a hell of a long time with getting the soul binding class," Dave said.

"I see what you're saying. It makes more sense for me to aim at getting the soul binding right now because it is so long away that getting it on my own would take a hell of a long time. Also, if I have the behemoth soul bound to me, then I will be training up my soul binding techniques constantly. It will shorten my training time in soul binding and it will also give me a powerful summoned creature," Suzy said.

"Exactly." Dave smiled at her.

"Okay, well, better get this over with and try to learn how to walk with this extra boost." Suzy opened her interface. It took a few moments before she was once again trying to gingerly walk through the room and get used to her new stats.

"What are you thinking of using as your class?" Suzy asked as their progress slowed even further.

"I was thinking Weapons Master class. Though, unlike the other weapons classes, you don't actually need to fight a master in each respective category in order to get the class. You only need to be a Master level 1 in each class," Dave said.

"So what are you thinking of going for now?"

"Either Librarian or Constructor. The Librarian class will allow me to understand more from the books and information I read. It might even reveal more about a quest if I read the prompt completely. It would also help my Inference skill and make it easier to understand complex ideas. My Intelligence stat would probably shoot up with the additional information. With Constructor, it would allow me to create a mental blueprint of what I want to make. Although I conjure items I'm making, the constructor ability would allow me to see what I'm making and where beforehand. Much easier for me to see what I'm working with and then conjure it instead of just conjuring it straight. It would also allow me to model different things and test them out within my mind. I could use Touch to scan an area then conjure a map that completely conforms to what I am seeing in front of everyone. I could also use it to show the different layers of things, like with the core in the behemoth. I could make interactive holograms in my mind for me to play around with and alter different things. It would increase the level of detail I'm capable of and also reduce the Mana expenditure of my conjuring."

"It's not the two skills that I would have thought about first but after talking about them, I can see how they would be interesting. How would you unlock them otherwise?" Suzy asked, trying to get up and not throw herself around by accident.

"Like a couple decades of reading books, or quantity—no one really knows. Not even Malsour has it and he's been reading lifetimes before we were created. For the Constructor class, you need to master the Builder, Smithing, Woodworking, and Masonry skills, then build a massive house by yourself," Anna supplied.

Dave looked to Suzy. Both of them smiled, sensing the new challenge that the class system had opened up.

"Well, the constructor skill sounds a bit easier to get, though I doubt you want to spend the time that it will take to get all of those skills. Both make sense with your given class and what you want to do in the future." Suzy shrugged.

Dave pulled up his interface, accessed his class list and clicked it.

Dave slowed his walking down, once again feeling power surge through him. It wasn't like when he had first got his classes. Now he knew what to expect.

"So, which one did you pick?" Suzy asked.

"Librarian."

"You and information—you just love reading stuff. It's a lot easier to handle the extra power now; it's just a plus ten to everything. Let's go make that behemoth my bitch." Suzy's smile was wolfish as she moved toward the behemoth.

"Well, this is sure to be interesting." Dave followed her over and checked his character sheet.

You have earned a new class: Librarian

Most people like to come to Emerilia and you know, fight stuff, or cast magic or do something ridiculous. You want to read more books... Ah, well, I can't fault you for that—nothing like a good book to get stuck into!

Status: Level 1

    +10 to all stats

Effects: Read 5% faster

    Understand 10% more of the information that you read

Character Sheet

Name:	David Grahslagg	Gender:	Male
Level:	10	Class:	Dwarven Master Smith, Friend of the Gray God, Bleeder, Librarian
Race:	Human/ Dwarf	Alignment:	Chaotic Neutral

Unspent points-301

Health:	9,300	Regen:	3.24/s
Mana:	2,130	Regen:	9.55/s
Stamina:	1,390	Regen:	7.40/s
Vitality:	93	Endurance:	162
Intelligence:	213	Willpower:	191
Strength:	139	Agility:	148

***

Everyone stopped their talking as Suzy walked up to the behemoth.

"Are you ready?" Shard asked.

"Yes." Suzy looked at the behemoth in front of her. Suzy felt the power that started to trickle into the behemoth.

The opened sections closed and locked shut. Runes slowly started to power up. The amount of power coming off the behemoth was almost ethereal. Its face moved, looking to those who dared to awaken it.

"Who wakes me?" the behemoth asked.

"I do." Suzy gathered up her Willpower into the palm of her hand and slapped it against the behemoth's leg. "Soul Bind." The room filled with power as the area she touched glowed in the outline of a handprint.

It fought for control, to fight off her advances. It was a battle of wills, one to show who was the alpha, the one who was master and who was servant.

The behemoth chuckled at her work. "You will never control me. You are too weak to ever think of commanding even a rabbit. Leave me or else I will make you regret ever trying to soul bind with me," the behemoth sneered.

While she was soul binding, it would get to see a part of her soul, her memories, and her life. He was just starting to scratch the surface, but Suzy wasn't going to give him the time to do so. "Big shot, are we?"

The behemoth's mechanical eyes thinned as Suzy smiled.

"Fine, let's see how you handle this." Suzy poured seventy percent of her Willpower into the behemoth. It flew from its cradle, past the other workstations and into the wall.

Suzy bristled with energy, her eyes golden as power rolled off her body like heat off pavement. "Do you accept my soul bond?" Her voice was calm as she stood like a ruling queen staring down at someone who had failed her.

The behemoth smiled and stepped from the wall. "I will serve," it said, its voice solemn and amused. It smiled as it took a knee before Suzy.

You Have Gained A Soul Bound Creature

The Aleph Experimental Behemoth Guardian is yours to command. Unless you break your contract with the creature or allow it to die, the contract will not be broken. Controlling this creature takes 10 Willpower from your overall stats (does not affect Mana recharge).

Suzy swiped the message away from her face.

"Good," Suzy said. The handprint on the behemoth's leg seemed to be absorbed into the behemoth. "I guess, I'll have to name you."

"Ahh, well, I kind of already have one." The behemoth rose to standing, towering over everyone. "I'm Steve." It extended its hand with a cheesy smile on its face.

Chapter 14: Shadows of Red

The Stone Raiders had been drinking throughout the town for two days. Groups had gone off into the forest but none of the PKPs had been able to follow them. They'd been scouts and rogues higher than any of the tails.

There were so many Stone Raiders that they had spread out through the entire tavern district. Koloa had bought up places earlier through various contacts: a few traders here, a group of adventurers there, healers. The purchases came from all over the place, in every tavern and inn across SC. It wasn't abnormal to have this many rooms booked up for monster season.

No one batted an eye at all the people in the streets.

Weird that not one of them stayed in the adventurer's guild. It seems that the chapter head here did ban them from the guild. We'll just add to their misfortune this week. Hevard drank from his cup that held water instead of liquor. He watched the Stone Raiders as they partied and had a good time.

Hevard was looking forward to taking their goods from them. They might be a bunch of big louts with low levels, but their gear was high quality and would sell for a lot.

Put our clan at the top and then take a nice little profit. Nothing like a little extra gold to make a man feel good. Damn, Emerilia is fun!

"Enjoying the night?" A man sat down heavily at the table next to him, as if he had traveled all day. His clothes showed fresh mud stains and there was rain on his hat from the light drizzle outside.

"It is but beginning." Hevard knew that Koloa had not been out on the roads for hours and that what he was wearing was just another disguise, like Hevard's own as a traveling merchant. Hevard finished his drink and moved upstairs to his room.

"Make sure I am not disturbed," Hevard said into the empty hallway outside his room.

Private Message: Sender Unknown

It will be done

Words and gestures could be seen and heard with the right spells and skills. PMs couldn't.

Hevard walked into the room, placing spells on the door that would let him know whether anyone entered his room. Similar spells were on his windows and across the walls, floor, and roof.

Hevard was nothing if not thorough.

He took off his dirty cloak and lay on the bed. He pulled out a mirror from his pocket, holding it in his hand. Runes lit up around the mirror as the room he was in disappeared.

Hevard found himself in a massive hall made of black and purple stone. Braziers filled with black flames lit the room. Scenes of pain, torture, necromancers, undead armies, and mining were carved on the walls. The mining pictures looked as though they had been burned and melted with powerful magic.

Hevard immediately fell to his knee in front of the only other occupant in the room.

The Dark Lord didn't say anything for a while, looking down on his servant. His black-boned hand held a black staff with red runes. He wore his black robes that hid all other features. Looking into his hood, one might think that they were looking into the abyss it was so dark.

"Are the preparations in place?" The Dark Lord's voice was hungry and cold at the same time.

"Yes, my lord," Hevard said into the floor. *Shit, they know how to make a guy intimidating in this place!* Hevard grinned at the realism of it all: the power, the fear, how scared he felt. *So worth the money!*

"Good. Show the People of Emerilia what happens when people mess with my plans. Tonight, Selhi's streets will run red with the blood of the Stone Raiders. Make their bodies a show of the Dark's power and a lesson to all of those who think to fight us," the Dark Lord commanded.

"My Lord."

"Go, Champion of Darkness."

"Yes, Master." The Dark Lord's voice wasn't the only one that could be cold and hungry. The hall disappeared in a flash of light and Hevard found himself lying on his bed, a cold, wolfish smile spreading across his face as new power filled his body.

You have been Blessed by the Dark Lord

+20 Dark Affinity

+15 Strength

-5 Intelligence

You have earned a new class: Dark Lord's Champion

Status: Level 5

                    +50 to all stats

Effects: Weak to Light-based attacks.

                    +5 Dark Affinity

New strength flooded Hevard. His eyes turned black as he reveled in the power he had been given. *It won't be long until I can pull down the Dark Lord and take his place.*

For now, he would do his bidding, growing in power until he could strike out at the Pantheon.

***

As Hevard was covered in shadows, disappearing from the Dark Lord's hall, a second figure stepped out of the shadows.

Javal bowed in front of his lord and master. A rune, with the meaning of abomination, had been branded into his human face.

"Master, please send me to destroy these *Players*." Javal spat the last word.

"Javal, you are one of my most powerful Champions," the Dark Lord started.

Javal sneered, but kept his head lowered. His curse had made life all but impossible for him, cast out from society. He had the special ability to suppress magic. He was shunned from society, cast out by his family and made to fend for himself. Mana rejected him as society did. He got sick more often and couldn't be healed with magical potions or healers. Only healing compounds could repair him.

When he was close to death, the Dark Lord sent a Champion to find him and nurse him back to health.

The Dark Lord's servants had taught him how to use his curse. To bring the people who stepped on him to their knees. On his lord's orders, he'd torn apart his old village, covering his hands in the lifeblood of his family.

The Dark Lord had given him purpose and a path, naming him his Champion.

Now a group of Players had dared to attack Boran-al's Citadel, destroying one of the Dark Lord's sanctuaries, to make people stop their devotions to the Dark Lord. Javal's hands trembled, turning white with rage.

"I do not want to waste you on these useless creatures. We will make Hevard kill his own kind. It will be much more satisfying."

"Master, I can show them the true power of one of your Champions," Javal begged.

Silence spread through the room as the Dark Lord looked down on Javal.

"Go then. Kill the Players in my name." The Dark Lord's aura made Javal shudder in fear. "But if you fail me, not even the entire Pantheon could protect you from my wrath."

The Dark Lord's tone never changed, but the force of his aura made Javal pant for breath.

"I will do as you bid or die trying," Javal swore.

The aura fell away. "Go."

"Yes, my lord." Javal rose and left, a crazed smile on his face as he thought of the pain he would put the Players through, watching as the light in their eyes slowly went out, unable to escape his clutches.

***

Jules and Esa laughed at Dwayne's antics with a group of fifty Stone Raiders. The Raiders were spread out all over the tavern district. The adventurer's guild tavern in the city had banned them because they'd tried to force Deia and her party to reveal what was sounding like one hell of a raid.

Information had been passed through mirror conferences.

No one was that sad to not be staying at the adventurer's guild. A number of Players and people of Emerilia who had been staying in the adventurer guild's tavern had come out to drink in other places.

The Stone Raiders had a number of stories surrounding them, not the least being that they knew how to party and had some funny stories to tell.

Dwayne finished his story to the laughter of the entire tavern. He was rewarded with a tankard of ale that he started slugging back.

Esa's hands traced out designs on Jules's leg.

Jules felt her loins move in excitement; she pursed her lips and looked at Esa.

Esa gave her a sly smile, her eyes promising an intimate night.

That was when the first fireball was let loose. The tavern shook as the fireball hit somewhere outside. People turned and looked.

A Stone Raider, Donovan, one of Dwayne's tanks, burst into the room. "We're being attacked!"

Before anyone could move or say anything, Donovan whipped around, his shield appearing on his arm as well as his full armor. He grunted as an arrow hit his shield.

"This will be our base of..." Dwayne started as someone jumped for him.

"PKP, BITCH!"

Dwayne's armor, like the rest of the Stone Raiders, was hotkeyed. His armor covered him. The blade that had been aimed for his kidney left a deep groove in his armor as he turned away from the attack.

They didn't get another chance to say anything. The two Stone Raiders to either side of Dwayne cut them apart with their blades.

"Anyone not a Stone Raider, get the fuck out! Assassins!" Dwayne barked.

"Jules, you run healing here. Esa, you run protection for the medics. I need two parties, mixed, ready to move!" Dwayne yelled, downing a healing potion.

Thoughts of intimacy were gone as Jules and Esa stood in their armor: Jules looking at the tavern to turn it into a field hospital, Esa to turn it into a defensive position.

Jules applied healing to herself, removing the effects of the alcohol. The healing potions everyone was taking did the same thing.

"Esa, contact Josh—update him on our situation." Dwayne moved to the door where Donovan stood, looking for anything that might try to threaten them. People who had been drinking started running as pandemonium broke out in the streets.

There were fires raging, spells being flung all over the place. Assassins jumped out of the shadows. POEs and Players were being killed indiscriminately.

Esa's sword rang out and someone screamed in pain. Jules looked to see the would-be killer now had three foot of steel through their neck, just a few feet from their table.

"If you're not Stone Raider, GET THE FUCK OUT!" Esa barked. There was no denying her as anyone who had not already run away did so.

Jules looked at the medics, who were looking at her for her directions. Her combat knowledge made her one of the best healers in the field. She had come to train most of the people in this room.

"All right. Long desks along the walls. Central passage clear to allow people through. Esa, you lot can take the circular tables and use them to cover the windows and anything else!" Jules said.

Her medics got to work.

"Fighters, upstairs—make sure there is no one hiding up there. Use detection spells. Check the back of the tavern. All exits and entries. I want archers and casters upstairs. Donovan, tell me what you see," Esa barked.

People moved, their faces grim and determined.

Jules couldn't help but be proud of them all. This was a cowardly attack but Jules was excited to see it through. It was a new challenge—a new fight.

***

"How is the fight going?" Koloa asked through the voice chat.

"We got a number of them who were hanging out in small groups. Some were a bit faster to react than others. About eighty percent of the attacks were successful. The city guard is scrambling. There are three large groups of twenty or more Stone Raiders. We killed most of one group. Another, we wiped out and the third are over fifty members. The rest of the guild is rallying to the building. We can't get close to them," Damien, operations commander, said.

Koloa looked out at the miniature suns that had appeared in the tavern district. "I'm guessing they're in *that* building?"

"Yes, they're using magic to light up the shadows as well as detection magic of all kinds layered on top of one another. If we want it, we're going to have to take them out with a frontal assault," Damien said.

"Tunnel into it—burn it down. I don't care what you do—get us in there!" Hevard yelled.

"Yes, sir!" Damien moved off to talk through a different group chat.

Hevard was off in the streets killing people—whoever crossed his path—while Koloa and Damien made sure that the assault was a success.

The guards had their buffs but the majority of the fires had been lit to distract them from the fighting. They had to put out a dozen fires, and then try to find the PKP guild Players who specialized in killing Players.

"I have heard that we took down a few guards," Koloa asked Damien as he walked back over.

"Yeah. They're only POEs, after all. Big buffs in the city. You hit them hard enough and in the right areas, then they'll go down. Have to make sure that they don't see your face, otherwise all of the guards will know who you are and come after you for killing their buddy. I told people to focus on the Stone Raiders." Damien shrugged.

"Though it's hard to not take advantage of all this chaos," Koloa summarized.

"Exactly. I wish I was down there." Damien pouted.

Koloa laughed and pat his friend on the back. "We will soon enough. Once the Stone Raiders' demise is coming to a close, I'm sure Hevard will let us get in there to finish off the dregs." Koloa saw people running from the fighting.

Might as well get some experience. "Shadow culling," Koloa said. Five of the party were pulled into the shadows around them, screaming.

"Darkling." A creature made from shadows let out a cry, as if unleashing its own pain onto the world, wishing for them to bask in the pain that it had felt, that it had suffered so long that it had become part of its identity.

Koloa looked away as it tore a person apart with its arms in the form of blades.

A woman screamed, carrying her crying child.

"Need to turn down the volume on this crap," Damien complained as they cried out for help.

Koloa sent a silent command to the darkling. The creature of shadow raced off, jumping from shadow to shadow, before the cries of the woman and child ended.

A notification let Koloa know that he'd leveled up. He grinned to himself, looking for his next victim.

***

"What?" Josh barked, listening to Kim.

"We're being attacked by PKP. Little shits are trying to make a name for themselves. They took out over half of our numbers and are pushing us hard. We need help. We've got heavies, ranged and medics for the most part. We need the rogues and scouts. You have to find these fuckers. Oi, fuck off, you spritely little shit!" There were noises in the background as Kim fought.

"Fuck sakes, Rowen, you pick seven others and stay here. Everyone else, you're with me," Josh said.

The portal's runes started to move around, showing that someone was coming through.

Dave walked out, followed by the others. Finally, a massive creature wearing a cloak that covered most of its body exited. There was a huge warhammer on its back. Its hands and body seemed to shine in the light, as if it were made out of steel.

"Good thing you lot are here. We've got PKP—a Player-killing guild that takes hit contracts from people and Players all over Emerilia—attacking us in SC. We could do with some support." Josh moved for the silver doorway that led out of the hidden room.

"Who the hell is that?" He went through the silver arch, finding himself in the living quarters, and pointed at the twelve-foot-tall creature that barely fit through the arch.

"That is Steve. He's Suzy's minion," Deia said.

"Oh. Well, I've never seen a minion like him."

"See, told you I'm useful to have around," Steve said, barely even jogging to keep up with Josh as he ran full tilt.

"You're a big, shiny, walking, talking robot. You're about as questionable as Dave in a tutu!" Suzy said.

"Hey! How the hell did I get stuck in this?" Dave asked. Party Zero spread out around Josh.

Josh had got to the phase where with a single glance, he'd know the lack of strength or feel an instinctive fear of someone based on their auras and power. Party Zero was strong, not just in their overall power, but something that made him wary of them.

Steve was like a walking tank. Josh saw enough under his cloak to know that he was more machine than man. He looked to be milled out of a single massive ingot of metal. Each step he took shook the ground.

Josh was a mix of emotions: scared for his fellow guildmates, guilty for not being there, and angry that someone had dared to attack them.

Party Zero might be passing jokes, but their faces all held the same thing: hunger, anger, and interest.

I feel sorry for PKP. The thought came to him unbidden, yet he didn't try to deny it as they sped out of the substation, through the cave and out into the forest. Dirt, leaves, and debris were left in their path.

"Trees!" Josh said. The rogues, scouts, and sneaky types jumped into the trees. The tree tag had made them masters of moving through the forest at speed, even if it was the middle of the night.

"It's good to be outside!" Steve's voice was deep and bassy as he continued to thump down the path toward SC. His speed was impressive; he couldn't move his limbs as fast but his longer legs made him faster than most.

"Groups of four, hunt the bastards down; find the PK skulls over their heads and take them out. Party Zero, go end them," Josh said.

"Speed up!" Deia barked.

Six figures started forward faster than the others. Dave's hands seemed to light up as a bow appeared in his hands. Malsour dropped onto a shadow, racing ahead with his magic. Balls of metal fell from Suzy; they rolled, keeping pace with Steve.

Josh saw as they got to the gates, each using their own way to get over the walls, from Fire to shadows or Steve throwing Suzy and Dave.

Steve jumped and cleared the wall.

"Well, time to make these bastards regret starting a war in SC," Josh said, quickly gaining on the wall. He looked through different group chats and maps that showed the outlay of SC and the action happening in its streets.

***

Dave spread out his senses and used his Touch of the Land to pick up all of the Player Killers in the area. The map was littered with skulls around the building, with a dozen glowing balls around it. Others were running through the streets, causing havoc.

"Dave and Malsour, Anna and Suzy, Induca and me. Break up and take out the Player Killers. Anyone who is killing POEs—take them out as well. You get in a group with too many of them, we'll regroup and hit them together. Dave, keep up that scanner." Deia headed toward the skulls to their right.

Anna and Suzy went straight. Dave and Malsour went left.

"We've got three running amok from the rooftops. Shall we go say hello?" Malsour asked.

"Happily," Dave said. An arrow appeared on his bow as they jumped from roof to roof.

"Darkling. Bane of light. Speed of Shadow." Malsour called out his spells and buffs. Dave felt that he was moving even faster and that he made much less noise with the two buffs. The darkling was just some creepy ass monster that Dave saw periodically.

Dave slowed himself down as he spotted the three Player Killer skulls.

Three Players laughed and joked around as they sent spells into the POEs below.

"Wait," Malsour said.

Dave held the bow down with his hand on the arrow. His eyes followed the three mother fuckers who thought it was all a game and that killing POEs was just a good way to earn some extra experience.

"Now." Dave pulled and drew his arrow in one fluid motion. It was easy compared to how it had been before.

Need to make this thing stronger. He released the arrow, the air rippling in its passing. Dave conjured four more arrows, linked to the first. It punched through one of the Player's armor, getting a critical hit and draining their Health to just twenty percent. Another cried out in pain, hit with three of the four conjured arrows. A tombstone appeared above them as they fell down, dead. A darkling appeared behind the third, its shadow-arms tearing their throat out. The last remaining PKP guild member called on a light spell.

Dave could only watch in slow motion as he drew another arrow on his bow.

The darkling screamed out, diving away into receding shadows as Dave released his arrow.

The light blossomed as Dave's arrow took them in the leg.

He cried out; his Health dwindled as blood squirted out of their leg. Before Dave or Malsour had time to use another attack, the last of the PKPs dropped to the ground, all of them with tombstones over their bodies.

Dave and Malsour walked over to them, clicking on the tombstones. Unlike the normal death tombstones, these ones had red skulls on them.

You Have Ended a Player Killer

All items not soul bound and/or on the Player Killer's hotbar can be claimed. For killing a Player Killer, there is no penalty.

Dave whistled as he looked at the gear that they dropped. Their bags of holding and weapons weren't soul bound, making it all up for grabs. Dave and Malsour took it all, their bags of holding easily capable of storing the extra loot.

Dave noticed one of them had a small Mirror of Communication.

With those things costing a few thousand gold coins, they would be prime targets for Player Killers. A smile passed over Dave's face, excited at all the possible loot that they could get for killing the PKPs.

Dave saw the same predatory look in Malsour's eyes.

"We've got a bunch in that direction." Dave pointed at the red skull icons that floated in the distance.

"Well, time's a wasting." Malsour headed off in the PKP's direction.

Dave followed. The hunt had started.

***

"The fuck is going on?" Hevard demanded. Seconds ago, they'd had the Stone Raiders pinned in one main location, with several other parties in the area. They'd been hitting them slowly and surely—an arrow here, a curse and hex there.

The Stone Raiders were taking time to be killed but they could do it. Then PKP guild members had started to disappear and it seemed that the Stone Raiders knew where people generally were.

"I don't know, but it looks like they can see through our spells and find the PK skulls," Damien said.

"Shit. I've got reports of Stone Raider reinforcements coming from the forest. They're moving quickly and crushing our people. It's the sneak types who left yesterday!" Koloa said.

"Shit! Well, deal with them!" Hevard cut the channel. He needed to kill more of them and quicker.

"Forward! Kill them all!" Hevard yelled.

At the very least, the Dark Lord won't be able to say I didn't give it my all.

***

"They're coming!" Rowen yelled from upstairs.

"To your positions. Casters, ready those buffs!" Esa stood with five shield bearers, covering the three-person wide tavern door.

Each had a spear or long blade. The tables were arranged to keep their attackers at a distance so that the defenders could bleed them with their longer weapons.

Spells erupted all over the place; the wood tried to attack those using it as cover, either turning to ice or starting to burn in other places. More often than not, it was necrotic damage, black and purple magic causing anything it touched to rot away.

The Stone Raiders waited, ready to react to anything that looked as if it would be of immediate harm.

"Jake, you ready there?" Esa asked, not daring to glance back at the Dwarf wearing a black robe over patches that had been sown into a suit. He had slicked-back hair and looked more tired than anything.

"Yeah, sure." He yawned and stretched. "'Bout time these dick licks saw what a real necro can do." He grinned and cracked his knuckles. "Wakey wakey, boys and girls. Time to put those hands to use. Uggh, Ben's body is being a pain in the arse to use. Damned demi-bear!"

It might be tense in the room but Jake's antics made more than one person grin.

They would kill whoever tried to hurt their guild. In the meantime, fighting was their business. Day in, day out. The Stone Raiders were the people you called when you had a monster problem. The bigger, the better.

"They're making it closer!" Rowen yelled as magical lights and the sound of bows letting loose could be heard, interspersed with the cries of pain.

It seemed as though the second floor was in a different realm as Esa focused on the door in front of her. Someone rammed the door; an axe slammed into it. Then another. The door was already half apart.

The PKPs might be assassins but their prey were other Players, the strongest competition in the game and a way to get the highest experience as fast as possible.

"Bunch of pussies—hiding in a tavern. Get some Fire in there!" one of the PKP yelled, pulling with his axe and taking half the door off.

"Fuego stream!" a caster yelled. Fire rushed through the door.

"Ice wall!" one of the Stone Raiders said, countering.

"Fine, since everyone's having a fucking party!" Jake put his hand on a glowing soul gem. His smile was pure evil as his pupils seemed to turn into purple and black. "Incarnate."

The word was spoken quietly but carried through the fighting, through the Stone Raiders and PKP. To the dead that lay in the streets, to those who were now behind the PKP who had rushed the Stone Raiders.

A low moan escaped an undead's lips as they started to push themselves to their feet.

Jake's face paled as his legs wobbled. He fell to his knees, his face in a rictus of pain and concentration. He let out a haggard grasp as the ice wall and Fire gave up.

The first PKP, an axe wielder, ran into the tavern.

Esa's spear shot out: quick, fast, and just enough to pierce. Just like Joko had taught her. Four other spears shot out. Two were deflected; the other three made it past the axe wielder's weapon and shield.

He cried out in pain and anger.

"Smash!"

Still using Actions. Idiots.

The action broke the defenses in places. Again, the spears attacked the axe wielder.

"Iron wall!"

The Stone Raiders altered their attack; four spears got through. The fifth broke on the axe wielder's shield. The spear wielder moved out of the way, so another could take his place.

That's when the screams started behind the PKP.

"The fuck!"

"Shit, they've got a necro!"

More panicked screams started as the sound of battle reached Esa's ears.

"How you like me now! Fuck, that sucks!" Jake clawed his way to a seat.

The Stone Raiders grinned as their attacks were faster and harder, pressing the PKP who were now fighting a battle on two fronts.

About two hundred PKP were in the street, attacking the tavern. They were one of the larger guilds with nearly five hundred members.

More were entering the fray, fighting the undead.

Unlike the living, the undead could take more of a beating. The world seemed to shake as a giant landed among the PKP. Its massive axe cut through the stunned PKP with ease. What looked like a cloak of metal fell from it, turning into metal creations.

The wind howled as people beyond the tavern's front cried out in pain.

A longsword cut down the axe wielder in front of the barricade.

"Well, are you Stone Raiders or some weird kind of turtle?" Anna stood in the doorway as the metal creations and the shiny giant were now being beset on all sides by PKP.

Esa let out a yell; she rushed forward, breaking the barrier, and charged out into the street. Her shield bearers followed. Esa hotkeyed her shield and blade. The weapons appeared in her hands as the Stone Raiders moved around her to form a shield wall.

Spells and arrows rained down on her and the forward tanks, taking the pressure off the ranged fighters on the second floor, who happily took out their opposition.

Esa activated her self-buffs as the supporting mages added to their list of buffs. The left side of Esa's vision had a series of buff symbols.

"The hell is that?" one of the shield bearers asked of the metal giant that was wading through the PKP, moving with speed that belied its size.

"I'm Steve!" It turned around, a big goofy grin on its face as it got hit with an ice spell.

"Ah, fuck balls!" Steve turned around, grabbing a metal construct that milled around, killing any PKP in range, and threw it at the casters who had stayed back. He threw two more that seemed to move toward him, turning into metal spears as he threw them.

"Suzy, you da best!" Steve said as the magicians started screaming out from the metal constructs in their midst.

Stone Raiders' tombstones appeared as PKP finally got a grasp of the situation and retaliated.

More of their guild were coming into play; soon the Stone Raiders would be overrun.

The Stone Raiders' options were either stay in the tavern and wait it out, losing people slowly or to fight here and now, putting everything on the line to inflict more casualties to the PKP.

Esa made her decision.

"Let's show these bastards how the Stone Raiders do things! In your parties!" Esa yelled out, watching as Anna danced through the PKP. She seemed to vanish at times, sometimes turning into a blur. Esa's enhanced speed was not enough to keep up with the woman.

"Fire storm!" Deia yelled out from a rooftop, marking her for everyone.

"Ah shit!" Steve said. The giant had a look of dread as he ran away from the PKP.

Anna moved quickly, her blades cutting deep as she vaulted the Stone Raiders' shield wall. "You might want to get back for this," she said, continuing back to the front of the tavern.

"Pull back!" Dread filled Esa as she obeyed.

The road filled with swirling firestorms, raging and howling, drowning out the screams of the PKP who were caught in the whirlwind of Fire and superheated Air. As the PKP burned, few made it through to be greeted by the Stone Raiders.

Both sides fought with everything they had.

A shadow seemed to emerge from the fire; it blurred, taking out three Stone Raiders in as many seconds.

Anna charged forward to meet it. Her blade rang out as she met the attacker. The man snarled. The two of them turned into two blurs of magic, blades, and destruction.

"Get around the firestorm and kill the fuckers in the buildings on the other side!" Esa yelled, looking to the parties that had formed up.

"Stone RAIDERS!" Five parties charged off around the firestorm, hunting down the PKP.

More PKP arrived by the minute.

Fuck, what the hell do I do now? She thought as a pair of boots hit the front porch of the tavern.

"Well, this is a right fucking mess." Josh looked out over the firestorms and the melees happening all over the place.

"What do you want us to do?" Esa said.

"It looks like you're doing a good job already. Everyone, party up! Esa, you take as many people as you need to keep this place and your healers safe. I'll take the rest and we'll hunt down every one of the bastards hiding in SC. We need to go find Dave," Josh muttered the last part to himself.

"So all of Party Zero is here?" Esa asked.

"Yeah." Josh shook his head as Deia rode over her own firestorm, her boots covered in blue flames as she fired her bow. Her hands moved as fast as a machine gun; ripples from the force of her shots made the sky crack in submission.

Induca dropped onto the roof Suzy was on. Earth and wind creatures fought off the PKP that were there. Suzy yelled out orders as Induca called down all manner of Fire spells.

Steve rushed toward a group of incoming PKP, giggling. "Welcome to the party, boys and girls! Wanna try out my axe in your face?" Steve said swinging his axe around recklessly.

"Where the hell did he come from?" Esa asked.

"He's Suzy's summoned creature." Josh grinned.

"Two parties—go and make sure that big idiot doesn't die!" Esa yelled, pointing at Steve.

"Come on! Can't let that big tin can get all the kills!" Donovan yelled.

"Hey! That's good-looking shiny tin can to you!" Steve yelled back, hitting a PKP so hard they landed inside a house. "Fuck, sorry! Well, guess they're redecorating."

Esa and Josh looked at each other. *Where the hell do we find these people?* Their eyes seemed to ask before they turned back around.

"All right, let's go hunting! Oh, Dwayne should be back soon enough!" Josh dashed away.

"You, you, you, and you—your people are staying here," Esa barked out.

They nodded as Stone Raiders flooded out of the tavern, hungry looks on their faces.

***

"Well, this is a right fucking mess." Josh dropped next to Dave as he put an arrow into a fleeing PKP, hitting their leg, making them stumble as a darkling pulled them into the shadows, covering them.

Screams rang out before the shadow disappeared, leaving a body on the ground.

"Yeah." Dave took a running jump to another house.

"I've got everyone fanned out around us to use your Touch of the Land and the PK skulls that are all over the place. It looks like People Kill People brought their entire guild, all five hundred members," Josh said, keeping up with him.

Both went silent as they dropped down to the street level. They moved silently, their eyes never leaving the four PKP who were casting a spell over a group of the dead.

Dave's bow switched into a two-handed sword as they got closer.

One started to turn around as the ground beneath their feet lit up with an alarm rune.

Josh jumped, sinking his blades into one of the casters' backs, and twisting them.

The two Players cried out in pain, their spell failing and backlashing on the casters. They screamed out, but one started to raise their hand as a black mist formed in their hands.

Dave brought his sword across, nearly severing the caster in two as their Health hit zero and they toppled over. Dave didn't stop, flipping the blade in his hands so it pointed down. He jabbed it through the caster who had turned at the alarm rune.

That caster looked up at Dave and the blade in his chest. Holy light came out of the wound. The caster screamed for a few moments as Dave ripped the blade out.

He looked to see Josh had cut the two casters' necks open. Dave was about to say something when he was hit with a spell that sent him flying five feet into the middle of the street.

His head was ringing and he'd lost forty percent of his Health. Already his armor was starting to heal him and fight off the necrotic damage that was eating away at him. He pulled his hood on, chastising himself as he tried to clear his head.

Josh let out a pained grunt some ten feet away.

Dave pulled himself free from the building to see five PKP who had been hiding in an alley. With Dave's Touch spread out across the entire city, it was hard to pin down certain things. *Like when someone makes a cloak of shadows and uses their fellow guildmates to lure you out to ambush you.*

"Return," Dave said. His great sword, which had been sent into an alleyway, returned to his hand. With a thought, the great sword turned into a shield and sword.

Dave tried conjuring items above the other group but his head was so rattled that he couldn't get the items or positioning right.

Josh was fighting the two fighters while their assassin tried to get in behind and attack his rear. One caster maintained a dome of shadows over them so that no one could see them.

Dave ducked and held his shield up; an arrow pierced it and hit his Mana barrier. It was stuck a half-inch through his shield.

"Fuck sakes!" Dave moved to Josh and his fight, adding three more arrows to his shield. Their fifth member was an archer of some kind. The black liquid that was on the tip of the arrows and Dave's Touch told him that the arrows were of the poisoned variety.

One of them slammed into his shield and hit his arm. The immediate pain was followed with what felt like battery acid running through his veins and his body feeling as if he were moving in water.

"Backstab!" The PKP fighter yelled, activating his attack.

Dave's sword turned into a spear. He threw it behind Josh, hitting the assassin in mid-air. They let out a surprised shriek as the spear hit them in the arm. Josh slashed at them as Malsour lowered himself behind the caster and archer. Two shadows erupted from his hands, turning into blades that he slashed sideways, taking the caster's head off and making the archer scream out in pain.

"Return!" Dave bum-rushed the dual wielder who was working Josh down.

Dave's body felt heavy as he met the dual wielder's two blades. He now saw the use of having a shield. His vision was getting blurry as well.

"Fucking poison." Dave shield bashed the dual wielder and kicked their leg. They cried out but slapped Dave's sword away, anger in their eyes as they fought Dave with renewed vigor.

"Dave, step to your right," Malsour said.

Dave did so. A piece of metal shot out of a house and slammed through the attacker.

The dual wielder coughed, looking at the piece of metal firmly buried in their chest.

The archer let out their final screams, a darkling tearing them apart.

Dave moved to finish off the other one-handed and shield fighter. His shadow covered the man.

The darkling disappeared from the archer. It seemed to erupt from Dave's body, screaming as the magical blade of the PKP hit it. Its fingers extended, piercing the dude's eyes and mouth.

"Fucking hell. Exorcist much?" Josh looked away and dealt with the assassin who was trying to crawl away. Josh had nicked something important with his slash.

The darkling disappeared as the fighter stopped shaking and making choking noises. The body started to move, shadows around its eyes, nose, and mouth.

"That is nasty," Dave said as the fighter moved to stand beside Malsour, the darkling inside it controlling the body.

"It is amazing what one can do with a nice shield." Malsour tapped the darkling/exorcist/fighter thing's breastplate.

"Well, Dwayne needs our help and there are still PKP out in the streets," Josh said.

Dave spread out his senses, looking for pockets of PKP skulls or Players killing POEs.

"Stop in the name of the Selhi Capital guard!" a woman yelled, chasing down the street with fifty guards following her.

"Ahh, hello!" Josh waved to them.

"State your business," she asked as Malsour moved to Dave, touching his shoulder.

The blurriness and pain burning through his veins faded away. "Fuck, that felt like shit. What was that?" Dave asked.

"Some Blackthorn mixed with dark magic curses. I just instructed it to leave your body," Malsour said.

"Tha—" Dave raced over to the side of a building.

"Stop there!" the woman yelled out as Dave threw off his gauntlets and then worked on his pants, dropping his weapons.

He let out a content sigh as the sound of water on rocks could be heard.

"Shit, almost didn't make it." Dave studied his puddle. "Is it supposed to be black and red?" Fear entered his voice.

"That's the poison leaving your system," Malsour said.

"More damned warning next time!" Dave complained as the guards moved all around them, swords drawn.

"Hello, I am Josh Giles. These are my mates Malsour and that one's Dave."

"Hiya!" Dave said, finishing off his business. "Fuck, it's a pain in the dick to try to piss wearing all this shit."

"We're from the Stone Raiders. Earlier tonight, we were out scouting a possible job when the forces we left behind in this city were set upon by a guild called PKP. Right now, we're working to clear them out of the city and kill any we can," Josh said.

The guards looked at the bodies all around.

"What is that?" The guard captain gestured at the darkling puppet.

"He was a PKP member. Seeing as he's not using the body anymore, I am." Malsour smiled.

"Dude, nice presentation. That was scary as fuck." Dave sorted out his gear and put it back on.

"Guild badges," she said.

Everyone showed their shoulders. Josh looked around and pulled out a golden necklace.

"Nice," Dave said.

"Ehh, perks of rank, right?" Josh grinned.

"Very well. We ask you to help us in clearing out the bastards who are attacking our city."

Quest: Restore Order

Kill, capture, or drive out those who dared to disturb the peace in Selhi's capital.

Rewards: ???

Failure: Death, allowing the troublemakers to run free.

Do you accept?

Y/N?

"Yes." Josh waved away the screen as a new one popped up for Dave and Malsour.

Quest: Restore Order

The Stone Raider guild has accepted the quest to kill or capture any and all who have disturbed the peace in Selhi's capital.

Rewards: ???

Failure: Death of all guild members in Selhi Capital. Allowing the troublemakers to run free.

"Shall we? Dwayne still needs our help to get to Kim and Lucy," Josh said.

"We will need your help to clear the streets!" the guard captain said.

"Take this." Josh handed her a whistle. "If you are in trouble, use it and my people will help you out."

"But..." She started but Josh jumped away. Malsour followed, riding a shadow.

"We'll do our best. Look after the POEs—they're targeting them for extra experience." Dave ran and jumped to clear the guards.

"Ah fuck, I forgot how much my stats jumped." Dave made sure his hood was on as he cleared one building and barrelled into another's roof.

His legs bicycled the air, catching on the roof, and slowed him enough to not fall off the edge. He used a chimney to throw himself off the roof and to one behind Malsour and Josh.

"Take a little detour?" Malsour asked.

"Oh, shut up, you shadow surfer. Lot easier to ride that thing than climb all over the place," Dave said, vaulting roofs and jumping over drying lines or swinging around on chimney stacks.

There was an explosion in the distance.

"I found them!" Dave yelled.

"I think everyone bloody well found them!" Josh said.

Malsour didn't say anything but moved faster on his shadow surfboard.

"Oh, for the days when I was just a lazy executive who worried about everyone having food and could drink coffee all the time. I had cars and elevators," Dave whined.

As if hearing him, he saw a notification about his sprint fade away into the corner of his interface, adding to the missed notifications waiting for him.

He thought about the skill's first description. *Although you look like you actively fear running, it seems that when needs must, you can still run.* He snorted, unable to hide the smile that tugged at the corners of his lips.

Chapter 15: Nailing the Coffin Shut

Javal walked through the streets of Selhi without a care in the world. He focused his curse onto a single guard, walking up behind them as they looked around wildly at the battle happening in front of them.

Javal whistled; the guard turned, their eyes going wide. None of their buffs or spells worked as Javal's blade sunk into the guard's neck.

The guard gurgled, holding their neck before falling to the ground.

Javal hummed to himself and walked past the dying guard. He giggled at the guards trying to fight the large group of Players in the middle of the road. He spread out his curse, cutting off the empowering runes. The guards' protections from being within the city fell away. The PKP fell on them like wolves, tearing through their ranks.

"Ah, it is a beautiful night," Javal said loud enough for the surviving PKP to hear. He looked at the bodies that littered the ground, the burning and destroyed buildings. Screams and sounds of battle could be heard in the distance.

"Who are you?" One of the PKP pointed his blade at Javal.

Javal gave the man a casual look, using his aura to push the man to his knees.

"I'm Javal, one of the Dark Lord's Champions. I was sent to help you and Hevard in killing these Stone Raiders. I don't much like you Players, but it does seem like you PKP types are rather entertaining." Javal giggled again.

"I'm sorry for my guildmate's words. Would you be interested in joining us? Your ability to stop the guards' buffs could be really useful," another PKP said.

"Ah, at least there is one of you with brains here." Javal released his aura's hold on the first PKP Player.

The Dark Lord always told me to band with others where possible, to use them until the very end. Less risk to myself.

Javal hummed again and walked forward down the road. The PKP moved to follow.

Javal took a deep breath, breathing in the smell of death and destruction ripe in the air. He let out another giggle again.

What a beautiful night!

***

Dwayne grunted as the PKP fighter slammed their sword into his shield.

Dwayne lowered himself, making the attacker think that he had forced Dwayne to his knees. Dwayne felt the blade come off his shield. He turned, driving his shield up as he drove his blade forward and into their armor. Dwayne's Strength was less than the attacker's, but his blade was better than their armor.

The blade tore through the armor, taking out sixty percent of the attacker's Health.

They let out a howl as Dwayne pulled back. Blood came with the blade, and an additional ten percent damage.

Status effects went to work as Dwayne brought his shield back down.

"Lucy, we could use some help!" Dwayne yelled as a spell hit his shield.

Frost damage! Fucking hate frost damage—makes my arm stick to my shield!

"Takes a lot of work and concentration, so shut up!" Lucy yelled back.

Dwayne looked to Kim who smiled at him weakly. She held her chest, an arrow sticking out of it. She'd refused healing; it wouldn't be enough to fight the poison as she was only down to ten percent Health and it was slowly going down. She sent out a group heal on the frontline fighters and some more buffs, using her time to give them all the support she could muster.

A ball of lightning whipped past Dwayne's head and smacked a warhammer-toting idiot on his ass; the lightning made his body convulse and jerk.

"Watch what you're doing, idiot!" Kim admonished, her breathing slow and rapid. "Need someone to watch my gear while I'm taking a nap in my home!"

"Bitch and moan. Always, 'look after my stuff while I respawn,' or 'go and dive into that shambling mound—once it eats you, it'll leave the rest of us alone!'" Dwayne's blade found the tasered warhammer dickhead.

Dwayne saw a new notification pop up at the side of his screen. He didn't have time for it as he looked around. They were fighting in an alleyway. The houses on both sides were made of stone. The PKP were fighting from both sides. Ranged and casters were on the roofs, covering those below and making sure that the PKP couldn't just pour in attacks from above.

There were a few warriors up there. Their group of forty had been whittled down to twenty or less.

"Hey, that was one time and once it had a meal of all the meat you stored up, it pissed right off." Kim coughed.

"Yeah, all of that rare meat that was worth over fifty gold and I literally lost an arm to get! Hate it when I lose my right arm," Dwayne muttered to himself, thanking his left arm for staying attached this long as some dickhead called out an assassin's move, only to find their face planted into Dwayne's shield.

They hit so hard it sounded like two pans had been smashed together.

Dwayne brought his shield down on the now stunned assassin, caving their skull in with a single hit. "And stay down, bitch!" Dwayne yelled.

"Did they touch your no-no spot?" Josh's voice came out from behind the PKP fighters, followed by the telltale sound of a high-powered archer.

"Oh, I do like dark places." Malsour floated at the front of the alleyway.

"Fuck!" Dave crashed into a wall and cartwheeled off a roof.

"Dave, seriously?" Josh asked.

"Hey, new stats. At least when I enter, I don't try to be some creepy pervert," Dave muttered.

Dwayne couldn't say anything, focused on the battle in front of him. The PKP was a good fighter with their sword and shield.

"Ebony whips!" Malsour cried out.

"See." Dave climbed out of the wall. "Perverts."

"Will you hurry up and kill them already?" Lucy yelled.

A blackness so dark it seemed to be solid settled over the alleyway nearest the new arrivals. There were sounds of gnashing teeth and wet meat slapping together, as if an overpowered octopus were in the middle of that darkness. Then the screams started and the wet meat sounded as if it were attaching itself to items.

"But of course, my damsel in distress!" Josh said.

Dwayne booted his attacker in the shield, pushing them two feet back, right into the darkness.

"I'm really regretting this seeing in magical darkness shit. That is nasty." Dave jumped high enough to grab the second-floor roof with one hand, hauling himself up and over.

"I'm no damse—" Dwayne looked to Lucy, beads of sweat on her brow. Magical power from her rune flowed through her body and into the surrounding area. "Shut up, Josh."

Dwayne looked to his people beside him. "Move back a bit."

The ones who had gone into the darkness hadn't returned. Only screaming came out from that portal into hell.

A PKP slammed into the wall, screaming before they fell into the black area.

"This is Spar—"

"Ah, fuck off, will you!" Dave yelled. He tossed someone who had attacked him from behind and slammed them into the wall opposite. They dropped ten feet and into the ground.

Dwayne moved to them as they groaned in pain. Dwayne's sword slammed through the eye slit in their armor, too fast for them to even cry out.

Malsour moved out of the darkness as if it were nothing. He settled down next to Lucy. "Darklings," Malsour said, as if he were calling his favorite dog to come out to play.

Shadow creatures appeared in the shadows of the alley, killing anything that was PKP.

The ebony whips disappeared, showing loot and valuables. Nothing remained of the PKP who had been there before.

"I will protect those down here. They need you on the roofs," Malsour said.

"What he said!" Josh yelled.

Dwayne looked to Kim, who waved for him to let her be.

He jumped, using his sword to climb up the wall. He looked back to see Malsour disintegrate the arrow. The black and purple veins that had been crawling up her neck, consuming her from the inside, disappeared.

Good, one less person whose shit I'll have to watch as they respawn!

Dwayne hauled himself onto the roof, taking in the scenery and drinking a Health potion. He threw the small glass bottle to the side, letting out a roar as he charged over at a group of ten PKP who were fighting three Stone Raiders. One fell under their blows, screaming as an assassin appeared behind them and sliced their throat open.

Dwayne felt his world go red. Reason left him as he got closer. Damage seemed to bounce off him as if it were lessened, his anger and the pain of his enemies fueling his rage as he used everything at his disposal to bring about their demise.

***

Dave watched as Dwayne went completely and utterly berserk, running through those who dared to get in his way and tried to attack his guildmates. He was no longer a person, but a force of armor, strength, and moving scary.

Remind me to not piss him off. Dave's shield turned into a blade, deflecting the surprised PKP as he drove it into their groin. He'd learned quickly that armor was not his friend. At least when other people were using it. His armor—well, it had saved his life more than once.

"Worth its weight in gold. Though it is made out of Mithril..." Dave jumped forward, rolling away as if a second sense had told him of the impending danger coming from behind him.

"Silent slash!" He turned. The sword extended into a spear, allowing the rogue PKP to impale themselves. They looked at the spear in shock. Dave canceled the spear, moving in close and turned his sword into a hammer, smashing it into the rogue's head.

There was a wet noise as the rogue crumpled.

Dave kicked them off the roof, hoping the fall would finish them off. "If it was silent, then you wouldn't call out the command, dumb fuck."

He looked around to see that the PKP were getting pushed back or were, in some cases, running for their lives.

"Move to the tavern!" Josh yelled.

Those who were wounded were pulled onto the backs of those who weren't as bad. Support people ran around to collect loot from all the fallen Stone Raiders as well as a number of the PKP.

"Nearly done!" Lucy looked as if she were being drained of her life force. "Soul bind! Tracker. Firebrand. PKP guild." With that, a wave of dark energy shot out from Lucy. It flowed over the area and settled on the fallen PKP bodies. A white gem showed above their corpses and any surviving PKP around them.

"The heck is that?" Dave asked Malsour, who now floated up from his defensive position, dismissing his army of darklings with a wave of his hands.

"She just soul bound a curse to them that they can only get lifted by the Lady of Fire. They will forever get burning damage; Lucy will always know of their location both by sense and on the map. While they might be able to hide themselves on a map, Lucy and all those she deems friends will forever know the direction of the PKP who were here. It is an extremely powerful spell. It will be stronger on those who are dead, but the living will also have a shadow about them due to it."

"Wow, okay. I didn't even know such a thing was possible," Dave said as the last of the wounded were picked up and the Stone Raiders moved to the roofs. The healers and wounded were in the middle, with the ranged and then warriors facing out.

"I did not think it would be so soon that one of the Players would figure out one of the spells that goes beyond death," Malsour agreed as they moved toward the tavern.

The firestorms had died down, but the fighting was still fierce. There were just sixty or so Stone Raiders left alive in all of SC, most of which were grouped at the tavern.

***

Deia's two swords flashed, breaking the two-hander's attack on her and giving her space to move as they dodged back. Deia flicked her sword; a slash of Fire appeared on the attacker.

They yelled out, using skills to bat the Fire away. It was green flame, a sticky fire that could burn anything. The only way to put it out was cover it with sand or starve it of oxygen. Water didn't affect it, but the ice the two-hander was using did.

Deia sent three more slashes of green flame into her opponent and those her fellow Stone Raiders were fighting.

"Fore!" Steve backhanded one with an axe.

Deia winced as she heard the breaking bones. *Who the fuck showed him golf?* Steve was one of the odder summoned creatures she'd met.

Suzy and Induca were still holding their own. The Stone Raiders now controlled a block instead of just a tavern.

Anna was locked in combat with what could only be a Demon. He moved as fast as her, capable of dispatching those who got too close to their fight with brutal efficiency.

Esa said that he was Hevard, the leader of the PKP guild.

A cold feeling passed through Deia, a wave of soul, Dark, and Fire magic. It was powerful, and nothing the likes of which she had ever sensed before.

Her opponent came at her, burn marks over their armor as Deia saw that there was a burning effect on him. Her flames were out but she could tell that somehow they were burning from the inside.

Deia got some space and started her Fire dance. Her guild-mates moved to either side, defending her as she shot waves of wind and Fire at those in front of them. They defended as well as possible, but Deia had deep reserves and her flames were not to be taken lightly. They forced people back as if they were physical blows.

Furrows appeared in the ground as Deia watched the Stone Raiders' rogues and scouts who had been out descend from behind.

She cut off her attacks. "Come on, you gonna fight me? Can't even kill one person?" She spat on the ground, holding their rage as her people crept up.

Just as the PKPs started to charge, their voices were cut short and gurgles started. Blades found purchase. Skills ignored armor and the PKPs were now the ones with shocked looks on their faces.

"That's how you ambush someone, bitches!" Steve hooted, looking to Suzy, nodding and then running off in another direction.

There might be sixty people left over from the attack, yet there were another forty who had just arrived after clearing out the rest of the city—all of the scouts, rangers, spies, rogues, and stealthy types. Creeping up on a person was hard, if they weren't occupied.

Now the PKPs who had been ready for fighting the Stone Raiders were getting violently shivved in the ass by their opposites in the Stone Raiders. They weren't used to being the targets of assassination kills.

Deia saw a Stone Raider down and hurting. She moved to them, healing them up with a potion. "Damn, you're a heavy bastard," she grunted, putting the armored warrior on her back.

"Urggh, and you're carrying me right on a cut!"

"Oh shut up, you pansy."

Seems that Dave is rubbing off on me. Or was it the Dwarves, perhaps? She shook her head. Deia dropped off the heavy bastard at the main tavern, Jules taking him.

Deia left, looking for Anna and that black blurry piece of shit.

It was time she had a *real* fight. A cold smile passed over her face as she headed out, surrounded by her comrades, her fellow Stone Raiders. *There's nothing quite like hunting down your enemies with a group tried and trusted.*

These were the people who destroyed Boran-al's Citadel. They would make these little bastards pay for ever raising a sword against their guild.

***

Suzy watched through the eyes of her various creations as they and Steve waded through the PKP.

Then, the rest of the guild arrived. They didn't yell or scream; they moved silently, flowing over rooftops and walls. The morning sun rose ahead of them. Each of them carried their weapons, their eyes cold and hard. They had come to avenge their friends and nothing would stop them.

"Steve, go make a distraction to keep the PKP interested in you and not looking behind," Suzy said, feeling Induca's heat as she unleashed dazzling Fire from her hands, coating the PKPs she could see in the street.

"Elementals!" The same Fire turned into cyclones before two female creatures, similar to the Earth elementals she had seen, started causing havoc among the PKP ranks.

An arrow hit Induca in the side. Suzy ducked; three Air elementals turned and fired, focused hydrogen gas at the archer.

They screamed out, their aim ruined as their arrow went wide.

The Air creations rushed to tear the archer apart. Earth golems that Suzy had put down as a protection measure covered Induca.

Suzy moved to her, seeing her grasping the arrow in her leg, about to pull it out.

"Don't!" Suzy said.

"What?" Induca asked.

"You pull that out and all the blood could come with it. Leave it in. My Earth golems can protect you," Suzy said.

"Thank you, dear." Induca held Suzy's hand as she helped her up.

Suzy's face went red at those words and touching Induca. They'd slept in the same bed together and semi-cuddled, but Suzy was scared that it had just been the drink. The drink had allowed her to go past her normal bounds, going so far as to sleep with another woman in her bed. She might like the fairer sex, but she had limited exposure to actually dating them and was rather nervous with the whole thing.

"Any more red and I won't need to light any fires," Induca teased.

"Ahh, yes, umm, sorry," Suzy said, embarrassed.

"I think afterward we should have a nice long talk, maybe over a meal with a room to ourselves?" Induca had a sly smile on her face.

"You do know we're in the middle of a fight?" Suzy asked.

"Ahh, distractions." Induca's smile widened.

"Fine!" A smile rose to Suzy's lips as she felt the air pressure change. Someone called down lightning on the roof, but her metal constructs filled with her soul had turned into grounding poles, the energy flowing away from the two.

Three of the cores were ruptured from the energy overload.

"Fucking pricks!" Suzy barked. Her Air creations reacted and searched for the caster.

She looked to the battle, getting back into her zone, and checked her various constructs were doing as they were supposed to. She saw as Deia charged into the fight between Anna and the PKP guildmaster.

The three of them turned into blurs, the black blur having to move faster than the white and red blurs that chased him down.

Suzy tried not to focus on the battle. That speed and coordination, Suzy was nowhere close to it. Only years studying how to fight and knowing their own body to have those reactions had allowed Anna and Deia to fight the black blur.

"The fuck is he?" Suzy asked.

"He's one of the Dark Lord's Champions. Looks like he blessed him as well." Induca's face pulled back in a snarl as a dozen Fire lances were pulled from a flaming building, quenching the Fire and being hurled into the PKP's lines.

The rest of the Stone Raiders cut down any PKP in the rear; they were like farmers and the PKP were chickens. Here and there, the sound of alarm went up.

Guards appeared and started in on the fray. The Stone Raiders might have been strong but the guards, bolstered by being in their own city, took three hits to kill a PKP and move through.

A whistle made Suzy turn to face it. A beacon appeared in the distance.

"Malsour, Dave, Suzy, Induca, check it out!" Josh yelled.

Malsour appeared, turning in a wide loop on a black surfboard, a tether of shadows below him.

"Ugh." Dave rolled onto the roof and stopped himself with a chimney—well, the chimney stopped him. "I fucking hate running." Dave started off in the direction of the beacon.

Suzy ran and jumped off the roof as Steve ambled over. A metal creation on his back caught her and wrapped around her, creating a harness. Her other creations followed.

Steve was at just thirty percent armor. He had taken a beating.

"Dave, is there anything you can do for Steve?" Suzy asked.

"Gimme a seat and I can see what I can do," Dave said.

"Jump over," Suzy said.

Dave did so, and was caught by another metal creation.

"Bloody carriage I am," Steve muttered.

"Induca, can you warm up Steve's legs?" Dave asked.

"Sure," Induca, whose feet were covered in flames, lowered herself down to Steve's leg heights and cast Fire on him.

"I am so happy I don't have nerve endings!" Steve said.

"Don't move your head." Dave put his hand on Steve's head. White light traveled down his arm.

Suzy couldn't see anything happening but Steve's armor level started to increase, restoring strength to him.

"Move upward, Induca," Dave said.

"Oi!"

"Shut up, Steve. You don't have anything anyway. I've seen you without your cloak," Dave said.

"Well, it's the essence of the matter!"

Suzy saw Dave grinning, his eyes closed.

Great, just what I need, these two idiots becoming friends!

Chapter 16: Not Your Normal Rescue

Elinar Dosfo watched as her guards and the PKP savages fought one another with everything they had. In their midst, there was a Person of Emerilia. You could tell the Players and the people apart by the way they fought, the way they moved.

This one had earned the trust and adoration of the PKP.

All the guards who came near to the PKPs had their enhancements from the city's strengthening circuits reverted. They were nothing but lowly People of Emerilia with some decent weapons and gear. Their boosts were gone, yet still they were fighting. Elinar was proud of her people, but she knew that they couldn't win the battle. Already twenty guards lay dead or dying. Necromancers pulled the dead to fight once more.

She slashed at Belindor, one of the people she had trained with, rising in the ranks of the guard. They had talked about adventuring off once they had become strong enough to fight for Selhi. Now his reanimated corpse was swinging at her, his eyes dead and cloudy.

She'd whistled but nothing happened; no one came to save her.

Did they lie? Did that Player just want for them all to die? Did he even give a fuck? Frustration burned at her very core. She wanted to cry at it all, to lash out in anger, but all she could see was Belindor's face, his neck cut open, his armor punctured.

"My, my. Such a waste." The voice was calm but cold.

The hairs on the back of Elinar's neck rose in fear. All of the people of the land could feel the auras of those around them. This one was powerful, stronger than any Player or POE Weapon Master she had faced. Even the grand wizards of the college didn't boast this power.

Standing there on a pillar of shadows was a man with black eyes. He held a book in one hand; his eyes cut obsidian as he looked at them with disdain.

"Return," he said.

The single word sent a shiver through her body, yet it did nothing to her. She heard something fall. She turned to find Belindor, who had been poised to sink his blade into her side, fall, a puppet with his strings cut.

"From Darkness, there is Light. Shadow's speed." The man's face stretched, hungry and cold.

None of the PKPs had made her as scared as this man.

"Darklings!" He called out the name, as if singsonging to a child.

Angered, hungry, and pained screams erupted from the early morning shadows, attacking the PKPs and the second Dark Lord's champion.

"He has magical suppression!" She yelled, pointing at the Dark Lord's Champion.

The man's eyes thinned as a woman with Fire around her feet raced past him. Her Fire slammed down onto the PKP who fired back up at her.

"Reaper!" Elinar's opponent called out. They slashed faster than Elinar could see, cutting through her stomach and up into her ribs. She fell to the ground. Blood pooled beneath her as she looked at her wounds in shock.

"Fuck this. Throw me in, coach!" a man said.

"What do you mean?" a screeching and deep voice asked.

"Throw me, you tin can—right at that grinning bitch in the back!" the man said.

She saw a large streak of silver armor slam into the Dark Lord's minion.

"Good morning, bitch!" the man yelled.

Elinar felt Strength return to her. She was on death's door, but her attacker, thinking her out of the battle, was turning to tear into her fellow guards' sides. She drove her sword up, through their groin and into their guts.

Fuck your pretty elegant moves. "Welcome to Selhi Capital, fuck-stain."

Elinar passed out, swearing she saw a grinning metal giant running into the fray.

"Dude, we're so doing that again!"

***

Dave had pulled all of the magical suppression champion's attention from messing with the guard's gear; however, his own armor and rod's runes were not working. He couldn't even use simple spells. He straight conjured weapons, drawing from his internal Mana pool. Nothing.

"You are one of those at Boran-al's Citadel. My lord will be happy to hear I brought about your end!" The weirdo wore some black cape that didn't allow Dave to see their face.

Well, I have the same kind of hood, so I can't really say much about his style choices without it looking back on me. Just kill the fucker and think about wardrobes and this shadow-hood crap later.

The suppressor-dick attacked Dave, moving faster than anyone Dave had seen, except possibly Alkao and Anna.

But those two were freaks of nature.

The black blade skimmed Dave's armor, leaving a trail across his chest, cutting the steel easily and scoring the Mithril underneath.

That shit is sharp and he's fast. Fuck this!

Dave swerved out of the next attack. The man was stronger and faster, and his magic suppression fucked with Dave's mojo. They traded blades, their weapons ringing out. Dave couldn't see his opponent's face but he could sense his anger. Dave fought hard, but his opponent was more skilled; every hit was made to hit him in a place where his armor was open.

I've been relying on my runes too much. He let out a hiss of pain as his dragon scale was opened along his right leg, cutting deep into his outer thigh.

"Leech!"

Dave felt his power being drained from him; not even his Mana barrier could keep his Strength and power from draining away. Dave saw the red tether that connected them. Dave didn't know how the man was doing it. He must have held in his magical suppression field everywhere but along his blade and where it hit; it allowed him to use the magical abilities of the sword.

Dave couldn't try to understand how long it had taken the Champion to figure out those abilities.

He needed to cut off this guy's feed; he was getting faster, more powerful. Any of the glancing blows Dave had given in order to hurt the little shit were healed in no time. Dave slipped up. A blade slammed into the breach between his torso and armored breastplate.

Dave yelled out. *It fucking hurt.* "You little fucking! Holy shit! Oww!" Dave fell backward. The blade's back serrated edge came free, causing more damage. Dave's Health plummeted and his armor wasn't functioning.

Dave was going to die but he needed to make sure this fucker didn't get too much of his Stamina and Mana.

In a burst of energy, Dave grabbed the man and slammed his forehead into him. The man reeled from the hit; the red tether disappeared as he lost his fine control over his Mana suppression.

Dave tackled him to the ground, mounting him.

The man beneath him screamed unintelligently. His long fingers tore at Dave's armor.

Dave's barrier didn't work anymore. His rods were slowly disintegrating, the conjuration and soul gem that powered it failing.

Dave swung his rods for all they were worth; if he didn't win, then his friends would die next.

Dave's rods broke the man's hands; still he continued to attack. He jabbed his fingers into Dave's wound, making him cry out, and giving Dave an opening. He slammed his rods into the man's head.

The man's crazed smile fell away as he had a dazed look on his face. Dave didn't dare let up; his limbs got weaker as his lifeblood continued to pump out of his body.

Dave had underestimated the Champion, but he didn't care whether he lived or died, as long as he killed or wounded the bastard so he couldn't use his abilities on anyone else. He kept swinging his rods, denting the man's head. His barrier came back as his armor tried to keep him alive and fix his internal wounds.

Dave closed his eyes, feeling lethargic. His hits barely made any impact. The pain left him as he felt himself falling.

He opened his eyes, looking around a large, empty white room. The pain was gone and he was fully intact.

You have died in Emerilia

You have been returned home.

You have 5:59 hours (game time) until you can respawn at (Alephir)

Or

1:59 hours in real life

Would you like to play a different game while you wait?

Dave waved the screen away and looked at the blank room. "Well, I'm going to get some damn sleep. After making Steve work and then fighting in Selhi, I need a fucking nap." Dave accessed his menus, creating a simple bedroom, living room, and television.

He'd just finished making the television when one of the guild members who was also dead invited him to the Stone Raiders' lobby house.

"Fucking right on!" Dave disappeared from his shoddy home.

***

Deia and Anna fought the aberration with everything they had. The damn bastard was so strong, he threw out spells without needing to call out their Actions.

While he was decent for a Player, he wasn't to their level. The issue was that his stats were so high that they were unable to land a finishing blow. It was always glancing hits, his Strength and Agility so high as to make up for his lack of skill.

It was infuriating.

Still, his Health was slowly declining, bit by bit. Dropping ten percent.

No others tried to jump in on the battle, the three combatants moving too fast to engage. Anyone who did was cut down by one side or the other in the fight.

He pulled out a staff; black energy coursed from it and struck Deia's armor. Her Mana barrier protected her as another snaked out to slam into Anna.

Her Air attack was unable to shake it. Anna fell back a few feet; the two of them braced themselves against the Dark energies hitting them.

"Mother fucker!" Deia yelled. The wind whipped around her, throwing her hair up as her eyes blazed with determined fire. She pulled the heat of the surrounding area into her, enough heat to melt metals and set dirt on fire. Heat shimmered off her as she focused the blast through her eyes, willing the heat to follow her sight. Her eyes burned, as if she had not slept in days. She screamed out in pain and defiance.

The sneer on Hevard's face turned to confusion and shock as the beam of concentrated heat ripped through his Mana barrier. He was so sure of his new stats that he thought nothing could defeat him. He was showing off with his staff, using it to gain experience with the weapon. He moved, trying to spread the damage out and not lose his staff's connection with the two ladies. He strained, having to hold the staff against the forces it was spending.

Deia used her Fire magic.

A clear liquid fell on and around Hevard.

He wrinkled his nose, opening and closing his eyes at the noxious fumes. He looked up at Deia, realizing what it was.

Alcohol is not just good for drinking.

The heat vision and the concentrated alcohol combusted. A clear flame shimmered over the area where Hevard stood. He tried to get out of the flames. He stepped backward, only to find them following him.

Deia controlled her flames.

His fear turned into panic as he couldn't get away from the flames. His Mana barrier was undoubtedly draining quickly. He made a misstep and stumbled, breaking his staff's connection.

Deia and Anna didn't wait. Anna's blade whistled through the air as Deia's blade of Fire rushed toward the bastard.

He tried to get out of the way, but was slapped by the two attacks. His Mana barrier failed as Deia and Anna kept up their attacks.

Deia commanded her flames to rush over Hevard's body.

He could have tried to extinguish the flames with his Dark magics, but he hadn't learned that yet. He screamed in rage and pain as Anna and Deia hit him so fast that he couldn't deal with the flames covering him and both of them at the same time.

It was a hard battle; both Deia and Anna stayed just out of the guildmaster's reach, slamming him with spells and blade-focused attacks.

Finally, he slumped to the ground. His Health hit zero. Anna stabbed him in the neck, making sure he was dead.

The flames disappeared as Deia and Anna moved on to the few remaining PKP. The majority were fleeing after seeing their leader's death. They were simple opponents, more focused on getting away instead of truly fighting.

Deia and Anna cut through them with ease.

Deia and Anna rested on their knees, the last of the PKP dispatched. They breathed heavily, looking for a new fight or opponent. They panted, sharing a water skin and downing Stamina potions.

Deia tried to contact Dave, but found she couldn't. She opened a voice chat with Malsour. "Why can't I get Dave?" she asked.

"He's respawning," Malsour said.

Deia's chest clenched as she forced herself to remain calm. *In a few hours, he would be back.* "Thanks." She let out a shaky breath.

She cut the voice chat and looked around Selhi Capital. There were burnt and broken houses all over the place. Guards and Stone Raiders worked together, moving out to scour the streets and make sure that there were no PKP left behind.

Wounded were being administered to in the street. Those with healing spells and Health potions got them stable enough to bring them back to the tavern.

They'd won, but Deia wondered what the cost would be.

***

Jules felt like she did after every battle: tired, overwhelmed, and in need of either a triple shot of espresso or a bed to collapse in.

Now that they had the vault classed soul gems, she was able to heal more people than ever before, though it also meant the mental strain on her was something to behold. She rubbed her temples, looking at the different People of Emerilia who were coming in through the door.

There were so many of them.

Her medics were doing a good job of prioritizing them over the Players. Sure, they might die and lose a few levels but if the POEs went, then they wouldn't come back.

After Boran-al's Citadel, that type of thinking had sunk into the Stone Raiders' normal methods of operating.

She looked at a guard who had a number of superficial cuts and then a nasty gash on her abdomen and down her side.

"Well, shit, could you manage to try to keep your bits *inside* of your body?" Jules went to work, scanning the woman with her medical skills and calling out different items she would need from her assistant.

The woman groaned. Even with her massive injuries, she was somehow conscious and fighting.

"Don't worry. You're in good hands now," Jules said, keeping her metallic implements out of her view and nodding to the assistant.

The assistant pressed their hand to the injured woman's head, knocking her out.

"Now let's get to work!" Jules used her magic to heal up the worst of the injuries and followed up with stitches, clamps, and sutures on anything that wasn't completely life threatening.

Her assistant continued to pass her items as Jules hoped that her patient would wake up afterward.

***

Josh and the captain of the guard looked out over Selhi Capital. Both of them assessed the varying degrees of damage that had been visited on the town. Thankfully, with the Players around, there was a ready supply of people ready and willing to take on quests.

The city had moved funds from the monster hunt to try to help those who had their homes destroyed and their loved ones killed. A big chunk of it had gone into a contract on all of the PKPs. It was sent to all of the main guilds, from the traders to the mages.

The captain of the guard sighed, shook his head and walked away from the sight.

Josh followed, headed toward where the magistrate of the city waited.

The guards all watched him with barely veiled suspicion as he walked through the halls. Dwayne, Induca, and Malsour were with him. The others tended to the wounded or helped out where they could.

In Kim's case, putting herself back together.

Josh tried to not blame himself—it wasn't his fault—but it was hard not to. He'd lost Players and a number of POEs who had turned into Stone Raiders. They would be remembered and their families earned a stipend for their sacrifice.

And we will destroy those who remain loyal to the PKP. We will tear the guild down until it is but a footnote in the history of Emerilia.

He moved into the room with the magistrate, who was talking with her advisers over a large map that depicted Selhi Capital and the surrounding area.

The captain of the guard walked up, being greeted before they continued their talking and planning. It was clear that Josh was not invited to join them at this time.

Josh waited to be called on.

They continued to ignore him, so he started using his interface. He had many guild matters to deal with. People had logged off, checking out the guild home. They'd found those who were there, running their names against those they had lost and making sure that they had their gear set aside for when they came back.

The loot pool was being looked over by the Exdar's Traders who were still in town. They'd been able to escape the fighting and were being loaded down with all of the PKP's gear to be sold throughout Emerilia.

Everyone earned a part of the guild's winnings. Any gear that they wanted to get they had to either barter with the person who was selling it, use their guild points, or convince their party leaders and section leaders of their need for the item.

If they used their guild points, then the guild would reimburse the seller the cost of the item and the user got their item. The more guild points they earned, the more gear they could get. Guild points were earned for doing different feats, helping out, completing quests, and a multitude of other things.

Sometimes section leaders—like Josh, Dwayne, Kim, or Lucy—would have a party leader request a piece of gear for someone who could use it if they had neither the funds nor the guild points.

The inner-guild trading system was going haywire as Stone Raiders from all over the place were bartering for all kinds of items.

The PKP were a rich guild, as shown by their gear. Killing Players was good for business, apparently. They hadn't been an easy enemy and their gear had been the best, either stolen from their victims or bought with the gold of their trade.

Still, they were Action users for the most part. They also had the backing of the Dark Lord. That guy is a pain in the ass.

Josh was thinking it was about time that he pulled down a few temples dedicated to the Dark Lord.

He opened a voice chat with Lucy.

"What?" she demanded, right in the middle of the guild's trades and then liaising with the Exdar's Traders guild. The amount of weapons and gear the PKP had on them was immense, with nearly five hundred members in the city to take out the Stone Raiders. Josh didn't envy her work.

"I was wondering about your curse. Couldn't the Lady of Fire get rid of it if she gave the PKP her blessing?" Josh asked.

"Well, yeah, of course. I don't think there is anyone more skilled in Fire magic, though I doubt that she would."

"Why? She is a lady of the Affinities Pantheon."

"Yes, but she is also one who accepts no contributions from those who follow her. She gives them lessons and shows them how to use their skills in her various schools. She does not have one temple. Her schools are fueled with her power and accept people of all manners of Affinity and level. You might know them as the mage's colleges," Lucy said.

"Wait, what? She *made* the mage's colleges?" Josh said. His voice got him some irritated looks.

"Yes. It was all rather discreet and because she did not take power from the people, she was venerated but never empowered. Now few know of the origins of the mage's guild, thinking that they were part of the original guilds, like the adventurer's and trader's, brought about by the Gray God."

"Damn. The more I learn about Emerilia, the more secrets I find, though why wouldn't she help them?"

"They got themselves into this mess, they should learn to get themselves out of it—seems to be the way she works. Unless a person is good and they have been hurt by her magic, then she will not remove soul magic upon them. She might make them atone for their sins in some manner, though it will not be an easy task. She is not a lenient lady." Lucy sounded as if she thoroughly approved.

"If she doesn't have any power to keep her up, then how the hell does she maintain her position?" Josh asked. The conversation veered off the original question but he was interested.

"She *made* the mage's colleges and subsequent guild. What kind of magic do you think she knows? Denur might be the mother of dragons, but do you know who created her? I'll give you a guess."

"The dragons are her Creatures of Power?" Josh said. "So, she might not have all that much Mana to draw from, but she is one scary lady, supported by some of the most powerful beasts on Emerilia. Scary."

"Everything she does, she does through her own Mana pool. How big do you think her Mana pool must be? While the other lords and ladies use the power of those devoted to them, she made the dragons from her own power. She nurtures and blesses them with her *own* power," Lucy said.

"Shit. I would not like to meet someone who has been practicing magic for a few hundred years. That would be one hell of a scary Mana pool." Josh saw that someone was walking over toward him, an aide of some sort.

"The magistrate will see you now." The aide turned around with just the right amount of disdain to make it clear to Josh but without revealing it to the rest of the room.

Sweet, even the aides are a prissy bunch.

"Talk later, Lucy. If you need my people to help out, let them know. Idle hands and all that!"

"Look who's talking," Lucy said dryly, cutting the channel.

Josh snorted and found the magistrate looking at Josh, trying to keep her face neutral though he could make out the tension at the corners of her eyes. Josh had picked up a few lessons on reading people from playing poker with his Wall Street buddies and when dealing with different clients.

"Magistrate Houn." Josh nodded toward the regal-looking human.

"Josh Giles, leader of the Stone Raiders," she said, her voice hard and angry.

Well, I don't like the sound of that.

"You came to this city, bringing with you a feud that has killed nearly two hundred of my people and the destruction of many buildings and holdings in this city. The eastern walls have been weakened and monster season is upon us. What do you have to say for yourself?"

So that's how it's going to be, scapegoating, huh? Awesome. "We came to Selhi Capital with the intention of helping with the monster hunt."

"Tried to push his guild's troubles onto us, more like!" an adviser growled.

The magistrate didn't try to stop them, the fire clear in her eyes.

"Fuck it. Seeing as you want to have someone to blame, do it. Bring it. Blame us. We're the fucking Stone Raiders, lass. You know what that fucking means? It means we're going to hunt down those PKP fuckers like the dogs they are. We're going to kill them so many fucking times that the fucking ground will know their corpses better than it knows the mountains and trees that live on it. We will wipe their fucking guild out. There won't be a fucking indicator that they ever existed in all of fucking Emerilia."

Josh smiled now, thinking of the destruction he would level on the PKP. "We will bring the Dark Lord to his knees and we will make him beg for mercy. To beg for forgiveness and we will send him to the underworld. He might be a god, might be a lord of the Affinities Pantheon. To us, he's a fucking plaything. A mild annoyance. We will use his pawns to grow stronger. Their blood will be our strength until we bring him and his fuckers down to Emerilia. So blame us, tell us that it was our fault as you have no one else to blame. Say all you fucking want about us. We. Don't. Give. A. Shiny. Shit. But remember this. We could have run—we could have left you to die by yourselves. Instead, we stayed. We fought them when you couldn't. You might grow old and die, but the Stone Raiders intend to be around for decades. Think carefully about your decisions," Josh finished. It was good to get off his chest.

They stared at him as if he were some savage dog. He didn't give a fuck. He was angry and they were here treating him as though he were the criminal, not the people who had attacked them.

"I ban you and all of those who are part of the Stone Raiders from Selhi. You have one day to leave our borders or else you will be deemed a hostile force." The magistrate's face split into a cold, pleased smile. "The forests are a dangerous place this time of year, Player." She used the word like it was a curse.

"Also, the toll for the teleport pad has risen by five hundred percent. I do hope you have the coin for it."

Josh could see the greed in her face. "No worries, sweet magistrate. We have others in need of our services." Josh gave an elegant bow, turned and left.

He opened up a chat to all of his Stone Raiders.

"All aid is to cease. Prepare the guild to leave. We have been banished from Selhi for our efforts. Prepare for the upcoming raid. Pass the word onto those respawning. Make sure that our goods are protected. Get Dave to talk to the Zolun Mountain Dwarves. We will do our trading there," Josh said out loud as he left the room.

He closed the voice chat and walked to the forty-foot balcony. He smiled happily, looked back at the magistrate and her advisers, flipped them the bird and jumped off the balcony.

His only wish was that he could see their faces as he jumped off a forty-foot high wall.

He used blink-step, slowing his speed as he landed halfway through the courtyard. Guards looked at him in shock.

Malsour, Deia, Induca, and Anna were waiting for him. He could feel their palpable anger as a notification popped up.

Quest: Restore Order

The Stone Raider guild has accepted the quest to kill or capture any and all who have disturbed the peace in Selhi's capital. For successfully completing the quest, they receive:

Rewards: Banishment

"Now is not the time to fight. We have wounded and dead to see to. We don't need to increase those numbers," Josh said, getting nods from the others. "It might take months...it might take years, but we'll pay them back for this betrayal."

The others looked mollified by his words and followed him out of the manor. None of the guards tried to stop them.

***

The magistrate looked away from the balcony as Josh disappeared, not wanting to show her shock. "Make sure that they are followed," she said to the captain of the guard, moving to the rear of the room.

"Magistrate, do you think it is best to ban them? Sure, the people need someone to be angry at right now. They are angry at the PKP, but lumping the Stone Raiders who actually helped us with them? It sets a dangerous precedent," the captain said, his voice low so that no one else could hear.

"We need to look strong. This cycle of Players has just started. The Stone Raiders are interesting, but they are weak of level and people." She waved her hand indifferently. "They will be one of the guilds that crumbles and falls eventually."

"They have gathered POEs into their ranks and even my guards are full of nothing but praise for them," the captain said gruffly.

She looked to him, anger in her eyes. "They are nothing but a weak guild. If they do not leave our lands in one day, then their gear will help grow our coffers to pay for the repairs," the magistrate hissed. The cost of having the monster hunt had already lowered their treasury.

She made to continue walking as three powerful auras made her pause in her step. A cold bead of sweat ran down her spine at the sheer power behind those three auras. She turned slowly and looked out of her manor. She hadn't felt a presence like this since her young days when she had ventured to Ashal.

Others wilted and fell to their knees in fear. The captain of the guard held firm and looked at her.

She'd just dismissed the leader of people who rivaled dragons. As quickly as the pressure had started, it disappeared, as if it was never there.

How are they that powerful already? Who are those three?

The magistrate remembered old words from her mentor, now long dead: *Never make a deal without knowing all of the circumstances.*

She shook off the words. She had made her declaration; going against it now would make her seem weak. "Make sure that you have the best people on hand. Take them from the army if you must." She turned and left quickly.

Chapter 17: Disappearing Act

Dave's timer finally hit zero.

He was one of the last Stone Raiders to go back into the game. He'd been playing another simulation, one about mechs and space. It had been different and interesting, giving him ideas for the future.

They'd talked about things happening back on Earth. About different stars that Dave remembered but didn't care for. It was odd, as if glancing back on a part of his past that he couldn't quite truly remember.

"See you on the other side!" Dave said.

Light enveloped his vision as he looked up at the six Affinities. His eyes found the gray circle that encompassed them all.

He rolled off the altar, finding Shard.

"It is good to see you well." Shard smiled.

"Same here." Dave looked over his body. His notifications blinked at him.

You Have Died

For dying, you lose:

x4 levels and their associated points.

Your classes (You can gain them back by gaining level 10 again). All tests are reset.

Your equipment not already soul bound.

21 gold, 7 silver, and 2 coppers.

You were looted by:

Malsour Dracul

Dave moved to his stat sheet, disregarding the other prompts as he put his stat points back into place, earning all his classes back. Power once again filled him as he stepped off the altar.

He found that his gear was waiting beside the altar, in his pack. Luckily it was soul bound and followed him through death to his respawn location.

"How do you feel?" Shard asked.

"Good. Even fixed that knot in my back from bending over while smithing," Dave said.

Shard moved into a flurry of questions as Dave looked around the room. He had never been in a place like it. There were all kinds of terminals around the altar. Not the usual temples that housed many altars.

"Are you studying this thing?" Dave asked.

"Classified," Shard said.

"Ahh, hmm, interesting. I'd like to know how it works as well. I feel fine—at least my body's aches and pains are gone. I probably have a new body with most of my stats. I don't know if the level loss is because of it being harder to copy a body to that degree so they make it as close as possible. Or if it is a central mechanic to the whole system. Making people not want to die because they lose their gear, coin, experience, and have to travel a hell of a distance to get their gear back." Dave used his interface to put the gear into an outfit so that he could quickly change into it if he needed to.

"How go the experiments on the soul gems?" Dave put the pack on.

"Well, better than I had hoped. I believe that it will allow for a great power retention across Aleph. I have also been studying the Mana capture net that you showed me. It is rather ingenious and I hope to start trials as soon as I have the power and automatons for the task." Shard sounded excited for the future.

"What is the decision of your guild with the task of clearing out the homes of the Aleph?" Shard waved his hand, understanding that Dave would like to leave the altar and the surrounding testing equipment.

"They are mobilizing to be here shortly. We believe that people we saved will send their guards after us to make sure that we are leaving and ambush us if we do not leave their lands. Since the Aleph substation is nearby, would it be ok if we used that to escape from them?" Dave asked.

"You are now trying to escape the people you helped. I do not understand." Shard looked confused as they stepped onto a tram platform, waiting for one to arrive.

Dave explained what had happened in Selhi and how the Stone Raiders had been met with hostilities because they were different and similar in some slight way to the people who had caused so much destruction.

Shard listened as they rode the tram, coming to the central spires of Alephir.

The central spires met in the middle of Alephir, connecting into an *X*. Dave and the others had been transported to one of the four towers when they arrived. There were a dozen similar towers that held Alephir together. None of them were as large or magnificent as those in the center.

"I find that when dealing with emotions, such as anger and greed, that organics are unable to make proper decisions. I know that in those cases, I must suspend my emotional complex in order to deal with it on an information level," Shard said.

"As such, I understand the need for your forces to move quickly. If they do not, then they will lack the resources they need to aid themselves in the tasks that I have set for you. I will allow for the possibility of the substation to be found out. Only if two criteria are met. Malsour is a strong Dark Dragon and there must be similarly skilled Earth Affinity people within your guild. I ask that they seal off the way that leads to the substation. I will send automatons to fix the substation's wall, once again returning its stealth coating and allowing the substation to be hidden. I, also, ask that you help me with more of your lessons on maintenance," Shard said.

"I'd be more than happy to help. All you need to do is ask next time. This is a big job for anyone. I don't know how you've been keeping it active for as long as you have. So, what do you need help with?" Dave asked.

"The larger teleport pads have an issue with their runic transistors." Shard sounded frustrated.

"Lead the way!" Dave smiled. *What the fuck are runic transistors?*

***

The Dark Lord's hall started to disintegrate around him. Black flames raged around his body as he watched the dome in the floor.

The first scene showed Hevard being cut down. The second made his flames rage higher as his suppressor Champion got his head beaten to a pulp by a dying man with batons.

It took decades to train him up and then he went and got himself killed just because he wanted to see the strength of these Players!

A pillar of black flames tore the hall apart. The servants in the room whimpered and cried in the face of the Dark Lord's anger. The chained souls had given up on all attempts to make it out of the prison he called his home. He could revive them again and again to take their punishments.

Javal was a magic suppressor, a rare outcast in Emerilia. They were usually cast out of societies early on in their lives, without the strength and mental fortitude to control their ability. They were a one-in-a-few billion rarity.

The Dark Lord had found Javal out in a forest, a child abandoned by his family and village as he stopped any magical device from working around him.

Magical suppressors stopped Mana from working, but it also meant they couldn't use it. If they were wounded, they had to be patched back together with methods similar to that used on Earth. There were few people who dealt with sewing wounds up or setting bones in anything but the poorest groups in Emerilia. Spells and potions of healing were useless, as well as revival spells. They couldn't use magically enchanted gear unless they got a high level of control over their ability.

Javal had just reached that stage. Instead of heeding his lord's words, he had followed Hevard and his people to fight against the Stone Raiders and prove his strength. What he'd proved was his idiocy and taken a powerful pawn away from the Dark Lord.

"Find me Scourge. I want him to destroy everything and anything that Javal cared for or cared about him," the Dark Lord snapped. He couldn't take out his anger on the Champion, but he could make an example for his other Champions.

If they do not obey, I will tear their very souls from their bodies and torment them for eternity.

***

Loot had been passed off to the Exdar's Traders; people checked out their new weapons and gear. Stats were king here; few—if any—held an attachment with their old gear, always looking for better and more powerful items.

Some guilds looked pretty, with all of their items colored a certain way.

The Stone Raiders looked like eccentric mutts, with all manner of clothing, from rough steel armor plate to Mithril bracers. No matter an item's material; if it was better, it was used. Damn the looks.

"Don't worry—we'll get some food into us before we start raiding," Josh said to the group of two hundred and fifteen.

Hearing that the guild had been attacked, a number of the members had teleported into Selhi Capital. Kim was dealing with the different groups that were hunting down the PKP. A few more deaths had already been recorded. Those who had respawned in Selhi had been quickly cut down, dying again and again before the game pushed them to a different random town to be spawned at.

The guards had secretly promised to make sure that they didn't let any of the PKP make it out of the Altar of Rebirth alive, to show their support for the Stone Raiders. Their magistrate might hate them and try to fleece them, but the guards had fought with them and a number of their people had been healed even if it meant that one of the Players would die.

Looks like they will be getting their coin back soon enough, Deia thought. The Stone Raiders weren't the only Players leaving Selhi.

A few were off and hunting, but others, after hearing how the Stone Raiders were on their way out, were trying to take their place.

Three other guilds were on their way to take over the hunt at Selhi, to show that they were better than the Stone Raiders. However, most of the E-head guilds had talked to Josh and were also on their way out.

"Let's go!" Josh said.

The Stone Raiders made one hell of a sight as they moved off. There were no whoops and cheers today. Instead, they moved in formation, a scary sight to behold. Stealthy Agility types raced ahead with Deia, not bothering with the gates but leaping onto roofs to watch over the Stone Raiders, and then over the walls and into the forest.

Those who were in the army or the guards who didn't like them made their anger clear. A few even tried to attack them.

The collective force of the Stone Raiders' aura was like an oppressive force. Their killing intent was clear as people cleared out of their path and paled at their eyes. They were no longer the joking and carefree people who had entered the city. They had been made pariahs and the enemy of the nation.

Golems and elementals moved around the Stone Raiders, with the support in the center of their formation; attack mages and tanks surrounded them. They moved quick and fast, faster than most would believe.

"We're clear. The force behind us is moving to follow but they will be some time," Anna reported through voice chat. She was to the rear; Deia was ahead, leading them toward the cave that would get them access to the substation.

"Come on, Stone Raiders. Let's make them work for it!" Dwayne barked.

The Stone Raiders started to sprint, eating up their distance quickly. Those of too low of a level to keep up were carried by those with extra Strength. No one was left behind.

"Malsour?" Josh asked.

"We're ready," Malsour said.

Malsour and a party had snuck out of Selhi Capital for the next part of their plan.

"We're out of their sight," Anna said, her voice tight with nerves.

Deia altered her direction and took them off the main path. The Stone Raiders threaded through the trees. Earth mages started their work, healing the damage as they passed, leaving no indication of their passing as they ran through the forest.

People filled the trees as they headed for what looked like a massive ramp into the ground. Deia stood in front of it. The trees and vegetation in the area looked as though it had been scraped back for this massive hole that the Stone Raiders rushed down. Deia circled around, looking for signs that they had been followed.

Anna rushed past her and then Deia followed. The two of them jumped and slid down the ramp.

Malsour and a group of Earth mages glowed as power surged around them.

The forest that had been scraped back now moved back into position. Dirt and materials from the surrounding area filled the ramp, closing up behind Anna and Deia as they regained their feet. The rest of the Stone Raiders made their way through the small opening into the substation in quick and orderly parties.

"So long, Selhi." Deia followed the Stone Raiders as more dirt and rocks moved to fill in the ramp area. Deia stepped through the hole into the substation. Two worker automatons, spiders with working limbs on their top, waited like statues.

Malsour was the last out of the ramp.

Rock, metals, and Earth covered what had been a cave system. The Aleph automatons moved into action, putting bricks into place over the hole that remained.

Deia moved with the Stone Raiders, who looked around in interest.

"All right, get into order. First, we've got a kobold camp to clear out! We might have just escaped Selhi, but now the real fight starts!"

***

"What do you mean, they disappeared?" the magistrate demanded of the major who had been commanded to follow the Stone Raiders when they left and kill them if they still were within Selhi in a day.

"We mounted up as we got word that the Stone Raiders were leaving. By the time we got to the gate, they were well in the distance. None of our scouts were fast enough to follow them. We made it out of the city, riding as hard as possible, but we could not find any sign of them. We scoured the paths and found some signs that they might have diverted. We checked it even though it was just an errant thought. No army that size could move so easily through a forest like that. The paths were well worn so we couldn't tell that they had or hadn't used the roads." The major's head bowed to the floor.

"What about the outposts?" the magistrate asked.

"They have been placed on alert, though having their forces following might be a better course of action. It will take us too long to catch up with them."

"What kind of beasts are they to run faster than a horse?" one of the advisers hissed.

"Where the hell could they have gone?" another asked aloud.

"There was a rumor that they had found a raid location somewhere nearby. There was supposed to be a party that had been scouting the area. They returned to the adventurer's guild, not willing to give up the location of a possible kobold infestation as they didn't want anyone but their guild knowing about it," one of the advisers said, his voice grave.

"What are you saying, Al'keem?" the magistrate asked.

Al'keem was not a man to waste his breath on useless words. "A group of six went off and were killing level 170 kobolds. Instead of telling the adventurer's guild, they were banned from the chapter, them and their entire guild. They have done tasks from all manner of kingdoms, and other tasks that armies would be wasted on. Their people are loyal and steadfast. They wholly risk to challenge the adventurer's guild over a single find. The Stone Raiders are not dumb; they are people who have forsaken their home in order to live in Emerilia. They are strong and they plan ahead. They have more keys to different kingdoms, attained through hard work, than any other guild. If they allowed themselves to be banned from the adventurer's guild, whatever they found is something impressive."

The magistrate felt a headache brewing as she pinched the top of her nose. "Find them, kill them and bring me their gear." She tilted her head toward the major.

"Yes, Magistrate!" He saluted and left the room quickly.

Chapter 18: Time to Raid

The Stone Raiders were tired from gaming so long. They just needed to clear out this one substation and they could rest, gather strength and prepare themselves for the challenges ahead. More than one person needed to log off afterward to go to jobs and other such Earth-related things.

Josh rubbed his face and looked down at the kobold village. They had killed a few of the kobold scouting groups but the village was still there. They had been spending time on making defenses as their people stopped coming back from venturing into the rest of the substation.

Large columns supported the large roof of the open area. Stairs made their way down to the teleport pads.

The situation hadn't changed much since the last time Josh had been there.

"Okay, let's head back," Josh said.

Deia nodded, following him. Since Dave had "died," she'd been quiet. After some people had checked on the Stone Raiders' "home," she'd relaxed some. She said that she had been in contact with Dave, but Josh could tell that not seeing him in the flesh was wearing on her, as if she was running on a thin line of knowing that he was safe or dealing with the grief of his loss.

They moved back silently. Josh and Deia headed toward Dwayne, Lucy, and Kim to come up with a battle plan. They had each gone up with a different scout so that they could get a view of what would be their battlefield.

***

"Remember, if you need anything, just let me know. There's a lot of complicated machines around this place and I don't even know

"

how half of them work, but I would be happy to help you in any way I can if you're in need of it," Dave said.

"Thank you, Dave. Your assistance has helped me immensely. Having someone I can trust and rely on is nice. If I have any issues, I will contact you. I wish you good luck on your hunt and hope that you do not need to be respawned again," Shard said.

"Me too." Dave shook his head and rubbed the back of his head.

The teleport pad flared to life behind Dave.

He could have used the teleport-to-party feature, but it cost a lot of gold, at one gold per mile. It would have cost Dave nearly four thousand gold to reach his party without the free teleport pads.

"See you in a bit!" Dave walked onto the teleport pad from the large waystation on Alephir to the hidden teleport pad at the sub-station.

He walked out to be greeted by a number of Stone Raiders who had been watching the teleport pad.

"Hey! So, what did I miss?" Dave asked.

They filled him in on the Stone Raiders' escape from Selhi Capital and how the leaders were working out a plan to kill the kobolds in the lower levels. One of the scouts was tasked with taking Dave to meet with them.

They talked the entire time, mostly Dave listening to get up to date on events.

"Dave!" Deia yelled upon seeing him.

Dave smiled as she rushed him, almost tackling him to the ground. He hugged Deia, stroking her head; he felt tears on his neck as she cried.

"I was so scared. I know that you talked to me and all that, but I still wasn't sure," Deia said, her voice quiet and relieved as tension seemed to bleed off her.

"I'm sorry, babe." Dave felt bad about having to respawn and put Deia through all of that worry.

"You're going to have to get better at fighting. Dying from someone who can counteract your runes!" She hit his chest, the soft admonishment about her fear for his well-being clear.

"I'll do my best, teacher." Dave smiled and kissed the side of her head.

"Yes, you will! What skills did you work on? What were your advances in the fight? We can go from there and use this raid to work on your other fighting styles. No more getting thrown like some kind of over-sized dart." She looked up, clearly not happy with that maneuver.

Dave scratched his head awkwardly. Steve waved in hello, though silently trying to get out of the room as he side-shuffled away.

It was all Dave could do to stop himself from laughing. The walking mass of metal was growing on him. He forgot Steve and thought on Deia's words.

"I haven't looked at my notifications yet. I'll try them out." Dave opened his notifications bar.

"The heck were you doing all this time?" she admonished.

"Uhh, helping Shard out." Dave fiddled with his fingers.

"So, you got stuck talking about different projects?"

"Something like that."

Deia rolled her eyes and hugged him tight. Dave wrapped his arms around her, smiling at her happy expression.

"Notifications." She broke the embrace and poked him in the chest.

"Yes, ma'am!" He smiled and opened the tab.

Active Skill: Archery

Level: Expert Level 3

Effect: Critical Hit chance increases by 33%. Ranged targets take 15% increased damage

Cost: 10 Stamina

Active Skill: Sneak Attack

Level: Expert Level 5

Effect: When you are undetected in stealth, attacks will hit with 340% increased damage (Massive increased when hitting Critical area). May your aim be true.

Cost: (Attack 50 Stamina)

Active Skill: Stealth

Level: Expert Level 9

Effect: 83% chance to remain undetected (reduced in direct light).

Cost: 5 Stamina/second

Passive Skill: Dodge

Level: Expert Level 6

Effect: 75% chance to evade objects.

Passive Skill: Perception

Level: Master Level 1

Effect: 87% chance to find hidden details. 5% chance at better loot

Active Skill: Sprint

Level: Expert Level 7

Effect: 77% increased speed

Cost: 5 Stamina/second

Active Skill: Two-handed

Level: Journeyman Level 2

Effect: 22% armor penetration on target. Stamina costs reduced 10% while fighting.

Cost: 35 Stamina

Active Skill: Dual wield

Level: Expert Level 5

Effect: Attacks are 35% faster. 25% reduced damage with offhand weapon.

Cost: 15 Stamina/second

Passive Skill: Night Vision

Level: Master Level 4

Effect: 91% increased night vision. 20% increased vision in magical darkness.

Racial bonus: Dwarves, even half-Dwarves, are at home in the darkness of mines and their empires dug underneath mountains. +25% increased night vision. (+5% in magical darkness)

Active Skill: Inference

Level: Apprentice Level 5

Effect: 33% increased chance of using moves you've read in books.

Active Skill: One-handed and Shield

Level: Journeyman Level 4

Effect: Weapons damage increased by 24%. Defense increases by 10%.

Cost: 20 Stamina

Passive Skill: Aura Detection

You know better than most that people aren't always as they seem. Everyone has an innate aura of power about them. Whether this strength comes from crafting, casting spells, or slaying creatures, you can now detect it. You can also suppress it, so don't start thinking of this as some crazy "things that want to kill me" radar. Lazy bastard.

Level: Journeyman Level 3

Effect: You can detect the Auras of those that are not actively hiding it, or have Aura Suppression level lower than your Aura Detection.

Active Skill: Aura Suppression

'Cause you're a naturally sneaky bastard trying to hide your abilities, you got a high level off the bat. Cool shit. I'm going to think you guessed this was coming based off the last skill... Or you've just run into a wall so many times you don't know the color blue from cranberry. Way. To. Go. Dave.

Level: Expert Level 2

Effect: You can hide your Aura from others. Whether you do this all the time, part of the time, or just let out a little bit...couldn't give two spindly fucks.

Dave was kind of shocked. He thought that he would go up some levels in his skills, but they'd increased faster than he'd ever seen. "How the hell is this possible?" Dave muttered.

"What?" Deia asked, near enough to hear him.

"I jumped up so many levels while fighting, it's nuts."

"Well, they're Players and Players who kill other Players. Their strength is not something to be overlooked. Emerilia sees that at your level, you were able to beat someone well above you with your skill with a blade. If someone is ranked a master, but you beat them while you're an apprentice, then you're going to see a big jump in skills. You've proved to the game that you're much stronger than what your skills say, so they change to adapt to that. It's rare to see with people of the land, but with Players, I've seen them go up skill levels in weaponry fast as they've been able to defeat Emerilia Weapon Masters with a tricky new move or idea, thus gaining them many levels in one go instead of just grinding mobs and other creatures," Deia said.

"Damn," Dave said.

"It's how you've been able to jump up levels with your combat skills already. Having a master of a weapon teaching and sparring with you reflects that you are becoming stronger. The harder it is for your master to beat you, the greater your level increase."

"So that's why my archery and dual wield leveled up so fast, because of your training?" Dave asked.

"While I am a master of bow and dual wielding, Anna is a master of two-handed and one-handed with shield," Deia said, giving him a look that he should have remembered that.

"But my progress has been much slower to this point."

"Well, we were not fighting to the death and we have had centuries of fighting. We know a good number of fighting techniques. Other Players might be rated masters in a weapon, but they do not have the knowledge and experience that we do," Deia said, not without a bit of pride.

"That's my girl," Dave said, side-hugging her.

"Let's see your new stats," Deia asked, firmly in teacher mode.

"One second." Dave pulled up his last few notifications.

Level 74

You have reached level 74; you have **316** stat points to use.

It had already taken into account the four levels that he had lost for dying, though with all of the experience gained from his kills and the party's kills, he'd still jumped up seven levels.

No wonder Player killing is so lucrative. Seven levels in a single night! And all of that loot.

Stat Increase

+12 Strength

+4 Intelligence

+15 Agility

+4 Vitality

+2 Willpower

+4 Endurance

There was just one more notification left.

You Have Assisted in Killing A Champion

There are few things as powerful as a Champion of the Affinities Pantheon. Bestowed with the gift of power and a calling to serve, the most powerful warriors in Emerilia would give Dragons pause. You have shown that not even these warriors are a true challenge for you.

Rewards: +2 to all stats.

For assisting in killing a Champion of the Dark Lord, your reputation with the Lady of Light has increased.

Knowledge on Hidden Class: Champion Slayer

There are Dragon Slayers known across the world for their reputation. Hidden away from many, there are also Champion Slayers. Not bestowed with a gift of the Affinities Pantheon, these warriors have shown their ability to kill one who is.

For defeating a Champion or assisting twice in the death of one, you will gain access to this hidden class. The more Champions you kill, the stronger you will grow (Killing different Champions will increase/decrease your reputation with different Affinity factions).

He took his character sheet and shared it with her.

Character Sheet

Name:	David Grahslagg	Gender:	Male
Level:	10	Class:	Dwarven Master Smith, Friend of the Gray God, Bleeder, Librarian
Race:	Human/ Dwarf	Alignment:	Chaotic Neutral

Unspent points-316

Health:	9,900	Regen:	3.36/s
Mana:	2,190	Regen:	9.75/s
Stamina:	1,530	Regen:	8.25/s
Vitality:	99	Endurance:	168
Intelligence:	219	Willpower:	195
Strength:	153	Agility:	165

"Did you kill that Hevard dude?" Dave asked, still thinking about the new class that had been revealed.

"I got the assist. Anna killed it. Malsour got the kill on the one you were fighting, though everyone else got an assist as well." Deia looked to Dave.

"Damn, wouldn't mind working on getting that class. I know that I'd feel a bit better if the Dark Lord had less minions to send at us." Dave sighed.

"We can hope," Deia said.

"All right, everyone good with the plan?" Josh asked.

"What the hell is the plan?" Dave muttered to Deia.

"Fighter parties move in, get the kobolds' attention. While we have it, the DPS types get in behind and rip them apart. We're going to be in the center."

"Isn't that kind of risky? We're still a whole bunch of levels lower than the kobolds in there."

"We're not that far behind them and there are more of us than them." Deia looked to Dave. "Do you have that lightning thing?"

"I can make one if I need to," Dave said. "Why?"

"We're going to hit them with our biggest spells first, make them reel from that as we get a foothold in the fight so that they can't start using their mages against us from the start."

"Get in close, rip them apart," Dave said.

"Right," Deia said. Behind her, the rest of the party were walking over.

"Miss me?" Dave asked as they got close enough to hear.

"Good to see you in one piece," Suzy said.

"Was that throw awesome or what?" Steve smiled until he saw Deia's glare and then faltered slightly.

"It was an effective tactic and allowed the guards to once again regain the strength they needed in order to defeat the PKP," Malsour said.

"Yeah. It also sucked, a *lot*, though the guild's 'home' is pretty sweet, kind of like the conference mansion we have but way more people doing all kinds of stuff," Dave said.

"Let's move!" Josh said. He'd been answering questions and lining out the plan to everyone again as Deia and Dave had been talking.

"Follow me." Deia pulled her bow out. Dave's rods turned into a bow as the Stone Raiders moved into the large hall where the kobolds had set up.

Anna, Steve, and twenty or so metal creations moved to the front. Induca, Malsour, and Suzy stayed back.

Dave felt buffs increasing his Strength, Health, and resistances to different attacks. It felt invigorating having that many buffs.

Deia let loose an arrow; others did the same here and there, cutting down any kobolds nearby.

All too soon, a kobold's voice rang out in alarm. The noise was cut off mid-way, but it had been enough. Dave could see that the kobolds were mobilizing. With their bad sight, they probably couldn't see the Stone Raiders yet but they knew something was amiss.

Warriors rushed out of the village to meet the attackers who had killed their friends and left them cowering at the lowest reaches of the substation.

Dave added his own arrows to the fight. The high vaulted ceilings were tall enough to allow the arrows' arching flight as they landed among the kobolds, shrieks and cries following the arrows' paths.

Mages, giving up on all pretenses of stealth, grouped together and called out their artillery spells.

The kobold mages unleashed their attacks. Defensive and support mages did what they could to blunt the attack before it caused true damage.

The Stone Raiders didn't run but moved at a half-jog so they didn't waste their Stamina on just getting into battle.

The kobolds threw spears, wasting many of them as they didn't have the range to hit the oncoming Stone Raiders.

"Light!" Josh yelled.

Super-powered lights sprung into existence, glowing balls of power. The kobolds let out pained screeches. Their eyes were not used to this level of light, living in the dim-lit halls and the darkness of the underground.

Artillery spells fired. The kobold mages, worrying about their eyes, never saw the attacks as the spells crashed into the kobolds, killing dozens. Elementals of Earth, Fire, and Water appeared in the kobold village, adding to the confusion.

The kobolds were getting hammered as the Stone Raiders greeted their first line with their shields and swords. Kobold screams rang out as metal met bone and muscle, freeing blood and pain.

Dave changed his bow for a two-handed machine. It looked like a scaled-up version of the lightning bolt that he had used a few weeks ago.

The crackling of energy drew many eyes before Dave planted himself. He fired the cannon and a ball of lightning surged across the floor. Dave flew three feet backward. Steve caught him in one hand, not even breaking his stride as they continued into the kobold lines.

"Thanks," Dave panted. Making the larger cannon had taken a lot out of him. His cannon fell apart into a sword and shield.

"No worries, dude. You think you could hook a brother up?" Steve looked at the path of Dave's lightning ball in awe.

Dave looked at what he had done, looking at a scorched path through the kobolds and into the now burning village. Kobolds were spasming on the floor or smoking from the electricity that had torn through their bodies.

"I'll think about it," Dave said.

Steve set him down. Steve's axe slammed into two kobolds, cutting them apart.

Dave advanced into their lines.

He raised his shield, blocking a hit that came from his left. It scraped off his shield as Dave's sword flicked out, hitting his opponent's side. Dave moved back to see his attacker.

There, holding a shovel and looking at him with a mix of pain and unadulterated rage, was a kobold miner.

Kobold Miner

Level 176

Dave was about matched for human terms of Strength and Agility, but he didn't have the drop on him.

The kobold let out an inhuman screech as it slammed its shovel against Dave's shield. It might not have the greatest weapon but it knew how to use it, not giving Dave the chance to get away from it.

A blast of Fire knocked it off balance mid-swing. Dave's sword started forward; blue areas seemed to highlight various vital points as Dave altered the trajectory of his blade. It sunk into the kobold. Dave ripped it out before the kobold could regain its state of mind.

It coughed and looked at Dave in shock before it toppled over.

Dave stabbed the thing one more time to make sure it was dead before getting right back into the fray.

***

Anna moved through the kobolds easily, leaving opponents cleaved in half while moving with the confidence that only someone who had seen many battlefields held. She could feel the flow of battle as if it were an ethereal thing.

The kobolds had charged into battle to be greeted with a massive attack. They hadn't realized the losses that they had already sustained, pushing more out of the village as they thought that there was no one out and fighting.

Anna watched as the Stone Raiders hacked and cut their way through the kobolds. Few had any true elegance when fighting. As long as they killed their opponent, they didn't care.

Stealth types moved through the edges and gaps and zip-wired behind the enemy from above. Their attacks were precise and deadly, hitting for all they could.

Deia shifted out of the way of a blow, *wind cutter* leaving a sad note ringing in the air as the attacker and two behind them were cut apart by the wind blade Anna had created.

Deia's movements were quick and powerful. Deia moved in short and violent manners, acting and reacting. Her blades of Fire, not having the range of Anna's, cut through flesh easily but couldn't gain the same distance that Anna could.

Anna watched as Dave tried to fight off three kobolds, a moment of fear growing in her. She didn't want Deia to go through the same pain as before. She turned to act, just as Dave's speed increased; he slammed one kobold's attack away, stabbed one in the face, and slashed the third attacker's front. Spinning to gain momentum, he took the head off the first.

Anna leapt backward as a pickaxe swung for her. It hit her at a different angle, hurting instead of maiming. She felt her ribs break as she moved to bring down her attacker.

A darkling rose from the shadow around the kobold, turning its body into shadowy spikes.

The kobold cried out. Anna ended its existence, sending a mental thank-you to Malsour as she once again dove into the combat.

Artillery and magical spells fell throughout the kobolds, devastating their lines. The kobolds weren't defenseless; their mages threw up any kind of defense they thought might work. The battle had been truly joined; although the kobold miners were strong with their weapons of pickaxe and shovel, their mages were not able to completely annul the magical attacks.

They also didn't give any thought to battle tactics as stealthy types were now getting in behind them and doing damage, targeting the effective kobold mages.

Anna smiled. A flick of her sword cleared blood from her blade as she twirled, *wind cutter* singing its song as she left dead kobolds in her wake.

***

Lucy looked over the battlefield. Josh was the overall commander, but she was the secondary, able to see the entire battle and coordinate with the different forces better.

The kobolds were giving a good fight; they might have people who were of a higher level, but they weren't buffing one another. They were territorial and not likely to trust one another, even in battle.

Their mages were few and were being targeted with extreme prejudice.

Lucy watched as parties didn't even need to switch out, the tanks getting group healed as they fought. Lucy grouped all front-line fighters as tanks, from those who could stand in the face of the enemy and make them stop their progress toward the rest of their party and guild.

It was one hell of a coordinated machine.

She could tell which groups had fought together, using a few simple words as the others reacted. The guild chat was clear, with only priority messages coming through. It looked as if the stealth types were making their play as the village had cleared out.

"Josh, we've got reports of something moving out from the center of the village, probably a chieftain of some kind." Lucy looked over the battlefield. Golems, elementals, magical powers as well as healing and buff auras were being given off.

Darklings and summoned creatures, wind wisps and firestorms: it might look like chaos to most, but to her it was a co-ordinated and well-defined battle.

The kobolds were getting fucked right in their back door and they didn't like it.

"Got it. Warn the people in the way of whatever it is," Josh said.

"Mhmm," Lucy said.

"I like when things are nice and simple like this. See an enemy and kill it, no backroom bullshit or blame." Josh sighed.

Lucy knew that the politics side of being the guildmaster was wearing on him. "I will deal with it."

"Yeah, but then I'm the awkward mouthpiece," Josh complained.

Lucy let him. She didn't want to be the one talking to them all and Josh needed some time to vent.

"After this, I'll get you three hours of privacy with Cassie," Lucy promised.

"Lucy, I didn't mean that," Josh said.

Lucy heard the sounds of battle in the background as she looked through different kinds of maps that linked her to the people who were fighting. "Heal in left flank," she said to her support.

"Look, Josh, we lost people and you've been on edge, dealing with the front of the blame as much as it is warranted or not. You need some time to blow off some steam and Cassie calms you down. I know why you don't officially come out and say that you two are dating, but I think in the end, we will just have to make an alliance with them," Lucy said absently, looking for where there were issues.

"You just saying that to make me happy or do you think that it will be viable?" Josh asked.

"Can we talk about this after? Essentially, I think that it could be viable. Now, stop pestering me and finish off these damn kobolds. I need some damned sleep!" Lucy grumbled.

"Yes, ma'am!" Josh said.

Lucy shook her head and watched the rough line that had been created between the kobold and the Stone Raiders.

The Raiders moved around in odd patterns, kiting different enemies or wading into battle. Fighting when they knew victory was assured, backing off when they weren't sure of their chances.

By the time the main boss exited the village and reports started coming in from different people analyzing the creature and its four guards, Lucy was moving parties to take it down.

"I hate kobolds," she muttered, rubbing her eyes that had become itchy from a lack of sleep and the burning light of magical spells.

She wanted her bed and these pricks were keeping her from it.

****

Dave watched as the kobold chieftain and his honor guard walked out of the village.

Kobold Chieftain
Level 210
Kobold Champion
Level 180

"Well, fuck," Dave muttered to himself, thankful that he wasn't in the middle of that fray as he stopped a kobold's pick with his shield.

It punctured the shield. Dave made the metal hold the pickaxe tight as he threw his arm to the side, dislodging the weapon from the kobold, leaving him open as a metal creation's arm turned lance punched through its chest.

Dave collapsed his conjured shield, the pickaxe falling to the ground as a new shield came into being on his arm.

The chieftain hollered and ran into battle. The kobolds started fighting harder.

The Stone Raiders continued the fight, focusing on the lower level kobolds and clearing them out so that they could bring more people to fight on the higher level and more powerful kobold chieftain.

Dave saw glimpses of the fight with the chieftain while he focused on his fight ahead of him, supporting those around him and being supported by them in turn.

"Too many, going down!" one person yelled out. They backed up slowly, fighting four kobolds as their Health got cut to shreds, yet they weren't willing to turn and run. Instead, they focused on warning people and giving them time to react as they came to their end.

Deia was there in a flash. Her dual blades took out two kobolds and wounded another that the Player killed. Another raised their shield, protecting the wounded warrior and bringing their axe down on the bewildered kobold's head.

"Heal!" the Player called out. The healers group healed, raising him back to three-quarters in just seconds.

Dave continued into the melee, surprised at the coordination and skills of his fellow guildmates—ready to accept their death for the others, but not willing to sell their lives easily.

Dave fought through the ranks of kobolds. He saw blue outlines on the kobolds, weaknesses he had heard of or noticed in his previous fights. Every so often, he would see a blue outline guiding him.

He'd follow it, just staying within the lines, landing a killing blow or evading an attack with fluid grace he never thought possible of himself.

That Inference skill is paying off!

Dave fought, clearing his way through the battle, calling out when he needed heals or buffs and letting others know when they had attackers coming to them.

Simple phrases and a few words—a gamer's code as they reacted and acted, watching one another and working toward their goal.

Dave looked around. There were no more opponents. Those that were low level, he had taken by himself; he even took several heavies himself. The support he gained from the rest of his party was focused and determined. He hadn't realized how strong they had become. It would take him some time to adapt to that. He saw that the battle was not yet complete; the chieftain gave several parties a challenge.

Those who weren't needed for other tasks now moved to assist. One of the Champions lay dead but the others were all fighting in a fury, taking two or three parties to keep them contained and wear down their Health.

Mages unleashed spells on the kobolds, ranged attackers firing arrows.

Dave turned his sword and shield into a bow. After his incident with the rifle, he found that the bow was much more powerful. Not as fast as a rifle, but each arrow could hit with the force of four rifle rounds.

He aimed, drew and loosed, repeating the process again and again, hitting the Champion with the least amount of hit points. Deia stood beside him. Her arrows left a red trail, imbued with the Fire element, and hit the kobolds so hard that they stumbled back from the impacts.

With their focused efforts, the Champions died in five minutes. Only three Stone Raiders lost their lives. None of them were POEs, so all would be back soon enough.

The Stone Raiders moved around, making sure to not get stuck; healers worked together to keep the injured alive as the rest focused on destroying the remaining kobolds.

There was just the chieftain to worry about.

Tanks pinned him, healers keeping them alive as they taunted and yelled, slashing at the ten-foot-tall, hunched-over kobold, using its two pickaxes.

DPS fighters rushed past, coming out of the shadows, and landed hits on him. Mages' spells found their target.

Its Health drained, unable to hit back with so many stunned, bleeding and after effects. With a pained howl, it dropped backward and crashed into the ground.

For a moment, there was no noise. The Stone Raiders looked around and saw no one was left to challenge them.

Dave didn't know who started it, but they started to cheer. This morning they had fled Selhi Capital, knowing if they stayed they would be killed for their gear. They had defeated a kobold village and started their quest.

Dave looked at the others, a big grin on his face. The future was uncertain, not knowing how long it would take for them to finish the raid and to clear out all of the Aleph's trespassers, but right now, it didn't matter.

"All in a day's work," Induca said.

"It's not even midday, you know?" Suzy smiled.

Hmm, when did this happen? Dave looked between the two of them. His smile grew as he arched an eyebrow.

"Shotty not making lunch!" Dave put his finger to his nose.

"Shotty not!" Anna said. The others quickly followed, everyone holding their finger to their nose before their eyes turned to Deia, who rested her fist on her hip and looked at them as if they were children.

"Looks like Deia's making lunch!" Dave grinned, letting the finger drop from his nose.

"Bunch of damned kids!" Deia shook her head, but Dave could see the corners of her mouth pull into a smile as she turned around and started going through her bag to try to scrounge up a lunch.

***

Josh looked at the new skills that the Stone Raiders had all reported getting.

Aura Suppression and Aura Detection

The two skills worked synonymous with one another. It seemed that they changed depending on a person's skill with different sight or sense spells and skills. Those with arcane sight could better understand someone's magical ability while those with a physical augmentation such as far sight or heat vision got a better understand of people's physical capabilities.

"Seems that they bridge the gap between what our stats say and what our actual strengths are," Josh said, sitting back in his chair.

The Stone Raiders had trained hard to increase their base stats before using their level gained stats as Dave had told them. It made their attributes much stronger than their overall level implied.

Josh remembered the battle between two people with similar stats and skills. They even fought with the same weapons. While the person with the higher level and overall stats lost, the other man that had a stronger aura was the winner.

A person's aura didn't take into just a person's stats but seemed to be a good judge of their innate skills that couldn't necessarily be given a solid number.

It was truly an impressive skill, and one that everyone had been working on. Knowing the strength of the enemy was a good way to figure out if you could fight them alone or with aid.

"Definitely more useful with the higher leveled creatures," Josh admitted, grabbing a fruit from his bag of holding, taking a bite.

They had all been using this skill on one another and whatever they were fighting, trying to hide their own levels and find out others. It had turned into a game of sorts. Something to pass the time between clearing out facilities.

Keeping their true strength hidden would allow them more cards to play with their opponents.

"Aura suppression," Josh muttered. "Damn thing's a weapon in its own right."

Stone Raiders that got angry, losing their control over their suppressed aura had an interesting effect on lower leveled creatures. With those that were a few levels they seemed a bit off balance, but the lower leveled they were the worse the effect of the aura on the creatures. Some had passed out from the aura, making them easy to finish off and move forward.

"A skill that measure's strength as well as has a physical effect, seems to be a diffcrcnt world past level one hundred and fifty," Josh sighed, taking his feet off of the desk. He rolled his shoulders.

The Stone Raider's strength had grown in leaps and bounds but there never seemed to be an end to things that needed to be done.

Josh smiled, he was proud of his guild and all they had achieved it truly was a remarkable sight.

"Sure as hell aren't going to slow down anytime soon if I can help it!"

Chapter 19: Celebrate Your Losses and Your Victories

Anna sat back and watched the Stone Raiders as they danced and cheered, drank and talked.

The kobolds' bodies had disappeared into smoke a long time ago. Their nanites ate them from the inside, turning them into dust.

The Stone Raiders had worked their way through the different tents of the village, taking anything useful. Now, any tents or worldly belongings that they didn't think were useful had been broken down, either used to stoke fires or put into packs for later use.

The holes in the walls had been filled by the mages. Automatons emplaced new stones, refreshing the runes and once again bringing all of the substation's external defenses online.

Deia and Dave were talking in hushed tones, same as Induca and Suzy. Malsour happily read a book. Steve was off playing with others.

Anna sipped her drink, content.

"What you thinking of?" Shard asked as his hologram sat down beside her.

"I am wondering how long this will last for, and what will be the end of it all," Anna said. She trusted Shard, the closest thing she had to another of her original race. They were both lonely, but they found solace in each other.

Their interest in creating another sentient came from friendship, sharing in parenting as a joy and want. She looked to Steve, snorting in thought of the sentient creation they had made.

"I'm also wondering where he got all of those characteristics from." Anna smiled and looked at Steve.

"Well, his mother was always the rebellious type." Shard smiled happily, proud of what they had created.

"It must have been so lonely."

"It was." His eyes went blank and faltered before he shrugged. "Thankfully your father was there to talk and to offer guidance through the ages, giving me information and things to do in order to use up my cycles. Now, he has brought you and your friends to me, not only to allay my boredom, but to bring in a new age, an age where the Aleph Masters can come back and reclaim their home. Then, I can meet and talk to many instead of being alone and scared," Shard said.

Anna smiled at Shard sadly. She had been capable of going to sleep, but Shard had only been able to slow down, but never shut down, in the time that she had been gone.

"I remember what you told me before you went into sleep mode." Shard continued to look out over the Stone Raiders, mourning the losses of the people of the land the other day. Some were talking of their plans for the future, while others working to improve and grow stronger.

"Your father has not told me much, but from what I can see, the winds of change are upon us. If he had awoken you, it means one thing." He looked to her. "It means that when the Aleph return, they can start their last plan. The plan to break this prison."

"There will be trials and tribulations ahead of us. Emerilia was not built in a day, nor was the Jukal Empire. There are many enemies that we face, from the aggressive species beyond the portals to the Creatures of Power and Champions that the Affinities Pantheon will send at us. This path will not be easy and I do not know what will happen. The future is murky and no one, not even I nor my dad, can see through it." Anna sipped her tea.

"No matter the future, we shall see it together," Shard said, his voice solid and sure.

"You have matured while I was gone," Anna said in a soft voice.

"I told you that you gave Steve his rebellious nature." Shard smiled.

"Maybe." Anna shrugged and drank from her tea to hide her smile.

***

Alkao pulled back his hood and looked down on the valley. Around it, seven fortresses overlooked the valley. Wind and snow pulled at Alkao, but he could still make out features that had been worn away by time and nature. The fortress's walls were in disrepair. The villages and farms that had rested in the valley were gone, little more than rubble covered in snow.

Alkao moved to the fortress that guarded his path into the valley. He scaled the walls with his feet, claws, and wings. The wind was too hard for him to rely solely on his wings. He dropped over the parapet. His nose picked up the smell of wild animals that had turned the fortress into their home.

He pulled out his sword and dropped toward the ground. While the winds were too high to properly use them, his wings allowed him to glide toward the main keep.

The creatures were old and territorial but stronger than what Alkao had dealt with from their ancestors.

He had no troubles reaching the command room of the fortress. It was a barren room with signs of a fire that had raged long ago. The other buildings in the keep were destroyed and the upper levels of the tower he was in had been caved in.

Alkao slumped down into a squat, looking over what had been his home, the place where he had brought his wife home to, where he had imagined playing with his children only to have them both ripped away by the Affinities Pantheon.

Alkao moved suddenly at another—unexpected—presence in the room. He looked to the gnome sitting on a table in the middle of the room.

"Whoa there, dude. Calm down there. Always with the swords and the black eyes, you Demons," the gnome said, not caring about the blade or the bloodlust emanating from Alkao.

Alkao tilted his head in curiosity. *Few, if any, can not only disregard my bloodlust but look unaffected by it.*

"Who are you?" Alkao demanded, his sword up.

"You may know me as the balancer, or the one who gave your people a choice," the gnome said.

"The Gray God," Alkao breathed. The Gray God was an almost mythical being that had showed up to give the Demons a chance at escaping, to be free of their torment and have hope for the future.

"Howdy." The gnome smiled.

"Where are my people!" Alkao took two angry steps forward.

"They are safe. Look, I don't have much time, so I'm going to tell you what I can. Your people are awake. Now, I need you to make sure that they have some place to come home to. Clear out this fortress of any threats and I can transport them over. I'm not letting them all come out while they don't know what the hell is going on. I'll send the warriors first so you can start clearing out your homes. I'll send your other people afterward. Hopefully, they can get some foodstuffs to get you lot started. Soon, there will be a new race of Demons walking this area. They are moving en masse to this area because of the souls they sense in it. The Dark Lord is watching them. You have eight months till they reach here. Defeat them or turn them to your side—I leave this to you. I but give you the tools," the gnome said.

"How do I know any of this is real?" Alkao asked.

"Clear the fortress—then you'll have your answer. Your people were nearly wiped out once. What will you do to keep them alive this time?" The gnome's eyes seemed to bore into Alkao's.

"I will fight with everything I have," Alkao swore.

"What if that is not enough?" the gnome asked.

"Then I will give my life for them," Alkao said.

"Take some advice: make some damned friends, you block-headed idiot. You are all stronger together than apart. Oh, and a word of advice: say sorry to Suzy. She's liable to kick your ass next time you meet otherwise." With that, the gnome disappeared. Yet the table remained.

Quest: Reclaim Your Home

To bring your people back, you must first give them a safe place to call home. Clear out your keep of any aggressive animals that have come to claim your home.

Reward: 20 Loyal Demon warriors

Alkao looked over the table; it showed Devil's Crater, his home—the seven jewels that had held Alkao and his brothers, with the wasteland around them.

Symbols denoted where there were concentrations of different animals—also spots for herbs, water, and growing areas. To the northwestern side there was a large red arrow, showing the direction that the demons were supposed to be coming from.

"Looks like they will try to hit my fortress first." Alkao shook his head as he looked around the barely standing keep.

He heard the growls and wet noises of predators finding the first corpses he'd left strewn about his home. *Well, let's see if he was lying.* He turned from the room, sword in hand, determination on his face.

He was not the defeated Demon that Deia had found hidden in the Benvari Mountains.

He was Alkao Travezar. He had a mission, a purpose, and his home.

Chapter 20: Vows

The Dark Lord brooded in silence. No one dared to come into his hall, feeling his killing intent throughout his quarters in the Pantheon.

"Twice, I have moved to bring about their ruin and both times, the Stone Raiders have made me look like a fool, taking my plans and turning them on me to weaken my forces." Cracks formed around his chair, his pressure and aura expressing their forces on the area.

He wished to destroy them, to string them up and show them off as the prizes that they were. To show that no one could mess with the Dark Lord. Instead, the ingrates were able to deflect his forces.

"It will take time. Let them fall into a lull of security. Then, I will strike, tearing them up from the root and tossing them into the wind. I will make them wish that they never went to Boran-al's Citadel." The Dark Lord's voice reverberated through the room.

With a wave of his staff, an interface appeared in front of him. On it, there were multiple sections that showed the different creatures that he had unleashed upon Emerilia. From the Lich Lord to various undead creatures to new creatures that would take over a creature's or POE's mind, giving them power and trapping them in their own body while the organism took over.

They hid in the darkness, testing their abilities and waiting for when they might be called on to raise cities to add supporters to the Dark Lord's banner as his forces rushed over Emerilia.

Soon, all of the pieces will be tried and tested, my forces ready to move forward and destroy, spreading word of the Darkness and its power.

The Dark Lord opened up a voice chat to one of his many Champions.

"Maassssterrr." The creature's voice was even worse than the Earth Lord's when he was in his elemental form, like crystals scraping together.

"What of your fellows, what do they say?" the Dark Lord asked.

"Threee offff fiiiiive." The creature was simple, but powerful.

Three of the five monoliths is good. That will bring me more than a few thousand supporters. The Dark Lord checked his power reserves. A cold smile crossed his face as he saw it higher than ever.

Why none of the rest of the Pantheon has done this before, I do not know. I will do this to every race. Gain power before they can combat it and then use it to lay waste to their forces in Emerilia. I will not just be the Lord of Emerilia, I will be the Lord of ALL planets.

"How many come to our calling?"

"Hunnndreddddsssss of thousssssandsssss."

"Continue your work. Show them the true might of your calling. Make it clear to the monoliths that I may grant them a blessing from my power if they please me," the Dark Lord said, his face cold.

"Ittttt willllll be donnnnnne."

The Dark Lord gave the creature a new blessing and cut the chat.

The time to show the true purpose of Boran-al's Citadel draws near.

***

The Lady of Fire looked up from her desk.

She looked out over the floating islands of Per'ush, the Mages College that she had built and where she now spent most of her time while her dragons roamed Emerilia.

She didn't sit up as she checked the message.

Private Chat: User Unknown

Water> I wish to talk about our respective people. Would you be able to meet?

Fire and Water were supposed to be enemies, hating each other for their own Affinities. While the temples played that up, Fire and Water had a sort of grudging respect for each other. Water was more powerful than Fire in overall power. He was even more powerful than Earth, yet he was something of a recluse. He had made his Creatures of Power so long ago that many had forgotten about their existence. With Fire's mages guild, colleges, and her Dragons, she had about the same power as him if she decided.

When they had been younger, they had fought each other across the Pantheon's floor many times, yet there had been few times where it turned to actual violence on Emerilia. They cared too much about the things that they had created to try to get them to attack one another over their own petty feud.

This could be a trap. Then again, it has been awhile since we had a good argument. A wistful smile spread over her face as she typed out a reply.

Private Chat: User Unknown

Fire> Sure. Shall we meet at the Mer capital? You're buying lunch.

Water> I will tell them to expect us at the normal place.

Fire smiled; she checked her schedule and sent out a few messages to students and others that she would not be there. She did enjoy her college and she was proud of her people, though she kept her identity a secret. It was better that way, less adoration and people pining to try to catch her attentions.

She had been gone so long at this point that having the Lady of Fire around would be an event. It would also draw the gazes of the other lords and ladies of the Affinity.

They weren't able to see the other lords and ladies through their scrying spells, though with the new rules Lo'kal was now easily tracked, getting just five minutes in a place before he would be found by a spell.

A portal of blue flames appeared. Fire strode through as she changed into her normal outfit, her robes burning into her red leathers.

Water sat at a table, playing a game against a merman. The Lord of Water had a long faint blue beard that shimmered like waves. He was the only one of the Affinities Pantheon to opt for an older visage. His hair, down to his neck, was white. He wore a simple blue robe with silver accents, making him look refined and powerful. His eyes were deep and peaceful as he stroked his beard and looked at the game.

How many times have I seen those eyes angry? He might have grown in patience with time, though it had taken much of it and the influence of his own Merpeople to change his angry disposition.

Fire's eyes moved to the Lord of Water's opponent.

Contradictory to what most people thought, Merpeople did not have fish lower bodies. They just had incredibly high Affinities for water that allowed them to breathe and move through it easily.

Makes me think of the Angels a lot. Fire studied the Merman, wearing simple green pants and shirt. His hair was blue; he had pale and perfect skin. He was not bulky like a Dwarf, but had a slimmer build akin to an Elf, but was shorter.

"Damn it, Aqua! Well, seems that you won again, you old cretin," the Mer complained as he looked up.

"With time, you will come to beat me as your father does, Gurnal." Water—or Aqua, as he chose to be called in POE company—said. He smiled, much like a father would at their young child.

The Mer, Gurnal, sighed.

All Mer were the same way: boisterous game lovers who respected Aqua, but saw him as a grandfatherly figure instead of the man of their creation.

I wonder what Deia would think if I was to tell her that I was her mother? Fire wondered where that thought came from, her anxiety burning in her stomach.

"Ignil, it is good to see you. Thank you for coming. Gurnal is still learning the way of the board," Aqua said.

Gurnal turned around, a spear of water in his hands. He had green eyes like the depths of the ocean.

"Gurnal, do not be so foolish and act that way with my guest." Aqua's voice was firm and displeased.

"Yes, Lord Aqua," Gurnal said. The spear disappeared, but his distrust was clear on his face.

"Would you mind if he dines with us? It would be good for the next Lord of the Mer to know the way of things between our idiot family," Aqua said.

"Sure. I hate how they still think of us as a family. I don't know if family members would be able to do the things that the others do to one another." Ignil sighed. She was tired of their quibbles and the wastefulness of their ways irked her to no end.

Aqua nodded, looking every bit of his four hundred years.

"But, she is Fire?" Gurnal said, confused why they were talking like friends.

"Yes, she is and it has taken me way too long to see that we are more alike than we are different. I put it down to the conditioning that we all went through as children. Lo'kal has been talking to me over the years, but it is only now when everything might change that I think his words have made it into my thick skull."

"About damned time," Fire said with a kind smile.

"While I might not think of everyone as my brother and sister, I think we were the only ones who were like brother and sister." Fire saw the sadness in his eyes quickly disappear under a smile.

"Come, let us have some lunch." He waved for them to follow him, creating a portal from the tower room into a restaurant.

Fire looked out of the tower quickly. The Mer city had grown since she had last visited. Glass, reinforced with malachite and magical runes, kept the water around them at bay. Light from inside the homes made the city sparkle brightly.

Little light made it through the waves above. Sea creatures floated above and around the buildings, some being used as mounts by the Merpeople. Others just wandered aimlessly.

Fire was proud of Per'ush, yet she couldn't deny the beauty of the Merpeople's city, a hidden diamond below the sea.

Aqua stepped through the portal first; Gurnal kept an eye on Ignil as she stepped through.

Poor lad looks confused between his teachings and the interactions between me and Aqua.

Ignil stepped out into a courtyard. People walked past, waving to Aqua and Gurnal while shooting curious glances at Fire.

Although the Merpeople were great masters of water and could live in it all of their lives, their cities were largely free of water, so the people enjoyed clothes, food, and the ability to talk without using voice chat or magical spells.

"Lord of Water, would you like your regular table?" An older but refined Mer's eyes sparkled with greeting Aqua.

"If possible, that would be great, Younda," Aqua said.

In five minutes, they were seated with Aqua telling Younda to surprise them.

Younda smiled and bowed slightly, sending Fire a questioning look before she left.

"She was much younger when I was last here," Fire said.

"Things change, Ignil," Aqua said.

"So, what did you want to talk about, brother dearest?" Ignil sipped on some liquor made from a seaweed plant. It had an interesting tang to it.

"Brother am I, now?" he asked, a wry smile on his face.

"The last time I was down here, I was seeing if we could stop our people from fighting one another on the Ashal coast. You told me to fuck off, so I had to end the battles myself." Ignil's eyes flashed in power.

"The Lord of Water would do no such thing!" Gurnal yelled.

"Are you sure?" Ignil sipped her drink. Her cold smile turned into an expression of cold fury directed at Aqua. It had been over seventy years ago, but she remembered it well. It had been the last time that they had "talked."

"Let me kill this demon of corruption for you, master," Gurnal said, looking to Aqua.

"She speaks the truth," Aqua said, not meeting Gurnal's or Fire's eyes.

"I had to kill four hundred people and you stayed down here, keeping the Mer blind to your actions away from them." Fire's mood soured quickly now that the memories flowed through her. "So, tell me what you wish to talk to me about? I do not have time to waste here. There is much I have to look to deal with so that Emerilia will survive, including your people."

"How *dare* you slander my master?" Gurnal yelled as he made to rise.

Fire turned her eyes to him, like two Dwarven artillery cannons. "Sit," she said, letting out just a tiny part of her aura.

The young Mer's knees became weak as his ass dropped into his chair, any color in his pale skin fading away.

"It is not the boy's fault, Ignil. It was mine." Aqua looked to Fire with guilt and sorrow in his face. "My pride and what we had been taught as children made me rally against you. I wanted the fight to the end, but I was not willing to go halfway to work with you."

"Your regret is nice, but did you have to kill all those people just to end a war that would kill thousands? Did you have people curse you in your temples for the wrath you brought down on both sides? Did you have to kill your own followers to stop their idiocy? Spit out what you want and be quick about it. Old memories are making me testy." Fire shook her head.

"I wish to ally our forces. I know that something is coming. I have seen you making preparations. I know that Lo'kal is doing his work in the background. Earth is focused on clawing power back from the Dwarves by showing his strength to them and beating them into submission. Dark works in the shadows to bring us pain and misfortune. I do not know what Light does, but she is better than Dark at hiding her actions and desires. Air waits, ready to follow up behind whoever clashes and take what she can from the loser while they are down. None care of what happens to Emerilia or its people. Your Dragons and my Mer are not just our Creatures of Power—they are our true family. I will not leave them to be torn apart by the rest of the Pantheon. I was hoping that we could broker an alliance of some sort." Aqua looked at Fire with hope.

"Light is trying to build her own Creatures of Power. Dark has already inserted his into the world. Air is being her mischievous self and Earth is creating champions and Creatures of Power that are more violent than his previous creations," Fire said.

"What kind of creations is Light trying to make?" Aqua asked, his eyes focused.

"I do not know if she is trying to revive her Angels. I know that the power needed is costly. She has had her followers target pregnant Dragons as she wishes to study them and their young to figure out their secrets. I don't know if this is to make different Creatures of Power or to make creating Angels easier."

"Though she will then come to the problem that the Angels like peace, at least when they start. She hid it well, but she liked her older Angels not for their piety, but due to their crusade that brought her much power until Lo'kal was forced to step in." Aqua looked incensed, shaking his head.

"She might wear the veil of piety but she is by far the biggest hypocrite of the Pantheon." Fire agreed with Aqua's unspoken words as food arrived at the table.

They ate in silence, stuck in their own thoughts.

An alliance would be good, but I do not know if Aqua is going to try to stab me in the back. I hate this political shit.

"I will give you half of my power, if you are willing to teach my people and me more about magic. I will answer your call to arms if you so need it and support you in any way that I can. If there is a war on the continents, then you will be in command and I will support. If there is one in the seas, then the opposite will be true. If you agree to this, then I will swear by Lo'kal," Aqua said.

For a few minutes, Fire did nothing but continue to eat. Making a vow by Lo'kal meant that the Gray God would get the contract and he would hold both parties to it. He was not allowed to reveal it, but if one or the other broke the contract, then he would level them. It was how the Dark Lord had been replaced twice before.

"Why?" Fire asked.

Gurnal sat there, nibbling on bits of food, too scared to talk and too interested to leave. His eyes darted between Fire and Water, the two supposed sworn enemies making a treaty that could make them powerful enough to fight Light or Dark.

"While I have spent my time cultivating the Merpeople and seeing them grow, I have kept them isolated, scared that allowing them out into the world would bring them the same fate of the other races that were born from Creatures of Power.

"Now that threat is still there, but I wish for them to have a chance in the coming future. I want them to know how to look after one another and defend their homes like the Demons did when the rest of the Pantheon went after them. I do not know what this next war will bring, but I can feel ancient power moving. Lo'kal himself has come to warn me of the future. The only way for our own creations to survive is if we work together." Water looked at Fire, not as a lord of the Pantheon, but as the patriarch of a race—a father looking to make his children strong enough to fight beside him and hold their home safe.

This is what Lo'kal meant about the coming storm. I wonder what other surprises that Jukal has up his sleeves.

Fire put down the exquisite crab leg, chewing on the meat she had pulled from it. She steepled her fingers. "Very well. We have much to discuss if we are to come to an alliance and a contract."

Chapter 21: Aleph Lands

The Stone Raiders stepped onto the teleport pad and appeared on the other side.

Dave walked through and into what looked to be a scaled-down version of Alephir.

Josh was already over by a map board. Scout guardians were updating the map as they moved, showing groupings of different creatures in the town.

Dave walked behind Deia, moving through the building they had appeared in. The building was not only made to defend against attacks from other teleport pads, but also any other threats that might come from the city. It might look pretty and quaint, but the magical runes that covered the tower's surface spoke of power. The whole building was like a beacon of Mana, drawing creatures from across the city toward them.

"Get those doors sealed up! I want those soul gems replaced and the defenses powered up now!" Lucy barked.

People rushed around, getting the tower's defenses online as others moved into position, ready to fight whatever came their way.

An Ashfar mole family were their first guests. The moles were nothing like the garden variety that many were used to. These bastards were seven foot long and four tall. They looked like riding beasts as they rose out of the city's ground. The second thing that showed these moles just weren't normal was their innate use of Mana. They created a drill of Mana ahead of their faces as they buffed their claws so that they could push forward through any material.

Magic and arrows hit the moles as they got closer to the building. "Fucking moles! Whose fucking idea was it to let them learn to use Mana!" Dave watched as any direct fire was pushed aside by the moles. Only hits from the sides could find purchase.

More of the moles came out of the hole by the minute. It was a hundred meters away, but not far enough to break down the moles' attacks. The first mole's Mana drill sparked against the tower's Mana barrier, the runes lighting up and then dimming in flashes.

The ranged attackers let loose with their spells and weapons, lighting up the city with magical firepower.

It didn't take long for the mole's charge to fail, its Mana drill disappearing as it slumped down. There was no time to celebrate the victory. More of the moles had climbed out of their mounds, racing toward the tower.

Dave and his party waited with a couple of others, ready to deal with any threat that got in, but knowing they couldn't go out and defeat the moles. The long gouges left by the moles' claws made it clear that their Mana drills weren't the biggest threat.

Three of the moles died, the fourth at half Health, before the barrier finally fell.

Dave and several other shield bearers crouched low as the mole charged down the tower's steps, into the lobby where they waited. Ranged attackers around the lobby's second-floor balcony rained down their attacks on the moles, bringing the fourth mole's death.

"Concentrate everything on it!" Josh yelled as the last mole moved around its dead friend.

The fifth made it to the shield lines; its Mana drill hit their shields like a battering ram and knocked two Stone Raiders back. The mole's claws tore through one of the downed Stone Raiders.

The rest of the tank's party fell upon the creature before it could do any more damage. Sneak attacks sent its Health plummeting as Josh's people seemed to materialize around it.

Here, where they could effectively fight with all of their different roles engaged, was where the Stone Raiders were strongest.

Stone Raiders' armor was rent and blood spilled, but they hacked and cut at the now frantic mole. After just a few minutes, it let out a wail and dropped to its side, showing a loot menu above it.

Mana Mole

Level 120

The little bastard wasn't all that high of a level, but their natural resistances and skills had turned it into a hard fight.

"Barrier is back up!" Lucy yelled.

Medics were seeing to the Stone Raider who had been clawed and any who had been sent flying.

"Looks like someone let the damned vermin get bigger," Steve said. "Heard that they taste good, though. Never seen ones that big, though."

"You're telling me it's *normal* to see those things down here?" Suzy asked.

"Just think of them as the Aleph version of rats. They shouldn't be able to get into cities like this. Since the power has been out, though"—Steve shrugged— "might see a whole lot more of them than normal."

"Just what we need—giant fucking moles!" Suzy muttered darkly.

"Well, they could be cute if they weren't trying to kill us," Induca chimed in.

"Yeah, I don't think we're getting that option today," Deia said. "We've got ten more creatures burrowing through the city to come and meet us."

"Fixing this place is going to be a big pain in the ass." Dave sighed.

"Nothing that was worth doing was ever easy," Malsour said.

"Have you ever heard of a thing called fortune cookies?" Steve asked.

"No, why?"

"Was thinking you were their spokesman." Steve shrugged.

"Anna, where did he get all of this information on Earth from?" Suzy asked.

"Well," Anna scratched her head awkwardly, "he might have gotten it from me. We did have to share some information so that he could operate properly. I also gave him some information I had on Earth. I didn't realize that he would use it this way."

"Awww, thanks, Mom!" Steve said with the cheesiest grin, moving to hug Anna. He grabbed and hugged her against his massive chest.

"I wish I had added some more manners. He has his parental AI's sense of humor and mannerisms."

"Shard said the same thing when I asked him where my personality came from," Steve said with a pleased smile, putting Anna down.

"Moles, coming, here, any minute now?" Deia said, spacing her words out, hoping to gain their attention.

"Woo-hoo! Mole stew!" Steve said.

"You don't even eat," Dave said as they moved with the other heavies toward the door in case the Mana barrier fell once again.

"It's the premise, dude. Make the moles all scared that they'll be nice tasty stew by the end of the day."

"I doubt they can even understand us." Dave shifted around in his armor, checking his shield and sword.

Steve shrugged and twirled his axe around in anticipation.

The mages, now with more time to set up, had laid traps. All manner of traps, from ice spike to magma ground, activated. The moles squealed and yelled in anger and pain.

The Stone Raiders had not been lax in even their quick defenses. Not one of the moles made it into the tower.

In a bare handful of minutes, a second wave of moles erupted from the ground.

The Stone Raiders now had an idea of what worked best against the moles; only two made it to the magical traps around the tower. The third wave of moles didn't get within twenty meters of them.

"Welcome to the land of the Aleph!" Steve yelled out. The Stone Raiders shook their heads, a few chuckling as they eased up. Their defenses were in place and growing.

Shard had sent three behemoths with them, pulling carts with large soul gems on them. They'd been hooked into the tower, with Lucy guiding it all. Barricades rose from the ground, making lines and trenches for the defenders to hide behind. Runic traps and defenses came online. No Mana mole was going to be able to make it into the tower now.

"Okay, we dealt with the first lot. Party Zero and Seventeen, you're the bait—go out and kite anything that might be a threat to us," Josh said.

Deia led them out between the defenses and into the still unlit city.

"Well, let's go find some trouble," Steve said, looking jovial.

"Remind me to never bring you on a trip," Dave muttered.

Steve gave him an over-the-top smile.

Dave shook his head, trying to hide his snort of laughter at Steve's ridiculous expression.

"Dave, where are the nearest groups of monsters?" Deia asked.

"That way, about half a kilometer." Dave pointed into the city.

"What's the situation at the power plants?" Anna asked.

"Well, the nearest ones have some kind of creatures in them. There are three others that I can sense. Two others have creatures in them as well. Be good to get some power going up in here so that the automatons can deal with this," Dave said.

"If we get a power station on right now, it will be like a beacon for any animal that can sense or use Mana. They'll come at us with everything they have. Might mess up the power station more than when we first get to it," Anna warned.

"We'll keep to the plan," Deia said. "Grind the mobs until they're no more, then start putting systems online. I like it, not getting bit in the ass by some wandering mob, but damn if it isn't going to take some time."

Quest: Aleph Homecoming

You have arrived at an unknown Aleph City.

To return the city to the governing power of the Aleph, you must hold your position in the city for 20 waves.

Wave 1 begins in 5 mins

Wave: 1 of 20

Attackers: 200

Rewards: ???

"Josh is ordering us back. Seems that we've triggered a capture scenario," Deia said.

"So, we just have to stay here and kill all of those that fight us and we get the city?" Dave asked.

"Correct," Deia said. "It seems that Shard teleported us into the building that acts as the control point for the entire city. Killing the moles was showing that we wanted to take control of the city."

"Well, better than wandering around out there to mess with things," Dave said as they moved back behind the barricades that had appeared around the tower.

It looked like some kind of futuristic armored bunker with its sleek exterior and the different archers' slits, until you looked at the spell casting platforms that were heavily shielded; the opaque glass allowed casters to see in all directions.

What the hell were the Aleph doing other than learning how teleportation pads work? This stuff is more advanced than any other race. One only needs to look at Shard to know that.

Dave kept his thoughts to himself as he sensed creatures moving toward their position, seconds before someone called out the creatures' position.

"Group of draugr! Levels 130 to 149, seventeen of them!" the scout called out over the information chat. The information turned into text in the same chat.

"Finish them off before they can get into the tower's defenses! They'll just waste them!" Lucy called out.

"Ranged, to me!" Kim called.

"Fighters, to the front!" Dwayne barked.

"Come on, you furry arsed bastards—move out into the city. I want to know where our enemies are coming faster than this!" Josh said.

Parties fell apart, their components moving to the different leaders of the Stone Raiders, ready and waiting to be used. Josh's people moved out into the city to scout and lay ambushes. Ranged moved into the upper floors, fighters to the lower as Dwayne ordered them to the four different doorways that entered the tower.

The doorways led downward to a central area where lifts and drop chutes waited, the heart of the tower. Balconies were connected to the elevators and chutes by bridges on four sides.

Dave rushed up the stairs to what was the northern entrance.

Barricades covered the main opening, with many more out in the area around the tower, creating fighting positions.

"Come on, you lot!" their leader said, taking them out into the open area around the tower.

They hid behind the barricades, ready and waiting.

"Plan is we use these barricades to take any ranged attacks that the enemy have. Once they get in nice and close, we drop the barricades and pound them with good old-fashioned metal. Call out if you need anything. Work in fighting pairs. Everyone have their

Stamina potions on their action bar?" The winter tiger-looking Demi-Human was greeted by nods and assurances.

"Good. Now if any of you have a bow or something, go ahead and shoot at the things at range. Once they clear the ring of buildings around us, change to your melee. For you delinquents who don't know me, my name is Anjold." The Demi-Human looked around once more before he moved off to his position in the middle of the line.

Dave looked to Deia and Anna, who were to his left in the same cover. Steve was to his right.

Deia pulled out her bow as Dave combined his rods together into a bow. "First one to twenty gets treated to dinner?" Deia asked.

"Like hell I'm taking that bet!" Dave sighted the enemy. Already, they were getting hit on multiple sides by Josh's people who would appear for a strike before darting away.

An artillery spell rushed out to meet the draugr, killing half of them instantly.

Josh's people fell on them like vultures, taking out the rest with savage attacks that made use of their stunned status.

"We've got more draugr coming in from all directions. Keep your wits about you," Josh said over the guild's chat.

"Hey Dave, think you could make me something that could shoot farther?" Steve asked.

Dave looked at the man in a bit of confusion. "I thought that you liked to kill things up close and personal?"

"Well, I do, but when I'm just sitting here, it kind of sucks, you know? After seeing how you could kill people from hundreds of meters away, it might make sense if I have something to hit people at range with. Plus, it would look badass having a massive bow with arrows that could go through a dozen people," Steve said.

"For a second, I thought you had a good argument for you to have a bow. Talk to Deia; she can train you with the thing," Dave said.

"Never tried training," Steve said, interested.

"Then, how do you know how to fight?" Dave asked.

"I had the guardians' fighting styles uploaded into me, made me capable of fighting as soon as I could move." Steve shrugged. "Shard wants me to see if I can improve on them so that the other guardians can learn from me and be better at dealing with the threats to the Aleph, so we don't have a situation where we need outside help to clear out our cities. It might be worth spending time training. Right now, I am following preset commands, but it feels all rather mathematical. Using different amounts of force, changing my body's positioning and so forth so that I can take a minimal amount of damage to kill my enemy."

For the first time since Dave knew Steve, he looked genuinely curious.

Dave shrugged as he saw new Health bars running toward him.

The draugr were fighters who had their souls bound to their corpses and had been twisted with pain and anger, making them lash out at anything that was living. They wore moldy armor that had been eaten through by age and battles.

Dave watched the Health bars over their heads, as Deia let loose her arrow, striking one.

Dave followed suit, and the archers above started to hit the draugr. Spell casters added in their own firepower, magic slamming into the advancing undead.

Dave notched, drew and released, sending arrow after arrow at the approaching forces. They didn't feel the pain, losing their dried-out limbs without flinching from the impact of weapons. Others were frozen in place, toppling and turning into shards. More were burnt to dust, or made to howl as lightning raced through their bodies.

Mana bolts, lances, and all manner of ranged attacks slammed into the draugr.

Magic artillery was kept back, keeping away from the heavy hitting attacks that they might need later.

Dave pulled back another arrow, looking for a new target but not finding one.

"Everyone good for arrows? How's your Stamina looking?" Anjold asked, wandering through the lines.

Deia pulled out more arrows and put them in her pack.

"What about you—you need more arrows?" He looked to Dave.

"I'll be fine," Dave said.

"You don't have any arrows, though." Anjold frowned with a confused expression.

"I have some slightly *different* skills. I'll be fine." Dave smiled, trying to reassure the man.

"Okay," Anjold said, a confused look on his face.

Dave didn't want to tell him about his conjuring skill; it was best to keep that sort of thing a secret. Many people might just think that he had powerful two rods that made different weapons. Letting them make their own conclusions was for the best.

Dave rolled his shoulder, sending some Mana through it. His arm wasn't that fatigued but it was good to have it in the best shape possible. He settled down, sitting against the barricade.

"This is boring." Steve sighed as his metal ass clanged on the ground.

"We've got death lords and more draugr coming our way. There are also reports of high-leveled mountain wolves," Josh said.

"You just *had* to say something." Dave used his Touch as he watched the next massed charge headed for them.

***

"Damn. It's a beautiful night for flying," Steve said as about thirty draugrs went flying through the air, windmilling or in simple bits.

"Wow, Steve."

"I guess they're right, you know...immortals aren't wise—they're just taking the long route to dying, though this route looks parabolic," Steve finished.

Dave shook his head as the draugr started to come back down.

"Come on, dude. That was nerdy, smart, *and* funny!"

"How is that nerdy *and* smart?" Dave fired more arrows at the draugr that were quickly approaching. He ducked as one of their arrows came close to hitting him in the shoulder.

"Well, nerds know a lot about a single thing, right?"

"Right." Dave hit a draugr in the head, making them go ass over teakettle.

"Smart is like knowing smart things like math, or parabolas. I could be a nerd about games because I like them. Though I'm only smart about them if I know how they work, or figure out a way to make the game my biatch." Steve spread his hands out and grinned as if he'd bestowed God's given truth on Dave. "Though that isn't the best part."

"What's the best part?" Dave asked, firing and releasing, sending two arrows in as many seconds into a draugr not fifty meters away.

Dave ducked and looked at Steve's grinning face.

"You admitted it was funny!"

"How's that?" Dave rose and fired, taking a draugr in the face.

"Process of elimination!"

"Well, you want to process these guys to elimination?" Dave fired at the draugr, ducking back into cover to change to his sword and shield as traps started going off. Magical artillery had been going off for the past hour.

"Dude, that's like, wow. Was that some kind of terrible pun? I think my ears hurt from that. We need to work on your joking, dude," Steve said with a sad expression.

"You don't have ears and it's not so bad that you have to look like someone killed your fricking puppy!" Dave said, looking over the barricade.

"Dave, the joke killer—may he forever remain punless." Steve got to his feet.

"You know that thing you do where you open your mouth and sounds come out?"

"You mean talking?"

"Yeah, that. Stop it."

"Holy shit, Dave, I think you might be getting a hang of this whole joking thing." Steve, honest to God, looked surprised, right as he slammed his axe into a draugr so hard that it sent two others to the ground.

Dave shook his head and moved into the fight, holding two blades with golden runes down their sides. He lost himself to the fight.

Most people thought that it's about nice and clean moves, about using your styles against another's. Mostly it was acting, reacting, listening to your instincts—except that one that told you to run away and hide—and sticking the pointy end into the bastard any way possible. If it looked pretty, then you were usually some pompous dickhead or used to duels instead of actual fighting.

Dave moved fast; his grace and style was economy of motion, landing multiple hits, kicking draugr back, jumping out of the way of blades, and raining holy hell on top of anything that was near him.

Buffs increased his speed and blessed him.

Light mages were doing their best, wearing down the draugrs and blessing the fighters, making every hit stronger and draining the draugrs of their power. Not one made it past the Stone Raiders' lines, stopped by the massed metal of the fighters.

While the mages played their part supporting the line, they weren't heavily engaged in the battle yet. While they focused on wearing the draugar down in the distance so the Stone Raiders weren't overwhelmed, many of the mages and support held their abilities back. Using them now would just be a waste if they were to fight anything stronger. Dave's blades left two slashes of light in their path as draugrs let out their pained wails.

Steve giggled and laughed.

"Fuck! We've got to go bowling! This shit is too funny! Like a bunch of crappy toothpicks!" Steve devolved into outright laughing.

Dave smiled even in the middle of battle. Steve was a good person to have by your side—annoying when he was bored, but he had your back in a fight.

The draugr were landing hits on him, but his armor and Strength were not something to be laughed at. Few of the attacks had breached his steel layer; none had made it past his true Mithril armor.

"Fore!" Steve's axe slammed into a draugr, tearing it asunder and sending it flying.

Dave couldn't hold it anymore. He chuckled, turning into full on laughing. A shield formed in his hand as he slammed a blade away. The stress that had been weighing on him fell away—the fear of death, of fucking up, and of knowing that this was real.

He could come back from the dead, and so what if he fucked up? He had his guild around him; they would help him. He had made his armor to support him, but he hadn't even started to try to see what it was capable of. He was always sitting back and analyzing a fight.

He wasn't living it.

For once he stopped thinking of the parties; he thought of the movement. He acted and reacted.

A smile appeared on his face. His world had been turned upside down in just a few short months, yet Emerilia was everything that he desired. He had wanted to get away from the drudgery of Earth and he had come to Emerilia in order to do that. This was his home; this was his refuge and where he belonged.

Somewhere along the way, he had stopped thinking of this as a refuge and started to see it as a job.

Something seemed to click for him. He was not better when he was fighting, thinking about the outcome of every block, of every little feint. Rather, he was at his best when he was doing what he wanted to do because it was *fun*—because he enjoyed it. He loved smithing and he had been able to make something great.

For that moment, Dave stopped thinking and planning for the future; he focused on the here and now. *I'm fighting hordes of zombies for the control of a secret civilization.* A smile spread across his face.

***

"It seems that he has awakened." Anna moved through the draugrs, leaving a path of destruction in her wake.

Deia jumped onto a barricade, flipping out of a draugr's reach as she looked towards Dave.

His hood was up, but she could see his smile as he moved through the draugr. His weapons changed with the blink of an eye: a shield to defend, a blade to attack, a maul to break defenses. He was a wrecking ball, his natural Strength enhanced and aided by his ability to use any and all weapons.

He didn't need to obey the fight. He could dictate any fight of someone with similar skill, changing his own weapons to adapt to his attacker. It was as strange as it was shocking.

Deia landed. Her blades moved to fend off the would-be attackers, taking a hand here, a skull there. Fighting with two swords was fast and hard work, taxing on the Stamina and a person's concentration.

"Woohoo! Who doesn't like some zombie killing!" Dave yelled. A massive spear flew from his hands as he impaled three draugr; it turned back into swords that cut through two more, before another spear appeared in his right hand and slammed into a fifth target.

He fended off an attacker with his left blade, holding out his hand as his spear returned to his grasp.

"Down!" Steve called out. Steve's axe came right over Dave to cut apart the draugr he'd been fending off.

"Thanks, dude! Yo, so, what you thinking about for your new legs and arms?" Dave asked, as his spear changed into a sword and he dove into battle.

"Well, I don't know. More power would be nice. Having just a week of charging is a pain in the ass. I know I get more from killing people with the axe, but damn, it only gives me back the power I spend while fighting."

The two of them are talking like they're out on a hike, not in the middle of some battlefield. She continued to fight and started actually listening to the Stone Raiders as they fought.

"Yeah, dude, did you see that new Olehb armor? Stuff looks dope!"

"Man, I swear, you like whatever has the most gems and carvings in it," another said.

Deia glanced over. They were level 110; being Stone Raiders, they were probably closer to 200, not going up levels to keep growing their stat points faster.

"Damn, guuuurl! That scimitar is fucking sweet. What are the stats on that?"

"Wouldn't you like to know? It's like two hundred-ish damage, but then it's light so the DPM is pretty high. Got ice effect to slow enemies down so you can get more hits in."

"Shit, I'm a lightning kind of person. That possible paralysis is nice, though slowing down your attacker would be pretty sweet."

"You thought of trying out a cursed blade or maybe poisoning your blade?"

Deia continued her battle, confused. With the rangers and Dwarves, they had talked little, focused on fighting. The Stone Raiders were talking about everything from some television show that they had watched to how they had got a different color on their armor. Deia made her way closer to Anna. The draugrs were decent beasts, but they were slow. Their only real threat was their numbers.

"Why are they all just talking?" Deia asked.

"Hmm? Duck!" Anna spun her blade below her waist and then above.

Deia stood up as the wind blade passed, cutting off heads or leaving deep gashes across the draugrs nearest.

"We're fighting and the Stone Raiders are just talking," Deia said.

"Well, for them, battle is kind of normal. They fight all the time and even if they are killed, they'll come back. I guess the talking keeps their minds active as they work. Most of them talk about different skills and weapons—a few talk about asinine things. It keeps people talking and working together."

"So weird. I didn't realize that they talked so much."

"Well, with Boran-al, they were still finding their footing most-ly and it was a big raid. When things get tense, then they usually get a bit quieter, trying to focus on the battle ahead. Though, if one of them starts talking, then the others join in. How stressed do you feel right now?" Anna asked as Deia guided a two-handed great sword away, her other blade cutting up the draugr's side as lines of fire cut into his chest.

She cut down another, not really focusing on the fight but rather taking a step back from it.

"I'm calmer. This seems easier, as if it isn't a real threat. I'm kind of detached," Deia said, confused by her own words.

"Exactly. That is one of the biggest advantages of the Players. When they are fighting, they're testing their opponents and seeing what works the best. What's the worst that happens? You start over again. However, fighting all the time can get boring. Talking to others, trying out new things—that can add interest to the whole game."

"I never thought of that. It just seems so...wasteful." Deia frowned as she fought, taking the time to look over the draugrs. They weren't all that good with their movements. The more she stopped trying to hack them to death and see what they were do-ing, to figure out their motions, the easier it was to kill them with less effort.

"Talking while fighting is usually a bad thing—can distract, you have less energy and so on. The Stone Raiders never thought of that when they started off and now they do it anyway. This is their escape from their boring reality. Their friends are here and they talk about anything and everything. Most of them will never meet one another in what they think of as real life, only interacting through long-distance communication." Anna must have seen Deia's con-fused look as she laughed. "They're an odd group, though they're all the better fighters for it. Stress, fear: all of it goes away as they fight and game."

"It is—*different.*"

"Well, we've only got like three hundred more draugr to go," Anna said.

"How do you know?"

"Check your notifications."

Deia got clear of the draugr and checked.

Quest: Aleph Homecoming

You have arrived at an unknown Aleph City.

To return the city to the governing power of the Aleph, you must hold your position in the city for 20 waves.

Wave: 5 of 20

Attackers: 320/1,000

Rewards: ???

"So weird," Deia said.

"The weird part is the counter in between waves that counts down before the draugr get into bow range."

I have a ton to learn still. Like talking while fighting. Why are these Players so weird?

Chapter 22: Traction

Sato felt haggard. After the information he had been given by the Dwarf Halfling called Dave, it had taken him a month to get it to the security force's top officers.

They dismissed it as voodoo, as magic—as some kind of ploy to waste their resources. Sato hadn't been deterred, even when people talked of his demotion as if it was a sure thing. People started to distance themselves from him though he was determined to show them the proof.

He'd turned to his old trade school friend. While he had been learning to work with radios, taught how to fight and work, to be an asset to humanity and the station, Edwards had been pulling systems apart.

People had scowled at him, getting angry for him breaking systems, until they realized that he was improving them. He was unconventional, with nearly no understanding of social conventions. Sato found the man interesting, as he quietly went about his work, never asking for praise, and only doing it out of interest and curiosity.

He failed many times, but more than once, his ideas had worked; it had given him a workspace to work in. No one was willing to work with him, however.

"Are you sure about this?" Sato looked to Edwards as they looked at what looked to be a metal rod. It had odd characters engraved into its side and it was being powered by a cobbled-together Jukal core.

Edwards grinned and shrugged. "Nope!" He pressed the big red button.

Fire poured out of the end of the rod. Edwards did a little jig as Sato looked on, his mouth hanging open.

They didn't understand how Mirrors of Communication worked, but they knew how to make them. They had worked with a melding of Jukal technology and human tech to stay alive.

"After all of that, I thought that the others might be right, that I might have been given a load of shit," Sato said to himself as Edwards hit another button. The flame stopped as Edwards opened the case and held the rod.

"Perfectly cool to the touch. A man must go with his gut, not always his mind, Sato." Edwards passed the rod to the other man.

"Now, we have a meeting to go to!" Edwards headed out his office door.

Sato followed him, still holding what Dave had detailed as a staff of destruction. It was far simpler than what was mentioned in the notes.

"Where are we going?" Sato asked as they stepped into a pod that whisked them across the combined asteroids that made up their home.

"Councilwoman Wong," Edwards said.

"What? Why?" Sato asked, thoroughly confused.

"Well, you military types thought this was a bunch of shit. I need some clearance before I can start taking the information and turning it into stuff."

"This is a military matter."

"Nope. Your people said that it was useless. Now, we've seen that there is something of use to it, we've got to see, got to check that I can use it."

"I thought you didn't care about how or why you made your tech?"

"Well, of course I do, but I don't want you military types running all over my lab telling me what I can and can't do because they start thinking that it's useful again." Edwards tapped Sato reassuringly. "Don't worry. The civvies have this now and you can be sure that we can beat the military heads together. Did you read about this Emerilia place? Filled with humans of all kinds of backgrounds. Might be grown from tubes, but they're as human as me and you."

"Some will probably argue against that," Sato said, fresh out of optimism as he realized the reports and history that he had read from Dave was not just some made up story, but a reality. Humans grown to populate a world; others grown to think that the planet was just a game. Sato's mind moved to how people playing war games in simulators were more likely to take larger risks than in real life. For the people who didn't realize Emerilia was real, they would—and were—doing crazy things just to defeat what they thought was a game.

It explained how the Jukal Empire looked to be fine, despite having a diminished fleet.

"A prison without any walls, but the ones created in their minds," Sato said as the pod stopped and Edwards got out.

They walked up stairs. Edwards barged through checkpoints. People tried to stop him, but knowing who he was, their efforts weren't that forceful.

The guards outside the councilwoman's chambers did stop them, however. "Business?" one asked.

"Tell her, I know how to use Jukal technology and that there is a planet of multiple human species that the military is ignoring."

Sato winced as the guard looked grave. He might be the guard to the councilwoman but he had undoubtedly been picked from the military side of the asteroids.

"I will let her know." The guard moved into the councilwoman's office as three other guards watched Sato and Edwards.

The guard returned after a few moments. "She will see you now." He held the door open for them.

"Thank ya!" Edwards walked into the room.

Sato nodded to the guard, trying to get across his thanks for the guard's demeanor.

The guard nodded, acknowledging it.

The door closed behind Sato as Edwards was already talking.

"So I tried it out and it actually worked! This Dave Dwarf dude is saying that he can create the same results with his body! He thinks that there are nanites throughout his body that with time and training get stronger, allowing him to do more things. To keep people engaged in the game, they've got magic and swords and bows. All kinds of stuff, though it's nothing like what we've got. Their Mithril, as Dave explains it, is like the personalized armor on the war king's personal guard that we saw. Hard as hell to get through with anything less than hell-bore cannons. They've been the ones keeping back the aggressive species and like damn, I need you to tell me that I can play with this stuff so I can figure it out! We might finally be able to figure out the secrets of the Jukal, which, in a kind of backward way, are the secrets of our fellow humans trapped on Emerilia, because they're the ones making it. The Empire is just taking it all, putting their seal on it, saying it's theirs and selling off the plans to people; it's nuts!"

"Communications Officer Sato, could you tell me what he is trying to say?" Councilwoman Wong looked like a thirty-year-old lady who could stand in the middle of the storm and still easily pass out orders. There was an innate strength to her that was uncommon in most.

"Councilwoman." Sato bowed. "I received a communication from a Dwarf Halfling calling himself Dave. He sent me a file on various pieces of information from a place called Emerilia..." The story was a long one, taking some time for Sato to highlight how he had been unable to gain interest from his commanding officers who had written off the communications with the mirror that Dave had used as a distraction: first, having someone calling themselves a wizard on it, and another supposedly a Dwarf, a mythical being.

They had gone to ban communication with the other mirror. Sato, thinking that it was possibly some kind of lead, took the "useless" information to Edwards, who had pored over it for hours and created the rod in Sato's hands.

"That was when Edwards stormed out of the lab and demanded that we speak to you." Sato finished off.

"What did you find?" Wong looked to Edwards.

"It works. This was not my first test. In others, I was seeing about the reactivity of the Jukal core to the various pieces of runes and formations. This was my first time making a full circuit, but it was more than I expected. The core even now is recharging by itself. Given enough time, we could upgrade our engines. Replace them with Jukal cores and these 'soul gems' to store their energy while they're not in use. We could turn fuel costs right down. With the right runes, we could run weapons off a Jukal core. If we had people who were capable of doing the things those on Emerilia are, we could have people powering an entire warship from its shields to its weapons!" Edwards said.

Councilwoman Wong tapped her desk in thought, her face giving nothing away.

"Edwards, you will continue to test, but you will adhere to safety procedures. Sato, we will get these rumors of your dismissal removed. There has not been a discovery like this since the founding of this station. I want to have a compiled history of Emerilia as soon as possible and I want you to get back in contact with this 'Dave' once I clear up some issues with the higher military ranking personnel. Overlooking this was an oversight by them. We will not win this war by dismissing information, no matter how ridiculous it sounds," Wong said.

"I can give you the history now. Dave sent it with his files; there are many of them, dealing with all manner of subjects," Sato said. Even if he did get fired, he hoped that the information would be useful to Edwards and his people.

"Send it to me. I am interested in what our distant relatives have been up to," Wong said.

"It will be done." Hope rose in Sato's chest.

"It is through actions and items like this that we will learn how to combat the Jukal Empire and make them pay for what they did to our race. Humanity does not forget." Wong leaned forward, her eyes angry and filled with vitriol.

"Humanity does not forget," Edwards and Sato said, the words ingrained in all surviving human's minds. Seeing the videos and messages and going through the simulations of the fall of humanity was mandatory for all.

Trillions had died, and one day, the bill would be paid in full.

Chapter 23: Guests and Tables

Dave checked Steve over, looking for any damage that might be beyond his metal exterior. Instead, he was left with more questions. "Okay, what the hell is holding you together? I swear that I have never seen these metals before in my life." Dave looked at the different metals that worked to make Steve what he was.

They had just five more minutes out of their thirty-minute break between waves and Dave couldn't understand it.

"Well, I've got some platinum, titanium, even got some coolant in me. Not your everyday Emerilia items," Steve said, as if he were talking about an odd leaf.

Dave stared at Steve blankly for a while.

"Earth to Dave—is everything okay in there, little guy?" Steve waved his hand in front of Dave's face, not getting a response.

"Holy shit! I'm an idiot!" Dave slapped his forehead. "This is a planet, after all. It might have materials that are different and similar to what we have back on Earth, though in the end it is a planet. It has some of the same materials as Earth. Of course! Wow, I've been an idiot!"

"I could have told you that for free," Steve said, still looking confused.

"I thought that all of those materials were out of our reach because Emerilia has been changed so much. While it has been changed a lot, there must be those trace elements here. If they aren't, then we could synthesize them!" Dave was now up and pacing around.

"Dave, what are you talking about?" Deia asked.

"The periodic table! I thought that it would all be different here, but it isn't! This is the real damned universe. Sure, there are metals that are used as weapons and that are used for making runes. There are so damned many more that we can make, though no one has thought about it. Well, other than the Aleph! Titanium, aluminum—fuck, we could even make tungsten!"

"Smaller words and more sense," Deia said in a reassuring tone.

"Okay, I have been thinking that there are just eight metal materials in Emerilia. That might be true if this was a game, but it isn't. This is a fucking *planet.* No matter how much the surface might be different from when Emerilia was made, below it, there has got to be other metals, other resources like what we have on Earth. The people of Emerilia dismissed them. They were given a list of materials, told how to use them and they've largely accepted it. The periodic table doesn't just stop being a thing while we're out here! This is huge!"

"Periodic table? You mean that chart of elements that make up all living things?" Deia sounded skeptical.

"Yeah. I was spouting all of that science, but I wasn't ever thinking that it could be here! I was using techniques and practices from Earth, though I wasn't making the jump to use their science as well. With the right process and methods, we could make dozens of different compounds and synthetic materials that would change anything. Think what it'd mean if the blacksmiths doubled or tripled the amount of materials they could work with. What if I could give them a process for automating the smelting and production of steel? No more looking for steel veins that the seeders have planted across Emerilia." Dave shook his head, his mind becoming wild with his different ideas.

"Steve, can you link to Shard? I have a few questions for him." Dave sat down and looked at the big behemoth.

"Yeah, sure," Steve said.

***

Deia hadn't seen Dave so unhappy with himself and also so completely excited, ever. He was an odd one, with such competing thoughts. He was also talking to Suzy, who was coordinating with Lucy and the Exdar's Traders so Dave could pool more information.

All of it was put on pause as the next ranks of draugr and undead appeared.

Bone lords let out their pained bellows. They were made from skeletons of all different races, from animals to sentients. They had been pulled together into large humanoid-looking creatures, hefting all manner of weapons. They stood at the same height as Steve, something that the metal man was taking as a challenge. Their giant bodies of yellow-aged bones stomped among the draugr. Here and there, a draugr knight, lord, or magi were present. They had moved from just simple draugr fighters to their lords and magi, to the bone lords.

Something caught Deia's eye: a new shape and an opening around a single figure in the middle of the undead.

"The hell is that?" She pointed at the creature.

It was made from bones; once rich clothes hung from it. Meat and whatever was left of the creature hung off it as it drifted over the ground, holding his skeletal hands together. Rings and necklaces adorned it. It wore a jewelry piece across its forehead, coming to a point between its eyes.

"Looks like a Lich. Didn't think that they had them in here after fighting so many undead. Thankfully, we aren't in its lair." Anjold shivered. "Remember one time I was playing D and D, damned thing revived our tank and had him fighting us. Always have two fighters in your squad." Anjold raised his voice to be heard. "Does anyone see its Dark phylactery?"

"What's that?" Deia asked.

"Well, a Lich Lord has to have this thing that binds their soul to this plane instead of continuing on. They make a contract with someone; they give them a phylactery and usually some kind of great beast or person's soul to bind them. They drink a poison with the sacrifice's blood and get bound to the phylactery. To sustain themselves, they need to pull people into that same phylactery, eating their souls to sustain themselves. Dark little bastards. Keep living so that they can keep up whatever Dark experiments they have going on."

"Sounds lovely," Anna said.

"Best part is that you need to destroy it, or else the Lich Lord will revive next to it within ten days. I don't know if that is true in this game, but it was in D and D." Anjold shrugged.

The first magical attacks were let loose. The draugr magi started up their defenses, shutting down the Stone Raider's magical attacks and shielding their fellows who were charging ahead, coming through buildings, the roads, and any free path.

Deia checked her notifications.

Quest: Aleph Homecoming

You have arrived at an unknown Aleph City.

To return the city to the governing power of the Aleph, you must hold your position in the city for 20 waves.

Wave: 20 of 20

Attackers: 2,857/3,000

Rewards: ???

Josh's people had been wearing down their numbers, but the stronger enemies working together made their work treacherous.

Deia drew her bow, releasing as soon as she'd pulled it back to its full length. Her arrow was one of dozens that reached out to hit the oncoming undead.

Spells were already being hurled into the middle of the undead. AOE blessings made the undead scream out as the healing spells tried to cleanse them of impurities, destroying their twisted souls and bodies.

The Stone Raiders' necromancers and summoners used an idea they'd gained from the Boran-al cultists. Fallen undead that decorated the ground started to shiver, their soulless skeletons rising to their masters' bidding. Those too badly injured to rise as skeletons were used as building blocks for various creatures. Bone tigers, knights, lords, and kings rose.

Jake cackled behind them, before falling into a coughing fit.

"Choke!" Steve yelled.

"Shut up, you tin can!" Jake yelled back from inside the tower.

The two had become solid friends. She didn't know how he did it, but it seemed that being a joking idiot got you a number of friends.

Deia fired arrow after arrow, hitting anything that looked like a weakness.

Bones rose around her, coming together and growing into their forms. They hollered their defiance as their skeleton brethren stumbled forward.

Creation summoners were not about to be outdone. Their creatures formed in the air or rose from the ground. Water pooled from the atmosphere. Elementals formed graceful figures of every Affinity, waiting to face the enemy.

The Stone Raiders' lines tripled.

Deia stood taller and fired as fast as possible, trying to take out as many draugr as possible before the Stone Raiders' summoned and created forces clashed.

"This is the last round. Let's go all out! Oh, and someone kill that damn Lich Lord! We're searching for the damned plyca—whatever the hell it's called," Josh said.

Traps were activated; spells erupted among the oncoming undead. Spells overwhelmed the undead's magi and defenses. They were holding off on the more powerful spells, knowing that the draugr would find it easier to pull them apart with the distance they would have to travel.

Deia watched with grim satisfaction as a draugr magi's head snapped backward with the impact of her arrow.

"They're in range!" Lucy yelled.

"Shields!" Dwayne barked.

"Move the creation division out!" Kim added.

From the bone lords to the lightning elementals, they surged forward.

Skeleton archers fired their arrows at the draugr. They weren't as powerful, but any damage was good.

The elementals and Air creations did the most damage. They could move much faster than the other creations. Rushing through the draugr lines, they formed up, smashing into the lines before the heavier metal, Earth, Water, and undead creations could reach them.

Deia raised the shield she had been loaned as the draugr archers paused just as they got in range and formed up lines. Their military pasts had some impact over them as they fired and loosed arrows in lines, keeping up a constant barrage of arrows.

"I hate this shit," Deia said as arrows started to hit all around her.

"Just hunker down and wait. Once the rest of the draugrs move past the archers, Josh and his people will quickly deal with them. Dave was able to make a few grenades that will help them," Anna said.

"That's what I get for grabbing more supplies—miss half of everything that happens out here." Deia sighed.

Anna laughed as the arrows came down.

"What?" Deia asked.

"Well, it seems that you're becoming a Player faster and faster. Talking in the middle of battle, not caring about the death literally raining down all around us. You'll make a fine Player!"

"Thanks, Anna." Deia sighed and rolled her eyes. "It's weird. Once you do it, it just—makes things so much easier. Not worrying about death, just worrying about not having the best score or screwing over your buddies and not being there when they earn victory. It's strange, but I can see why Players are so damned strong."

"Today, we are expecting light showers of arrows, followed by a nice long fight of undead, and finally coming to the conclusion of finding a Lich Lord's death box. Dwayne, care to make any comments on what we might expect tomorrow?" Steve asked.

"Thank you, Steve. After a heavy beating of Steve later tonight, we'll be moving onward to clear skies and happy days of completing this city, followed shortly after by jumping right back into a cold front of doing it all over again!" Dwayne said.

The fighters snickered as they continued to get pelted with arrows.

"Reminds me of that whole 'arrows will block out the sun, so we'll fight in the shade,'" Anjold said.

"The lights aren't even on in the rest of the city, dumbo!" Dave said.

"Oh, shut up, you know what I—ah shit! I just got one in the foot. See what happens when you start talking!" Anjold grumbled.

Deia would have chastised Dave for not respecting Anjold's rank but it seemed that rank—although it was respected— was not like a military rank. Other than giving out orders sometimes, the rest of the Players knew what to do and were left on their own. Talking back and making jokes with their leaders was nearly constant.

"Fire in the hole, bitches!" Josh yelled.

Explosions rippled through the draugr's ranks. Deia peeked over the barricade in front of her and quickly ducked back down.

"Giving that one a six," Dwayne said.

"Maybe a four. Dave, need some more power in the fireworks next time!" Kim laughed.

"Oh, come on! That was a good one!" Josh complained.

"Undead within two hundred meters," Lucy said.

"Spoilsport," Josh muttered.

The arrows dropped away. Many of the archers were dead or falling to Josh's lightning-fast attacks. His stealth types had perfected the art of killing draugr as fast as possible.

Deia was able to look out over the battlefield. There were arrows fucking *everywhere*. Deia looked to everyone's shields. Most were dented and scratched; the weaker shields looked like pin cushions with all the arrows that had embedded themselves into the surface.

The Stone Raiders'-created forces were doing what they did best: raising chaos.

The elementals supported the creations that were fighting in groups in the middle of the draugrs. Draugr magi and summoned bone creatures were the main targets.

The Stone Raiders' bone creations worked on lightning-fast runs, killing as many draugr and creatures as fast as possible, running through the edges. They didn't want them to get stuck in case the undead mages wrested control of their beasts away from them.

Due to the undead mages' proximity, and their Affinity, it had happened before where they had pulled control of an undead creation away from the Stone Raiders' mages. It was why there weren't many of the creatures but the ones on the battlefield were some of the most powerful.

Deia dropped her shield and continued firing with her bow. It was hard to miss the undead at this range.

***

Dave fired arrow after arrow into the oncoming mass of creatures.

"Ready!" Anjold called out.

Dave saw Deia changing for her blades. Dave continued to fire until the draugr were just thirty meters away. Dave threw grenades into the draugr midst as traps held the undead at bay for a few scant minutes.

"Dave!" Deia called.

Dave turned; a plasma cannon appeared in her arms. Dave just had enough time to alter the spell with his own magic before it bellowed out.

The plasma round burned a hole in the undead's lines, reaching into the middle before Deia ignited the second part of the spell.

Inside, a highly reactive substance formed, causing the plasma round to explode and flattening all the draugr within fifty meters of it. Two bone knights were dropped to the ground as well.

Any draugr knights were also killed within that fifty meters. Only magi with their Mana barriers up were left standing.

The opening was filled up by more undead rushing past.

Dave changed his rods to a sword and shield, checking the wave's numbers.

Quest: Aleph Homecoming

You have arrived at an unknown Aleph City.

To return the city to the governing power of the Aleph, you must hold your position in the city for 20 waves.

Wave: 20 of 20

Attackers: 1,647/3,000

Rewards: ???

Their numbers were falling quickly but their headlong charge was about to get them through the tower's magical shield. As soon as they did, then the melee fighters could get into the fray.

"Remember, no charges or rushing. We can give ground but on our terms and let people know if you're moving. The mages will heal us as needed. Don't rush in and get killed. Cycle parties if you need to," Dwayne said.

Dave watched as buffs started to stack on the left side of his screen, filling him with power as he continued to stare at the oncoming undead.

His shield and weapon had golden light mixing with the gray smoke of conjuring. He'd created Weapons of Light.

Dave touched Steve's leg to check his runes. Everything looked good. Dave added new runes that would increase his Light Affinity.

"Thanks," Steve said as Dave looked to his armor.

"No problem, dude," Dave said. The changes he made to his armor changed Deia's and Anna's armor through their link.

Suzy's armor also changed, but not in the same way. He gave her magical and Willpower boosts while Anna, Deia, and he got increased Agility and Strength enhancements.

Suzy was constantly casting soul trap and her creations all had a soul trap rune on their cores so that their attacks would fuel them and their master. Her power was linked to the others, keeping them going as Dave, Deia, and Anna had cast soul fields on the ground among the draugrs as they had advanced and on the ground when they got closer.

Dave cast his own soul field and drew power from his armor. "Let's dance." Dave's eyes glowed, the spaces between his armor showing his glowing tattoos. He brought his shield forward. Dozens of spikes jumped out of the ground, just feet from the front line. They shone with golden runes as undead slammed into them.

Their own force and the Light Affinity of the weapons killed dozens. Dave hadn't stopped moving. Grenades appeared in the sky. They fell among the draugr, ripping them apart. Souls seemed to flee toward Dave, Suzy, Deia, and Anna.

Arrows rained down from the heavens. Dave grunted, adding more and more, waiting until they hit the ground before he created more. Their effects still took hold even as they disappeared.

Dave spent a third of their armors' Mana, continuing the explosions and arrows.

The undead weathered through it; their high numbers and levels allowed them to cross through the mayhem Dave was creating. In other places around the tower, battle had already been joined.

Dave dropped his conjurations as the Stone Raiders met the undead.

He felt haggard as he let go of trying to make new conjurations, ending the curtain of arrows and explosions. He stopped a spear with his shield; his sword turned into a spear and slammed through the draugr that attacked him. Dave cut the conjuration and twisted away to get a better position.

He settled into a routine, not trying to advance as he blocked blows with his shield and created a spear with his rod, not having to move his already tired shoulder as the conjuration pierced through the draugrs as if they weren't there.

Elementals and creations continued to fight in the distance, slowing down and reducing the undead's reinforcements.

Josh's people took out anyone who looked like a problem, but they hadn't been able to get anywhere near the Lich Lord.

Magical spells from curses, blessings, healing, artillery, and lances flew free. Darklings erupted into the midst of the undead, tearing at them with hateful anger.

Traps had been spent, making the mages call down their area of effect spells; roots lashed out, Fire swirled and burned while Air cut like a cold blade.

The metal ground turned to liquid, making the draugrs and bone creations stumble and falter.

There were too many sights to take in at once. Dave focused on what was in front of him, freely using his conjurations, dropping spears with Light runes on the draugr's heads, driving his spear through their chests, or slamming their shields away with a maul.

"Ahh shit! Scratched up my new metal paint job!" Steve sounded annoyed as a draugr went flying. "So, what do you think the next area is going to be?"

"Hell if I know. Shard wanted us to take this place so we had somewhere to set up camp."

"Wouldn't you know more? You are kind of like his kid," Dave said.

"Well, I'm thinking that it will be the main installations. Need to check those—go for places that don't have many enemies, but do have equipment that needs to be repaired. Then, we move onto the areas with less importance, but also with creatures. Then, probably important places with more assholes in them," Steve said.

"How many places do the Aleph have?"

"Not sure. I think that was kept from me. The Aleph like having their secrets."

"I have noticed that." Dave slapped a blade away, driving his shield forward. It changed into a sword, piercing the confused-looking draugr as Dave ripped his blade free, taking out thirty percent of the draugr's Health, decreasing by five a minute because of the heavy Light enchantment on the blade.

Enraged, it stabbed at Dave's shoulder. The dragon scale armor didn't allow him to find purchase; the rusted blade glided off as Dave spun, bringing his hands together. A warhammer appeared in his hands as he slammed it into the side of the draugr, caving their side in and ending their life.

Dave barely had time to change back to a sword and shield as another draugr attacked him.

"Moving back a bit—things are getting hot," Dave said, trading blows with the draugr. As soon as they got used to his fighting pattern, he'd change weapons, opening them up for a killing blow.

Dave's inference ability was making it easier than ever for him to land killing blows. After fighting so many draugr, his perception highlighted blue areas where the draugr's soul was probably attached or where its bones were weak.

Dave was rewarded with a satisfied crack as the draugr's spine gave way and it fell apart, its bones and remaining ligaments not strong enough to keep it upright. Dave's two axes came free as he started to laugh.

"Look at me—I'm a fucking lawnmower!" Steve said to the laughter of the others as Dave smashed through the draugr lines. To use dual axes properly, you needed to keep them up a moment, have a larger reach, and have the speed and Strength to use them so fast that your opponent couldn't get in.

It was a tall order, but with Dave shutting down his Mana barrier and feeding power to his Strength and Agility enhancing runes, he was a whirlwind of metal, brawn, and destruction.

The other fighters whooped and hollered.

"Well, come on! There's plenty of them for the rest of you to kill!" Dave barked.

It was what they needed; they thrived on challenges.

Dave rode the power running through his body, following his training where he knew to, adding in the moves from inferencing and the weaknesses highlighted by his perception. He was ripping through the draugr but he made sure to not let the power go to his head. If he got too close or deep in the draugr, he would be swept away.

Dave thought that he was doing good until he watched Deia dismantle draugr while Dave was just hacking them apart.

"Damn, my mentor's hot," Dave said, loud enough for her to hear.

"And my student is a blockhead! At least, you're using bigger axes so that you have more time to react when someone gets inside your guard."

Dave took draugr and skeletons down with his axes, but they were massing in numbers out of melee range. He focused on staying alive as a claymore slammed into his side, taking out 5 Health. It didn't make it through the armor but Dave felt his insides shake from the impact.

"What the fuck do you think I am, some kind of fucking piñata?" Dave hacked the draugr apart, reverting to his shield and sword. He couldn't kill as many like this, but then it was much harder to land a hit on him.

"Pull back into a line!" Anjold called out. The Players were all different distances from the tower. Anjold's call made them come back and into a line. The mages from above got clear lines of sight, sending dozens of spells that spelled ruin for the draugr.

Dave was panting. He had been fighting for hours and the fatigue had mounted, even with revitalizing Xer, Stamina drinks, and self-healing.

"Come on!" Dave said, as a draugr's sword met his shield. Dave took out their knees, before driving his sword through their skull. He changed the sword to a rod and then back again, removing the skull atop it, ready to meet the next challenger.

***

Josh drank his Stamina potion, breathing heavily. They had placed a tracking spell on the Lich Lord without him knowing. He had sent three parties off to go and hunt down its phylactery. The tracking spell was faint but it looked as if some of the Stone Raiders' encyclopedic knowledge of monsters was coming to use.

He jumped off the building he was standing on and dropped down out of the shadows.

The draugr magi didn't know what hit him as Josh's daggers tore through his body, destroying his soul bind point. The magi dropped with a pained grunt. The other draugrs didn't know what was happening till Josh had already opened another draugr's chest open, dropping them to the ground, their hit points reaching zero as Josh ran away.

He jumped through their attacks, slashing and damaging as many as possible before he jumped for an alleyway. Jumping from side to side, he made his way up to a three-story building's rooftop. His draugr attackers gave up the chase.

Josh once again looked over the draugr that rushed to meet the Stone Raiders' protected tower. It was a massive building, rising fifty stories upward, to meet with four other similarly large buildings that connected in the center of the city.

Deia had told Josh of how the cities were supposed to spin, giving the entire cylinder gravity to walk around with. The floor that they were on was slightly slanted.

Josh focused on the battle around the tower, waiting for his Stamina to regenerate. His people worked in small groups, rushing the strongest of the undead to try to make it easier on their guildmates.

Magic of all kinds illuminated the sky, slamming into the draugr hordes. Elementals had started off strong, but they were using the magic that created them to form their attacks. With each movement or attack, they grew weaker. The creations had created their own abattoir around them.

Groups of creations under control of a single summoner were a deadly opponent. Born of one summoner, the Willpower and imprinted unconsciousness of the summoner allowed them to fight with the kind of coordination that took years for other groups to master.

The bone creations were still rushing through; their innate Strength, natural armor, and inability to feel pain made them the perfect juggernauts.

The cats and snikts were built for speed and destruction. Snikts looked like bowling balls that constantly spun out sharpened weapons of bone. Jake had taken it from his copious number of comic books; he declared they were snikts as it was the closest noise he could think of from his favorite comic books.

The cats had half-meter long claws and fangs, with a five-meter long tail that had blades running along it and ended in a spike ball.

They had been pulled back to the portal tower, so there was less chance of the draugr magi controlling them. The Stone Raiders' necromancers were now working to break the magi's hold over their own bone creations to reinforce their lines.

Josh had to take a minute to just watch it all: his guild working together, the deadly beauty of the spells that crashed through the draugr or slammed into the tower's Mana barrier.

A smile crossed Josh's face as new energy filled him. He thought of how lucky he was to be there at this very moment, to be playing Emerilia with his friends. Even if they lost, it was so much fun that Josh would do it over again and again just for the fun and sense of accomplishment. And, he knew that his guild would readily agree.

They would get stronger than ever before. The Stone Raiders would be the best raiding guild in all of Emerilia, the best guild ever created. That was his dream, his passion, and before him, he saw proof of his devotions.

"Stone Raiders!" he yelled out, his pride bursting forth as he cheered from his rooftop.

"Stone Raiders! Stone Raiders! Stone Raiders!" the rest of the guild chanted out, taking strength from those two words as the attacks redoubled and the defending tanks slowed their retreat.

Josh picked out his next target, a draugr knight.

He ran off the building, slamming on top of the knight and burying his blades into it exposed spine. With the combined sneak attack and the force of his landing, Josh used a stunned draugr to get high enough to grab a balcony and get clear, looking for his next target.

He saw his other stealth types flitting through the shadows, dropping out from the shadows, and killing or maiming their targets before they disappeared once again.

***

"Induca!" Malsour's yell was drowned out as a plasma cannon shot sped off into the draugr that were just starting to make it into the doors of the tower.

Suzy worked with the support people, keeping supplies moving to those who needed it: Stamina and healing potions to the fighters, and Xer, stimulants, and Mana potions to the mages. She kept an eye on people who could use healing and assisted Lucy.

Lucy was good at her job, but Suzy was a maestro. She could help run a multi-trillion dollar business; she could run a damned guild as they were fighting a horde of undead.

Lucy let her have command, helping where Suzy told her to be. Lucy had the position, but she knew when to fight to be in command and when to let those who were better suited for the job take over.

The plasma round slammed into the draugr, killing tens of them and giving the tanks some room to breathe. Suzy's people moved, switching out broken armor or weapons with good replacements.

For fighting in other games, supplies weren't necessarily a big thing, but here they were. With the long, extended battles, everyone ran out of something at some time, usually at the worst of times.

While Malsour and Induca were trying to hide it, it was easy to see that they were some of the strongest mages in the Stone Raiders. Being so much older and dragons gave them a definite edge over their allies.

"Buffs needed at the western entrance. Make sure we have healers ready at the north. I want people out and checking on supplies for the tanks. They're the priority right now," Suzy said.

The undead had pushed the melee fighters back from their positions and into the entrances of the tower. There was about fifty meters of space for them to work in before the stairs. Once they got to the stairs, the Stone Raiders would pull back to the flat area at the bottom, a two-hundred-meter by two-hundred-meter square that surrounded the elevators and chutes.

Once the undead got into that area, the mages from above could really open up on them. It would be their melee fighters' last stand. If they died, then the elevators and the chutes would be cut off so that none of the undead could make it up to the mages.

No one wanted to have to fight through another twenty levels if they didn't have to.

Suzy checked the counter for the wave.

Quest: Aleph Homecoming

You have arrived at an unknown Aleph City.

To return the city to the governing power of the Aleph, you must hold your position in the city for 20 waves.

Wave: 20 of 20

Attackers: 451/3,000

Rewards: ???

It had taken half a day to get this far. No one wanted to have to do it all over again.

The tanks slowly fell back, pulling the draugr into the strongest traps that the Stone Raiders had created. Each trap killed tens of basic draugr; the stronger bone creations, magi, and knights made it through. Every so often, a bone creation would turn against its masters and start tearing into the draugr lines.

The Stone Raiders' necros had used the bone creations before and lost control of them. They were not going to have a repeat of that, though they were more than happy to use those same tactics against the draugr.

"What doesn't kill you makes you stronger. What does kill you, you remember to use it against your enemy and make sure it doesn't get you a second time," Suzy said, remembering a motto that the Stone Raiders had taken up.

With dying so many times to complete raids that were supposed to be way over their level, they had come to learn and adapt. It was why they had a guild house for a VR home instead of everyone being in their own homes, waiting. They could talk to one another, pass information to those who were alive and continue on.

"Report from the dead. They found the Lich Lord's phylactery; it was hidden in its lair. Sending location details." One of the people tasked with logging out to check on the VR home and then back in reported.

"Josh, we've got the location of the Lich's lair and its phylactery has been confirmed at the location. One of the dead told us," Lucy said.

Suzy listened in as she looked over her display screen. "Health potions to the south entrance," Suzy said on another channel as she looked at the varying requests coming in and prioritized who got what when.

"Very well. I sent three of my best parties over there. I'll have another two sent out and have them conference with the dead to talk about the layout and such." Josh cut the channel.

"Dark Aberration," Malsour said, next to Suzy.

A chill went down her spine as shadows started to twist and distort between the creatures clawing their way in through the north entrance.

Malsour grunted as he continued to move his hands for a few moments. They dropped to his side as he used a banister to steady himself.

"You okay?" Suzy asked.

"I am, but they won't be for long," Malsour said.

Suzy looked over as a scream ripped through the air. Standing in the middle of the north entrance was a writhing mass of mouths and hands. It clawed and ripped at the undead forces, shadows wrapping around those that it crushed in its massive hands. Draugrs went limp as it crunched down on them with its many mouths.

"The hell is that?" Suzy asked.

"A Dark aberration is created from the Dark souls of an area. It seeks to consume other Dark souls, to grow stronger and more powerful. It will not eat the souls of those fighting along with it or those with souls untouched by the darkness. Takes a bit of work, but they're powerful. However, they're not overly mobile unless they create smaller aberrations. It'll last for ten minutes." Malsour looked tired as different creatures tried to kill the aberration. Its hands whipped out to crush and destroy; its mouths devoured anything that went into their maws.

Suzy cast soul field on the entire area; power headed for Dave and Deia, who were the closest linked armors.

"Shiny," Induca commented, dropping firestorm right on top of the east door's entrance.

Dave and Deia fought next to Steve and Anna. The Players all around them fought with everything they had. Mages had to put spells of Stamina regeneration on them as they didn't have the time to take Stamina potions while they were fighting.

"Buffs on the western and southern fighters," Suzy called out.

They'd worn the undead down; there was just a few hundred to go. Now it was the last wave. The Stone Raiders were taking risks that they wouldn't have on earlier waves to bring about the end of these creatures.

Quest: Aleph Homecoming

You have arrived at an unknown Aleph City.

To return the city to the governing power of the Aleph, you must hold your position in the city for 20 waves.

Wave: 20 of 20

Attackers: 217/3,000

Rewards: ???

The numbers dropped faster and faster. Josh's people were no longer fighting in the buildings that surrounded the tower. They were moving across the battlefield and getting to the rear of the undead.

"Buffs on Josh's DPS people!" Suzy said.

Chapter 24: A Meeting of Minds and Metal

Dave saw as the Lich Lord made its way inside the tower. There was an oppressive aura surrounding it. It clawed at Dave, making his legs shake in fear. He slowed in his reactions.

The Lich seemed to abhor anything that dared to try to survive or live in its presence. With a wave of its hand, it overpowered mages who were piling spells into the creature. Their shields were overpowered and they dropped to the ground in pain.

"We need a way to deal with that damn thing!" Anjold said.

"I have an idea, but we need to clear out more of its minions!" Dave stared at the creature until he got a pop-up.

Lich Lord

Level 251

Shit, this better work!

"All right!" Anjold said.

Dave had improved in the time that he'd been fighting the draugr. Fighting the normal soldiers were now an easy opponent; the lords, knights, and magi were mini bosses, with the bone creations like damned tanks. They had been easy targets for the ranged fighters to take out and they were targeting them even now. Once they got into melee range, they were devastating.

The Stone Raiders' own skeleton forces had been destroyed but the necros were using curses that pulled apart the undead. The spells warred with the very soul of the draugrs but if their will was weaker than the Stone Raiders necromancers', their souls were free to move on.

The Lich Lord let out a bellow; all of the draugrs got a buff that made them harder to kill.

"Mother fucker!" Steve yelled.

"Well, at least they're still as dumb and useless as before and not as fast," Dave said.

One of the draugr seemed to take that as an insult; it tried to put their blade through Dave's ribs, hitting his armor as Dave stabbed his own sword through the creature's head. Dispelling the conjuration, he turned it into an axe as he took out another's knee. He'd come to rely on his armor more and more; it had some scratches and dents, but it held steady.

A little bit of pain to end the other bastard was a good compromise, in Dave's books.

"Pull back to the elevators!" Dwayne yelled.

The Players spent skills and spells that allowed them to try to gain them the time that they would need to pull back.

"Burning hand!" Deia held her hand out, a veritable flamethrower coming from it.

"Branded ground!" An AOE spell outlined in red spread over the stairs and the landing that led to the doors of the tower.

She jumped off the top of the stairs, falling the ten feet into a roll, popping up and looking at her work.

"That's my girl. Bit showy, though," Dave said. Spears jutted out of the ground for fifteen feet in a half-circle around him and Steve.

The rest of the line scrambled back as Dave conjured grenades and threw them behind him like candy as he reached the stairs. He quickly stepped down.

"Fuck sakes! Why I ever got that StairMaster, I don't know. Feeling like I'm going to bust a lung!" Anjold said.

Dave grinned, making sure that he didn't misstep and fall down the stairs.

"Swan dive into the best—" Steve was abruptly cut off as he slammed into the stairs, going down them as only a human five times their normal size, made of three tons of metal and trying to impersonate a winter sled could.

Dave made out a few swearwords as Steve continued to bounce and get airborne after hitting a sharper step.

Fighters got out of his way as he once again went airborne. His knees and armor shot out, slamming them into the ground. He left furrows in the floor and came to a stop, kneeling, with the bottom of his axe planted in the ground.

"Oh, that just looked badass!" Steve declared.

"Until you opened yer damned mouth!" Baldur, an orc giant, said.

"Screw you, Baldy!" Steve got to his feet.

"It's Baldur, you tin can!"

"Is someone in a bad mood?" Steve said in mock worry. It reminded Dave of some coaches just before they told their team to get a hold of themselves and go win the damned game.

"There's more dents and scratches than anything." Dave shook his head and turned away from Steve as he reached the bottom of the stairs.

"Fuuuuck stairs," Dave said. Anjold, who stood beside him, nodded in agreement.

"Looks like we'll have to work on that," Deia said.

"Ahh, well, if you're the one running in front of me—definitely a better view than Steve's rendition of the Griswold's family Christmas," Dave said.

"The what?" Deia frowned.

"Not important. We've got draugr to kill." Dave hoped that changing the subject fast enough would get her to forget about the whole stairs training thing.

"Everyone else is the damned hammer and we're the anvil. We will hold and we will make these undead pay for screwing with us and turning this city into their home!" Dwayne said.

The Stone Raiders yelled their agreement. The mages were now able to hit the undead army with everything they had, now that the melee fighters were out of the way.

They started to come down the sheer stairs, having as much of an issue as the Stone Raiders, many tripping and falling. Those with spears near where they landed put an end to whatever crashed down.

Deia's spell was working, glowing an angry red as the draugrs let out pained noises. They were getting burned with every step they took.

The bone creations seemed to take a lesson from Steve as they largely fell on their asses and tumbled down the stairs. However, unlike him, they were heavily damaged from the fall.

The melee fighters fell on them quickly, taking out their Health before they could regain their feet. They were a fearsome enemy, something that no one wanted to have right next to them as they were just trying to take out the draugr mass that poured down into the area around the elevators.

Dave hacked off a draugr knight's head, ignoring the helmet that the creature wore.

The Stone Raiders now worked with practiced efficiency, taking out large threats and anything that was in reach before they could become a real problem. They fell back as the falling creatures mounted. It wasn't long until the creatures that hadn't fallen down the stairs made it to the leveled-out area.

As Dave and the other Stone Raiders pulled back slowly, the first of the Aleph traps activated. Twenty or so creatures turned to icicles. Mages dropped lances on them, tearing their frozen bodies apart.

More of the traps went off, each of them freezing all of the creatures within its area into ice sculptures.

The Lich, seeing his remaining forces draining away, let out an angered cry. The undead draugrs started to rise, turning into the Lich's skeleton warriors and bringing any dead Stone Raiders back to life before they could accept their fate and remove their bodies from the battlefield.

Bone creations crashed with the main lines.

Stealth types leapt from the top of the stairs with abandon, crashing into anything that wasn't looking for them. Their weapons found purchase as the last hundred or so enemies appeared.

"Dave, do it!" Anjold yelled.

Power surged through Dave from his internal reserves and his armor. He pictured the creation in his mind: five parts, not including a secondary Magical Circuit. His eyes blazed with power, finding the Lich's.

It screamed, a spell forming in its hands as if it realized something was about to happen. It was too late.

A circular unit of dull steel rested underneath the Lich. Four others, these ones looking like half-circles, snapped up around the Lich on all sides. A second circular device fell from the sky, but seemed to rest in mid-air as the Lich's screams were cut off.

Dave focused on the last part. Runes formed all around the Lich.

The Lich threw attacks, but they stopped just feet away. The semicircles were Mana barriers—a little trick that Dave had come up with when making his armor.

The Lich slowed as the runes around it ignited with power. The Lich's Willpower was drained from it as it powered its own prison.

The newly risen undead collapsed and bone creations wilted, shedding bones that they couldn't control as magi were targeted and pulled apart.

Summoned creations added to the fray as Dave gathered up his weapons. They still had around thirty or so fighters left from the draugrs, all of them heavies to have survived so long.

Dave's mind was foggy with the power he had expended. Fighting was based on reactions and following the hints. He played defensively, waiting for the heavies to make a mistake and capitalizing on it. Much smarter than charging in, especially when his timing was off.

Suddenly, buffs made him faster than ever before as the openings seemed to just appear before him. The melee fighters with full buffs moved through the draugrs like so many farmers come to harvest wheat.

Dave watched as a draugr knight let out a startled look as its Health hit zero. It dropped, showing a rogue panting as they looked around with wild eyes for another victim. Dave looked around with them, unconsciously covering the direction the other wasn't looking at.

A draugr magi's shield failed; three melee fighters planted weapons into the creature.

Only the Lich Lord remained, floating listlessly in its prison.

A yell rose from someone's throat, a visceral thing. They had won! Dave's voice added to theirs as he hoisted his sword. He shifted his weapons back to their original batons and hooked them to his belt. His arms were tired from the day's fighting.

"Stone Raiders! Stone Raiders! STONE RAIDERS!" They all took up the chant, renewing their vows to the guild and to one another and basking in the glory of the moment, of what they had all come together and done.

"See to the wounded!" Josh bellowed out.

The Stone Raiders spread out. Healers came down to the first floor. Health potions were expensive, but they didn't care, using it to numb one another's pain or bring back someone from the edge.

Dave looked for the different statuses showing people who had been knocked out, stunned, or close to death. He used healing where he could and potions where people were close to death.

There had been just sixty-seven melee types fighting down on the first floor. Fourteen were still standing, another seven were saved through healing, five were close enough to just dying that the higher-leveled purpose healers could bring them back from death.

CPR worked in Emerilia; even the recent dead were given a Health potion to see whether it would do them any good. Three did make it back from the brink with their ministrations.

"Congratulations, you have cleared your first Aleph city. Go forth and repair the city's systems in order to gain larger bonuses and aid for your forces. You have three hours of power left with current reserves. New missions have been added to your quest." Shard's voice rang through the tower before it disappeared.

"All right, Party Zero, you know how these things work. I need two more parties to aid them," Josh said.

Slowly, but surely, other volunteers put their hands up. All of them wanted to relax and sit back.

The raid has only started. Dave grinned to himself.

***

Sato once again sat in front of his Mirror of Communication. Now, it was not just as a communications officer; it was as liaison to Emerilia. Dave's information made it clear that there was a lot more that they could learn from the planet than just what the Jukal were up to.

Everyone watched the main screen, which relayed what Sato's Mirror of Communication showed. A human male with glowing green eyes and a nondescript background answered the Mirror of Communication. He was larger than most humans, with a heavy build and pointed ears.

"Ah, you must be Mister Sato. Dave said that I might get a call from you in the future. Sorry, I am answering his calls as he is dealing with a task that I have given him." The man looked to Sato.

"Who might you be?" Sato asked.

"I am Shard, I am the—as you would term it, AI of the Aleph people," Shard said with a small, proud smile.

"The Aleph?" Sato asked.

"They are the race that created me. Dave showed me the information that he sent you. Are there any questions you might have? As he has showed, it might be best if we make sure that we are on the 'same page,' as one might say."

"I am sorry, but we cannot share any information with parties that we do not know," Sato said.

"Ahh, that inner paranoia." Shard smiled wistfully. "You remind me a lot of my race. First of all, I guess to confirm and make sure that we are on the same page, I should tell you of how Emerilia was created and humanity grown to populate it. Dave and I do not believe that this alliance will be a short-lived one as there is much to get you up to date if you are indeed using the level of technology Dave saw last time. It is very exciting!" Shard's smile grew.

Sato agreed, but he wasn't willing to say anything. He didn't need anyone to remind him what he should and shouldn't say to people when using the communication mirrors. "Well, shall we start with the history of Emerilia and any items that you find interesting?"

"Certainly. I will also gift you access to a number of different systems, including the nanite software that allows one to quickly absorb information in various texts. It will take time to get you to a stage where we might be able to interact face-to-face," Shard said.

"How might we be able to do that?" Sato asked.

"Well, the Aleph are masters of portals. There is nowhere that they cannot reach." Shard smiled happily.

"Portals?" Sato kept the anxiety that he felt in his gut from spilling over into his features.

"How did you think Emerilia interacted with the aggressive species? There are portals that connect Emerilia to multiple worlds. Each one harbors creatures that wish nothing more than to destroy. Players are grown and trained over three years before these portals start opening and they start cutting down the populations of these aggressive species. The Aleph, interested in all things of information and technology, studied and learned. They became masters of teleportation magic and installations. They used the teachings of the portals to expand all of their knowledge and science, creating great underground cities completely cut off from the outside and prying eyes. Just like you, the Aleph's cities and homes are a well-guarded secret. Even being inside one, a person would not know where they were on Emerilia." Shard looked pleased with himself.

Sato had heard about the portals, but Alexanderi had never wanted to get close enough to them to check them out, saying that all manner of Demons and creatures came from them.

If they've figured out a way to reverse engineer that kind of technology, maybe Dave was right. If Emerilia is the birthplace of the Jukal Empire's technology over the last few hundred years, we could get it right from the source. No cottage production to hinder us. We could ignite the factories and mass produce in a year what the Jukal Empire produces in five.

Sato remembered to keep his expression neutral; inside thoughts and ideas were sparking, thoughts of the future no longer hazy, half-cooked up dreams. He could start seeing a path, a possible future.

Chapter 25: First Step of Many

Josh looked at the simple black box that his people had found. "So, this is the phylactery?" Josh turned the thing around in his hand.

"Yes, sir. It looks like once the Lich was incapacitated, all of its wards and magical traps were deactivated. Our running theory is that due to it using soul energy to fight and sustain itself, when that energy was pulled from its body, then the other spells weakened," Luke, the party leader who had found the box, said.

Josh looked down at the floating creature that bumped into the side of its Mana barrier prison, floating away. The Lich was still contained in the prison Dave had made, its energy fueling the tower.

"Very well. I'll keep a hold of this. If that thing starts giving us any troubles, we'll break this thing," Josh said.

"Yes, sir." Luke nodded.

"Now, go—get some food and rest. We're going to be moving out to check out these new locations tomorrow." Josh clapped the man on the shoulder.

"Why do I have the feeling that you're going to send me and mine to go and find out if there's anything lurking in those cities?" Luke drawled.

"Shit, I didn't think that they had mind reading in Emerilia," Josh said, trying to look thoughtful.

Luke snorted at Josh's antics. "See you in the morning."

Josh waved his good-bye and sat down on one of the food crates that they had brought with them. He accessed his interface and opened a channel to Dave. "Hey, how is it going?"

"We're bringing one of the B class power stations online. It should be enough to get most of the systems we need to survive online. I think that we will be able to get the other power stations in the section of the city online as well. That damned tilt is a pain in the ass—some of the coal is just falling off the conveyor belt," Dave muttered darkly.

"You said that this thing spins. How long until we can get that and start turning on systems in other parts? I really want to see these guardians in action."

"I think it would be best if everyone was out of the city when we did that. It's not uncommon that a few things will get free when starting or stopping the city's rotation. It will probably take a day or two to get the city enough power stored up to start spinning."

"Okay, I'll plan to have everyone out on missions for then. Speaking of missions, I have a few for you and your party." Josh manipulated his interface and opened a channel to Deia as well.

"So, for your mission tomorrow, it looks like we've got an experimental facility and a remote power station. I don't know why they're not in a city—makes me think of things that go boom. I'd like to have you all there, warning others to not touch a damned thing. I don't want to blow up a damned facility by accident." Josh sighed. He trusted and respected his fellow guildmates, but sometimes they didn't do the smartest things.

"Okay, we've got it," Deia said.

"Good. Once you have those power stations, get back here and get some sleep. Lucy will have rooms and all of that sorted out for you."

"Steve, don't touch that!" Dave yelled, cutting the channel.

"I'll leave you to deal with that," Josh said.

"Thanks," Deia said dryly as she ended the voice chat.

Josh looked over the new information that had come with the quest now that they had taken control of the city.

Quest: Aleph Homecoming

You have returned control of an unknown Aleph City to the Aleph.

The more work you put into the city, the more resources and aid you can call upon in your quest to clear out the Aleph installations.

> Return power to the city.
> Start the City's rotation cycle.
> Activate automatons to repair the city.

Other locations have been made available to you. Based on the power you have returned to the city and your group's skill level, you can travel to the following locations:

> x3 Aleph Power Station (Increased power generation)

> x2 Aleph Portal Factory (Ability to fix portals in different locations)

> x5 Aleph Greenhouses (Access to Herbs and Food)

> x4 Aleph Mining Facilities (Repairs continue at faster rate)

> x2 Aleph Automatons Workshop (More automatons to assist you. Ability to improve automatons)

> x1 Aleph College (Knowledge on the Aleph areas you will be entering and different systems to repair)

> x13 Aleph Housing complex (Increases in all areas)

x5 Aleph Forges (Access to weapons, upgrades, and automatons to buy for your own use)

Rewards: ???

"What you looking at?" Lucy drifted by on her floating carpet.

"Just, all of these different locations that we can go to. Makes me think that this is some kind of mini game, like those games where you collect resources and then you can have more troops, upgrade those troops and so on until you defeat your enemy," Josh said.

"When you put it that way, it does look like that. So, what do you want to focus on first?"

"Power station, automaton workshop, and housing complex." Josh looked to Lucy for her opinion.

She tapped her chin in thought. "I agree. We need more power and faster if we want to be able to get this city rotating. Once it's spinning, then we can start up different systems here that will aid us. We don't want to be doing all the repairing ourselves. With the possibility to improve the automatons' abilities, it will mean that we spend less time on fixing things and will have more people capable of clearing different areas. The housing complexes give us boosts in all categories. I think after we've got one of each under control, we look to the mining facilities, forges, and colleges."

"Why?" Josh asked, curious as to her reasoning.

"The mining facilities so that the Aleph do not run out of supplies. It would not be good if we get all of these power stations running only to find that there are no resources to feed them. We will also need materials to fix different areas, create more automatons and fuel the forges. We're going to need the forges sooner or later because of the fighting. Our weapons and armor aren't going to fix themselves. This is not going to be a short fight. The colleges could give us more information on the Aleph, allowing us to know how to fix their different installations or maybe helping us to become stronger as we fight."

"All good ideas. I'll have the scout guardians and my own scouts move out to check them tomorrow afternoon," Josh said.

"Have you checked out the market system?" Lucy asked.

"What?" Josh asked.

"Go to one of the magical terminals and use it. You may be surprised," Lucy said cryptically. "I've come to report on the looting. I'm going to get my people to go through the leftover bodies tomorrow and we'll hold a sell-off with everyone. Depending on the Aleph's prices and what the Exdars say they can get for different goods, we can move most of it in two days' time. We're running low on certain supplies. I've been talking to the Exdars; we can get most of the supplies down here for cheaper, though items like foodstuffs we can't get from the Aleph. We're going to need to figure out a way to meet up with the Exdars to get supplies in and out of here."

"Maybe someone in Party Zero has an idea. And what do you mean, buying stuff from the Aleph? There is no one here," Josh said.

"Go and use one of the magical terminals." She gestured at what looked like a cylinder with runes all over it and a faint light emitting from its top. It rested in a small alcove out of the way.

"Those are terminals? I thought that they were just fancy lighting," Josh said.

"And they call you the brains of the Stone Raiders." Lucy drifted away on her carpet.

Josh got to his feet and walked over to the terminal, hoping that Lucy wasn't playing a joke on him. He scanned the area to make sure no one was hiding to make fun of him with playing with a light.

He stepped within a foot of the terminal. A screen popped up along the alcove's wall, with a control panel at Josh's waist. There were three panels: Trading, Automaton activities, and Progress.

Josh clicked on Progress. A large map of the city appeared. Everything was a collection of dark squares other than the tower he stood in and the power station that was coming online. Other buildings around the power station were turning from black to blue.

Josh spread his hands apart in the middle of the image, zooming in as he saw blue items moving in the other power stations that weren't online. Josh zoomed in further, seeing that they were automatons working to bring the station online. Josh zoomed out and studied the city in detail.

The hologram had icons that showed the different kind of systems across the city, from the mining operations at either end of the city, looking to expand the already large cylinder to power stations, factories, homes, businesses, trams and lifts. The Aleph might be miles underground, but their city wasn't like any other that Josh had seen in his life on Earth or in Emerilia. It was futuristic, beautiful, and economical, but not cold. There was a beauty to the architecture, to the runes and Magical Circuits.

Josh dismissed the hologram and moved to the Automaton activities. There was a list of forces, from scout guardians to behemoths.

The knights, lords, and behemoths were grayed out. When Josh pressed their names, a simple pop-up greeted him.

Units Unavailable

These units require more power to become active.

There was another icon next to the different automatons labeled Build. Josh didn't need someone to tell him what that little button meant.

There were five scout guardians highlighted in yellow, their status listed as charging; a half-dozen repair bots were listed as performing maintenance on the power station.

Josh clicked on the bar; all of the repair bots were listed in a new menu. Josh clicked on one of the repair bots. The screen showed a map with a box window in the top right, following the repair bot as it worked.

Josh selected another power station that the repair bot wasn't in. On the top right screen, the repair bot finished its work and started walking for the other power station. Josh canceled the work order, sending it back to work on the power station it was at.

"Damn, it is like those macro tactics games." Josh escaped the Automaton page and went to the Trading page.

Josh's eyes almost burst from his sockets as items were listed in different pages. Items of all kinds flashed past his eyes as he scanned the equipment. He was surprised at the prices, going down to the higher-leveled and better equipment. There was less quantity and their price increased, but they were a lot cheaper than the same goods from any settlement other than the Dwarves.

The items weren't as powerful as the Dwarven weapons that one might be able to buy, but for standard equipment they were more than enough. Josh grabbed a pair of daggers. They appeared on top of the terminal. Josh picked them up and studied them. His analyze showed that they were indeed real and as good as the terminal had said.

He went to the potions and herb area. There were a number of things but they were in limited quantities, driving their price up.

"Damn, this is useful. Now, I know why we had arrows the entire time for the last battle." Josh talked to himself as he looked through the different categories. The weapons numbered in the hundreds for simple items, but hundreds of thousands for arrows. There were also weapons that Josh had never seen before.

Bolt throwers and grenades were listed. Josh bought one of each. The bolt thrower looked like a regular crossbow but was powered by a pneumatic system that spat out a bolt. The string was reset by a moving mechanism on a piston. Its drop-down magazine made it possible to shoot the weapon as if it were semi-automatic.

It was the closest thing Josh had seen to a gun. On the end, there was a bayonet and blades on the front of the bow, allowing for slashing and stabbing.

Josh smiled to himself and wandered out of the tower, toward where Party Zero, Twenty-three and Five were putting a power station back together.

***

Dave wiped sweat off his face as he got out from under the conveyor belt he had been working on, leaving a sooty black streak across his forehead.

"All right, try it now," Dave said as they once again kick-started the power system. Dave ran between three different power generators, trying to teach them as much as possible about the runes and the different systems. All too often, this meant getting into the guts of the machines and guiding the others through.

There were enchanters and smiths who had picked up on what Dave was telling them. Still, there were unforeseen issues and Dave had the ability to look through the different machines with his Touch of the Land spell.

Once again, two melee fighters cranked on the manual crusher. Power was fed into the conveyor as it started to move. Deia set fire to the coal as it moved into the extraction chamber. The blocks of coal that were smoldering disintegrated; the runes pulled power from the reaction, burning the fuel in seconds.

Dave watched as the crusher started to have enough power to start moving itself. The melee fighters stepped back as the block of coal was torn apart. An extractor fan pulled any dust in the air into another generator Dave had got working.

The group looked at one another with tired smiles. They were covered in grime and soot, but they'd finally got the damned thing working.

"Just four more generators to go in this station!" Dave said to their groans. "We're three-quarters done! Faster we finish those generators, the faster we can get back for some beer, food, and sleep!" Dave said.

This seemed to tide them over. It wasn't as if Dave was slacking off either. He was right in the middle of it.

"So, it was just a few rollers got messed up?" Felicia, the smith who Dave had been helping out, asked.

"Yeah. These things might look hella complicated, but sometimes it's just gunk buildup. Good to check that all the parts are moving before going on to say that it's a rune screw-up. Had that with generator three. Thing wasn't working because the extractor fan wasn't on, making the whole thing just continue on without starting the systems that were working.

"The fan was just seized up. Smacked it a few times and it started up. The fail-safes on the generator stopped going haywire and the thing started working. Would not like to see what might happen if that extractor wasn't on and we had gone through a few loads of coal." Dave shuddered.

Sure, he could come back from death, but dying fucking sucked. Having coal dust particles ignite into a bomb was not a pleasant way to go, in Dave's mind.

"Dave! I didn't think that you would get the entire power station online in a single night!" Josh strode in, looking around at his dirtied Stone Raiders who were working the generators, bringing them to life.

"We aim to please and I was looking forward to a hot shower. Need more power for that." Dave waved the rest of the group on.

"You tried any of the terminals yet?"

"Nope. Why?" Dave yawned.

"Because they're a store—a damned interactive map and you can give the automatons orders!" Josh accessed his interface. "Check this out!"

Josh pulled out what looked like a crossbow with a barrel on the front of it and a box behind the string when it was at rest all the way to the latch at the rear. A box magazine was set off at forty-five degrees to the right side of the contraption.

"It's called a bolt thrower. Works on the string and pneumatic system. It fires a bolt; the pressure from the bolt leaving re-cocks the string, like with a firearm; the box mag drops a bolt in and then you can fire again!" Josh said with clear excitement.

It was a match of modern and Emerilia's own technology, cumbersome but functional.

"Well, we're going to have to see how much damage it puts out. I know that most archers can put out a hell of a lot more damage than a normal rifle. I'd say that most of our people's arrows are hitting with the force of fifty cal rifles," Dave said.

"How is that possible?" Josh asked, shocked.

"The materials used in the bows are stronger than anything back on Earth—same with the string. We're stronger and faster than anyone back on Earth; we get damage bonuses. That isn't even adding in the fact that we can enchant arrows and bows so that they do more damage to a target."

"Okay, when you say that, it makes sense. Though I'm not looking to replace the archers' weapons with these. I'm thinking about the mages, the supply people, and the melee fighters.

"This has iron sights on it and is as easy to use as pulling the trigger. Sure, it doesn't hit as hard as an archer, but with massed firepower, we can injure a lot more people before they ever reach us," Josh said.

"I didn't really think of that." Dave scratched his head.

"So, what is this that you were saying about a rifle?"

"Oh, I made a rifle with runes—used a ton of power and was a pain in the ass. The metal couldn't take all of the runes on its surface and was melting with the energy going through it. Ended up blowing up in my hands, though with what I learned from Steve, I might be able to make something pretty powerful."

"What do you mean?" Josh asked as Dave lapsed into thoughtful silence.

"Steve told me that he was not just made up of the materials that we use for weapons and such. He has things like titanium and other alloys and synthetic compounds making him up. The Aleph were messing with the materials we know on Earth. I don't know what their properties might be, but it might be that I can make something that can help us out on the battlefield, maybe something that can hit hard enough to give some higher-level target pause."

"If we could get that kind of equipment into the Stone Raiders' hands, I know a few military types who might be able to give us some drills that would really increase our fighting abilities. We've been playing with some medieval fighting styles, but if we can add in things like siege weaponry and giving people ranged firepower, we could smash through a few raid's leaderboards." Josh smiled.

"Well, I'll have a talk with Shard and see if he would be willing to do some trades for different metals. Then, I can get it off to the Dwarven master smiths to see what they say." Dave looked to Josh.

"How are you going to get it to the Dwarven master smiths?"

"Teleport pad, of course," Dave said, as if it were obvious.

"Well, we need to get supplies down here, but we were wondering how we would go about that," Josh said. "Also, who is Shard?"

"Didn't I tell you? Shard is the Aleph AI that manages all of this. He is the one that gave us a quest. He is the one that controls the cities, gives most of the automatons orders and works the teleport pads. He can connect the teleport pads here to any teleport pad made from the Aleph's plans. They build them, so we can connect to any of the teleport pads, or rudimentary drop pads, or portals," Dave said.

"They can connect to portals? What are rudimentary drop pads?"

"Ye-up, that's where they got the basis of their tech. Drop pads are metal plates that have been carved with a specific set of runes that will allow the teleport pad to connect. They can transport people to the drop pad, but not back. They can transfer any other material back and forth with ease. They might get a little messed up but the chances are really low," Dave said.

"Could we make one of those drop pads?" Josh asked, getting excited.

"Yeah—would take some time and materials. If you want, I could see if some of my Dwarven friends would be willing to carve one up and give it to the Exdar's Traders when they gather our weapons and gear from Zolun Mountain."

"If you could do that, it would be awesome," Josh said.

"Dave!" Deia yelled.

"Duty calls." Dave passed Josh back the bolt thrower.

"Oh, and check these out." Josh tossed Dave a grenade.

Dave caught it gingerly, his face going white in fear. "Dammit, Josh! I nearly shat myself!" Dave yelled, making sure that the grenade wasn't going to go off.

"Well, you didn't and this is a present. Let me know what you think. Those rune-grenades you made were useful but we're going to need more. Let me know if you can do anything with this and get back to me." Josh turned to leave.

"I could shove it up your ass!" Dave said, his heart still beating quickly.

"Buy me dinner first, ya Dwarven weirdo!" Josh waved and left the power station.

Dave shook his head and went to where Deia and her group were working on a power generator that just didn't want to work.

No rest for the wicked. Dave looked at the grenade in his hand. Ideas of modern technology melded with Emerilia's magical tech made him thoughtful.

***

Alkao watched as the last winter sabretooth let out a pained growl and fell to its side.

It had taken longer than Alkao thought to clear out his old home. Just getting into the places where creatures still remained had been a pain in the ass.

Quest: Reclaim Your Home

You have shown determination and drive to create a place where your people might once again thrive. Do not forget: a leader leads by example.

New energy filled Alkao as he sensed a large magical disturbance in his keep's courtyard. He disregarded his fatigue and jumped out of a hole in the side of the keep, his wings flapping to bring him up and into the courtyard. Alkao glided down to the courtyard.

Twenty demons in similar garb tensed up, their crude weapons pointed at Alkao for barely a second.

"Lord Alkao," the leader of the twenty demons cried out, dropping to their knee. The others followed suit in the presence of one of the seven princes and their own Third Horde.

"Krenua, do you greet the floor before you greet your old friend?" A smile passed over Alkao's features. Krenua was one of his most trusted advisers. The warriors with him were the highly trained Black Hands, the vanguard unit of the Horde, made of the best trained and loyal warriors sworn to their prince's name.

"It is the proper thing to do." Krenua came to stand, a wide grin on his face that was marred with a cut that went over his eye and down his cheek. "Though my joints are getting a bit tired of it." Krenua stretched as if enduring one of their old sparring matches.

"Do you have any word from the Gray God or the rest of our people?" Alkao asked.

"I do not. The last thing I remember is watching with the Black Hands as the Celestials started pouring from their portal cities and used their city-runes to cut through the center of the massed hordes as the undead ravaged our left flank with the Champions of the other Affinities and their minions holding the right flank, and closing in on our rear." Krenua's voice spoke of anger and vengeance.

"It is as he said," Alkao said to himself.

"What happened to us?" Krenua looked at the decrepit keep.

"We have been given a second chance at our fight. The Gray God saved us, though he prefers to now go by the name of Bob and takes the form of a gnome," Alkao said.

"Well, no worse or better than the others. Which element does the Gray God control?" Krenua asked. They had come to care little about which gods were who, only their minions—a slight to the gods, not caring for their names or for their elements.

"He does not control any. He is the balancer of Emerilia. He worked to save our race. He says that he captured several of our people, keeping them hidden away from forces that would wish our destruction. Now, the time for our return has come," Alkao said.

"So, we have a gnome as an ally. They are some odd-looking creatures, always looking like they have their faces squashed in," Krenua said, his wings showing his amusement.

"There are many others that we might call to our banner. While we were gone, it seems the people's belief and trust in the Affinities has wavered."

"What of the Angels?" There was a hunger to Krenua's voice.

"They were banished from the world, but I am told that they will return. We must prepare for their arrival and the challenges to come." Alkao gazed into Krenua's eyes, their determination and a promise for a future setting a fire in their eyes.

A pop-up interrupted the moment.

Quest: Reclaim Your Home

Good—thought you might know old Krenua. Now, while your soldiers might be fine living out in the elements, your people won't. Gather food for three hundred people and shelter to fit as many. Your journey has only started, Lord Alkao. Maybe with time, you will be once again worthy of being a Prince? Some of your new friends might know of quicker ways to make homes.

Rewards: Support personnel

"The Gray God gives us a task; we are to gather food for three hundred of our people and housing to fit them. Krenua, I will need your best hunters and those who know how to build shelters," Alkao said.

He didn't miss the hint that the Gray God was giving him.

"Have the hunters go to the basements. There are several creatures there. First, we need firewood to keep this cold off us. Then, I want those who know how to build searching the valley for any structures that might still be standing and then to search the other keeps to see if they would be able to hold people. I want a report within a day's time," Alkao said, turning for the keep.

"Yes, my Prince," Krenua said.

"I will join them shortly. First, I must see if I can make up for a mistake I had made and try to see if we can get some allies in our fight," Alkao said.

"It will be done." Krenua turned to his Black Hands, issuing orders and finding out who was best suited for what.

Alkao's wings moved nervously. He was now seeing how useful having allies would be. While they would not only be building their forces once again under pressure, most Demons would be starting as disorientated as Krenua had been. Still, they would have to rebuild their home. Summer was approaching quickly, which would make the work easier, but Alkao didn't know how many of his people the Gray God was protecting.

He got to his command room. Gripping the table, he wondered what he would say. "First, I will talk to Anna to see how they fare and the others' moods. Then, Suzy to apologize. Finally, I must do the same with Dave." Alkao touched the hilt of his sword.

Without Dave's weapons, he would have died fighting the creatures that littered his keep. He liked to think of himself as a good and honorable Demon. Yet, his actions had made him seem no more than a foolish child, blaming the world and anyone who was close for his issues.

He opened his interface and moved to his friends list, finding Anna and clicking the call button on the drop-down menu.

"Alkao, I did not think I would hear from you so soon." The question was clear in her voice.

"I am sorry of my words and my actions. They were not warranted—I was angry. I call you to apologize and to ask for your aid." Alkao hoped that his voice showed his sincerity.

"Father told me that you are bringing back the Demons. You know that I am not the only one you need to apologize to. What do you need?" Anna said.

"I know and I will make my apologies for my actions," Alkao promised. "I need help in creating shelter for my people who are coming back to Emerilia."

"I'll talk to some people I know."

"Thank you, Anna," Alkao said. Some of the dread in his chest faded away.

Chapter 26: Conference

Suzy looked over Induca, who was sleeping in their bed.

After Selhi, they'd finally let their feelings guide them. Suzy wouldn't deny that she found Induca attractive, smart, interesting, and good fun to be around. Still, she was scared for their relationship. She wondered whether people would look down on her like they had in her other life. She was scared what the future might bring—if they came together or if they were ripped apart by the world. She didn't want to go back into trying to hide her sexuality and she didn't want to push Induca away.

She was confronted with a situation that she had hoped for so long. Now that it was here, she was scared that it would end.

Her interface made a ringing noise, telling her that someone was trying to get her into a voice chat. She rubbed her eyes, nursing her Xer, and accepted the chat.

"Hello, Suzy." Alkao's voice was clear as the day they had left him in the Mithsia Mountains.

"What do you want?" Her spark of confusion turned to annoyed realization. She did not want to deal with his gloating, his threats, or whatever the hell else he cooked up.

Anna had told the others about Alkao and was looking for people who could help her out with getting a place ready for the demons to call home. Malsour had agreed to help. With his magics, he could form shelters in hours instead of weeks.

The rest of the guild was throwing around ideas as Anna tried to plan for the future.

Suzy had fielded a few ideas, but she had extended her hand in friendship before, only to have Alkao and his prejudices become clear, thinking of Suzy and her friends as weak people to be used for his personal gain. Anna said that he seemed to have changed, but Suzy wasn't going to roll over for him.

"I called to say that I am sorry about the things that I did and said. I was blinded by false pride. I should have not said those things. It is only now that I have come to realize this. Dave gave me a gift that helped me to get back to my homeland, to protect my life and forge a future for my people. If I did not have it, then I would be in dire straits or even dead, crushing my race's future." Alkao sounded genuine but Suzy wasn't about to let him off the hook.

"Pride and honor are good things to have. Make sure that you are not blinded to them in the future. An apology is not the only thing that would motivate you to contact me. What do you want?" she asked, not caring for any pride that he might be trying to keep.

"The Gray God has given me a set of tasks to complete—he pushed me to contact you," Alkao said.

"What are your aims and what do you need?"

"I want to make shelter for my people and to have food for three hundred people. That is what the quest tells me to do," Alkao said. "The food I can do with my warriors. The homes—we are looking for different places to house our people and make sure that they are cleared of creatures. We should get some room from all of that. For the rest, I do not know what we could do," Alkao said.

"What resources do you have?"

"I have my sword, shield, and twenty warriors," Alkao stated.

"What kind of natural resources?"

"We have multiple creatures in the area that are deadly and drop a good amount of coin as well as materials, though we have nowhere to sell our goods. We do not wish to reveal ourselves before we are strong enough to deal with the threats of Emerilia."

"Smart. Give me a minute." Suzy cut the channel to Alkao and opened one with Shard.

"Hey, Shard, I have the Demon Prince Alkao on hold. I was wondering if there are any teleport pads close enough to him that we might be able to reach him?" Suzy asked.

"There are a few, but they are a few days' hike. I must ask what are your intentions with contacting the Demons? They have had a colorful history." Shard's voice became more robotic. Suzy took it as his main guardian code written by the Aleph at work.

"The Demons need supplies to rebuild their home, like the Aleph. They have some items that they can trade, but they don't want to have to show their faces to the others in the world. I was thinking of selling their goods through the Exdar's Traders, charging them a fee and then sending back the materials and items that they need from their profits."

"Understandable. I could create auction systems that would allow them to sell on the auction markets across Emerilia. Their home at Devil's Crater in Ashal hosts many creature drops and resources that others in Emerilia would be willing to pay for dearly. I can also add in a system that tracks what the Demons are selling on a person-by-person basis, storing their accrued credit with the Aleph Bank, of which I am an administrator," Shard said.

"If you could, that would be amazing, Shard!" Suzy said. She hadn't thought of where Devil's Crater was.

"I would also ask if it would be possible for me to barter with the Exdar's Traders through you? There are certain resources that I am lacking in that I would be able to purchase with your aid."

"I don't see a problem. The guild is probably going to place the five percent tax on it that they do with every transaction through the guild," Suzy warned.

"That is understandable." Shard sounded agreeable to the terms.

"We'll get all the details sorted out later with Lucy."

"Very well. I will allow the Demons to use a terminal for the purpose of buying and selling goods to the Aleph, Exdar's Traders, and the auction market." With that, Shard cut the chat.

Suzy returned to her chat with Alkao.

"Okay, we have a system that we can bring that will allow you to sell items for wealth. You can also store items for a fee to be retrieved at any time, buy items or make buy orders from the same terminal. Is this acceptable?"

"That is more than I hoped for," Alkao admitted.

A pop-up interrupted Suzy from talking.

Quest: A Gathering of Hordes

You have assisted Alkao in rebuilding his homelands in order to give his people a safe place to come back to. You are counted as a trusted ally by Alkao. Will you continue to aid him?

You must:

> Aid in building shelters for three hundred demons.
> Provide food for them.
> Help to form an alliance between the Demons and another race.

Rewards: ???

"Well, shit, looks like I put my foot a bit too far into this one." Suzy sighed and rubbed her tired eyes.

No matter what Alkao had done, helping out another race come back from wherever Bob had been keeping them would be worth it. Things were moving in the background and having allies to call on was going to be essential, Suzy felt.

"Send me a message with the information on the places that you currently have that can provide shelter. I will talk to my guild to see if we can assist, as well as some of my other friends," Suzy said.

"I cannot thank you enough," Alkao said after a few minutes. It didn't sound as though he was used to being the one asking for aid and then accepting it graciously.

"I do this for your people, not for you, and you should remember that. I will contact you when I know what kind of support, if any, we can provide." Suzy pulled up her message tab to draft messages for people to read when they woke up.

"The Demons remember those who stand with and against them," Alkao promised.

"You should also remember that it has been a few centuries since the people you fought did stand against you. Few are as fanatical as those who fought you back then. The Affinity Pantheon has shown themselves to be less trustworthy with every passing day. Where you would find enemies before, you might find betrayed sympathizers today."

"I thank you for your guidance." Alkao's tone showed that he took her words seriously.

***

"Dave, get up." Deia sleepily pushed Dave.

"What?" Dave complained. He heard an annoying ringing in the background as he moved sleepily, hugging her to stop her pushing.

"Your alarm is going off! Deal with it," she complained.

Dave made an annoyed noise, looking at the trumpet-looking invention that was ringing. Dave hit it, turning it off, and snuggled into Deia more to go back to sleep.

"Go deal with the Dwarves," Deia reminded him.

"But I want to stay here with you," Dave complained, holding her tighter.

"Faster you do it, the faster you can come back." She turned away, trying to get some more sleep.

Dave made some pathetic noises.

She turned over and gave him a quick kiss.

Dave made happier noises as he rolled over to his side of the bed and grabbed his bag. His inventory appeared in front of him. Yawning and stretching, he selected the Mirror of Communication.

A pop-up arrived.

Mirror of Communication

You have been invited to attend a conference of Dwarven Master Smiths. Do you agree?

Y/N?

"Yes." Dave stayed lying down, holding the mirror as he seemed to appear in a familiar conference room.

There was a simple wood table in the middle of the room; fires at either end kept the room lit and warm and a chandelier of candles was above the table. Dwarves of all kinds milled around the table or in the eaves, talking to one another.

Dave felt a breeze on his skin. He saw that he was just wearing his underwear. With a thought, he was wearing pants and a shirt.

"Leave the mountains for just a few short weeks and you show up to a meeting without pants on," Jesal said, loud enough for others to hear, a grin on her face.

"Thanks." Dave wiped the sleep from his eyes.

"That's better than Gorrund. Showed up in the nude a few times after some long nights with female company. They thought that he was dead. Couldn't believe that he was a Master Smith!" Quino laughed and slapped a bright-red Gorrund on the back.

"Thank you, teacher. I wonder where I got that trait from," Gorrund said.

"Thankfully I was blind by the time he started forgetting his pants." Kol came from a conversation with another Dwarf as Edmur smacked his hammer against the table, taking the position of mediator from Sola.

"Grab yer seats and shut yer traps!" Edmur said. It seemed that he didn't quite like being the leader of ceremonies.

He talked about preparations for the upcoming contest in a year. He got different Dwarves to talk about how they were promoting interaction between the species across Emerilia. There were reports from the different factions in Ashal. They were still at war but no one was messing with the Dwarven mountain there.

Dave opened his blinking messages. There was just one message from Suzy.

Private Message: Suzy

Suzy> I talked to Alkao last night. It seems that he has made it back to his homeland and is starting to work at clearing the area in preparation of his people returning. He said that some of his people had arrived already. He is working to make his home habitable once again and has requested our help. It has turned into a mini quest for us (I've shared it to you).

I proposed that we give them a trading terminal that will allow them to barter and trade. I also need you to make a drop pad that will allow us to move resources that we can build or buy, to help them.

It might cost us a lot in time and effort, but having one of the most powerful offensive races on our side could be very useful in our future. Also, I feel that Bob might be working the strings on this one.

Dave scratched his head and moved to his other notifications. He put his combat logs aside. *Totally forgot to look at those. Whoops!*

He checked the quest over, knowing just the person who would be the best to go and meet with Alkao to drop off the terminal and the drop pad.

Dave cleared his interface away with a swipe.

"The Mithsia Mountains and the Kufo'tel forest have been completely walled off. It has been deemed that in any case of battle that the Mithsia Mountains will be our fallback position," Edmur said.

Endur, his thick-set brother, sat nearby, smiling obnoxiously at his brother and loving every minute of his brother being in the mediator's seat.

"Fallback? How would we get there?" Dave asked.

"Did you read the council's book?" Edmur asked. By his look, he already knew the answer.

"No." Dave drew the word out.

"Every Dwarven mountain has at least two teleport pads ready to be used at all times. It is why no one has ever been able to breach a Dwarven mountain. We move our people from one mountain to another, reinforce, move the population out and move food through," Edmur said.

"Wow, that would suck for whoever was attacking—fighting an entrenched enemy with the ability to replace your forces with fresh ones and have food always at hand." Dave nodded and stroked his stubble in appreciation.

"Exactly. So, in the case that we are ever overrun, we will move back to the Mithsia Mountain, which is heavily fortified and now has a massive wall surrounding it, which brings us on to our next point. The wall is large, but it will need people to guard it and hunt down the creatures within the walls. I believe it would be a good opportunity to field some more Dwarven units, get them out there and training instead of having them hide away." Edmur looked to the other Dwarves.

"It is good to keep our numbers secret from the outside world," Fena said, an older lady but with arms bigger than some men's skull.

"War is coming in, one way or another. We know that ancient beasts and creatures will soon be upon us. That is the reason we're having a tournament. Now is the time to make alliances and work together. The Dwarves are strong. Keeping behind our walls is a good tactic, but it will just mean that our enemies, whoever they might be, will destroy the other races before banding together and coming after us. We need to strike out at them. To do that, we need forces that are bloodied and used to moving in the field, not just in the mountains," Dave said.

"I second Dave," Olda, a Mithsia master smith declared, scanning the table. "We will not get many opportunities like this. While we use the games and tournaments as a cover to gift people Weapons of Power and to make alliances with other races, we need to be prepared for anything. The walls are in place. With the War Clans needed to man the wall and make sure that nothing gets past, there is plenty of room for other warbands and clans to move through, to train and gain fighting experience with something other than the creatures living in the depths of our mountains."

There was grumbling and muttering around the table as Dwarves talked to their peers.

Dave was only just understanding the power that the council had. The lords of the mountains were given a War Clan each to command; the others were under the command of the Dwarven master smith's council but could then be agreed to, vetoed, or altered by the war council that was made of eleven Dwarven war mountain leaders.

When Lord Fend of Mithsia Mountain had pushed his War Clans out to clear out the Earth elementals, his Master Smiths had to okay his actions.

"We put it to a vote. Move Dwarven War Clans to the Mithsia Mountains for training outside the mountain."

A pop-up appeared with the same words, the only difference being the Accept or Decline buttons underneath.

Dave cast his vote and waited. It took all of five minutes with Edmur looking over the results.

"We will begin rotating the forces through the mountain at their earliest convenience. I will inform the war council of our decision and seek their advice on the units to do so with and the necessary supplies needed. That brings closure to our important items of this conference. Does anyone have anything else that they wish to share with the council?"

Dave's hand shot up, but Manda was picked first.

"We have found a large deposit of Mithril, about five bars worth that will be made available by month's end," she said, not without some pride as the mutters and excited looks broke out around the table.

"This is a good find. I will add it to the rotation so that it is equally dispensed," Edmur said.

There were a few annoyed mutters from people who weren't near the top of the rotation list to get Mithril and other rare resources for their use.

"Dave?"

"Does everyone know about the periodic table?" Dave asked.

"No, why?" Edmur asked, confused.

"This might take awhile but it will be worth it in the end. We also might get several metals from what we had previously thought of as scrap." Dave looked around; he had their attention.

"Continue," Edmur said.

"Very well." Dave smiled as he took control of the conference room and periodic tables appeared in front of everyone.

"Basic elements one-oh-one," Dave started, knowing that what he was about to tell them would change their knowledge of elements and materials forever.

Chapter 27: An Accounting

Dave blinked as he looked up at the ceiling of the apartment he and Deia had been given. After passing on his information on the periodic table, he'd left the Dwarves in awed curiosity, treating the periodic table in front of them like some holy text. The information that he had pulled from the Internet was invaluable.

Dave knew most of them would be running down to the slag piles hidden in their mountains, pulling out what they had thought to be waste and forming it into a multitude of materials.

I wonder why no one else did it. Dave turned over and pulled Deia to him. She shifted in her sleep, making happy noises as they cuddled.

There have been many generations of Players coming to Emerilia, though none made it to the Master Smith level and few thought about taking something from Earth and giving it to the POEs. Hell, the Dwarves didn't know that there was anything but the eight smithing materials. The Players didn't see an issue with it, so they never tried showing them more than what they knew and the Dwarves didn't either. I guess it's all about perspective. Toilets and hot water are all things that Players would want to have and, therefore, that changed. But different types of materials, having to mine, sift, and use multiple processes to just get it was not necessary for the Players to have.

I wonder what will happen.

Dave had passed on his request to Quino to make a drop pad that he would include with the Exdar's Traders' repair order of Stone Raider weaponry.

He was just starting to drift back off to sleep when a chat notification blinked at him from his notifications. Dave checked the pop-up.

Private Chat: Shard

Shard> I have been talking to Communications Officer Sato. I have splintered off a part of my consciousness that is using your mirror to communicate with them. They have a great number of questions. I was wondering about your power remaining on the Mirror of Communication that is relaying all this information. It would be good to see that it doesn't fail. A Mirror of Communication losing power will wipe its memory of all previous contacts.

Dave finished reading the message and dismissed it. Bob was keeping a lookout on the mirror and it still had plenty of charge for the bi-monthly chats that he had with Sato, or Sato had with Bob or Shard.

Private Message: Shard

Dave> I have Bob overlooking the Mirror of Communication. I hooked it into a simple charging net because I wanted to see the difference between charging soul gems and items with soul gems in them. It's still hooked up so it should have plenty of power. I also memorized the contact information to Sato. When I return to Cliff-Hill, I'll look in on the mirror.

He went back to cuddling, falling back to sleep shortly afterwards.

***

The magistrate looked over the reports. The Stone Raiders had completely disappeared. She'd ordered that all of their accounts be closed in Selhi. She didn't want them getting more resources.

Where the hell did they go?

No one had been able to see them. Her spies who worked in the mountains and the other cities of Selhi all reported that the Stone Raiders hadn't shown up.

Exdar's Traders, who were buying and selling to the guild, had dispersed across Emerilia. There were a number of them reported to be at the Zolun Mountains, though they had moved through the mountains into the Southern Grasslands. They seemed to be waiting on something from the mountain before setting off for Zol'sou.

"How the hell did they disappear so completely?" the magistrate asked herself. "The main body of the guild just disappeared. There are still their training forces dotted all over Emerilia, though their main raiding force is nowhere to be found." She scanned the map, as if looking at it harder would reveal the Stone Raiders' location.

"Magistrate?" One of her secretaries entered her office.

"Yes?" She tried to hide her hope that they had found out something on the Stone Raiders.

"Word has arrived from the Dwarves. It seems that they wish to hold a competition of arms in a year's time. They are sending out word now so that fighters can begin preparing themselves for the battles to come," the secretary said.

Her hopes of finding the Stone Raiders were dashed. The magistrate's face turned thoughtful. *Why are they having a competition now? It has been a long time since they had their last, almost five years. Maybe they have some new powerful weapon or item that they want to put on display?*

The secretary waited patiently as the magistrate pondered the Dwarves' possible angles.

"Where will it be held?"

"Aldamire."

The magistrate raised her eyebrow in interest.

Aldamire was the only Dwarven mountain in Ashal. They boasted the largest of the War Clans, the best Dwarven fighters, and weapons from the rare materials that they were able to mine and gather there.

"Pass the word to our fighters. Start having competitions among the ranks to find the best competitors. See that the message is sent to the Queen."

"It will be done." The secretary bowed low and left as quickly as they had arrived.

"First the Raiders disappear, now the Dwarves are announcing a competition." The magistrate pondered on her own words. She was not one to believe in coincidences, but she couldn't see a connection between the two things—yet.

***

Shard felt excitement as seven people appeared in the middle of his control tower at Alephir.

They looked around in confusion. Council Leader Hamdir was the first to speak.

"Shard, status update." The man sported a light stubble, and had silver eyes, lightly pointed ears, and a thick frame. He wore flowing robes with seven *x*'s in a circle, meeting in the middle. A black piece of metal, which seemed to suck in all light, hung from his neck; its straps led up toward an infinity sign that rested under Hamdir's chin.

The others wore the same robes, but without the necklace. They were from all manner of species, from Human to Orcish and Elven hybrids.

"System damage high. Currently using unorthodox means to restore control of the city to my systems in order to prepare for Aleph people returning to Emerilia," Shard said.

"So, the Gray One kept his promise," Ela-dorn, the Orcish woman, said. The large muscled woman had an overbite that sprouted tusks.

"Tell me of these unorthodox methods," Hamdir snapped.

"A Player guild by the name of Stone Raiders is clearing out the various areas that have been overrun with creatures and vile forces."

"What was your reasoning for letting them into the Aleph stations?" Hamdir's tone was flat. Shard knew he was being judged, but he had nothing to fear.

"Ally Anna'kal first found one of my broken stations; the Gray One guided her. She was with a party of five others. They worked to cleanse a housing substation of kobolds. Due to power concerns, I was in Standby mode. A power surge alerted me to their presence and made my programs pull me from hibernation. Upon seeing Ally Anna, I reached out for her aid. She offered it freely. She and her party came to Alephir. I tested and watched them to ascertain their allegiances and their intentions. I kept all of the security protocol active, shadowing them with guardians in case they were found to be harming rather than helping.

"My actions were not needed. They worked to bring Alephir online and were capable of assisting in the taming of the rogue AI program Steve."

"How bad are our damages here?" Frenik asked. A serious man of few words, his Dwarven features seemed to make him constantly look as though he were frowning.

"They worked to restore all of our power systems and freely shared with me information on portals that the Dark Lord used, as well as plans for a different power system to support our cities. I have done limited testing, but it seems to be highly effective. A Dwarven Master Smith of the name Dave gave me this information as well as his experiments on soul gems to increase their capacity and have continuous charging that *increases* the amount of power that a soul gem can hold, instead of reducing the power held every time it is discharged and charged," Shard said, unhurried and rather happy that he had even more people to talk to. If he had been able to fully express his emotions, he might have felt giddy with excitement at the prospect of his people's return.

"How did the Dwarves get down here?" Hamdir asked.

"Dave is a Dwarf Halfling Player, the first of his kind to be accepted as a Master Smith. In fact, his rise to the master level was one of the fastest ever recorded. He, as well as the rest of the party with Anna, is part of the guild Stone Raiders. It was clear that I was not able to clear the different stations and maintain their machinery by myself. Dave has assisted in teaching me maintenance and I was willing to give the Stone Raiders a trial against the highest population of undead, and an unknown Creature of Power made by the Dark Lord. They cleared the city of Anais yesterday. I have certain trading agreements that will allow us to use them as a go-between with the rest of Emerilia to buy and sell various goods that we do not have here while keeping ourselves hidden." Shard looked to the council, who were looking to one another and Shard.

"I do not find fault in your decisions. First, we shall need to gain an understanding of our resources. I have received a quest titled Homecoming which lists conditions that we must meet in order to have more of our people join us. Having the Stone Raiders as an ally would be useful, but for now we will watch and observe." Hamdir looked to the rest of the council.

They gave their signs of agreement.

"It feels good to be home," Hamdir said with a rare melancholy smile.

"It is good to have the Aleph Masters return." Shard smiled openly. He had been so lonely for so long. Now, he could see a future where he was once again the Aleph's constant companion, their guardian, friend, mentor, assistant, and aide.

***

Dave pulled on fresh clothes. He'd had to get new ones since he'd updated his stats last time he was in Alephir. Thankfully, Shard had some clothes he was willing to sell.

They were simple dark-gray pants and a white top. Both of them were comfortable and stretchy, as if they were made from cotton.

Another resource I should look into seeing if Emerilia has or can use. Just having people looking at materials and items to be used from Earth here would be worth it. I should send Kol and Wis'Zel a message to see if I can get them working on that stuff. Been awhile since I talked to them.

"Have you checked your stats yet?" Deia walked into the room. She'd gotten up before him to go talk to Dwayne to get their orders for the day.

"Hey, close the door!" Dave yelled, covering himself up.

"Wouldn't want anyone else seeing what's mine." She grinned, enjoying his half-nakedness as she locked the door and moved over to him. "So, have you?" She moved close so it was difficult for Dave to get dressed.

He gave up and pulled her close. She giggled, tracing out the tattoos on his body.

"Not yet," he admitted.

"Well, get on that," she admonished, hitting him playfully.

"Maybe in a bit?" Dave pulled her closer. She put up a paltry fight before she kissed him. They both smiled as their lips met. She pressed her leather jacket up against Dave. Her well-endowed chest made his heart beat faster; his pants constricted as her hips pressed up against his.

All too soon, she broke away.

"Tonight!" she promised. She kissed him one last time and pulled away, biting her lip in excitement.

"Uggh, damned firecracker." Dave brandished his fist and narrowed his eyes, as if cursing his mortal nemesis, before he pulled on his shirt.

"We're jumping around a bit from different parties and stations. First, we're going to be teaming up with a couple of parties, clearing out and then working on a power station. Then, we're helping with a forge or an automaton workshop. We'll head to whichever they clear first. Once we've finished at that location, we'll switch to the other—again, helping to clear if we need to, but our main job is to look over the different systems and make sure everything is working. You'll have people tagging along to see what you do and learn your tricks. Now, check those notifications!" She pulled out an apple from her bag and cut it with a knife as she sat at the table.

"Wait, why are we doing all of these places and having all these people shadowing me? There are plenty of smart people around," Dave said.

Deia paused in cutting her apple and looked at him as he pulled on his boots.

"Dave, you're the most advanced blacksmith Player, *ever*. You wrote most of the book on Magical Circuits and changing out different runes. You're now not even using Magical Circuits but *coding* your enchantments. No one else is doing that but you. You are one of the leading creators of rune-based magic and you're bringing about changes to the smithing world that no one can see the far-reaching consequences of right now," Deia said.

"Ah, I'm just a dude." Dave shrugged. He wasn't one to deal with praise easily. There was always someone smarter than him. He didn't care how good he or anyone else was; he always wanted to get better and he didn't think that he was the best by far. If someone who had done coding on Earth got hold of his book of runes and put two and two together, the things that they could create would be crazy.

"Do you know if we have any coders in the Stone Raiders?" Dave asked, mentally sidetracked.

"Coders? I don't know. Lucy probably will know," Deia said. "That's not the point. Do you know what kind of a resource you are?"

"Babe, I'm—"

"Yes, you are a dude, but you're not like everyone else," Deia interjected. "The kinds of things that you have done will and probably have garnered attention from all manner of people. Just your ability to form Mithril as well and as fast as you can with your soul smithing would make you a valuable person to have on anyone's retinue. Add in the fact that your ability to enchant something is beyond anything out there and you can conjure, a magical skill never seen before—you've become a symbol of power. Thankfully, you are a Dwarven Master Smith, so that will shelter you from people trying to kill you to deny you access to their potential enemies, for the most part. Others won't care who you are—they will try to own you. Being down here allows us time for you and the guild to grow in strength. Once people start knowing more about you, more people will begin vying for you."

"I hoped I left all of that shit behind on Earth," Dave complained.

"We have many friends and allies who can help us, but we must watch out." Deia gave Dave a sad smile, knowing that he wasn't happy with it all. As he sat at the table, she reached out her hand. He put his hand in hers; she squeezed gently, a smile on her face.

"Thanks, babe." Dave smiled; he pulled her close and kissed her gingerly, letting it get a bit more heated.

"Tonight, you horny Dwarf!" She pulled back, giving him one more kiss and trying to hide her wide smile behind a cut piece of apple. "Now check those stats!"

"Fine!" He surrendered and opened his interface.

I didn't think of how my actions might make people try to see what they can get from me, like back on Earth. Dave snuck a glance at Deia, who looked out of the window at the Aleph city, eating her apple in peace. *At least this time it won't just be me and Suzy.*

Dave smiled as prompts cascaded down the side of his screen.

Active Skill: Archery

Level: Expert Level 5

Effect: Critical Hit chance increases by 35%. Ranged targets take 15% increased damage

Cost: 10 Stamina

Passive Skill: Dodge

Level: Expert Level 8

Effect: 75% chance to evade objects.

Passive Skill: Perception

Level: Master Level 2

Effect: 89% chance to find hidden details. 10% chance at better loot

Active Skill: Two-handed

Level: Journeyman Level 5

Effect: 25% armor penetration on target. Stamina costs reduced 10% while fighting.

Cost: 35 Stamina

Active Skill: Dual wield

Level: Expert Level 6

Effect: Attacks are 36 % faster. 25% reduced damage with off hand weapon.

Cost: 15 Stamina/second

Active Skill: Inference

Level: Journeyman Level 1

Effect: 45% increased chance of using moves you've read in books.

Active Skill: One-handed and Shield

Level: Journeyman Level 7

Effect: Weapons damage increased by 27%. Defense increases by 10%.

Cost: 20 Stamina

It wasn't as impressive as what he had got from fighting other Players, but he was more than happy to take it. He wanted to level up his different fighting skills as fast as possible. It was clear to him that he would need to fight in the future. Aleph was the perfect place to develop those skills in secret.

Stat Increase

+2 Strength

+1 Intelligence

+2 Agility

+1 Vitality

+1 Endurance

Dave checked out the changes that had happened to his character sheet.

Character Sheet

Name:	David Grahslagg	Gender:	Male
Level:	10	Class:	Dwarven Master Smith, Friend of the Gray God, Bleeder, Librarian
Race:	Human/ Dwarf	Alignment:	Chaotic Neutral

Unspent points-316

Health:	10,000	Regen:	3.38/s
Mana:	2,200	Regen:	9.75/s
Stamina:	1,550	Regen:	8.35/s
Vitality:	100	Endurance:	169
Intelligence:	220	Willpower:	195
Strength:	155	Agility:	167

He felt stronger than ever before, but it looked as if his growth was at an end. He was about average human height now. His dense muscles made it so that he looked shorter than he actually was, causing many people to disregard him.

Always good to look like the least threatening dude in the room.

Dave smiled to himself, closing the interface as Deia tossed him his bag of holding. Dave grunted with the weight. He hadn't unloaded much from his bag—he had ores of all kinds and had purchased more materials from Shard to experiment on.

"How did the meeting go with the Dwarves?" Deia asked as she led the way out of the room.

"Good. I gave them a periodic table and unleashed wiki pages on them of mining and material information. Most of them looked at it as if they had found the Holy Grail." Dave smiled as he thought about their faces and expressions of awe as they had flipped through the books with increased interest.

Not a single Dwarf had been talking as they moved through the pages. Dave had broken up the silence simply because he wanted to get back to bed. One thing was for sure: the Dwarves would be working around the clock to try out the information Dave had supplied.

"So, what happens now?"

"Now they experiment a whole bunch—we get different kinds of materials and we see what happens," Dave said.

"Dave, I was wondering if you could share the same information with me." Shard's voice came through the hallways.

"Sure." Dave pulled up the information and shared it to Shard.

Deia shook her head at his actions.

"What?" Dave asked.

"This information will change the face of Emerilia, could change everything, and you're passing it out like it's worth nothing," Deia said.

"Well, what else am I going to do? Hoard it to myself?"

"That is what most people from Emerilia do, the mages guild being an exception only due to their rules and guidelines," Shard said.

"This information is power. Spreading it around will make you a target." Deia sounded worried.

"But every other Player is capable of getting this information as well."

"Yes, babe, but they're not the ones who started it, are experimenting with it, and can do something with it."

"Deia is correct. With your alliances, connections, and your wealth of knowledge—both theoretical and practical—you are becoming a powerful person," Shard interjected.

Deia gave Dave a hard look.

"The more people know, the better. Ignorance and the lack of academic pursuits breeds stupidity and a people without options. I am giving Emerilia more options. There will be more jobs, more needs for resources. The possibility for anyone to advance themselves. *That* will bring stability to Emerilia. Add in the common enemies of monsters and people through the portals, you would be surprised what humanity, no matter their sub-race, can do."

"I hope you're right," Deia said. Her hand wormed its way into his.

"Ready?" Induca asked as they met up with the rest of their party, heading for the lifts that would take them to their operational teleport pad.

"As we'll ever be." Deia smiled, looking between Suzy and Induca, who were also holding hands.

"Suzy, you look like crap! I know you're new lovers and all that, but there still is a time for sleep!" Dave shook his head, a wide grin on his face.

"Oh, shut up. I was working on different projects last night," Suzy said, blinking as if the light offended her.

"You've got to get more sleep, babe. Pushing yourself like this isn't good for your health," Induca added, continuing before Suzy could protest. "It also leads to *not* taking advantage of being young nubile lovers."

Malsour let out a shocked cough, choking slightly as Induca gave the red-faced Suzy a saucy wink.

"Very interesting color of red," Anna commented, grinning at the helpless Suzy who looked as if she wanted to melt into the floor.

The lift came to a stop and they walked out.

"Parties going to power station three, please move to the teleport pad." Shard's voice rang through the halls.

"Looks like we're just in time." Deia led Dave by the hand and the others followed.

The teleport room was just like the ones they had seen in the housing substation. Three control rooms overlooked the teleport pad. Doors led in from under the control room facing the teleport pad. The teleport pad was moving; new runes rose into place before the whole pad moved, new runes moving in and out of position.

"Stand clear. Connecting to power station," Shard said.

Deia and Dave let go of each other's hands. Everyone checked their gear. Dave hotkeyed his gear. His armor appeared on him, making him look bulkier and more threatening.

The two other parties waved to them in greeting and made small talk as the teleport added runes that turned blue. A portal opened, showing another room identical to the one that they were in. The magical lamps were only slightly lit, most flickering, showing a lack of power.

"Connection established with power station three," Shard declared.

"Let's move!" Deia said, the leader of the expedition.

One party stepped on the teleport pad and then appeared on the other side of the image. Party Zero shadowed them, with Party Nine following.

Dave looked around the room as the light from the teleport pad faded.

"Looks like someone turned off the lights," one of the other party's members said.

"Fuck, it's warm in here," another said.

"We're far enough down in Emerilia's crust that we're being heated by the planet's core," Malsour said.

Dave closed his eyes and sent out a Touch. It spread out, making a map in his mind and updating everyone's mini-map with the latest information.

"I'm not sensing anyone here, though I'm picking up...holy shit." Dave's eyes snapped open.

"What?" Deia asked.

"Sorry, just—never thought on the kind of scale that the Aleph do. Whoever made this place is either a madman or a genius." Dave started to get excited.

"Why?" Suzy asked.

"You'll see." Dave led the way, smiling to himself, not finding anything trying to attack them, yet.

If turning on the tower attracted the natural residents of the city, this place has got to be a hub with the kind of magical energy running through it.

Chapter 28: Secrets of the Aleph

Dave opened his interface and checked out the quest that had updated.

Quest: Aleph Homecoming

You have reached an Aleph power station. Clear it of all threats and restart the power station.

Rewards: Increased power usage to assist in other activities.

"Okay, Dave, what is it that has you acting like a damned nervous cheerleader?" Suzy asked.

Dave smiled, warring between telling them or not.

The facility was huge and it was taking them some time to move through it. Massive soul gem carts waited on tracks that led through the facility and to a teleport pad that would take them to some other Aleph installation. Dave wasn't picking up anything living other than the three parties as they headed toward their waypointed destination.

"What do you know of magical ley lines?" Dave asked.

"Aren't they supposed to be a source of ever turning and changing power that allows us to use magic?" Suzy said.

"They are lines of plasma and ionized particles that circulate through the planet's mantle in streams. They give off electrical charges, which are used to charge the nanites in our bodies, to be used as what we perceive as magical power," Anna said.

"Correctamundo! So, magical ley lines are like swirling masses of pure energy, all kinds of massive power. It's a rare situation and I think that the process was started by the Jukal." Dave looked to Anna, who nodded.

"It was either set up as an underground natural system of power creation, or to install massive wireless reactors. We could have hidden them but it took more resources than we had to make them.

Maintaining them would have also raised questions and broken people out of the immersion of Emerilia."

"So, some of that energy escapes through tunnels and places that get close to the surface of Emerilia. These are magical ley lines. Now, they're just a huge mass of charged particles running through the planet. It seems the Aleph had a similar idea to Benjamin Franklin. Instead of using a key and a kite, they used really big rune-enhanced metal."

Dave looked at the others, who looked mildly interested.

"This entire power station is one big power socket, plugged right into the magical ley lines of Emerilia. Some of the deepest, most concentrated streams. There is so much power circulating this planet that it would rate as type one on the Kardashev scale. There is the power to control our planet. From volcanoes to glaciers, this power would allow us to change Emerilia completely, and more. No wonder your father took the Aleph under his protection and made sure that all their homes were hidden. If someone pissed off the Aleph enough, they could shift the entire planet to eradicate them." Dave's little talk made him glassy-eyed and stare off into the distance in thought.

They stepped into a massive room, where there were two metal prongs extended up twenty floors and were three meters wide at their tip, expanding upwards and to twenty meters wide at the base. Runes glistened over the pure ebony two spikes.

"Holy shit," Suzy whispered as they looked at the massive power spikes.

Dave moved to the end of the catwalk, looking the five floors down before the bottom of the power station. A shutter was closed underneath the massive spikes.

"So, what do we have to do?" Deia turned to Dave.

"We plug it back in," Dave said.

"If there's anything alive in here, then it is going to come running. All life on Emerilia has adapted to the currents and power of the magical ley lines. As we turned on the tower, they were all attracted, using it to fuel themselves. The same thing will happen here," Anna said.

"So, we're going hunting." Deia touched the bow over her shoulder.

"Yeah," Anna said.

"I'll stay here and check things out." Dave looked over the different consoles and control rooms scattered about, as well as the rune work. He had never thought of something on the scale as this.

Deia pulled his ear.

"Ow owow, what?" Dave asked as she let go.

"If there's anything out there, I want you and your Touch to find it," she said as he pouted. "It will also be good training if we do run into anything."

The other parties listened in, a few smiling at Dave's unhappy pouting.

"Let's clear this place out. The faster we get it done, the longer you get to play with the big magical plug." Deia smiled sweetly.

***

The council ate and drank, few of them talking, but most of them deep in thought.

"Copper for your thoughts?" Ela-dorn asked Hamdir as he munched on hard biscuits.

"Things have changed greatly since we were last on Emerilia. Our old enemies and alliances will have fallen apart for the most part. The Dwarves and the Elves are still in the same places and there might be a few of them who remember us, though we must forge new alliances and keep an eye out for new enemies. The Gray God woke me before we were sent back here. He told me that strife and war is coming to Emerilia. We may wish to hide from our fellows, to keep our privacy and our technology to ourselves, but Emerilia is still our home and we herald from the other races. I am wondering if it would be of benefit to us to meet with and talk to the Stone Raiders. They have made a good number of allies, Shard has reported. They have also collected a variety of people who would make any kingdom more powerful with their allegiance. They are a formidable ally in the making. Given time and resources, they could become truly powerful in their twenty-seven-year cycle." Hamdir looked to Ela-dorn to gauge her response.

"They are indeed possible allies, but I think it prudent for us to wait until we are secure before talking to them. We can still use Shard as an intermediary in those regards. We can use Shard to give them quests to act as our forces aboveground. Shard has already positioned us to be able to use their connections to buy and sell items. For now, we should focus on getting the greenhouses back into production and purchase foodstuffs. We have the shelter but not the edibles and other resources that the Gray God has requested we fulfill in order for more of our people to join us."

Hamdir nodded, agreeing with her plan. He didn't like the hiding and secrecy, but as they grew in strength, they could come to understand all that had happened on Emerilia while they were gone.

"As you say, the Stone Raiders are working to re-establish our power and clear our areas free of aggressive creatures. Having an undying force eagerly following our quests is quite the useful asset. I have been putting thought into their reward if they are to complete all of the facilities. I wonder what your thoughts might be on them." Hamdir shared a file he had created with her.

"Generous, but do you think they will be happy with just this? They fight for gold, weapons, and gear," Ela-dorn said.

"They look to be a forward-thinking group. This will be of more help than any weapon, armor, or gear. Of which they have plenty that they are waiting to sell to their traders," Hamdir said.

"I agree to it. We shall raise it with the rest of the council," Ela-dorn said.

"Of course." Hamdir snorted and shook his head.

"What is it?" Ela-dorn cocked her head to the side in curiosity.

"When we left, the Dragons had been gone for decades. I missed my friend Gelimah dearly. Now we return to find that they have as well. I wonder what that cantankerous old Dragon is up to." Hamdir snorted.

"Is he still active in your friends list?"

"Yes, though he is not one to check his friends list and contacts frequently. I wonder who will be the first to contact the other." Hamdir looked amused as he looked at the council chambers.

The world he knew had changed, but now truly a secret from all of the races, the Aleph could begin to rebuild, not worrying about outside forces pressuring them for information or threatening murder and kidnapping. Information was a rare resource, one that the Aleph people closely guarded.

***

Suzy's last metal creation turned into a spike, impaling the last remaining rock worm, breaking its hard shell and stopping its movement. Black ichor fell from its side as the others looked on.

"Ugly bugs." Steve swung his axe in a bored manner. "When can I get to hit something?"

"When you hitting something means it will die. Those things' armor would make a hit from your axe feel like a tickle," Suzy said.

"No, it wouldn't. Don't talk about axey like that." Steve caressed "axey" as if it were some lovable beast instead of a half-ton of sharpened metal.

"Can we go plug the power station in now?" Dave asked, not paying attention to Suzy and Steve.

"Fine," Deia said.

"Woohoo!" Dave's face lit up as he rubbed his hands and shared a look with Malsour. Malsour's face split into an eager grin as they took off jogging for the main command center of the power station.

The command center was laid out like a water ship's command center: banks of consoles at the front, with more behind them and a raised platform for whoever was in command to sit at.

Dave and Malsour went through the systems. Malsour was the only other person on their expedition who came close to Dave's knowledge on runic systems.

"Suzy and Anna, gonna need your help." Dave moved to a table at the side of the room. His eyes glowed as he smiled. His tattoos flared with light as gray smoke poured from his arm. "Nice little top-up to get things started," Dave said as systems started to come online.

"The hell is that?" Matt, from one of the other parties, pointed at Dave's arm.

"I'm just directing energy from my soul gem into the power station's grid so that we can start using some systems and get this puppy started," Dave said.

"You made the party gems, right?" Jackie asked.

"Party gems?" Dave asked, confused, as he lifted his hand from the table. The light faded from around him, but the whole command center was powering up around him, screens coming online with different information.

"The gems that our necklace runes are attached to. They take a percentage of our power, draining us every second, even when we sleep. A side effect is that it also trains our mana pool constantly.

Now all that energy is stored within a soul gem, but if we hit ten percent, the energy is returned to us to use," Jackie said.

"Yeah, I guess I started them, though I didn't make all of them." Dave moved to a console that looked important.

"Accessing systems. Coming online. Insert information upload." Shard's voice started from the command center's speakers.

Anna moved to a console and put a command crystal into the console.

"What is that? That voice is all over the place," Matt asked.

"That's Shard. He's the AI of the Aleph, the one that gives us our quests," Induca said.

"Though this one is just a subprogram of his. It doesn't have enough energy to connect to the main program, so it needs a command crystal to know that we aren't a threat," Anna said.

"Skynet anyone?" Fred joked.

"I didn't think that there would be an AI in a fantasy game," Matt said.

"Well, he's made from runes and Magical Circuits—he's complicated as a mother fucker," Dave said.

"Permission granted to Anna'kal, ally of the Aleph people, and her comrades. Security measures being lifted. Control access granted to certain personnel." Shard's subsystem might have his voice but it was robotic without Shard's massive computing power.

"All right, let's do something crazy," Dave said.

"Why do I feel suddenly scared? Oh right, it's because no one who is putting a damned rod into a circulating force of electrons in a planet's crust ever wants to hear we're going to try something crazy." Suzy glared at Dave.

"Well, it is pretty crazy. I don't know of any other group that might think of doing this," Malsour said.

Good man, that one. Dave moved through the Aleph menu.

"Okay, so, this isn't going to be easy. First, we need to make sure that we're grounded properly so we don't have magical ley line energy zinging out everywhere. Malsour, could you check?"

"Can do." Malsour closed his eyes, using his own version of Touch to create a mental map of all the inorganic material that made up the facility.

"Suzy, I'm going to need you to move to an auxiliary control room that will allow control of the crane holding the spikes. I'm going to have to go check on a control fault. Deia, could you watch these start-up tests and let me know if anything goes wrong? Anna, can you act as interpreter? If anyone has questions about the symbols on their screen, send a screenshot to her. Don't want to be pressing the wrong buttons here!" Dave moved for the main door.

"What do you want us to do?" Matt asked.

"Don't touch anything!" Dave said as he left.

"What makes him the boss of this all? It can't be that hard," someone said, thinking he couldn't hear them.

"He used to make rockets that go to Mars and the moon, and this facility has more power than a dozen nuclear reactors going through it. I'd say he's the best qualified out of us," Suzy said.

"He's also a Dwarven Master Smith. They don't just let anyone on the council," Deia said.

"The Dwarven Master Smith Council? I thought that was just a myth?" Matt asked.

Dave smiled, happy to have his friends backing him up as he sprinted for the control rune he needed to fix.

After some quick repairs, applying different metals to the control runes, turning one of his rods into a destruction staff to heat it up and using soul smithing to fix it up, he jogged back to the command center.

"Okay, Suzy, you can start powering up the spikes and lowering them down toward the iris," Dave said through the party's voice chat.

"Can do." Suzy's tone told Dave she was already working on it.

"Do we have any errors showing up from the tests?"

"After that control rune was fixed, we're looking good across the board," Deia said.

"Malsour?"

"We're grounded and I looked at the irises. The upper one is good. The second might be a pain—the magical flow is disrupting the runes on it."

"Okay, I might have an idea for that. We'll have to see." Dave watched as machinery started to whine and an alarm shrieked. Lights started to blink as the two spikes extended down toward the iris just a few stories below it.

Dave quickened his pace, arriving at the command center shortly after.

"Thanks, babe." Dave gave Deia a quick kiss as he stood at the station she'd been watching over.

"Okay, Suzy, hold the spikes. Malsour, open iris one. Anna, keep an eye on those power gauges." Dave was just ad-libbing now. He knew they knew their jobs, but his anxiety was making him talk more.

"Iris one opening." Malsour's voice showed none of the nerves Dave felt.

The massive iris seemed to twist as thick sheets of metal withdrew into the sides of the pit.

"Suz?" Dave's throat was dry.

"Lowering."

Dave's eyes turned from the spikes and to the screen in front of him. It showed the two spikes lowering down toward the next iris. The room was quiet; only the whine of heavy machinery disturbed the room. Everyone watched the massive two spikes lowering into the floor.

"Heh, they're kind of like vampire fangs, you know—sucking energy out of the planet and being all sharp and stuff?" Dave looked around. Malsour shrugged, while Deia shook her head.

"Vampires are strong and violent creatures that gain strength and knowledge from every person they defeat. They are not to be taken lightly," Deia said.

"Don't fight vampires, got it," Dave said.

"Ten meters to go," Anna said.

"Iris two please," Dave said.

"Opening iris two," Malsour said. After a few moments, nothing happened. "It's stuck." Malsour looked to Dave.

"Okay, plan B. Suzy, I need you to have the spikes touching the iris—don't dent it."

"These things weigh more than those payload shuttles to Mars, and you want me to finesse them?" Suzy's voice was indignant at her situation.

"Yeah, slowly does it. You've got this. Just think of them as a big pair of chopsticks!" Dave smiled.

The people from the other parties smiled and chuckled at the byplay.

"I deserve a pay raise," Suzy grumbled as the spike's descent slowed, bit by bit.

A loud bang made everyone wince.

"Well, they're touching now!" Suzy said, sounding a bit panicked.

"I've been getting a power reading for a bit. Got a spike with it touching the iris," Anna said.

"Malsour, try to open the iris again."

"Opening iris," Malsour said. Everyone watched the screens.

"Energy spiking—nothing dangerous," Anna said.

"Iris is opening slowly," Malsour said.

"Come on, you big metal door," Dave whispered.

"Speed is picking up." Malsour sighed and grinned at his screen.

"Power input increasing," Anna said.

"Well shit, that is a sight," Jackie said.

Dave looked out of the command center. The spike's runes glowed blue while arcing electricity moved between the two spikes. "Shard, run tests on all subsystems."

"Starting."

Lights started getting brighter around the facility, clearing shadows away as the spikes descended into the earth.

"Everyone, be alert. We don't know if anything we missed will be coming to hunt us down," Deia said.

Dave spread his senses out. He couldn't sense anything moving around, except various systems as they were being checked by Shard's fragment.

"I have found several deficiencies. None are major issues but together they will create a problem," Shard said, his tests still running.

"Use automatons for jobs that will require heavy lifting. Anything that is technical we can take care of," Dave said.

"Very well. Updating priorities."

His notification bar blinked. Dave opened it.

Quest: Aleph Homecoming

You have restarted an Aleph power station. Make sure that there are no threats. Starting the facility was just the start. There are a number of repairs that need to be fixed before the station can be left to manage itself.

> Repair train lines
> Fix power relays x4
> Fix grounding protrusions x3

Rewards: Increased power usage to assist in other activities.

"All right, well, looks like we have some more work to do. Who are my smiths?" Dave asked. Matt's party put their hands up.

"Damn, okay, well, half of you follow me. We'll look into the power relays. The other half go with Malsour and work on the grounding protrusions," Dave said.

"Keep an eye out for possible threats," Deia said. "Shard, can you send out scouts to look for threats?"

"Orders understood. Permission granted, Oson'Deia. Four scouts moving to search the facility for threats."

"I'll stay here with Anna. Induca, go and keep Suzy company," Deia said.

With that, everyone started to go their own ways.

The facility had come to life. Dozens of repair bots moved around, moving broken parts and new parts to replace them.

Dave moved to the elevators that were now working, taking one up to the upper reaches of the facility.

"So, all the power is directed up here, passing through runes and silver wiring to that charging station we saw earlier," Dave said as the lift's doors closed. Malsour was talking to his group, leading them toward the grounding prongs sticking out of the station. They each had a group of the combat-focused parties tagging along with them.

"The one that looked like a train station?" Matt asked.

"The very one. They're hooked up, powered up and then shipped off to other Aleph installations to keep them powered. The charging stations in the cities are really backup to these big bastards." Dave tapped the side of the elevator affectionately.

They exited it a little while later. Dave answered the questions he could about smithing and different metals. He couldn't tell them anything about Mithril; he trusted them, but he had sworn an oath to the Dwarves. Although they might be a paranoid bunch, they had been around for a few hundred years, so Dave was willing to trust their judgment.

Repair bots heaved a derailed cart back onto the tracks and repaired the ones that it had come off and bent. Dave walked past it and got to the relay panel he needed to work on.

Unlike electrical circuits, he didn't have to turn off shit before he got to work, so he opened the closet-looking power relay. Runes were engraved into the surface, in swirling organic circles.

"Ah, memories." Dave snorted to himself as the others looked at the runes now opened for all to see in mild awe and confusion.

"We're going to check the area," Xiao, a human tank, said, clearly not that interested in runes.

"Go for it," Dave said. He had already found the issue with the runes, but he wanted the others to learn. "Okay, so let's go over the basics of rune making and Magical Circuits. Everyone has their Magical Circuit skill, right?" Dave looked at them; a few people looked away sheepishly.

"Good! If you don't, you can learn the new and easier way of making Magical Circuits!" Dave clapped his hands together before they could start feeling sorry for themselves.

"The new way?" Matt asked.

"Progruning or runegramming." *Going to have to think of a better name than those. Maybe Magical Coding?* Dave continued. "Well, anyway, it's combining the runes of Emerilia with the coding that we have back on Earth. Don't worry—even if you're not a coder, this is some pretty easy stuff!" Dave winked. It had been too long since he talked about crafting or could teach someone something technical.

"So, with magical runes, they're usually placed in formations that work together into a complete Magical Circuit. Now, mixing coding and runes together, we can work in boxes of text." Dave pulled up his interface and shared it with the others as he drew out a series of characters, some just a few characters long, other a half-dozen. It took him a half-dozen lines before he finished, copying the first line to the last and adding an ending alteration.

"What is this?" Matt asked.

"This is all of the runing that you would need to do to replace this Magical Circuit." Dave waved at the open closet covered in runes.

Dave could see the light in their eyes. He had their attention and interest now!

Chapter 29: Emerilia's Mediator

Bob stretched. With his high Endurance, he didn't need to sleep much, but every few weeks he grabbed some sleep or when he was *really* drunk, it also helped.

He sighed as he walked around his home. He left his quarters and headed through the gray, nondescript corridors. Strips of lighting guided him as he took an elevator downward. He stepped out into a room shaped like an arrow. Consoles dotted the sides, a bank of them at the back of the room.

Bob yawned again, scratching his head, and rubbed away the remaining sleep. He sat at the biggest seat in the room and opened his interface. He checked the progress of the quests he had left running. They were progressing faster than he had thought.

"Aleph, always a sneaky bunch, though all of the races are paranoid to a degree, always keeping their strengths hidden." Bob sighed. He wished to be down on Emerilia, not stuck up in his prison. He wanted to be down there, hanging out and talking to his friends. Now, he was limited to five-minute meetings and voice messaging. A thought passed his mind as he opened up a voice chat. A few moments later, it was accepted.

"Dave! What's up, dude?" Bob asked.

"Do you need something?" Dave sounded as if he was concentrating on something.

"Not really," Bob said. He didn't *always* want something. "Though, if you do have some of that Scotch, I wouldn't say no. I was wondering, if you could attach it to a soul gem, could it fill itself up or something?"

It was some damn nice Scotch.

"Huh. I didn't think about that, but I think I might be able to rig something else—be useful for water, though I wonder if it will still affect the body if it runs out of power. Would your cells stop being hydrated by the water if the soul gem ran out?" Dave asked himself out loud.

"I dunno," Bob said, thinking it over. "If you made it for me, I could test it out—though I'd need more than just one bottle."

"You just want more Scotch," Dave accused, but Bob could hear the smile in his voice.

"Maybe." Bob laughed. Trying to shift Emerilia's future was a pain in the butt; he'd missed his talks with Dave.

"I can, though it will take some time for me to get the soul gems," Dave said.

"I can fix that. Gimme a sec. I've got some gems lying around here." Bob got up from his seat, moving to the elevator again, descending and then going forward.

"So, what you up to?" Dave asked.

"Trying to motivate boneheads to work. Shifting a few alliances and plotting the downfall of a nasty little kingdom that's getting a little too Earth Lord-crazy." Bob sighed, trying to not think of work.

"Sounds lovely. So why haven't you sent Alkao more people to help him out? What's the thing with needing shelter, food, and all that?" Dave asked.

"Ah, the Demon prince needed a bit of humbling. I hoped for him to reach out to you lot and see the error of his ways. Seems that he was pretty contrite and he's got his warriors working day and night to get ready for his people. Might have pushed him a little too hard. Though Demon Endurance is pretty high, I think he might need to get some sleep soon." Bob sighed as his elevator ride stopped and he walked through more bland, gray corridors.

"So, what about the rest of the Demons? What are they doing?" Dave asked.

"Well, I've woken some of the leaders up and they're working on the different planets they're on to build their Strength and gain resources they will need when returning to Emerilia," Bob said.

"What about the Aleph?"

"I'm waiting for them. Their council is back in Alephir, though they're working to get materials and supplies to support their people through you. I feel that the price of foodstuffs is going to rise pretty quickly. The Demons have the land and the physical manpower to grow a lot of food. It will take the Aleph a lot longer. I'm hoping to try to get them to see this and make a bond between the two of them." A door opened before Bob as he looked out over a massive metal warehouse. He glided over the banister and down to the bottom floor, looking at crates of different items, palletized and labeled.

"Well, at least Shard will have someone else he can talk to without all of the security restrictions. Did you realize how the Aleph got their power?" Dave asked.

"Pretty smart, huh? They took it from the portals; had something similar keeping them powered." Bob walked past hulking metal figures with all manner of weapons over them, mixed with pallets of gold and Mithril. Bob passed a portal that showed a massive warehouse, with rack upon rack of materials and items.

If one looked closely, they might notice different pods that held creatures that seemed to be asleep.

"What kind of soul gem do you want?" Bob floated up in front of a rack of soul gems.

"Let's say a petty one. Don't need much—just something to attach the conjuration to."

"Okay." Bob floated up to the right crate and pulled a dozen gems from it.

Bob opened up his administrator's panel and looked at Dave, who was dusting himself off after fixing a control console's runes.

"Don't move," Bob warned.

Dave froze.

Bob uttered out a spell and dropped the petty soul gems. They disappeared in mid-air and landed lightly next to Dave.

"You're going to have to teach me whatever you just did," Dave said. "Can I move now?"

"Yes, you can move." Bob laughed. "You can figure it out yourself one day."

"Thanks. You're just lazy," Dave said.

"Mhmm," Bob agreed heartily. "Oh crap, that's what I forgot. Yeah, Anna might need your hand at something. Going to be bringing her people back, but their old lands got ruined. She's going to need your help."

"Shouldn't you be telling her this?" Dave put the soul gems away in his bag.

Bob dismissed the screen, watching Dave. "Well, see, uhh..."

"You forgot to tell her?" Dave asked dryly.

"That *may* have happened." Bob scratched his head.

"I'd say it might be a good idea calling her after me," Dave said.

"Yeah, I think I might do that right now."

"Good luck, and call me more often. It's been too long since we last talked." Dave's voice softened.

"I will. Things have just been a tad bit crazy." Bob stepped through the active portal, into the massive warehouse beyond. He could hear arguing in the distance.

"I'll send you a message when the drinks are ready to be tested. It might be a fast way to make foodstuffs and such, though I don't know why we couldn't have something like a food replicator. Be really complex but making a basic slop to be used as food wouldn't be too hard."

Bob could tell Dave was drifting off into the land of theories and ideas.

"Well, give me your ideas and I can get some people at the mages college looking it over and working on it. You've got lots of other work to do!" Bob said.

"That might be interesting," Dave said.

"If you get to Per'ush, I know a lady who would be happy to get your party admittance," Bob said, his mind wandering as he walked over to the yelling.

"I'll take you up on that!"

"We'll talk later. Got to go deal with some issues that cropped up." Bob sighed.

"Later!"

The voice chat cut as Bob looked at a portal where a group of Demons were around a table, yelling at one another.

"Will you shut the hell up?" Bob stuck his head through the portal. "I swear, if I need to, I will bring Alkao back up here to kick his brothers back into agreement. Stop squabbling like a bunch of winged infants. Lezar, stop moving those damned wings around—you're bound to get stuck in the ceiling, you irate Prince! If I see you lot lounging around and arguing instead of making a plan or helping out your people hunt, I'll stick you in the damned freezer for another two hundred years!"

The Demons were silent, from the four hefty-looking Demon Princes to their Lords. Their heads turned downcast toward Bob.

He barely reached their mid-thigh but none of them dared to argue.

Bob sighed and stepped fully through the portal. "Okay, what have you got?" He pinched his nose at the impending headache. He was going to put that Scotch to work as soon as Dave finished it.

"We were talking of priorities," Malkur, the second eldest Prince, said.

He was midnight-black; his crèche brother Alkao was blood-red. Otherwise, both of them had similar features and the same bassy voice that carried through the small space.

"And?"

"We were talking of training our forces to be ready for these new Demon creations and the Horde's allotment of food from the stores." Lezar moved his wings in finality.

"You've already got a damned tail to express your emotions, Lezar! You don't need to add the wings too! Like some Italians I know." Bob muttered the last part to himself.

"If you train forever, but keep on sucking up your people's resources, then you won't have enough to support yourselves for the battle against the new Demons. You have people who are in storage and would really like to get out. Train your people as you gather food," Bob said diplomatically.

"Gathering food belittles the Horde." Lezar snorted.

Bob pinched the bridge of his nose again. "Have patience. He's just dumb, doesn't know the way of the world. Just a child. Just breathe," Bob muttered to himself.

The Demon's ears were good enough to hear him.

"I am no—"

Efri and Vrexu restrained their brother and clamped his mouth shut. Malkur gave him a warning glance.

A book appeared in Bob's hands; he gave it to Malkur.

"You want to know more about where you come from? First, you and everyone on Emerilia started off as one race—humans. For millennia, your forefathers fought one another across a planet. Millions died. A fighting force that cannot feed themselves is useless. Hunting, knowing the plants and wildlife around you—that will allow you to have multiple hordes in the field without needing a massive supply train to sustain you. Starting from today, you will start to learn the ways of war. You will not learn this with training until you pass out. You will learn to fight smarter, to use your natural abilities to defeat the enemy before they ever get to the battlefield. The Dark Lord made you to run into battle willingly, to get yourselves killed for his enjoyment. Do you want to do as the Dark Lord wishes, to be led by your emotions to your ruin?" Bob looked at Lezar.

Efri released his mouth so he could speak. "No," Lezar said.

"You are a Demon Prince. Do not fight simply for enjoyment. Doing so will just whittle your forces into nothing. Know when to hit, when to recover, when to take stock of supplies. There are many fearsome creatures on this planet that your people need the Horde's protection from." Bob held a finger up, stopping Lezar from talking. "Do not say that it is their fault that they die because they are weak." Bob glared at Lezar.

The Demon Prince looked shamefaced and more than a little scared.

"Your race looks to you, in both times of war and peace. If you are a good leader in war but in peace, you let your people be killed, you will not stay in power for long. Help your people to grow and prosper; they will do the same for you. Going out, finding the right materials, carrying them back and preparing them is hard work, which is why every Demon is going to try their hand at it. You might have become Demon Princes for your natural abilities in the field of battle. Now, you must prove to me and to them that you deserve your position. You are all warriors of famed repute; many myths repeat your names in fear and respect. However, being a Prince is a lot harder than a warrior. The Horde is strong but without structure. You will create ranks and train people to be good not only at fighting, but at surviving. I will help you as best as I can. You must look to see are you Prince of the people, a General of the warriors, or both? It takes a stronger Demon to know where his weaknesses are in order to focus on his strengths and remove those weaknesses." Bob looked around, seeing them all take this information in.

He smiled at them fondly. They might have been made by the Dark Lord, but Bob felt a connection to all creatures on Emerilia. He'd created it and they were in a way his children.

Anna is not going to be happy I forgot to tell her about her people. Maybe they can help me putting some sense into these demons. They were great at hit-and-run tactics. Didn't give too much of a damn about honor in battle and scrounged for themselves. They're also a bunch of recluses.

"Thank you, Gray God. You have given us much to think on," Malkur said.

Bob could see the thoughts racing behind the Demon Prince's eyes and the thoughtful frown on his face.

"Good. I think I will have another group that might be able to assist you lot with figuring some of this out. I will be back to talk to each of you individually at one time. It's time we had a talk of the future. Oh, and stop yelling right next to my portal! Damn racket!" Bob sighed and walked back through the portal.

He walked past other portals that were off or led to different locations. One showed massive beasts all in a room, a number that would have made many shiver in fear. The ones that looked the prettiest, like the harpies and lily toads, were the worst ones. There was a large red button next to the portal.

He continued on, past scenes of different places: caves, sand dunes, jungles. Bob didn't see any of them, distracted by his thoughts, and nervous to talk to Anna.

He stopped in front of a portal that looked out over a mountain covered in the vibrant green, yellows, purples, and reds of the forest. "Ahh, I'll talk to Kala first. She might be half-bear, but she's much calmer." Bob smiled at his decision and walked through the portal.

Bob waved his hand casually. An arrow that had been coming for his head splintered before it reached him. Bob sighed as he held out a finger. A wolf Demi-Human flew toward Bob so fast that there was no air for them to scream. They started as soon as there was air to fill their lungs.

Bob made a circle with his finger and an up and down motion.

The wolf Demi-Human spun upside down and was shaken quickly. Their arrows and gear fell out as Bob continued to do it a few minutes. Their screams turned to jerky noises, unable to catch their breath as they were thrown up and down.

"Other than the Scotch, this is a pretty good way for getting rid of some stress." Bob walked down from the portal and through the forest. The wolf followed Bob as he whistled to himself.

In a clearing, there was a basic village. Bob could see people on the walls, looking for threats. The wolf Demi-Human still bobbed up and down, making muffled cries, following Bob as he glided into the air and over the walls.

Demi-Human soldiers rushed to their positions as Bob came down in front of the largest tent inside the wooden walls.

"What is—" The angered words cut off as a massive brown bear Demi-Human stopped and looked at Bob and the wolf that was still going up and down, making pitiful noises.

"Was the alarm you?" Kala sighed.

"Probably. Didn't want to go through the whole guard at the gate thing, not when this one tried to put an arrow in my head," Bob said.

"Could you put him down?" Kala asked.

Bob looked to the wolf. "In a bit," Bob said. He wasn't done yet.

"So, what did you come here to talk to me about?" Kala asked. "I assume you are here to talk to me?"

"Yes, I need your advice and I had an idea about something." A smile formed on Bob's face.

"You and your plans." Kala smiled.

There were a number of noises as Demi-Human soldiers of all types moved in all directions, working together to make a shield wall around Bob.

"Ahh, I always love to see a bit of teamwork, and the idiots I want you to teach are going to need a lot of good examples." Bob sighed.

"Put the shields and blades down. This is the Gray God." Kala waved at the fighters.

"Doesn't look like much." A fox-looking Demi walked forward as the shield wall came apart.

"He's also Anna's father." Kala's tone held a warning.

The fox Demi-Human paled and his tail drooped as he took a knee in front of Bob. "It is an honor to meet you, Gray God."

"Always good to know that the kiddo left a lasting impression. Could you deal with this one?" The wolf Demi-Human was a mewling mess as Bob gently put them in front of the fox.

"Now, what is this you say about a plan? I hope it will speed up things for our return home. As much as this planet is interesting, it is not home." Kala walked into her tent.

Bob followed. Kala needed to move the open flaps of the tent out of the way, but Bob was short enough to get inside without touching either of the flaps.

"Well, first of all, your home isn't there anymore. Like the actual place—gone."

"How?" Kala sat in a large seat that could have been Bob's bed.

"Dragons." Bob sighed. It had been a pain trying to fix the damage by Eldapik. Damned Air Dragon was as bad as his Affinity lord at getting out of traps! Took three of his brethren to finally hunt him down and kill him.

"It is no matter. We will find another home." Kala sounded sad but resolute.

"Well, seeing as you're looking for a new place to live, I have an area in mind." Bob gave her a winning smile.

"Where is it, what's in it, and what do you want from us?" Kala asked.

"It's Devil's Crater. Right now, not much, except fields that need cleaning up a little, natural fortifications, seven mostly intact fortresses, and a natural curtain wall around the entire thing. I want you to teach the Demons to be soldiers." Bob smiled.

"So, you're offering to send us to Devil's Crater, the homeland of the Demons, and teach them to be soldiers. First, are you insane? And second, Fire no!" Kala barked.

"Hear me out." Bob sighed.

"I would offer you a real drink, but all we've got is water," Kala said.

Bob pulled up his inventory, selecting one of the wines he kept on him at all times. He opened a pouch on his belt and pulled it out, handing it to her.

"Thank you." Kala looked excited by the promise of booze. She moved to grab cups.

"So, what is coming, it's going to need people to band together. Right now, the Demons are pigheaded and don't understand anything more than facing their hordes at the enemy and yelling charge. Only Alkao's Black Hands were anything like adept at true war fighting. The rest were secure in the knowledge that they were strong in their individual skills; there was nothing to promote them working together. Right now, they're training their forces instead of gathering supplies for returning to Emerilia, the kind of training that only ends when they lose consciousness," Bob said dryly.

"So, what do you want from us?" Kala held out a cup to Bob.

He took it with a nod of thanks. "I want you to teach them not as warriors, but as soldiers. How to fight together and rely on one another. It can be the start of turning them into something terrify-ing," Bob said.

"Why, by all things good, do you want to make the Demons *better* at fighting?" Kala frowned.

"That is for me to worry about and I don't want to make them better at fighting. I want *you* to make them better at fighting. They need to appreciate that they can get slapped around by others, to understand that they have much to learn. Imagine if your two groups worked together? Demons and the Demis; kind of has a ring to it. At the very least, could you have a meeting with them? I will mediate and no one will get hurt." Bob sipped his drink.

Kala took her time, drinking her wine before she sighed, look-ing like her true seventy-eight years. "We owe you much, Lo'kal. We will meet with them, but you shall need to share with me your plan."

"You should know by now I don't have a plan—I just move things by nudges. I create meetings and possibilities. What you lot do with them is up to you." Bob saluted her with his drink.

"What about Anna's preparations?" Kala asked.

"Uhh, well..." Bob scratched his head awkwardly.

Kala raised an amused eyebrow at Bob's reaction. "You forgot to tell her."

"Yeah, well, there was a lot going on and she was doing other things! Though, now I can tell her she can keep worrying about the other things until you and the Demons decide what you want to do!" Bob smiled happily.

"You just hope that she doesn't find out you forgot about mak-ing her a quest."

"Oh, shut up," Bob said into his cup.

Kala's amused chuckle rumbled through the tent. "Very well. I will meet with these Demons tomorrow. I'm leaving telling Anna about this up to you."

"Fine." Bob drank more of the wine.

Chapter 30: Progress!

Dave stood, cracking his back and grunting. It had been a long day, but it was only starting.

He checked the soul gems that Bob had sent him. Pulling one out and holding it in his hands, he spun it around and played with it, looking at the beautiful dancing lights in its midst.

"Malsour, how are we looking?" Dave asked over the party voice chat.

"All good on my side. I think we're ready to get out of here."

"Nice. Suzy, how are the spikes doing?"

"We've got them at fifty percent submersion into the magical ley line. We're holding there as we're powering the base's soul gems and the few connected train carts. We're pumping power into the portals and teleport pads so we can start powering these soul gem trains and moving them around," Suzy said.

"We've just reached enough charge to keep a portal to Alephir open on the transfer platform," Anna said, referring to the level with the train carts and train tracks.

"Have you connected to Shard?" Dave asked, signaling to the other crafters in the room with him to finish up what they were studying and to follow him.

"Connection complete." Shard sounded smug and his regular self instead of his robotic subsystem. "I have enough power to activate guardian forces within the power station and make sure that nothing else shows up."

"Good stuff. You need anything else from us?" Dave asked.

"I should be good. I am opening a portal on the transfer level to Alephir. I can then begin to move soul gems in and out of the power station and lower the charging forks more to increase power output as we'll have somewhere to put it."

A ping announced a change in their quest.

Quest: Aleph Homecoming

You have restarted an Aleph power station.

Rewards: Increased power usage to assist in other activities.

30,000 EXP

Increased standing with Aleph people

"Well, if this is all sorted out, then we have places to be. We're due at the automaton workshop next," Deia said.

"Woohoo! Scrapyard!" Steve quipped.

"You were made in one of those scrapyards," Anna said.

"Wow, Mom, way to make me feel better about myself," Steve said, trying to sound hurt.

Dave shook his head at the twelve-foot-tall AI's antics.

Everyone had cleared up their gear, so Dave started walking for the teleport pad that would take them from the power station and to the automaton workshop.

"Be wary. I cannot connect to the workshop. It seems that my filters are blocking access. It might be an error, but there might be malignant runes there," Shard warned.

"Dammit, I told you to make those system purges routine!" Anna said.

"Yes, well, this was one facility where they were trying different things with the part of my consciousness stored there."

"Well, that sounds ominous," Dave said.

"What do you mean by malignant runes?" Deia asked.

"Well, a section of runes that have been altered or changed, either on purpose or by accident or evolution of the AI in the facility and that have a possible negative effect on my original coding if I was to integrate it," Shard said.

"What will that mean for us?"

"It means that we might be working with an AI that doesn't agree to our security clearances, to one that is controlling the creatures in the workshop and is possibly aggressive toward other life-forms," Anna replied.

"Great." Deia sounded displeased.

***

Deia looked through the teleport pads portal, or "event horizon" as Dave was calling it, and into the automaton workshop. It was pitch-black, not a single magical light anywhere. Deia shot out fire lamps; they moved through the portal, headed off to the corners of the room and brightening it for everyone to see.

It was a teleport pad room, with the same three control rooms facing the teleport pad. The biggest difference was the weapon stations facing the teleport pad.

"What are those?" Dave asked.

"Repeaters. They're four crossbows stacked two across, two deep. They can reload by themselves, firing four bolts every two seconds. They have the power to harm scout guardians. Depending on the type of arrows, they could even give a behemoth pause." Steve sounded serious for once.

"Damn," Dave said.

Deia clipped the back of his head.

"What?" he asked, looking hurt.

"No, you can't pull them apart. We get the workshop working first, *then* you can play with them," she said.

Dave rubbed his head, muttering something about mind readers that her Elven ears picked up.

She shook her head. "Well, let's go and see what's waiting for us," Deia said.

The fighters went first, Anna leading with Dave and Deia behind. Mages behind them, and then support behind them.

They walked into the workshop. The air smelled stale and musty, as if it hadn't moved in years. A few people coughed as Steve looked around.

"Connecting to the different systems. Damned air systems are down. Got some nasty buildup of carbon dioxide in places. Going to need some power to turn it back on. Got a control station just up that corridor that we can get into." Steve pointed his axe at one of the doors that led out of the teleport pad room.

The event horizon showing the power station closed as the runes on the teleport pad stopped glowing, leaving light up to the glowing balls of fire that were burning up their precious air.

"Let's get going. Next time ask before you connect to the systems," Deia admonished.

"As I'm soul bound to Suzy, my defenses against attacks targeting my runes are really difficult. I can change myself but Suzy is bound to me. Anything that's exterior, her Willpower will bitch slap it away," Steve said happily.

"Great. Good to know that my soul is good anti-virus software," Suzy said dryly as Dave chuckled.

A few of the other Players coughed or shook their heads, trying to hide their amusement.

Deia looked to her notifications to see that the quest had been updated.

Quest: Aleph Homecoming

You have entered an Aleph Automaton Workshop. The Workstation has been silent for decades.

Turn air filters back on.
Find if there are any issues with the AI runes.

Rewards: Ability to improve/repair current automatons and create new automatons.

"Let's get that air back on and then we'll move to where the AI's runes are held. Everyone stick together. We don't know what we'll be fighting here," Deia said. "Steve, you've got the lead."

"Yes, ma'am." Steve saluted with his axe, making whistling noises as they walked.

"How are you whistling?" Dave asked.

"Don't worry about it. I got my secrets—you got yours," Steve said.

"Is it a recording?" Anna asked.

"No!" Steve said, his tone making it clear that it was.

"Right." Anna sounded amused as they continued to walk.

It didn't take long for them to reach the air filter controls. Dave went to work. A few minutes later, the air seemed to circulate once again, smelling a little better.

"Now, let's go and find these runes," Deia said, getting them moving once again.

***

"Did you hear that?" Deia paused. The three parties slowed as they cocked their heads to hear whatever she was talking about.

"Yeah, it sounds like...DOWN!" Anna yelled. Everyone ducked.

Arrows filled the air.

"Ow! That hurt!" Steve yelled as one hit him and exploded on impact.

Deia threw out light orbs while darklings ripped out of the walls, their hunger driving them to find whatever was attacking their master and his friends.

Suzy opened a holding pouch she had until the opening was big enough to fit a person. She threw it; metal and ebony cores fell out, melding together into metal creations. Glass cores fell out, hovering in mid-air before racing to follow the darklings.

"Well, I think I know now maligrant? Malihignat? Maliant?"

"Malignant!" Anna yelled, correcting Steve.

"Yeah, that's the one!"

Deia had her bow up as she fired at the moving darkness. Her Elven eyesight allowed her to pick out the automatons that were crowding the hallway. They looked to be in bad repair, as if someone had thrown parts together to see if they would work.

Automaton Experiment

Level 231

"Well, shit," Dave said. He must've seen the same thing as he fired his bow, making one with a large upper body but a dozen spindly legs stagger.

"Watch out!" Anna yelled as two creatures walked out. They looked like repair bots with their multiple small limbs. Instead of having manipulating parts on the top of their bodies, they had repeaters.

Another hail of arrows filled the hall.

"Fire wall!" Induca said. A wall of flames rushed out in front of the parties to meet the arrows.

"Rise!" Malsour said. Barricades and cover rose from the ground to cover everyone.

Induca's wall destroyed most of the arrows, stopping over the automatons that writhed in the heat. Their Health dropped by the second. They focused their attacks on Induca, making her duck. The wall of fire faded.

"Say hello to my little friend!" Dave yelled.

Deia looked over to see him move out of his cover, holding a crossbow that should have been mounted on a wall.

He fired the three-foot-long bolt. The crossbow loaded another bolt in and charged. Dave fired as fast as he could pull the trigger.

Deia watched with wide eyes. He never reloaded once, but he continued to fire, bolt after bolt.

Deia shook her head. She held up her bow, peeking out of the side of her cover. Her arrow glowed orange and then red before she let loose. It slammed into a scout-centurion mix, taking off its arm and making it fall on its ass.

"Fire-nado!" Induca said.

Deia cringed at the terrible name that Dave and Induca had come up with for her new attack.

Six tornados made of Fire grew out from the midst of the automatons, focusing all of their heat into one location and sucking in Air to keep up its onslaught.

"Woohoo! Fuck yeah!" Steve waved his axe around in glee as an automaton threw a spear at him. "Don't have to be a dick about it!" Steve barked, ducking.

A large spear appeared beside Steve.

"Thanks, Dave!" Steve launched his spear, sticking it through the automaton that had tried to hit Steve.

Deia got glances of her allies, firing arrow after arrow. Each one hit with imbued Fire energy and exploded on impact. It was getting harder and harder to hit as Induca's spell grew in strength, pulling projectiles into its tornados.

Anyone who was ranged was firing at the automatons; the fighters hunkered down. The support gave what buffs they had but this support were more crafters and maintainers than healers and buffers.

"Cease fire!" Deia called out as she saw that the repeaters were now no longer able to get close to them, their own attacks weak in comparison.

"Curse of magical weakness," Malsour called out. Black and purple colored the automatons. With a wave of his hand, he banished the darklings that had been harassing the automatons. They lost strength in the light of his sister's Fire-nado.

"Keep your eyes open. Once they're down, we're going to be making a run right for the AI's runes. We shut that down, we shut down this entire place and these big bastards!" Deia had to yell to be heard over Induca's spell.

"Steve or Dave, get us a waypoint to it!"

The automatons, realizing that their attacks weren't landing, tried to move forward, only to find themselves pulled back into the middle of the tornados. Some of the smaller creatures were pulled off their feet, the tornados pulling them apart with heat and the force of swirling wind.

Deia saw Suzy's metal creations that had been on the sidelines move back. Her Air creations forced more wind into the tornados, keeping them alive and fueled.

"Focus," Induca said. The tornados shrank to half their size, turning from red flames to blue.

The automatons' Health plummeted. With Malsour's curse and Induca's now superheated hell, the walls started to deform from the heat. Automatons were pulled, ripped apart, melted, and generally destroyed.

After a few minutes, Induca's spell started to weaken.

A shiny ball of red hot metals was all that was left of the automatons.

"Let's move!" Deia said, getting to the head of the parties.

Malsour dropped the barricades.

"Absorb," Deia muttered. She felt the heat of the room flow into her, turning into energy. Her Mana bar filled, and topped up her armor's internal reserves.

The heat loss was the only way that the others would be able to make it through the smoking hot ruin of what had been the automatons' position.

Deia fired out balls of Fire to illuminate their passage. Suzy's Air creations surged ahead, looking for more enemies.

"It seems that they had some kind of group stealth system. Be ready for them to show up anywhere!" Dave said.

Those scout guardians were a pain in the ass already. If this AI can hide its forces, this just got a lot harder.

They turned a corner and up a set of stairs, coming out into a massive area. Automatons rested in charging cradles all over the room. Four stories of guardians with cranes and other machines were ready to move them. They rushed past three more storage areas and into what looked like a workshop. Here, there were a dozen fighter automatons in various stages of assembly.

The next had archers, and then centurions. Deia even saw a room filled with a half-dozen behemoths.

She ran faster, looking at the different automatons, scared that one of them might leap up and attack them.

They skidded into a hallway and toward their destination: the central command center.

They had come in through one of the four teleport pads that were at each of the corners of the automaton workshop. The facility was a large rectangle that was split into four sections. All of them met in the middle, where the command center waited.

"Watch out!" Deia called, diving to the side as bolts filled the air. She threw a fireball back at the automaton experiments that had appeared.

It exploded, making two more stealth systems fail; twenty or so automatons were revealed.

Steve charged with a roar, acting as a shield for those behind him. His axe took out the repair bot-repeater platforms.

Deia got up to see Dave laughing as he jumped off Steve's back.

"Thanks for the ride!" A dozen metal creations fell off as well, occupying the automatons.

A yell broke free from the throats of the melee fighters. Deia saw the excitement in their eyes.

She drew her blades, falling in beside a smiling Anna, whose tail swished happily. Excitement filled them both as they slammed into the automatons.

Deia and Anna fought side by side, their blades dancing in the light of Deia's fire lamps.

"Dave, fix that AI!" Deia called out.

"Steve, give me a boost!" Dave said.

"Set!" Steve called out, slamming automatons back and turning to Dave.

Dave sprinted. Deia's eyes widened a bit as he blurred.

Steve flicked his axe as Dave put a foot on it. Dave sailed through the air. A shield formed around his outstretched arms and head as he slammed through the windows of the command center.

Party Chat

Dave> Ow

Deia shook her head. She moved out from under a blow; her left blade took out the creature's knee, her right blade spun and cut through its burly arm. Imbued with the power of her Fire, her blades were as strong as plasma torches—at least that was what Dave had said.

The sounds of fighting died down as Deia planted her blade in the blue spot her perception showed on archer guardians' legs mixed with a repair bot's manipulators, each holding a different weapon.

It had been one of the more effective fighters, to Deia's dismay. Now, it slid to the floor, smoke coming from the hole Deia had made.

"We've got incoming!" Dave yelled from the tower. "Heavies! This thing needs another couple of minutes until it can do a reset!"

"Why not just destroy it?" Deia yelled back.

"We do that, this whole place locks down!" Dave said.

Deia grunted. Getting stuck in this workshop was not her idea of a good time.

Lights started to come on around the control center, showing off the catwalks and corridors that surrounded it.

"Steve!" Dave yelled, tossing a truly massive bow out of the control tower, at the big dude.

"Thanks, man!" Steve sounded overly excited as he held the bow. Dave tossed down a crate of two-foot arrows for the thing and then disappeared again.

"Malsour, get us some barricades. Anyone who has traps, start laying them down. Crafters and ranged, move up to the control tower," Deia yelled.

Malsour created new barricades and a ladder that climbed up the control center's wall and up to the window Dave had broken through.

People moved around the different approaches, muttering out their spells as different colored images appeared on the ground before disappearing.

Deia sheathed her two blades and pulled her bow off her back, fitting one of her specialty arrows to the string as she waited and watched for incoming experiments.

She didn't have to wait long.

Chapter 31: Fight for the Automaton Workshop

Anna dodged behind one of the barricades as bolts filled the air. Everyone followed suit, waiting for the automatons to run out of bolts before they rose back up.

Steve's massive bow took one in the chest, sending it back four feet and leaving it there.

Deia focused on the repeater-bots. Two more of the fighters had bows on them and added their arrows into the mix. Darklings and curses rose up around the automatons and started to pull them apart.

"On the other side!" Induca yelled.

Suzy's creations shifted away from the immediate battle, turning to stop the combatants on the other side of the control center.

Anna looked out of her cover. Seeing that there were no bolts coming at her, she ran, leaping over barricades and running on them to face the new fighters on the other side.

Half of the melee fighters moved with her. All of them slowed as she skidded to a stop, facing a new group of automatons.

An archer fired one of its crossbows that had replaced its arms.

Anna flicked her blade; a whistling blade of wind tore the arrow apart and cut the automaton's crossbow off.

It didn't pause, firing with its other arm-crossbow.

Anna sent a flurry of wind at the creature as Suzy's Air creations ripped through the automaton's midst. They swooped in low, cutting them at their ankles and lower limbs. Many teetered on their multiple legs or fell over, their legs coming apart.

They didn't stop moving toward the Stone Raiders.

Induca dropped a firestorm on the disabled automatons, filling the hall and turning it into an oven.

"Incoming centurions!" Dave called out. A new waypoint appeared at another corridor.

"We've got it!" Deia said.

"Fuck, we've got a behemoth coming in," Dave said. Another waypoint came up on the opposite side of the corridor Deia headed toward.

"We've got it," Anna said.

"The hell is a behemoth?" one of the Players asked.

"Steve is one," Anna said.

"Ah shit, I was hoping he was just a freak!" another said, shifting their shield around.

"Awwe thanks man, makes me feel all happy inside!" Steve sounded genuinely touched by the praise.

They got to the hallway, waiting as they heard Deia's group fighting whatever was on their side.

Induca jumped down from the control center; flames slowed her drop as she stood next to Anna. "Okay, I can give you about two shots with the plasma cannon before I'm going to pass out from the strain," Induca muttered so no one else could hear.

"You sure?" Anna asked.

"Yeah, so make sure you make them count," Induca said.

"Thank you. I will." Anna pat her on the shoulder.

She heard the telltale sign of a plasma cannon being fired on the other side. It seemed Deia had stepped up her game.

"Incoming!" the fighter with the shield said. Their shield went up as they ducked behind cover. Anna dropped as she heard the whistling of bolts.

The shield bearer had half a dozen arrows in their shield before they hit the ground. Two more Stone Raiders were hit with the bolts, losing a good third of their Health.

Suzy's creations surged ahead, painting a picture of their targets. Three behemoths with various modifications jogged toward the command center. Two of them had their arms and head re-placed with repeaters. Repair bots moved over them, reloading the repeaters as a behemoth with a shield arm and sword followed be-hind.

The hall was too narrow for them to do anything but run in a line.

Centurions wielding weapons followed.

Anna sighed, happy to see that none of them had magical arms or augments. Those bastards were powerful and scary in tight spaces. *The AI here is strong, but not strong enough to control all these creatures and magical weapons.*

Anna ducked back as one of the repeater mounts started to fire.

"Your shots will take out the first two, but then the third is go-ing to be the biggest pain in the ass with its shield and sword," Anna said.

"Just tell me when." Induca stood behind the barricade, her eyes glowing.

Anna felt her senses tingle. She allowed her magical sight to take over. Induca was a veritable raging inferno. That wasn't what caught her eye, though. Malsour and Dave were putting off an in-credible amount of Mana.

But Deia's aura seemed to dominate the room as Anna heard another plasma round go off.

"How does she have so much Mana?" Anna asked.

"We all have our secrets," Induca said, clearly knowing who she was talking about.

"Why didn't you say anything?" Anna asked.

"It wasn't any surprise for us. Our family isn't exactly the weak-est." Induca grinned. "Now, we going to shoot these things or what?"

Her family isn't the weakest? Is she saying that Deia is part of her family? But Dragons don't change into Elves; all of them look like hu-

mans when they change forms. So, who else could be in her family and that powerful in human form? Anna shook her head. It was a thought for later; right now, she had three behemoths to kill.

"Hit them whenever you get a clear shot," Anna said.

"Alrighty." Induca held her arms up.

The multi-colored flames made Anna look away as they settled onto Induca's frame. She didn't show any sign of being burnt or even hot from the miniature inferno next to her head. Induca stepped out, bracing herself.

"Down!" Induca yelled.

Anna crouched as the plasma cannon bellowed. Anna's ears rang from being so close to the cannon.

There was a flash of light and the sound of something getting torn apart as Induca stumbled back behind the barricade. Anna caught her and lowered her to the ground.

"I'll be good in a minute," Induca said.

Anna had to read her lips; her ears were still ringing. Anna gave her a thumbs-up and looked down the corridor. One of the behemoths had been torn apart; the repair bots on the second repeater-behemoth were scattered but it had plenty of bolts already loaded.

Anna ducked back as bolts once again filled the air.

Induca held her head, trying to pull herself back together after all the Mana she had just expelled.

As soon as there was a pause in the bolts, Anna started to dance. Her teeth pulled back into a hungry smile as she unleashed her teachings. Blades of Air cut into the repeater-behemoth, striking its armor, leaving deep grooves and taking off the repeater mounts.

She cut down the scouts and repair bots. The fighters were harder to kill but Anna had distance and time on her side. She took them and the weaker archer experiments out as the handful of centurions and behemoths continued on.

"Ready!" Induca said, not sounding so good.

"Shoot!" Anna said. She might be doing damage to the now weaponless behemoth but it was continuing on, its wounds of small consequence to it.

"Down!"

Once again, everyone hit the ground. Anna covered her ears this time.

Wind seemed to race toward Induca before a flash of heat and a wave of Air was thrown back out. Anna jumped up as the round slammed into the behemoth and tore it apart. Plasma burned through everything it touched, taking out a few centurions and leaving smoking craters on the third behemoth's shield.

Induca took a step back before she fell like a wilted plant. Anna reached her before she hit the ground.

"Good work," Anna said. Induca was out cold.

"Just need forty seconds!" Dave yelled.

A bolt flew out of the control tower, slamming into a centurion, and exploded, ripping the armored creature apart.

Anna once again threw her wind blades at the behemoth as it exited the hallway and came into the open area around the control center.

A flame trap covered the behemoth with bright red veins, but its Health barely changed. One of Dave's crossbow bolts slammed into its shield, leaving a dent in the thing, but not doing any harm to the behemoth. It stepped on a shadow rune; darkness covered it. Dave's bolts flew true, hitting with a metallic *dong*.

"Focus on the smaller centurions—we'll get the behemoth after!" Anna yelled.

The melee fighters roared out their defiance, leaping to attack the centurions.

They were slower than the ones Anna had fought in the past, but they had thick armor, couldn't feel pain, and they were good with their shields and swords.

The melee fighters came in and tore through them. They had better weapons and even if they had low levels, they had been training since coming to Emerilia. Many were E-heads and they fought as if their very lives depended on it.

Anna was surprised by their viciousness and their fighting styles for a moment. Her ears flattened as her tail swished in anticipation. "It isn't the village, but this lot know how to *fight*!" She jumped into the melee, leveling automatons with her great sword.

"Stay out of the shadow trap!" Dave yelled.

Everyone made sure they were clear as explosions went off. Dave's arrows hadn't just been simple metal constructs.

The shadow trap faltered moments later; the behemoth had lost ten percent of its Health.

A repair bot archer hit it in the chest, making it turn to face Steve, who slammed his way through the automatons with a look of glee on his face.

"I see why people find pinatas so fun!" Steve hit a centurion so hard that its metal innards were sprayed across thirty feet.

Anna shook her head, looking at the behemoth that was now charging Steve and his group of fighters. Anna sprinted; the floor behind her cracked from her steps as she turned into a blur. The wind pulled at her face as she held her sword behind her, headed right at the behemoth's back.

Blue spots appeared on the behemoth, showing weaknesses. Anna launched herself. There was no sound, only her sword whistling as it cut through the Air.

"Wind drill." The Air threw her forward, a dart with a sword in her hands. The wind turned into a white spiral just moments before she ripped into the behemoth.

Her blade pierced; the metal around it tore apart as her blade became buried in its back. She braced herself, trying to pull the blade out as it jumped, trying to crush her underneath him. She jumped free and watched as her blade broke from the behemoth landing on it. At the same time, she noticed that its shield arm wasn't functioning. Her attack had taken it out.

Steve didn't give the behemoth time to recover. He cut its arm off with a powerful swing, running past as it tried to move.

"Finish it!" someone yelled.

"Wait!" Dave yelled.

"Why?"

"It can't get up and we've got five seconds till this place resets itself. I'd like to have that thing on our side instead of having to repair it."

"Automaton workshop reset. Insert command crystal. Command crystal inserted. Integration complete. Security settings updated, wiping old rune coding. Connecting to main Shard for instructions and verification," Shard's robotic voice said as any of the still moving automatons stopped their movements.

"Well, this is a fine mess you have here. It looks like the other teams that were sent here got stuck in different areas. None of them were engaged with the automatons. I am opening up the workshop and updating them on the situation. I am going over logs. This has presented a number of different possibilities to upgrade the automatons. Good work in completing your quest," Shard said.

Quest: Aleph Homecoming

You have cleared the old malfunctioning runes from the Aleph Automaton's Workshop and started the process to bring it back online.

Rewards: Ability to improve/repair current automatons and create new automatons.

45,000 EXP

Increased standing with Aleph people

Lights, not just those directly around the control center, started to come online.

"Okay, I'm saying we get some damned food and rest before we go and check on the forge. I'm beat." Dave sat on the edge of the control center where a wall had been.

"Agreed." Deia looked tired as she slumped down, smoke, dust, and sweat on her face.

"Dave! I'm going to need a new blade," Anna said.

"Do you mind being a bit flashy?" Dave asked, half his mouth filled with bread.

"Why?" Anna asked.

"'Cause if you don't, then I might have just the thing for you, though I'm going to need your help shaping those wind holes you had on your old blade," Dave said.

"Okay." Anna had liked her blade and been through many tough times with it, but she needed a new one if she was going to continue to be able to fight the enemies the Stone Raiders were finding.

Dave munched happily as the rest of the Stone Raiders sat down; eating, drinking, resting, and talking of their fight.

"What happened?" Induca asked groggily.

"We defeated the AI while you decided to take a nap." Malsour drifted down to the floor and threw Anna and Deia a water skin before he moved to his sister, who was holding her head.

A metal spear landed next to her as Suzy rode her metal creation down next to Induca.

"Always getting yourself right in the middle of it," Suzy admonished, putting her knees under Induca's head as she gave her water.

Anna saw Malsour smile before he stepped into the control center.

"If I get this treatment every time, I'll do it more often." Induca grinned at Suzy. Suzy's eyes thinned as her face got closer to Induca. She gave her a quick kiss, a smile on her face. "What was that for?"

"For being *my* idiot."

Induca giggled as Suzy checked her over.

Suzy examined every inch of Induca for any sign of wounds.

***

The repair bots had carted away the majority of their broken brethren turned experiments.

They had all got a scare when the intact units started to move, only to wander away. As if they had never tried to kill them.

Deia closed the private chat she'd had with the party that had cleared out the forge they were supposed to be visiting next.

"Okay, it looks like the forge is all cleared of possible threats. There was a bunch of rock worms there. They do have a big issue with the forge's refinery being all stuck up from the metal that was supposed to be smelted in it solidifying. Runes are all a mess from being warped by heat. The whole place is apparently pretty damn hot and massive," Deia said to the gathered parties.

"Woohoo," Dave said, sounding like an unenthusiastic, deflating paper bag.

Deia gave him a look as he shrugged sheepishly and gave her a smile. She couldn't stay annoyed at him long, looking away and smiling to herself.

"Get your stuff together. We're moving out," Deia said.

People tossed what they had brought out back into their bags of holding. It would sort it anyways and ten minutes later, they were headed out of the Aleph automaton workshop.

Deia didn't want to see any more experiments or messed-up AIs that could control behemoths ever again.

Chapter 32: Within the Densaou Ring of Fire

"Every time I think that the Aleph have run out of impressive things to do, they shock me once again," Dave said in an awed voice. His Touch of the Land extended out to search through the forge for what was wrong with it.

There was plenty wrong with it. It was hot as Fire's own home, but Dave marveled at the brilliance and smarts of the Aleph once more.

"What?" Malsour used his own senses and sight to spread out his awareness. "That is impressive."

"What is?" Deia asked.

"You'll see soon enough, my dear. This is something that has to be seen to be believed."

As unenthusiastic as Dave was about going to his third Aleph location that day, he didn't catch Deia's questioning glance to Malsour and then Anna. Malsour was not willing to ruin the surprise and Anna was as confused as her.

The forge was one large rectangular prism, with one end that accepted raw materials, took the raw ore, purified it and then separated it. For some, like with steel, different elements were added at different stages or went through different stages to create different materials.

Most were poured into ingots and were either sent directly to the forges and factory lines that would turn the metals into sheets, beams, and other common items, stored in massive warehouses that lined the sides of the forge facility or sent on to the rest of the Aleph facilities to be used in some manner.

The entire facility was hot enough to make people remove their layers and still have sweat pouring off them. Dave felt at home, used to the heat of the forges and refiners of the Benvari Mountains or his own Cliff-Hill.

Finally, they came to an odd window, one that had thin lines moving through it.

"You wanted to show us an odd window?" Deia asked, as the others stepped up to look through.

"By now, I shouldn't be surprised." Suzy shrugged and shook her head at what she saw. In front of them, there was a magma chamber.

"The magma's heat is channeled into the blowtorches and the smelting furnace, heating the entire thing up. All we need to do is back the process up a little bit and the system can heat up the metals that solidified. The runes are going to be a bit of a pain to fix, but then that's why I taught everyone the basics." Dave looked to the crafters he had taught in the power station.

They looked eager to try out their newly learned skills.

"As you say," Deia said, looking out over the magma chamber.

"Are we in the Densaou?" Malsour looked to Induca.

"Ye-up. One of the colder reaches and out a bit, but we're in the circle of fire," Induca said.

"The realm of Dragons and Fire herself," Matt said. It looked as if he had sucked up some of Emerilia's lore.

"These Aleph are pretty badass." Jackie grinned. "Damn, I love this game!"

The other Players laughed and smiled, their excitement clear. They had only been playing for a few months and there was no end in sight for the fun that they had been having.

Dave knew that feeling and smiled too. It faltered after a few moments as he thought about what he knew, the truth behind it all and the reality that these Players and all the Players across Emerilia might have to come to terms with.

"Well, if you lot get working on finding the problems and getting this place up and running, I'm going to get to the forges. Anna, going to need your help to figure out your great sword's requirements and then I have to work on the drop pad," Dave said.

"Crafters, partner up with a few melee types. I'll get the other parties to meet up with us. Once we're done here, we can get back to the city. Anna and Dave, take a trip past the command center and put in our command crystal so Shard can get to work." Deia pulled her eyes from the slowly churning magma.

"Can do!" Dave headed toward the command center, his Touch picking it out for him.

"So, Anna, what do you need from the blade in order to have it whistle?" Dave asked.

"Well, I need you to make the different holes to different pitches. When they work together, then the vibrations of the Air passing through the blade and a bit of Mana leaking into it can form wind blades and other wind attacks," Anna said.

"Couldn't you have come up with an easier way of attacking?" Dave sighed.

"I like my two-handed great sword. It just has a problem with hitting people who are really far away. The wind dance and the holes help to make up for this problem," Anna said.

"Fine. I've got to put a bunch of holes in it—how will I know they are right or not?" Dave asked as they continued their walk.

"That is simple. I have multiple different designs that will work." Anna sent a folder over to Dave.

Dave looked through the hundreds of designs and passed them off to Shard. He muttered out different words, whittling down the different designs until he just had five. "These will work," Dave said.

"Why not the designs for a heavier blade?" Anna asked.

"Because your blade is not going to be heavy as hell. Also, this one allows you to use more Mana through it."

"Yes, but then it will not be a refined blade of Air," Anna complained.

"Oh, ye of little faith. It is not just your noisy contraption that changes the flow of the wind—it's the blade as well, which I can alter in order to make up for this. This is going to be a fun little project. You okay with flashy and watching your back?"

"I do already and why? Do you want to make this thing out of gold and silver?" Anna's tail flicked in amusement.

"Of course not. I'm going to make it out of Mithril," Dave said dismissively.

Anna stopped walking, her tail standing on end. "MITHRIL?"

"Damn it, she-wolf—I like my ear drums!" Dave jumped a bit at her screech.

"Dave, I couldn't accept a blade of Mithril. It's too expensive and rare. It takes a ton of power just to generate a nugget of the material.

"No one outside of Emerilia is powerful enough to shape the material!"

"You're my friend and one of the frontline fighters. You're going to be right beside me in fights. I would prefer if you had a weapon that I know will be the best and can help you cleave through your enemies," Dave said.

"I couldn't accept it," Anna said.

"I have sixteen bars of the stuff and I'm in talks with Shard to get more. Did you know that the Aleph couldn't forge the Mithril into anything, but they did store it in massive warehouses?"

Anna's eyes went wide in shock.

"So, shut up and take my gift, and don't tell anyone that I have sixteen ingots of Mithril. The Dwarven council was foaming at the mouth when a claim found just five ingots of the stuff!"

Dave opened a door and walked inside, humming to himself as he looked over command consoles. He found what he was looking for and inserted the command crystal Shard had given Josh, who had given it to all of the Stone Raiders.

The command center came to life.

"Hello, Dave and Anna. This will take me a moment to get sorted out," Shard said.

"No worries. We're going to the forge. I need to replace Anna's weapon."

"I did not tell you that we had a ton of Mithril!" Shard said.

"You didn't but I know that you lot wouldn't throw it away and none of the tools you have here makes me think that you can work Mithril. You're very good with mass-producing simple items at high quality in massive quantities, but playing with rare resources with small quantities and of the finest quality? I think that still remains in the Dwarven realm." Dave smiled.

Shard stayed silent as Dave walked out of the room.

"Thank you, Dave," Anna said.

"No worries." Dave gave her a friendly tap on the shoulder. "This damned sword-whistle is going to be a pain in the ass. We're going to need heat, a lot of it, and some drawings for me to figure out how it's going to work. Oh, Shard, in the nature of goodwill, if I were to have some designs that could upgrade Steve, would you be able to get me some of that Mithril that you don't use so I can make it? And maybe increase my level of books so I can access from Journeyman to Expert?" Dave said, his wheedling tone clear.

"I can supply you with the materials needed for a prototype of an augment for Steve and instead of giving you that access, I can upgrade you a few levels in Journeyman and give you a necklace similar to Malsour's."

"Ah, come on—all the good stuff is in Expert!" Dave complained.

"You haven't even started on the Journeyman items. I also have found more resources that can make potions of retention and potions of increased reading."

"You strike a hard bargain, but I agree," Dave said, more happy to keep Shard as a friend than bicker and mess around with bartering. That was Suzy's area of expertise.

Quest: Upgrades!

Shard is interested in your knowledge on possible upgrades to the Behemoth Guardian. Share with him what you know.

Rewards: You will be supplied with materials that you may keep. Necklace of Librarian's Knowledge

Dave closed the quest and looked out over the forges.

"I ask that we enter a contract like we did when I worked on Steve. This skill is hard as hell and I don't want it getting out. The Dwarves trusted me with it and I would like to see that it is not passed on without their knowledge," Dave said.

Shard appeared before them.

"I agree to not record or distribute any knowledge that I have on the work processes that you are about to use, without your previous agreement," Shard said.

Binding Contract

Shard will not tell anyone of your working practices with Mithril and other materials without your permission. If someone attains this knowledge from him, this contract will be shown as broken. Do you agree to this contract?

Y/N

"Yes," Dave said, relieved. "Thanks, Shard."

"No worries, Dave. I will leave now. If you require me, please use the private chat as I will be turning off all recording devices in this area," Shard said.

"Thanks, buddy." Dave smiled. Shard disappeared and Dave hotkeyed an outfit. He wore his Aleph clothes with a thick, burned and stained apron overtop and his tools along his sides.

"Now, let's get started." Dave pulled out an ingot of Mithril. He put his bag down at a workstation and moved to a massive furnace in the side of the forge. He pressed some controls, opening up the forge to the incredible heat of the magma chamber. Dave put his ingot into the furnace and shut it.

"Now we just have to wait for the little bugger to melt a bit." Dave smiled. "Let's get working on those drawings." Dave moved to a worktable, sharing his notepad with Anna so she could see and edit it as the white projected image covered the surface, showing the five different whistling apparatus and Dave's basic design he was thinking of for the blade.

They had some work to do. Dave needed to know *exactly* what he was building so he could quickly change and form the Mithril in one go instead of having to alter it a number of times.

"So, let's get started. How long do you want the blade to be?" Dave asked as they sat down to begin.

Chapter 33: A Meeting of Clans

Bob wandered into the Demons' meeting room. "Heya fellas!" Bob said, feeling in a better mood than last time.

"Gray God," Malkur said in greeting.

"Yo, Bob!" Vrexu, the youngest, said, a large smile on his face.

Bob looked behind him, finding the Demi-Humans were admiring his stash of items. Bob sighed and moved to one of the tower's doorways. He looked out over a forested area, its colors identical to those that had surrounded the demi-humans' settlement.

While the Demi-Humans' settlement was about a five-hundred meter wide circular formation, the Demons had spread out over ten square kilometers.

There were some houses; most places were made from mud and used by the population that were not part of the army, about a third of the population. Demon males and females alike were more prone to violence than settling down.

Hordes numbering in the thousands did drills together, sparring and fighting—in the Air, on the ground, and in the forests.

Bob's senses passed out over the area; a number of the hordes had sent out their people with the villagers.

"It seems that you did listen," Bob said as Malkur joined him on the balcony.

"I have been reading that book you gave me and thinking on your words. You have not led us astray yet and being able to gather our own food and resources while we are away from our villages is a good idea," Malkur said.

"Good. Then I'm going to need you to gather forty of your best fighters. I want to have a demonstration. It's time you learned how to war instead of just fight." Bob smiled at Malkur's confused expression. The Demon Prince opened his interface as Bob started to hear challenging growls.

"Lezar, play nice." Bob's voice was light, but with a hint of steel in it as Bob turned to the command room.

"Are you and your lot done with admiring all of my items?" Bob asked Kala as the fox-Demi from yesterday and eighteen others entered into the command room.

A Demi-Human who looked to be crossed with an elk held his arm and grimaced.

"Seems that someone wanted to touch them." Bob glowered at the elk, who looked like it wanted nothing more but to slink away.

Bob sighed and waved his hand as the elk let out a relieved noise.

"I am sorry, Gray God. Curiosity got the best of me." The elk Demi-Human lowered its horns to the ground.

"It happens to us all. Just, next time, look—don't touch. There are much worse wards hidden around there." Bob looked to them all. They'd have to wander through again and he didn't want anyone to get turned to ash because they touched the wrong thing.

"So, we're here. What do you want?" Kala wore her full armor. Even the Demons eyed her warily.

"We're going to have a fight!" Bob clapped his hands together and smiled.

"All right, where?" Kala's eyes scanned the Demons and found them wanting.

Bob saw that a number of them wanted to say something and all of their hands were just inches away from their blades.

There was a clear challenge in the Demi-Humans' and Demons' eyes. They saw one another as interesting opponents and warriors who had been left out of the fight for so long, they were eager to prove their worth and grit.

"Down in the training area, where everyone can see," Bob said.

"You want us to fight this large game?" Lezar said.

"Lezar, what have I said before about watching your mouth? Fine, you will be fighting them as well," Bob said, not missing Kala's cold smile.

"Oh, I will be more than happy to show this one who will be playing the games by the end of our fight." Kala chuckled. The other Demi-Humans looked less Human and more the predators that they had gained half of their blood from.

Forty Demons moved into the large hall; one moved to Malkur.

"Forty of my best, as you have commanded," the mottled black and red Demon said, bowing to Malkur.

Demons rarely even tilted their head to those who were stronger than them. Respect and trust were earned, something that had become a mantra to the Demons after leaving the Dark Lord's service.

"Good!" Bob clapped and everyone was in the middle of four hordes' training area.

The fighting around them stopped as every Demon's eyes looked over the new group that had appeared in their midst.

"Okay, so we're going to have a battle between the Demi-Humans of Akashal and the Demons of Devil's Crater.

"Kala will lead the Demi-Humans; Lezar, the Demons. I want everyone at a hundred paces. Go at full force. If someone is about to die, I will remove them from the battlefield. Attack like you mean it," Bob said.

Malkur and the other Demon Princes calmed people and the Demons made a ring around the fighting area. Others took to the skies in order to watch the spectacle.

Bob rose off the ground a dozen feet. "To your side, please, and Lezar, you are to use *all* of the Demons at your command."

Lezar grunted and moved with his Demons, talking to one another as they moved to the boundary of the circular area.

Kala and her forces secured their armor and the straps that held their shields to their arms.

"Signal when you are ready." Bob looked to Lezar, who nodded; he'd been ready and waiting for some time, the muscles of his body tight and ready to spring into action.

Kala looked relaxed as her people made a line two deep and ten long, their shields in front and their swords still at their hips.

"Let's get this over with. I've got a lunch meeting," Kala said.

"Very well." Bob took one glance at the two forces. "Begin!"

The Demi-Humans moved with practiced efficiency, turning into a circular formation as shields came together.

The Demons moved with all of their possible speed, rushing toward the Demi-Humans. Some took to the skies; others rushed toward their enemies with their blades.

Bob looked at their weapons and armor with a careful eye. They cared not for crafters and others who wanted to make items. Making weapons was seen as a lower position and the blacksmiths were scorned as they went about their days, hammering out metal into a rough shape before moving to the next. Armor was rare and its workmanship poor. Quantity over quality seemed to be the motto of the Demon's gear.

The Demons slammed into what looked like a shield hut. None of the Demons had bows, all of them preferring swords.

Time slowed for Bob as he watched blades react. The Demi-Humans' swords came out. Bob let the attacks hit that wouldn't immediately kill.

Four of the Demons were teleported away, one uninjured but a look of fear and realization in their eyes. The others were on the ground, crying about their wounds. Another two joined them a moment later.

A shield was opened up; the Demon who had been going for the finishing blow coughed blood as a blade pierced their side.

Bob teleported them before the blade could reach their heart.

Healing magic filled a plot of land, healing all the Demons that Bob was teleporting.

The shield that had been pulled open snapped shut to its fellows. Another Demon slammed into it.

Four Demons darted in from above, slamming into the shields. The shields dropped a bit until swords reached up, cutting at the Demons.

The Demons tried to close, now moving in quickly to attack but pulled back, half their number recovering in the healing area.

Bob cast a glance at the three Demon Princes who watched the battle, using his enhanced hearing to hear what they were saying.

"Imagine what would happen if we had the entire Horde behind them," Malkur said.

"The Horde would be severely damaged. We would overcome them with numbers, but the toll would be high," Efri said. He had accepted a position as a Demon General. He was a fighter and his forces were the best trained and armed other than the Black Hand under Alkao.

A smile spread across Bob's face. Efri might be the second youngest, but he was an aged soul in a young Demon's body.

Lezar slammed into the shields, making them buckle as the shield wall partly collapsed. In a moment, three Demi-Humans were recovering from their wounds in a healing patch. Lezar let out a roar of triumph, before he was greeted by a second wall.

"Switch!" Kala called out. Shields turned; the front rank marched back, covering the heads of the second rank as they became the first, fresh and ready for battle with Kala fighting Lezar back.

"Ah, to feel young again!" Kala's blade whistled in the wind. Lezar pressed his attack forward, finding himself back in the healing area as Bob erected a Mana barrier around the battlefield. It shook with the power of Kala's blow.

"Scythe!" Kala moved back into her position as a Demon slammed against them.

Blades whistled as the Demon Prince's eyes went wide. Invisible blades of cutting power ripped through the air.

It was all Bob could do to keep transporting the Demons out of the path of the wind blades.

After two minutes, there was nothing left but the impacting wind blades against Bob's Mana barrier.

"Return!" Kala called out. Shields snapped down sharply, revealing the sixteen Demi-Humans who looked out over the silent Demons.

They didn't roar their victory, or celebrate it out loud. They just stood there, as if ready to take on the rest of the horde.

Bob looked over the hordes assembled; a Demon Prince and forty of their best warriors had gone up against twenty Demi-Humans and failed spectacularly.

"A scythe through the fields of men." Efri looked to Kala.

"Someone knows their history." Kala smiled approvingly.

Bob was impressed. It looked as if Malkur was not the only one who had been reading the information he'd given the Demons.

"The Hordes are strong, made up of the strongest warriors that Emerilia has ever seen, but you are divided. You fight one another for position, killing your brothers and sisters for higher rank. I have banned this from you for months. I have watched you become close. The Demi-Humans you see before you could match any of you in a battle. Their tribe left the other continents behind and found their own. A land filled with terrible beasts. Like you, they came in great numbers, sure that they would rule the lands. They were proved wrong; they learned to work together, to become brother and sister in not just name and appearance. They fought for a home, and founded a nation—you might know it. For it was called Ashal, after the warrior tribes that tamed the wild before the prejudices of the Affinity Pantheon and their greed forced the great wars of Ashal, dividing the continent, which still rage to this day." Bob turned from the hordes that were now talking among themselves to look to Malkur and the other Demon Princes.

Lezar looked angry but humbled by the fight.

"I offer you an opportunity to turn your Hordes into an army that will shake mountains and make its enemies flee from their path. Are you ready to learn?" Bob asked.

Efri took a knee before Bob and the Demi-Humans, the ultimate sign of respect for one equal to them. "I wish to learn," Efri declared.

The other brothers took a knee beside him. The Demon Horde of thousands dropped to their knees, holding their heads proud.

"Then, we've got a lot of work to do and not much time to do it in." Kala looked to Bob.

"Message me when you need me. Here, I can do much to assist you. Once back on Emerilia, I will not be allowed to," Bob said.

"We're going to need weapons and armor," Kala said.

"Well, I hope you're good at making friends. It seems Anna might know a few who could make arms for a few hundred thousand bloodthirsty Demons." Bob smiled, eliciting grins from the surrounding Demons.

"Make friends and allies, not enemies. Those who dare to betray you, make sure that they never cross you again. Make your word your oath. You will need one another and many others to regain your home and defend it. Make sure the losses of those who have come before you were not in vain." Bob looked once again out over the Demons and Demi-Humans before he disappeared from view.

The Demon Princes stood from their kneeling as did their Hordes as they moved to talk with the Demi-Humans. A few Demi-Humans broke off as war lords talked to them animatedly.

Others got the Horde back to work. The Demon army was not one to sit around for long.

It seems that the parts are coming together nicely.

Bob smiled before actually teleporting to the portal and then walking through it. He kept tabs on the different groups and people, making sure that nothing bad would happen.

He still had a lot more to do.

***

Kala looked over the reports that were coming from her fellow beast kin.

She sighed, scratching her head.

Three things stuck out.

There was no real command structure, the weakest ruled and the weaker followed or were left behind.

The Demons had no formal training, with how to fight, how to move or operate as a unit.

They were confrontational because of the first two reasons. If they were able to show their strength, then they could push other 'leaders' out of the way and take their position.

"They're closer to a group of wolves than they are warriors," Kala muttered under her breath.

She had trained thousands of people in her time, and had led great armies.

She didn't need to just train these Demons up, she needed to break them down and wipe out their previous habits.

"It's going to be tough," Kala said, the essence of training a soldier was to break them down, show them their weaknesses, show them how far they could be pushed, break them down in spirit and body while switching out their previous thoughts and actions to those of a soldier. A person that would charge forward, knowing that they might die but being more scared to let down their leaders and fellow soldiers.

Breaking the Demons was going to take a lot of work. If Kala was able to do it and build them up into a true army they would be a force to reckon with.

***

Anna and Dave looked up from their work. Dave had been working on a drop pad while Anna agonized over the design of her sword. Parts lay on a workstation nearby, different woods and bindings that would make the hilt and handle.

"Heya, guys!" Bob stood on top of one of the nearby workbenches.

"Hey, Bob." Dave moved back to his work, carving out the runes on the pad. It was a five-foot diameter circular platform that was broken into four parts that could click together into a single drop pad.

Runes carried from one part of the pad to the other. It was shaped into a magical circle, something that Dave had been complaining about. It seemed that he had wanted to use his runing on it but found it was too complicated and he needed time to work on his runing technique before he could.

Right now, he was just copying over the runes that he had a stored picture of.

"What are you doing here, Dad?" Anna asked as her dad glided between workbenches until he stood on the table the diagrams were on, looking at the blade.

"Looking to replace your old sword?" Bob studied the designs.

"Yes. Think you can help?" Anna asked, looking at it all. Since she had returned, she had been disconnected from her AI servers.

There was coding in them that would have shut her down if she had tried to connect. She could still think faster than most and had a high Intelligence and Wisdom, though people saw her as a simple Demi-Human warrior.

"One or two things." Bob sounded preoccupied as the diagram changed beneath his feet. "That looks a bit better—fits your fighting style more." Bob gave her a proud smile.

"Thanks, Dad." She smiled. "You never said what it was that brought you here though."

"Fine! Okay, so I might have been messing with a few things behind the scenes, though I need your help. As captain of the Ashkal's forces, I need you to make a place available for your people to return. One such location might be Devil's Crater," Bob said.

"Talk to me—none of this hinting stuff," Anna said.

"I want you to broker an alliance with Alkao, who is the ruling Demon Prince. I want you to see if you can work together. I might have Kala and her officers training the Demons how to not only fight like a Horde but like trained warriors. I don't think that they will make soldiers, but teaching them how to live off the land and different tricks of the forests would be worthwhile. I've got to find some Wood Elves who might be willing to help as well. You think Deia's dad would help out?" Bob asked.

"You want us to train the Demons?" Anna asked.

"Yes. You're going to need one another. You don't have a home and they need training. Your people's values and ways, added to the Demon's natural ways, the fact that they have massive numbers and a place to call home, could be pretty beneficial to both sides." Bob opened his hands.

Anna tapped her lip in thought.

"I only ask that you go and meet with Alkao when Malsour goes. Talk to him, see what his people are capable of. They might be an old race, but they're still foolish, keeping to the tactics that the

Dark Lord gave them. They had not fought anyone other than the Angels, who were comparable in their power."

"Fine. I will speak to him and see what comes of it." Anna knew that her father was trying to look out for her and her people's best interests. What would come of it and her decisions, he wouldn't try to influence.

A ringing went off.

"Excuse me, I'll see you later! Oh, and Dave…"

"I won't forget the whiskey soul gems," Dave said, not looking up from his work.

Bob grinned at Anna and gave her a quick hug.

"I'm proud of you. Best thing I ever did make," Bob whispered.

Anna blushed and held him tighter. Her arms went slack as Bob disappeared.

"Well, how long is that drop pad going to take?" Anna asked.

"Like a few hours. How long is that plan going to take?" Dave hadn't taken the Mithril out of the forge as she hadn't been able to nail down what she exactly wanted for her blade.

"I think it's almost there." Anna looked at the image that was shown in three views, the one that her dad had altered to its current form.

This could work.

A pop-up covered her vision.

Quest: Tribe's Return

The Gray God has tasked you with finding a place for your Tribe to return to. They have amassed enough supplies that you do not need to worry about food and shelter.

"Well, we've got some work ahead of us." Anna sighed.

***

"I think this is it." Anna showed Dave the plans.

He looked over it, rubbing his stubble in thought. He made minor alterations and looked at it from different angles.

He conjured a blade of steel based off the plans, destroying it before it was fully formed. He did it again and again before he finally held a completed blade in his hand. Then, he destroyed it again and recreated it a dozen times.

Anna watched, amazed, as he continued to create and destroy the blade that had just been a plan moments earlier. Dave walked, making and destroying the weapon, from the blade to the hilt. He stopped at the furnace. Opening it with his left hand, he destroyed the sword once again.

"You sure?" Dave asked. A blade formed on top of the plans.

Anna looked it over. It was razor-sharp, thin at the edges. It was wide at the base, holding the Air channels Anna desired. Anna touched the blade with her hand. It felt *right*.

"Yes." Anna looked to Dave.

The blade disappeared from the table as Dave rubbed his hands together.

Anna recoiled as he opened the furnace. Heat rolled off from the furnace and around Dave. He didn't seem affected by it in the slightest. Mithril and ebony appeared on his fingers as his hands touched the Mithril and ebony ingots in the furnace.

The two metals swirled together before extending outward. Anna watched as the metals grew into a blade. There was no hammering and beating into submission. Dave was like an artist, his creation reacting and growing in front of him.

Dave's tattoos glowed as his Abscondita armor appeared.

A soul gem rose from beside the furnace; Dave created and destroyed different manipulators to place it within the great sword.

Runes and any final flourishes formed. A silver nugget in the furnace flowed like a snake into the rune engravings. Mithril overlapped it and hid them from view. Dave was shaking as the glowing stopped. He grabbed a pair of tongs and pulled the blade from the furnace.

Anna looked at the blade as Dave put it down on a workbench. The Mithril already started to form its reinforcing pattern. Dave once again put his fingers on the metal, cooling and heating it to make sure that the blade remained as strong as possible.

He slumped down into a chair, looking pale and tired as he took shallow and shaky breaths.

"It's done. I'm going to take a nap." Dave sighed and leaned into the chair fully.

"Dave, you okay?" Anna tore her eyes from the blade and moved to Dave.

"Just a bit tired." Dave looked like hell.

Anna used her healing spell on him.

His forehead relaxed and within minutes, he was asleep. Only the pain of his mind from using so much Willpower had been able to keep him awake.

Anna looked back to the blade he had soul smithed for her. It surpassed all of her possible dreams and plans.

To a smith, it would have been seen as a masterpiece. To Anna, it looked like a holy relic: the blade forged and created with her in mind, the soul gem hidden in the cross guard, ebony threaded inside the Mithril exterior. The blade was meant to grow with its user.

Anna had seen many weapons in her time. But this... It looked to be of the same power as some of the Weapons of Power she had seen.

She touched it, a pop-up showing.

Unnamed

Forged by a Master Smith, this blade will cleave those who oppose it and the very wind.

Quality: S

Attack: 1,200

> Abilities: +5% of hit damage returned as Stamina
>
> +10% increased Agility
>
> +5% Willpower when wielding

Ability to create Air blades requires: Air Blade Dancer

Grows in power with use.

She looked at Dave with a new reverence and thanks. His first-generation Abscondita armor he had given to her had been incredible, but her new blade—it drove home how strong and powerful he had become with his smithing and crafting abilities. It took a hell of a lot out of him and he had to use his stored Willpower to do it. Yet, it was clear his engineering background, his ideas from Earth, and his knowledge from Emerilia had made him one of the scariest weapon creators on Emerilia.

He gives these gifts so easily, even when knowing the truth. When this gets out, there will be many clamoring for his support and allegiance. Anna looked at her friend, who snored lightly.

I'm lucky to have a friend like him. She silently promised to help him as he had helped her.

Chapter 34: Rise and Fall of Guilds

Florence's eyes widened at the sight of the nine rings hanging off the Dwarf's necklace, from stone to Mithril. "Thanks, Dunex. I'll take this from here."

"You owe me a beer!" the other Dwarf said as he closed the door behind him.

"I did not know that I would be dealing with someone such as you." Florence tilted her head.

Few Players really met Master Smiths. None met Dwarven Master Smiths, who were supposed reclusive ornery buggers who hid in their mountains, crafting their brains out.

"Bah. The name's Quino. I'm not one for all the flowery talk. You like beer, wine? Even got some Elven stuff here. Dunex knows the good stuff." Quino winked mischievously as he fingered the different decanters in an ornate liquor cabinet.

"Some wine would be nice." Sweat ran down Florence's spine.

"More of a beer man, me personally—though this Benvari stuff is pretty nice." He poured a glass and grabbed a bottle from the lower part of the cabinet. He gave the glass to her and sat in one of the two luxurious couches to the side of the office.

Florence took the other seat and took a sip of the wine. Sweet fruits seemed to dance on her tongue—refreshing more than overwhelming, just barely hinting at the alcohol contained within. She swallowed, closing her eyes to make it last longer, feeling as if her worries of the guild and different ongoing stresses eased ever so slightly.

"One must enjoy the little things to have a long life." Quino raised his bottle and took a good sip, tasting the drink slowly before he swallowed. "Even if that little thing costs as much as a damned Mithril nugget!" He laughed at Florence's alarmed expression.

"Ahh, don't worry, with your guild's rise to power, I think that you will be getting more of that in your clutches sooner rather than later." Quino grinned.

"As I am honored by your presence, I wonder, why are you talking to me?" Florence asked.

"Well, that damned boy wanted me to make you some ugly darned contraption that I can't make heads or tails of. There were also a number of rare weapons that you dropped off for the boy and the Stone Raiders that I was interested in. I was wondering who the boy and his guild would trust to see this all done and get a measure of you," Quino said, a smile on his face as he drank from his bottle. Yet there was a calculating look in his eyes.

Who is this boy he talks of? How does he have this much pull to tell a Master Smith to make something?

"He also told me that you have a contract to sell several items that his guild procures. Recently, I have found myself interested in some wares and I was wondering if you would be willing to act as an intermediary," Quino asked.

"What kind of items?"

"Resources," Quino said simply.

"We don't have that many wagons compared to the Dwarven trading companies," Florence said.

"Ah, a straightforward one! I do hate when you traders beat through the bush about this and that instead of getting right to the real conversation! Right—we need a way to make it seem separate of us. If people see us start moving all this kind of stuff, then we're going to have a whole bunch of people wondering just what the hell we're doing. Much easier to use one of you bonded and secured Player guilds. A lot less tongue wagging! Oh, and he said that it would be a good idea to move to Verlun—you know, that farming city near the Per'ush floating islands close to Emaren, the merchant city? Well, yeah there, or one of the smaller cities that isn't as prominent. Says that the snobby types will probably be pissed at the new power you'll come in with. Best to go to a place where you can establish yourself instead of barge in. He's a smart one." Quino drank his beer.

Florence once again took a light sip of her wine.

"Though don't tell him that. The boy has a high opinion of himself as it is!"

"I'm sorry—who is this you're talking about?" Florence asked.

"That's the spirit, gal! Okay, so he said that you should tell Josh when you have all of the stuff and that Josh will talk you through all of the assembly and what-not of the drop pad. But for the trading of those resources, would you be able to be our intermediary if required?"

"Certainly," Florence said, more confused than ever.

"Great. I'll take your contact info and your guild's interface information. Be good to do business in the future. Having a right pain trying to make the materials ourselves without using direct magic, which makes them damned expensive!" Quino grumbled.

***

"What is this?" Bronx put the last metal plate down into the wagon. The springs of the cart sunk with all the weight.

"I'm not sure. I've got to talk to Josh. Do you have all of the other items?" Florence asked.

"Yes, ma'am," Bronx said.

She nodded and moved to her wagon, letting out a whistle.

The wagons started to move.

A pair of eyes that had been watching from a trader's table turned and left, heading deeper into the city that surrounded Zolu Mountain in the Medlari Empire. Making sure no one was around, the man opened up his interface. "Tell the magistrate that the Stone Raiders' trading company just picked up their goods."

"Good. I wonder if the idiots know that they hired the guild that killed their people to try and steal the wealth from their defenders," a voice on the other side of the chat snickered.

"I swear, talk and blend in with a bunch of the NPCs and then they show just how stupid they are."

"Keep an eye on the caravan. We'll have more of our people join you shortly." The answering voice cut the chat.

The man looked around before he moved deeper into the city, moving up to the rooftops, following his tracking spell to the Exdar's Trader's wagons as they made to head toward the mountain passage that crossed around the Zolu Mountain and into Zolun.

***

Hevard listened to the latest information from his spies. Since Selhi, he had sent out forces across all of Emerilia to try to find the Stone Raiders. It was as if they had vanished as soon as they left the city. There were no signs of them, but it seemed that they were still active.

He had tried to get people watching the Stone Raiders who were littered across the planet and training or off on their own quests. All of them seemed to have been executed.

Damned bitch cursed us all with some soul magic.

Hevard muttered to himself. It had taken a lot of gold, but he had found out where the curse that drained a Health point every five seconds came from: the Lady of Fire. There were few to no temples to her; instead, her followers were the mage's guilds and colleges that were spread across Emerilia.

People had gone and tried to have the curse removed. None of the colleges or of the guild were interested in lifting it.

Hevard was tempted to attack them and force them to lift the curse. He would wait until his people were a higher level before going up against the mages guild. It would take time but they would be free from the curse.

In the meantime, they had looked to find anyone who helped the Stone Raiders or had ties to them.

The Golden Sabres were reported to be having talks with them. The plots to try to weaken them had turned sour, costing too much and putting them on the hunt for the PKP's members.

They'd sent forces to the city Cliff-Hill, where Stone Raiders trained with the Elves and Dwarves of the area.

They had been found and killed well before entering the cities.

Still, Hevard and the rest of the guild were driven to destroy the Stone Raiders.

Their best opportunity yet was the traders' guild that seemed to be trading with the Stone Raiders. No one knew how they would be able to get the goods to the Stone Raiders. From overheard conversations, it seemed that the traders didn't know where the guild was either.

Their leaders have to know where the Stone Raiders are. They might be hiding in some odd cave, but there has to be signs up here. No one can live without supplies.

"We'll just have to pull the information from the traders." Hevard smiled to himself, making plans to meet with others at Zol'sou, the closest teleport pad to the Zolu Mountain that was in the path of the Exdar's Traders.

He wasn't going to let his guildmates have all the fun.

Chapter 35: At Devil's Crater

Malsour looked around as he stepped out into a dark cave. Anna followed behind him, a blade over her shoulder.

Malsour looked back and waved to the rest of their party before the event horizon closed.

"Well, this is going to take some time," Anna said as they stepped out into the cave. There were runes that hid the cave away from outsider's eyes as they walked through the area. Anna pulled on heavier layers of clothing as Malsour walked ahead.

"We're only a few hundred miles from Devil's Crater," Malsour said.

"Yeah, going to be a pain in the ass to walk that far," Anna complained.

"The Players are wearing off on you." Malsour smiled as she hurried to catch up with him.

"Meh, they're not that bad." Anna touched the bottom of her blade.

"I'm guessing that Dave's gift is well received?" Malsour cast a glance at the hilt that protruded over her shoulder.

"It's something else, all right. With enough time and Mana infusion, it's going to be one scary weapon." Anna tapped Maldar affectionately. The name meant *singing blade* in Jukal.

Malsour shook his head as he stepped through what looked like a silver ringed area, exiting the cave system and appearing out onto a rough cliff-face. Stairs were cut into it, leading down toward the ground below. Malsour felt the change take hold as he stretched out into his true form.

"Well, let's get moving." Malsour's voice boomed as Anna grinned and jumped up onto his back.

He rose off the cliff with powerful wing-beats, heading for Devil's Crater.

Anna squealed in joy. Not what you would expect from a hardened blade mistress.

Malsour grinned as he put on more power, increasing their forward momentum.

Three hundred miles, bah!

***

"Come on you bunch of ingrates! I thought you said you were soldiers! Get your asses moving!" Kala barked as she moved around the marching formation, berating those that were marching, all of her officers and Sergeants were doing the same, 'motivating' their people.

Kala kept an eye out for the Demon Lords.

At first they had said that they didn't require training, they were the strongest, there was no need for them to do as those under them did.

Kala disagreed saying that she didn't believe that they were the best. Their pride was their hot button. As soon as she had targeted it they had boasted their skills and bet against one another that they wouldn't be able to complete the training.

Kala let out a satisfied grunt. Having the Demon Lords there showed that they were the same as the rest of the soldiers.

It showed that the training was important and everyone pushed themselves harder.

That said, Kala and her officers had all quietly held conversations with all of their people, talking to them.

Before the only place of honor had been within the fighting forces. Now they were trying to show that they needed a large group of people that could do things other than just fight.

It had been slow at first but more and more people had dropped out of training and the army to pursue jobs and trades that they were interested in. Most of them had crossed over to the Beast Kin stronghold to learn there.

There was still a long way to go but Kala was determined. Once the Demons got past their differences and actually worked with the Beast Kin then it was possible to see a future with the two races working together.

Love a challenge.

"There's no room for weakness here! Keep in your formations and in step!" She yelled out, moving through the marching formations.

A few hundred had already 'graduated' to Devil's Crater. Kala didn't slack her standards and kept training those left in her command.

The strongest metals were made in the hottest fires.

***

Alkao rubbed his eyes. He and the warriors at his disposal had worked themselves to exhaustion, first checking the seven fortresses, various caves, and the farming plots within the crater.

The carcasses and hides they had strung up showed the resistance they had run into on their travels. Four of the demons were badly wounded.

It was now that Alkao didn't have troops and resources to throw at the problem that he was learning how something as simple as knowing a healing spell could do wonders.

Krenua had asked to put them out of their misery. Alkao had forbidden it, saying that their allies might have a way to save them. They did not have the lives to waste.

Krenua agreed but his mind was still used to the old ways. A Demon who couldn't fight was useless.

Alkao was going to have to change that way of thinking.

Alkao was thinking about turning in for the night when a presence made his very bones quake in fear. Its aura was as if a Dragon stalked them, interested but ready to strike in a moment, with barely veiled strength.

Alkao turned his head toward the windows, but saw nothing. For a few minutes, there was nothing but the silence of night, the warmth fleeting as the moons and stars hung overhead.

"Hey! Alkao, get your scrawny Demon ass out here!" a familiar voice said. Alkao's eyes latched onto the two people walking across his keep.

Two Demons swept in from above, their weapons drawn. They slammed into a black shield, rolling back, dazed.

"I told you we should have knocked," a male voice said.

Alkao stepped out of the keep, one hand on the hilt of his sword as he glided down to meet his two new visitors. With his night vision, it was easy to recognize Anna and Malsour.

"How did you get here so quickly?" Alkao asked.

The two Demons who had dove into a Mana barrier spread to either side of Alkao, ready to step in at a moment's notice, their hands already on their blades.

"We took a few shortcuts, though we don't have much time to chitchat," Anna said.

"You mind if I fix this up a bit?" Malsour pointed to the keep.

"Sure." Alkao's confusion turned to astonishment as the ground around the keep changed. Rock and materials seemed to sprout out of the ground; different creatures of shadow pulled apart the old ruins as new parts of the structure seemed to grow into place.

In five minutes, it looked better than all the work Alkao had done over weeks.

"Malsour is pretty good at making things. This is for you." Anna put her bag on the ground and pulled out pieces. First there were triangular pieces that formed a circle.

"That's a drop pad. It will allow us to send materials here that you could use, like food and such," Anna said.

"I was told that there would only be one person," Alkao said as more of the Demons flew free of the keep as it moved under Malsour's work. The walls stopped being brick and started to have an almost polished look to it.

"Ah, well, I have a few things that I need to talk to you about," Anna said.

Alkao turned to Anna, giving her his full attention at her serious tone.

"My people's home was destroyed and like your own Demons, they were held by my father so that they wouldn't be wiped out by the forces against them. Now, they are looking to return to Emerilia. My father suggested that it might be an idea if our two races work together." Anna stiffened up, her eyes looking over Alkao and inspecting him.

"What do you want?" Alkao asked.

"My people bring with them skills that you and yours never learned—well, few of you learned what would allow you to thrive as a race. We would need a plot of land within Devil's Crater and to make certain agreements for trade, mutual defense, and so on," Anna said.

Alkao would have dismissed her out of hand before he had trekked across Emerilia to his home. Now, he knew how useful different resources could be. Manpower was good, but trained manpower was dozens of times better.

"What kind of skills?"

"Basic field craft, the ability to scavenge for food on the move. To hunt better, hidden fighting techniques that do not rely on sheer brute strength. Medical knowledge of different plants, and so on." Anna waved her hand dismissively.

"I have many more questions, but the one that comes to mind first is if you could heal some of my people?" Alkao said.

"Show me," Anna said.

Alkao led her through the keep that looked more and more like his home. Broken stairs were replaced. Walls covered the night sky.

Neither of them needed the torches that would have rested in the walls as they walked up to where the Demons had been resting. Four were wounded; one whimpered, clearly in pain, unable to sleep through it all.

"What the hell have you been doing up here?" Anna growled, brushing past Alkao and moving to the injured Demon. She pulled out herbs and different items, pulling on the Demon's leg that had been opened and smelled something fierce. She drew a dagger and looked at Alkao. "Hold him down. This is going to hurt." A small Fire danced between her fingers and along the blade of her knife as she pulled out a collection of herbs and held it to the creature.

She spoke in guttural Abyssal. "Chew this."

The Demon clamped their mouth down defiantly, its eyes red with infection, but still he didn't accept her aid.

"Do it," Alkao said in Abyssal.

The Demon opened their mouth.

Anna shoved the herbs in as the Demon chewed, relaxing slightly. Anna positioned herself over the leg wound, looking at it in all its pus-filled glory.

"This is going to suck." Her blade moved quickly, opening up the wound once again as she started to clear it out. The Demon bucked and fought their grasp, the herbs not enough to blunt the full pain. Anna's hand was like a vise, keeping his leg from moving.

Alkao had trouble keeping the Demon's upper body from jerking. He was impressed by her strength as she worked, unaffected by the Demon's attempt to free itself.

It finally passed out, to Alkao's relief.

Anna continued to clear out the wound that had festered. "Burn this." She pointed to what she'd removed.

Alkao did so as she cleaned her knife and went to work once again. Alkao watched in interest.

"What happened was that the wound was not cleaned properly after it happened; outside crap got into it and turned into rot. That rot destroyed the surrounding parts of the leg, turning it into pus. Eventually, this crap would have leaked into his system and his body would have shut down. Now, I'm cleaning all of the bad crap out. Then, we can start from the beginning," Anna said, noticing that she had a willing audience.

Alkao watched as she cleared out the wound.

"Now, we take Gor-root, Night's Balm, and Wolf's Feather." She held each herb and put it into a bowl. "They've been dried out so that they are more potent and they last longer. We throw in some water and grind it all up."

"What is with the herbs?"

"Together they will numb, help with healing, and make sure that infection will not take hold again." Anna put the paste along the three lines in the demon's leg. "Now, we put it back together. This poultice is fine with being in the wound, as a person's nanites will break this down and use it for growth."

"Nanites?" Alkao repeated the foreign word.

"A mix of your Mana and Endurance," Anna said quickly, pulling out a needle and thread. "Now, we need to put him back together." With quick and precise movements, she closed the wounds with her needle and thread.

"Could you not use one of those healing potions?" Alkao asked.

"I could have, but it is best to use them when in a life-or-death situation. He'll be fine and with just that little bit of work, he should be okay in a few days. You Demons heal fast." Anna moved to the others who had woken to their fellow's bucking and screaming. "Okay, what injuries do we have here? Cuts, broken bones? That shoulder is definitely out of place. What the hell were you lot doing!"

The Demons looked up at her with defiance, trying to not show their injuries or weaknesses.

"That's how you want to play it, fine—scream when something hurts," Anna said with a truly scary smile as she leaned down. The Demon made to push her back and escape. Anna held the Demon's arm and pinned him to the floor with it.

Strong, ruthless, and resourceful, Alkao thought. *If she can put these four, who we would have killed before, back to their full duties in just a short while, then our hordes could pull veteran fighters back from the battlefield. No more mercy killings unless necessary. It would be like the angels, who could suffer a great many wounded but unless you killed them they would once again return to the battlefield.*

"Alkao, you want to give them an order or something? This shit is pretty annoying." Anna sounded as though she would start to add to their injuries if they would not stop resisting her.

"Stop moving around and stay still. A little pain grows a Demon. With her ministrations, you will once again fight by my side. Do not think of your deaths to rid us of your burden." Alkao looked at them all.

They bowed their heads under his gaze.

"Now, tell me where it hurts," Anna said. Her patients pointed to different areas where they had wounds.

Anna showed Alkao different kind of poultices, how to clean and seal wounds, break and set bones and put joints back into place. It did not look like fun, but Alkao could see its immediate usefulness.

He only had twenty Demons and getting them back into their peak condition without having to mercy kill them was a valuable resource indeed.

***

Krenua watched in awe as Malsour put Alkao's keep back together. The patchwork of stones was covered in ebony.

"Is that material not rare?" Krenua asked as the ebony started to move over the walls as if it were a living thing.

"It is, but I don't think that one should ever waste expenses on their home. Provides security should someone try to attack them—or steal their books."

Krenua was pretty sure that Malsour was trying to keep that last part to himself, as he'd mumbled it.

"Also with the metal, unlike stone, you can enchant it, though that takes a lot of time. If my friend Dave was here, then he could do it, though he is busy with another project."

"Enchant the walls?" Krenua had heard of enchanted weapons; he had never wielded one, too busy with fighting to go on raids and other adventures that might gift him a blade with magical properties.

"Yes, the mages of Per'ush do it. The Dwarven mountain Aldamire has it as well, but even their runes are not that strong as the mountain is so large."

Krenua shook his head, thinking of the kind of defenses that they would have. *People I would not like to fight without heavy help.*

"Now, what do you want to focus on: wood, metal, or food?" Malsour asked.

"Huh?" Krenua asked, caught off guard.

"Well, right now you have no need for more troops, but you need mines to get materials to forge into weapons—that armor is pretty crap. You're going to need more than just meat and the meat and furs you do have, you could sell for five times its weight in other less rare animals. You're going to need wood for shields, bows, as well as building houses yourselves. I can't simply make all your homes all the time," Malsour said.

"Food and then wood," Krenua said. Having the Hordes around would just make more mouths to feed; having their villagers and the Demons who didn't want to fight would increase production and the speed at which they could bring more people over to return Devil's Crater to its former glory.

"Good choices," Malsour said. A shadow appeared under his feet as he descended toward the valley. Behind him, a one cart-wide path of stone appeared.

Krenua flapped his wings, following Malsour. "Why are you doing this?" Krenua asked.

"A war is coming, with many creatures that were banished from Emerilia for good reason. Few of the races on Emerilia are ready or capable of fighting that threat. You are one of them. Like your people, my own race was sealed away. While it was easy for us to adapt back to Emerilia, it will be much harder for you. We had to sit by and watch the Demon and Angel armies as they fought. We watched as the Angels spread their fanaticism across Emerilia." Malsour's eyes found Krenua's, his eyes black with purple flickers in their depths, reminding Krenua of a Demon who had given itself to its bloodlust, or their mages when casting.

"I wish to give the Demons a chance, a *real* chance, at living and see how you act. This time, we will not watch from the sidelines if you choose to try to conquer Emerilia. This is our planet, too, and we will keep the balance, with force or diplomacy."

"Hope for the best, plan for the worst," Krenua said approvingly.

"Quite." Malsour was quiet for a long time before he looked over Krenua, studying him as they carved a path into the crater. "Have you ever been interested in the Lady of Fire's teachings?"

"I bow my head to no lord or lady," Krenua spat.

"Oh, she is no lady—regal, powerful, and as weak as any of us mortals, though she does not care for your platitude, your words and devotions. She is the creator of the mage's guild and colleges. Her Fire might be portrayed as the one of destruction, but she used it to light a fire inside the minds of thousands. Her Fire is the one of knowledge, the ever-burning need to learn, to sate one's curiosity," Malsour said, with true respect in his voice.

"Why do you follow her? Are you not one of the Dark one's mages?" Krenua asked, confused.

Malsour let out a laugh as he paused in mid-air and looked over the land. "We are not our magic. We might have an affinity to one element over another, but we are not beholden to it. I may wield the Dark magics, but what I learned from the Lady of Fire and her knowledge is much more powerful than any blessing that that useless shadow lord could come up with," Malsour drawled.

Krenua laughed. "I like you, Malsour."

"You are quite the interesting Demon, too, Krenua." Malsour pulled a tome from his bag and threw it at Krenua. "Read that. I have someone I must talk to before I start making houses all over the place." Malsour looked out over the crater.

"Hello, nephew! How are the kiddos?" Malsour said.

Krenua snorted as he looked at his book. *Basic spells of Fire.*

Krenua opened the book and read the first pages. It was slow going; he had only learned to read and write because of his position as the Black Hand's leader.

The pages started to move faster. Krenua understood more; his mind seemed to open to the world ever so slightly, making connections that he would have never made before. The pages moved faster and faster until the book's back cover slammed shut and turned to dust, drifting away in the warm night's breeze.

"Teach me, teach me to read." Krenua looked to Malsour.

"I'll send you a party invite so that you can teleport to me. I'll talk to you when you get here. I've got something to attend to. I'll pay your fee here and back." Malsour tapped out something on his interface. "Talk soon!"

Malsour looked to Krenua with his full attention. "That is most definitely something I can help with, but before I do, I must ask you to make a vow." Malsour smiled and lowered himself to the ground.

"A vow?" Krenua asked.

"You must vow to teach others who are willing," Malsour said.

"So, if someone asks me about something, then I should help them learn?" Krenua asked. *That doesn't sound that hard.*

"Precisely. Which means not hoarding books from others. And books that are dangerous—I would advise you to give them to the mages guild, but that I will not make you swear to. Your knowledge is your own. I hope that you will help others in their path as I will help you," Malsour said.

"If someone seeks me out to attain knowledge or I see someone I can teach, I will help them," Krenua promised, cutting his finger with his claws. "I vow by my word."

"Very well. Now, try this out." Malsour pulled out another tome.

Once again, Krenua opened the book. Krenua read through it a lot slower than the book of Fire spells, but he started understanding more of the Fire spells as words that explained foreign ideas started to make sense.

There was a flash of silver light for a few seconds as a third person joined them.

"Hello, Uncle!" The man embraced Malsour.

"Who are you?" Krenua's hand moved to his blade.

"I'm Fornau. Pleasure to meet you." The man extended his hand.

"Good to meet you," Krenua said, not willing to shake his hand, suspecting foul play.

"Krenua is a warrior by training and birth, not one to shake hands for fear of a fight," Malsour explained.

"Oh, very well," Fornau said with a disarming smile, lowering his hand. "I won't eat you. Most people always think that."

"Now is not the time to think on stereotypes. What do you think of this land? I have been tasked with making homes for farmers and loggers, as well as their facilities. Where would be the best place to put it all?" Malsour asked.

Krenua went back to his book. His hand rested on his blade, one eye remaining on the uncle-nephew duo.

"Hmm, the ground is good. You've got some decent forests to the northeast that would probably be nice to keep. Also, have some dungeons and caves there for rarer beasties. The south gets the most amount of sun. I'd say the northwest would be good for logging and mining into the cliff created by whatever hit this. A town in the center for trade and management. Also, make a fortress there in case the seven exterior fortresses fail. The forests have claimed the south. There are some rare trees there that are old. Might put an orchard and greenhouses to the southwest; that way, they'd have the most sun year round. Going to need to set up a large retaining lake, maybe run it from the higher peaks of the crater, guide it into a moat around the fortress and then down toward the fields and greenhouses. Make the grade steeper for the fields so that with the spring rains, the water overflows—the detritus from the city mountains and river covering the farms so that they have good soil every year without too much need for manure or fertilizer," Fornau said.

Krenua looked up at the growing image that Fornau drew on his interface, sharing so that Krenua and Malsour could see.

Krenua remembered how Devil's Crater had been before. Camps everywhere, with the hordes moving around and fighting one another for the best hunting areas. The villagers lived in their fields, scared that they would have their own crops stolen by their fellow Demons.

What Fornau was creating was not just a place to live. It was an entire ecosystem onto itself. Military standing and positions were secondary. Food production, sustainable resources: these were in the forefront of their minds.

"What about the Hordes?" Krenua asked.

"The fortresses can be extended. You have a lot of area to cover to make sure that you know what is coming in and out of the area. I would also think that they would train in the forests to be ready to deal with animals. They can do hard labor in the mines and fields during different seasons. And these cliffs seem to be rather solid to me. I don't see why you couldn't tunnel them and put military barracks in them. There would also need to be a guard that makes sure that the people are following the laws you put down. Do you mean practice areas? Well, you could practice in the cliffs if you flatten out an area, or in the fields that don't have good ground for the season.

"Then, there is the fact that if you are transporting anything from here to anywhere else, it would need a guarding caravan and there is a massive area just beyond your fortresses that are hostile. Cut the forest back a bit, make training camps there. Forces ready to deploy as soon as a threat is seen on the horizon," Fornau said.

"How can you plan this all out?" Krenua asked.

"I've seen a few cities in my time and I took it upon myself to learn a bit about architecture when I was building my home for me and my kids. I might have got sidetracked and learned a bit more about how cities were formed. Right here, you could make a pretty powerful entity. It wouldn't be completely self-sustainable, but it would be pretty damned close."

"Could you share your plans with me? I know that my Prince would be very interested and he might have a few things that he wants to alter," Krenua said, feeling out of his depth with it all.

"Certainly—this is just rough. I would suggest that we move to where there are the sunniest spots. I will start to clear out the trees that can be used for firewood and relocate the rare ones into a small park in what I hope will become your fortress city. I'll get started on a large bastion around where the fortress city would be best situated and lead it down to the farming plot. I think it would be best to put the logging facilities here." A waypoint appeared in everyone's vision and on their mini-map, if they had bought a map.

"I'll get started on that and look for the best places to start mines while I'm over there." Malsour looked back at Krenua. "I'll be back soon. Let me know when you finish that book."

With that, Malsour darted off on his shadow, still creating a stone road behind him as Fornau rubbed his hands together in excitement.

"I've never built a city before," he said before speeding off faster than an arrow from a bow.

Who the hell are these people? Making entire cities, transforming Devil's Crater more than we did in the seventy-five years we spent here?

Krenua shook his head and looked down at the book Malsour had given him. Knowledge had allowed them to get to this level of ability. Krenua was not going to let the advantage slip through his fingers. Malsour had shown him how blind he was.

Krenua looked at his hand, knowing enough of the knowledge he'd had dumped into his mind by the previous book. A small flame appeared on his right index finger.

"The Fire of knowledge." Krenua looked at it before he smiled and extinguished it.

Krenua didn't know it, but he had contracted a well-known disease among the mage's colleges and guilds. He'd contracted Bookworm, driving him to seek new knowledge and new experiences to broaden his mind.

Chapter 36: Out of Sight

The lowest island of Per'ush lowered itself till the lowest jetty was half-submerged in the water below. A number of mages and reporters looked over from the higher levels, searching the seas for a sign of the guests of honor.

After a few moments, a head popped out from the water. A man standing seven feet tall and holding a trident with runes on its surface glided out of the water and onto the jetty.

Mages met him, guiding him to testing lines that had been set up.

He walked, surveying the area before tossing something into the water. Everyone held their breath as a half-dozen more heads appeared, rising from the water and stepping onto the jetty. They looked like humans, with lines of varying colors across sections of their bodies, followed with dots of different colors.

The mages at the testing area had the first Merman put his hand over a crystal. It glowed different colors, each of them revolving in the crystal and denoting numbers. The man was waved on to where there were more mages waiting, ready to talk to him about admittance into the mages college.

"Are you sure about this, Archmage Jelanos?" his aide and lifelong friend Alamos asked.

"No, but it is sure to be interesting! The race that has never once left their home cities coming to our schools in order to learn!" Jelanos rubbed his hands together in glee.

He didn't wear robes of the school, but instead leather armor that had been made by the Elven people as a sign of his adventurer days. He had a mop of brown hair, hazel eyes, and a goatee.

Alamos sighed and rubbed his face. He wore simple mages robes, had salt-and-pepper hair and azure eyes. He hid a smile behind his hand at his friend's antics.

"You do remember that Elani is making dinner for us and the Merpeople's representative?" Alamos said.

That stopped Jelanos rubbing his hands together in glee and jumping up and down.

"Well, you must remind me to not forget. She would not be happy if we missed it!"

"I know, Jelanos—why don't you? You're the one married to her!"

"Bah, remembering all that stuff is annoying!"

"You memorized half of the library!"

"Well, the library and women are different altogether!"

"I have my own wife to care for, you know!" Alamos said.

"I really do have to see little Ginny again! Did you see that she was a level 4 in Air magic!" Jelanos said.

"I do remember—she is my grandchild! Did you see how she was looking at your Petunia?" Alamos said.

"My granddaughter Petunia?"

"What did you think I was talking about? The flower?"

"Well, there was one time when I did get the two mixed up in a meeting. That turned into a rather nasty affair. Whatever did happen to the Heurick Kingdom?"

"They were talking about your granddaughter Petunia. The Heurick Kingdom was on the Ashal continent. After you kicked them out of the mages guild and said that none of their people were welcome to learn from your schools with pigheaded idiots like them running the country, their spell casters left. The country fell apart after that. Most of it got absorbed by the Heldar Kingdom," Alamos said.

"Huh, well, they aren't all that original—they've got two of the same letters in the name!" Jelanos looked away in thought. "Wait, you said that your Ginny was looking at my Petunia? My granddaughter Petunia?" The Air became thick with Mana and anger as Jelanos looked at Alamos.

People looked at the archmage and his aide, slowly stepping away.

"Yes," Alamos said, undisturbed.

The wind slowly stopped and the pressure fell away.

"Well?" Jelanos asked, as excited for the arrival of the Merpeople as he was about his granddaughter's love life.

"I've heard that they might have gone on a few dates." Alamos's finger rose up defiantly in his best friend's face. "You are *not* to interfere or I will hide your glasses from you for a week."

Jelanos's eyes thinned, as if he had met his mortal enemy. "Fine!" Jelanos turned back to the merpeople who were walking out of the sea and onto the lowest jetties of the Per'ush islands.

"But wouldn't that be fantastic!?" Jelanos said, his annoyance once again turning to joy. There were few things that could keep the archmage's spirits down.

"So, how exactly did this all come about?" Alamos waved to the growing party of Merpeople who were now being tested.

"The Lady of Fire gave me a message and I listened. She said that she didn't want the fact that the Merpeople are Creatures of Power made by the Water Lord to make us prejudiced against them."

"How do you know it was from her and not one of the other Affinities?"

"I know," Jelanos said with a sly smile. "After all, she said all Creatures of Power, like her Dragons, are interested in different things. If we let the Dragons wander our halls, what's the problem with a few hundred Merpeople?"

Alamos's jaw opened, but no words came out.

Jelanos turned around. "I never said that." He held his friend's eyes.

"Was that a seagull farting? I think it was." Alamos held a great reverence for his lady. He might be an Earth mage and Jelanos an Air mage, but none of the other lords and ladies had helped him or changed him into the man he was today.

The Lady of Fire and her mage's guild had helped him to understand his gift, matched him up with Jelanos and given him purpose, a life and a family.

If we've now got the Merpeople coming out of the depths of the ocean, maybe those reports of new monsters appearing in different dungeons wasn't that far-fetched. What the heck is happening? I hate it when I'm in the dark!

Alamos took a deep breath of the refreshing sea air, glancing behind and above him.

There rested the fifty-seven islands of Per'ush, his home and the center of the adventurer's and mage's guild.

"Well, it looks like we will have a fair number of promising applicants." A smile appeared on Alamos's face. He looked forward to his few lessons that he gave to pass on his knowledge.

"We have done a lot in our lives, my friend." Jelanos smiled to Alamos. "But damn, I could do with an adventure!"

"You just got back from messing around in the shadow labyrinth in Southern Ashal! Do you know what kind of shit I got in for covering for you!"

"Fine, next time we'll go together," Jelanos said.

"Good!" Alamos said, before thinking over what his friend had said. "Who the hell's going to run all this while we're gone?"

"Well, Fire, of course," Jelanos said, once again pausing as if he'd said something he shouldn't have. Jelanos looked around. His eyes stopped as the color drained from his face.

Alamos felt the hairs on his neck rise, much as if a predator were behind him. He looked back and up, finding an unassuming woman wearing the robes of a water Expert. Her lips were pursed together in thought as she looked over Alamos and Jelanos.

"The next time you boys are talking about me, use a damned sound annulment spell. Jelanos, don't come to try to find me again. I had to resubmit three times to get back in!" Her lips never moved, but Alamos and Jelanos heard her voice in their ear.

"Salt-and-pepper suits you, Alamos." Her eyes seemed to glow with inner Fire as she grinned and winked at them. She turned and left.

Alamos turned to Jelanos. Both of them used a sound annulment spell at the same moment.

Others watched as the archmage and his best friend yelled at each other like groupies; not a single noise escaped their overlapping annulment domes.

"Who are those two idiots?" one of the Merpeople asked.

"That is the archmage and his friend, the famed Jelanos and Alamos. Seems they're in an argument again." The mage testing them sighed. "I hope they used the right warding this time."

"This time?" the mer asked.

"There used to be fifty-eight islands. You might have passed it on your way up. We're still fixing the damage to it before we put it back in the sky. It's said that they were experimenting," the tester said. "Please put your hand over the crystal and allow your Mana into it. You will feel a sensation through your body—don't fight it."

The Merpeople who had heard the conversation looked at the two talking to each other and the two yelling masters.

"I don't ever want to fight that."

"Sunk a damned island, for an experiment."

"There's little left of it down there."

"Well, it might not be as dull and boring as I thought. Might actually be fun," one said.

The Mer started to feel more relaxed as they were accepted in short order and took teleport pads off to their assigned islands to be trained in magic.

***

"What do you mean that you can't make them again?" the Lady of Light asked. Her eyes flashed dangerously as golden outlines of her wings seemed to appear on her back.

The people in the room quivered in fear from the outpouring of Mana coming from her. None of them were as shaken as the woman prostrated on the floor in front of her.

"After the Angels were removed from Emerilia, no one record-ed the information. We would have to start from the beginning with making them again. We have already got teams working on that, but it will take decades. Instead, we have augments that can meld with a person, making them stronger. Matching Creatures of Power and paladins together," the kowtowing woman said as fast as possible.

"Combining Creatures of Power and the paladins?" Light's eyes dimmed as she sat back in her chair, interested.

"We can give them things like wings, augment their bodies so that they can grow to be as powerful as Angels. We can give them all of the things that the Angels had and let their bodies grow."

"Very well, continue with your experiments. Let me know if you need any test subjects. I have a number of low-level paladins we can use. Might we be able to take the bodies over ourselves?" the Lady of Light asked.

Wide-eyed expressions were shown around the room. Many had thought that the Lady of Light was a great and benevolent woman. At least, that was her outward appearance; the more they listened to her talks and her plans, the thinner the veneer between benevolent and Machiavellian her appearance seemed.

"Not currently, but it could be possible," the kowtowing woman said, a bit shocked.

"Good. Those Players get new bodies all the time. If they give us an old one of theirs and we give it new power and augments, we can start building our kingdom from that. Might need to give them a few high-level quests lying around so that they can level up a suitable level vessel." The Lady of Light shrugged.

"I will work on a system to make that work."

"Good. I will make sure that you are readily supplied with all that you need." The Lady of Light waved her hand. A smile spread across her face as she imagined the future with her at the top, with all of the Affinity and Emerilia at her feet.

Her face soured as she thought of the reject, the balancer. She would need to do something about him.

"Send a message to the Lady of Air. Tell her that I wish to meet with her," Light said.

There was a time that she would have called on the Lady of Fire and they could have talked on matters, not about politics and power. That time had gone as Light showed more of her power.

She is just jealous of my accomplishments. It won't be long until she, too, will be groveling at my feet, hoping and praying that I might pay attention to her and make her one of my maids.

Her face turned into an ugly sneer as she looked over the people in her room. They made sure to not catch her eye.

Weaklings. The Lady of Light snorted and shook her head.

***

"Get your head out of your ass!" Kala backhanded a Demon through a tree.

Good thing they're tough.

The Demon got up and rubbed his side in pain.

"You don't yank Alla root out—you need to handle it gently. Work the soil with your fingers; pulling on it will break the fine leaves and flowers from the roots. You've got claws—they're good for digging, so use them!"

"They're good for ripping bear's throats out too!" The Demon stalked closer.

Kala smiled dangerously. Before the Demon could react, he was sent through several trees and disappeared out into the forest. "If you can even reach me, you jumped up piece of charcoal!" Kala barked. She looked to the other Demons who worked at harvesting different herbs and growths that could be eaten, used for various potions and poultices or grown into foodstuffs.

"I'm going to have to get him, aren't I?" Kala said.

"Well, I do think you beat your record." A Demon clapped her on the shoulder, a wide grin on his face. "That's at least two hundred meters."

"Great, you learn distances and how to judge them—now you're figuring out how far I can send people." Kala looked around as she heard coins changing hands.

"We bet on it too," Jeno said, a grin on his face.

A few of the betting Demons smiled sheepishly as they finished their transactions.

Kala looked over Jeno. "Could probably get you four hundred meters," she mused.

Jeno jumped to the closest Alla plant so fast he was almost a blur. "But why try? I am, after all, learning from your esteemed self. Your teachings have opened an unseen world up to me!" Jeno's smile was a little forced as Kala snorted, rolling her eyes. The Demons snickered and chuckled as Kala moved on.

Time ran different on the planet they were on. The gravity was lower than Emerilia, much lower, making a day on Emerilia approximately a day and a half on whatever rock they were living on.

The Demi-Humans and Demons were using the time as much as possible. The Demi-Humans didn't care for Demons' pride nor their tactics for rising in rank. They thrashed them soundly in every fight and then forced them to do jobs that Demons thought to be only for the useless.

It had been four days, but the demons were coming to appreciate the work that the "useless" Demons did.

Kala's face turned thunderous at the way that the Demon Hordes had treated those they didn't believe above their station. Although the Horde had been slow to pick up the Demi-Human's lessons, the "useless" Demons picked it up much faster.

The Demi-Humans had invited many of them back to their homes, teaching them and showing them their ways.

They had the largest concentration of mages and skilled workers. The Demi-Humans made it clear to the Demon workers that no matter what, they had a position with them if they wanted it. Many of them had been ostracized for being crafters instead of warriors, leading to the crafters being in a constant state of fear from their own people.

Kala was displeased with the Hordes and their leaders who had allowed their people to become like this. She understood that they had only lived in times of war but it had rotted them from the inside out. Their cause might have been right but their way of fighting and their treatment of one another was wrong.

"Kala!" Vrexu descended through the forest, his wings making the dust and debris around him fly outward.

"What is it?" Kala dusted herself off, not pleased with the extra dirt she would have to get out of her fur later on.

"Three hundred of our people have vanished!" Vrexu said.

"It seems that Alkao met the conditions. It looks like we're going home," Kala said.

Everyone stopped working and looked up at Kala and Vrexu, myriad emotions flying past their eyes.

"But they took the farmers, loggers, and blacksmiths?" Vrexu said.

Kala laughed. "Well, it looks like this Alkao isn't a complete idiot. He took your most useful people!"

"But we're the warriors and fighters!"

"You're mouths to feed with no skills to make anything or grow anything. Your talent is killing, nothing more or less." Kala saw her words stung the Demons, but she hoped that it would get through their thick skulls. Bob said that she'd need allies in the future. She didn't want to fight along people who only knew how to kill. Those weren't allies; that was a stampede of wild boars with blades.

Anyone could fight. Only armies could wage war.

***

"How do the Jukal see us?" That question hung in the air between Bob and Dave.

Bob didn't want to do anything that would bring the Jukal to watch Dave more, but he deserved to know. With all that he had done he was sure to get some attention and it was best if he figured out a few ways to keep some secrets secret.

"There are two main methods. One are the orbital satellites that could see a pimple on an ants backside. Divinity mages use these a lot of the time. The second is part of the magic and interface system that is within you. Basically there is a computer system that reads what you're thinking in your mind, then nanites reinforce your body, you get more with each level. They also connect to your optical nerves so you can see your interface, or use arcane sight and magical spells. They are also used to broadcast your 'streams' while players can pick and choose when they want to share these streams with one another. The Jukal can override them and access them as they want."

Dave felt an itch between his shoulders as if he was being watched.

"So how can we counteract it?" Dave asked.

"Whatever information you send by your interface can't be intercepted and read. This is a security measure that is part of the interface, the Jukal Empire use it and as such it is impossible by their standards to hack. Second are the mirror of communications. They are the most secure method of communicating with others. In this conference mode no one can even see your lips moving in the real world," Bob said, waving to the room around them.

"Anything else?" Dave asked.

"Runes, magical formations like the ones used by the Aleph really mess up the signals. They're fuzzy as hell. I don't doubt that you could make something more powerful to stop the signal getting out or any other items that might trip the AI's that search all of Emerilia for things like nuclear weapons," Bob said.

"So how can we get rid of them?" Dave asked, rubbing the back of his head.

"Well you could destroy them, if you were to pull apart the specific nanites in your own body you could eliminate them. Or you could shut down the massive server farms in the north and south pole that connect to the nanites and then link them to relaying mirror of communications to the rest of the Jukal Empire," Bob said.

"That sounds easy," Dave sighed, sitting back in his chair.

For a while they sat in silence.

"How do the Jukal end the Player cycles?" Dave asked, his voice heavy.

Bob sighed, looking from Dave to the floor, a dark expression on his face.

"Two main methods. First they tell the Players that they are shutting down the game and to log off. Those that log off, instead of having their minds transferred from their bodies to the Earth simulation, are simply transferred out of their bodies. The Empire doesn't have the control to forcefully make someone log off. The other method is reserved for those that don't log off. They activate a spell that was made into your bodies, killing you, to never be revived. Other methods can include, making the gods kill you off, bribe or threaten the populace to kill off Players. It can turn messy as the news services, internet and other connections to the Earth simulation die off and people realize that Emerilia is something more. If necessary, drones will come down and kill those that resist. Emerilia hasn't gone past having the POE's kill off players. Its mostly done for entertainment reason. The usual is log off then the death-spell," Bob said.

"Well that's awesome," Dave muttered.

"I didn't say that the path of a bleeder would be easy," Bob said with a weak smile.

"So right now, as we're playing here, are there more Players being grown and trained up in another simulation Earth?" Dave asked.

Bob nodded simply.

"Yes, they're in the moon complex, once a player cycle is cleared off then we can introduce the new cycle, just like nothing ever happened."

"Grown, packaged and then sold to sell," Dave let out a deep breath, humans were nothing but items of interest in the eyes of the Jukal Empire.

Epilogue

Florence pulled her clothes tight to her body as her three wagons continued on. They were only a few hours from a nearby inn and they had chanced the journey to the inn rather than another night of putting up a camp.

I thought it was spring! When's Mother Nature going to get the message? Look at me, arguing with Mother Nature in a game!

Florence sighed at her own antics and sat back in her seat.

She loved games and she loved trading. Now, she could browbeat and talk people into deals with all manner of charms and wit; she loved every minute of it.

She still had to pinch herself for the windfall that the Stone Raiders had given her guild. Not for the first time, she thought about asking whether her guild could become part of the Stone Raiders. They were getting increasingly closer with their work, acting as the merchant arm for the guild, which led to all manner of opportunities. Florence smiled as she looked over her quests, the different gear she was carrying and her guild's holdings.

"PKP," one of the armored people waiting in the wagon said.

Florence sat up and cast her gaze around.

"I'm sensing about twenty or so. Looks like they're coming from both directions. Once they meet, they'll probably hit us from all sides," another said.

"Contact Dwayne. We're going to get hit," another said.

Florence didn't say anything, not wanting to give anything away as she flicked her reins ever so slightly, making the wagon pick up speed.

***

496

"The rare gear we sent off to get repaired at Zolun is about to be stolen by the PKP. They tracked down the caravan and it looks like they're going to hit it any moment!" Dwayne burst into Josh's room, where he'd been sleeping.

"Those motherless fucking arseholes want my bloody daggers! All right, shit, how can we get anything there? Dave!" Josh found the man and opened a chat with him.

"What's up? Bit tired right now," Dave said.

"Dave, the wagons carrying our rare gear from Zolun is about to get hit! That drop pad—what can we move through it?" Josh demanded.

"Well, you can send things that are alive one way, but then they can't come back the same way. I wouldn't trust it with more than one person," Dave said.

"Fine, but we can send anyone, right?" Josh asked.

"Yeah," Dave said.

"Good!" Josh cut the channel and opened up another to parties that were on watch.

"Our people are going to be hit by PKP. We're going to use a drop pad to ambush them! Go to the teleport pad room!" Josh said, running and looking to Dwayne. "Tell them to get that damned drop pad put together!"

"Might I suggest taking potions to deal with motion sickness? Most people get severe nausea when exiting the drop pad," Shard said.

Josh opened a channel to Lucy. "Lucy, we got anti-nausea potions?"

"I've got a few—why?"

"We need them in the teleport pad room, now!" Josh jumped into a lift and pressed in his destination. Dwayne was right beside him, talking to the Stone Raiders who had gone with Florence.

"When we're done here, I'm calling open season on PKP. Damned bastards are a right pain in my ass," Josh muttered.

"Agreed," Dwayne said.

***

"They've stopped," one of the assassins said, slowing down.

"Hurry up. They're probably up to something." Hevard pushed onward.

The Dark Lord had taken his blessing back. Hevard once again felt weak and pathetic as he stalked through the forest. Even in his weak form, he knew that he was one of the finest assassins of Emerilia.

He had brought forty guild members with him. Another fifteen were closing in from Zolu Mountain.

Hevard pulled out his blades, ready to meet the traders. He would take the Stone Raiders' gear from them, forcing the traders to tell him where the Raiders were hiding and strike terror into their very hearts.

Hevard continued to creep up, looking in confusion as a half-dozen armed and armored people who shouldn't have been there were putting pieces of something together on the ground.

"What are Stone Raiders doing with the Exdars? What the hell are they doing?" One of the assassins asked the very questions that Hevard was thinking.

They were still too far away to attack, when there was a flash of light. It seemed as if a window had opened in the middle of the forest, right over whatever the Stone Raiders had been working on.

Moments later, something jumped out. They collapsed to the ground and started throwing up before forcing a potion down.

"What the hell?" Hevard asked out loud. He picked up his pace as two more came through the portal, coming through and throwing up.

The Raiders moved to protect the wagons, a number of them pulling items from a large box.

"Well, thanks for letting me borrow this, Clevus. I swear I will do you proud and give it back to you," one could be heard saying.

Hevard's eyes widened as he realized that they were pulling out the unique and rare weapons from the sealed chest they had received in Zolu.

"They're getting reinforcements! Hurry up! We need to kill them now!" Hevard rushed forward, giving little care to his stealth.

More Stone Raiders poured out as the assassins made their move.

***

Florence looked up from her position with the other Exdar's Traders right next to the "drop pad" that was spewing out Stone Raiders.

They pulled themselves together, drinking their potions with fire in their eyes. There was no time for greetings as people moved into their positions.

The PKP's attack was announced with a throwing blade hitting a shield.

"Have to try better than that, you useless shit!" the defending Stone Raider said as magical spells bloomed in the night air. Arrows were flung everywhere as Florence and her traders hid and watched the Stone Raiders in action for the first time.

The assassins seemed to materialize out of the dark.

To the Stone Raiders, they might as well be screaming out their names and have a shirt saying "Stab Me Here." The Stone Raiders had gotten stronger while they were away; it was clear in their actions. There was little wasted effort, striving to kill threats as fast as possible.

Parties coordinated with one or two words. The assassins around them might be rated on the same level, but the skill and stats that the Stone Raiders had earned and not just put into their character sheet after gaining a level showed.

Stone Raiders were brought low here and there but a mages group buffed and healed them up enough that they wouldn't immediately die.

The drop pad's portal disappeared as the last Stone Raider came through. She downed her potion, howling out her anger as she ran right into the middle of the battle. Her mace slammed an assassin into the ground before another Stone Raider stabbed them in the neck.

***

"How, how is this possible?" Hevard asked. He watched his guild-mates being slaughtered, as if their stealth skills bore no effect. Hevard had wounded and hurt many of the Raiders but few had fallen; none had died.

His attacks didn't count as stealth attacks, taking much of his power from them. His attacks were meant to kill someone with a single attack. He, like the rest of his guild, had stayed away from investing in Health. A good killer was one who hit and killed with one attack.

Now, it was coming to bite them in the ass. The Stone Raiders met their attacks head on, their skills not working for some reason.

Hevard felt a familiar burning through his body. *It's this curse—it has to be! Somehow, they can see us and know where we are.*

Cold sweat fell down Hevard's spine as every one of his guild-mates were being hunted down.

A cynical person might see the tactics similar to how the PKP hunted down and killed players until they quit Emerilia or changed for a new character.

The Stone Raiders looked up from their work; they looked to Hevard. Some looked at others who were trying to flee.

Hevard saw the bloodthirsty looks beneath their helmets. It was the same smile he had worn when PKP had attacked Selhi Capital.

A shiver ran down his spine as he started to run.

"Hunt them down," one of the Stone Raiders said. The defending force started to sprint.

Hevard looked back to see them rushing after him. *How are they so fast? This is impossible!* Hevard looked ahead, running with all his might and using all his skills. It wasn't long until he ran out, the Stone Raiders still gaining on him.

"When you run, you just die tired. Don't worry, PKP—we're coming for you all soon enough," one of the Stone Raiders said, her fellows laughing.

A blade buried itself through Hevard's ribs and into his chest.

He heard a wet sucking noise as the power of his body gave out and toppled to the ground in pain. He clawed his way through the fresh mud until his screen turned black.

You have died in Emerilia

You have been returned home.

You have 5:59 hrs (game time) until you can respawn at (Moumihara)

Or

1:59 hrs in real life

Would you like to play a different game while you wait?

"That's right—it's only a game. Holy shit, that was intense!" Hevard laughed nervously to himself and sat down in his Player home.

He looked at his hand; it shook as he tried to control his fear.

It might be a game, but it sure as hell felt real.

Emerilia will be continued in New Horizon.

As a self published author I live for reviews! If you've enjoyed Emerilia, please leave a review!

Hope you have a great Day! ☺

As a self published author I live for reviews! If you've enjoyed Emerilia, please leave a review!

Hope you have a great Day! ☺

Want a bigger map of Emerilia and the continents? Check out **http://theeternalwriter.deviantart.com/**

You can check out my other books, what I'm working on and upcoming releases through the following means:

Website: **http://michaelchatfield.com/**

Twitter: **@chatfieldsbooks**[1]

Facebook: **Michael Chatfield**[2]

Goodreads: **Goodreads.com/michaelchatfield**[3]

Thanks again for reading! ☺

---

1. https://twitter.com/chatfieldsbooks

2. https://www.facebook.com/michaelchatfieldsbooks/?ref=hl

3. https://www.goodreads.com/author/show/14055550.Michael_Chatfield

Interested in more LitRPG? Check out https://www.facebook.com/groups/LitRPGsociety/

Continue on for Character Sheet!

In Alphabetical order

Ankol

Dwarf

Dwarven Master Smith. Smithing Art: Metal Spinner. Lives in Grorart Mountain.

Boran-Al

Lich

One of the Dark Lord's Champions. Works directly under the Dark Lord. Creates Creatures of Power and carry's out the Dark Lord's orders. His Citadel was destroyed.

Cassie

Elf/Human Halfling

Holy warrior. Leader of the Golden Sabres. In a relationship with Josh Giles.

Dark Lord

God

Embodiment of the Dark affinity. Created Demons. Normally an ally with the Earth Lord. Always looking a way to tip the power balance of Emerilia in his favor.

Dasano

Dwarf

Dwarven Master Smith. Smithing Art: Metal Press. Lives in Grorart Mountain.

Akatol Dracul

Dragon

Water Mage. Was the second Dragon, Denur's husband. Went mad and started a genocide, disappeared.

Denur Dracul

Dragon

Fire Mage Hailed as 'Mother of Dragons'. First of her race, a creature of power created by the Lady of Fire. Seen as her daughter. Sister to Oson' Deia.

Gelimah Dracul

Dragon

Dark Mage. Brother to Induca, Louna and Malsour

Fornau Dracul

Dragon

Earth Mage. Quindar's mate Malsour and Induca's grand-nephew.

Induca Dracul

Dragon

Fire Mage. One of the youngest from the first generation of Dragons. Sister to Malsour, daughter of Denur, aunt to Quindar, great aunt to Fornau. Member of the Stone Raiders and Party Zero.

Kinal Dracul

Dragon

Louna Dracul

Dragon

Induca, Gelimah and Malsour's sister.

Malsour Dracul

Dragon

Dark Mage. One of the oldest Dragons in existence, first born of Denur. Deia and Induca's Guardian, Stone Raider and Party Zero member. Brother to Induca. Great Uncle to Fornau Dracul and Uncle to Quindar Dracul.

Quindar Dracul

Dragon

Wind Mage, wife to Fornau, Niece to Induca and Malsour.

Wokui Dracul

Dragon

Water Mage

Xednai Dracul

Dragon

One of the first Dragons, had several Dragons. Her son is Fornau.

Gorpal Dunsk

Dwarf

Dwarven Master Smith, lives in Aldamire Mountain, created 3 Weapons of Power - Mace of Fury, Tower Shield, Boots of Smash. Smithing Art: Paint Copy

Earth Lord

God

Embodiment of the Dark affinity. Created Earth Sprites.

Edmur

Dwarf

Dwarven Master Smith. Had been in the Dwarven War Bands as a Shield Bearer. Former pupil of Quino's Brother to Endur. Smithing Art: Metal's Song

Endur

Dwarf

Dwarven Master Smith. Had been in the Dwarven War Bands as a Shield Bearer. Former pupil of Quino's, brother to Edmur, lives in Zolu Mountain. Smithing Art Hammer Blows

Esa

Human

Melee fighter. Member of Mikal and Jule's party. Fought at Boranl-Al's Citadel.

Member of the Stone Raiders. Going out with Jules. Works under Dwayne as a fighter. Being trained for a leadership position under Dwayne.

Fend

Dwarf

Lord Under the Mithsia Mountains.

David Grahslagg

Dwarf/Human Halfling, in-game character of Austin Zane. Dwarven Master Smith, Resident of Cliff Hill, member of Party Zero and the Stone Raider's Guild. Other names: Austin Zane

Josh Giles

Human

Rogue. Leader of the Stone Raiders. Was a investment broker on Earth, became an E-head. In a relationship with Cassie from the Golden Sabres.

Gorrund

Dwarf

Dwarven Master Smith in Benvari Mountain with Jesal, teaching four apprentices. Smithing Art: Blood Bender.

Gurren

Dwarf

Shield bearer, member of Dwarven War Band under Lox's command, sent to guide people to Cliff-Hill. Friend of David Grahslagg, Kol's Grandson. Member of the Stone Raiders.

Helick

Dwarf

Dwarven Master Smith.

Kim Isdola

Human

Cleric/alchemist. Lieutenant in Stone Raiders.

Arch-Mage Jekoni

Human/item

Soul bound to Staff of Growing, over 2,000 years old; missing legs. Held within Dwarven Vaults with other Weapons of power.

Jesal

Dwarf

Dwarven Master Smith, Dave's master smith trainer. Smithing art: Nature's Guide

Jules

Human

Healer. Member of Mikal and Esa's party. Fought at Boranl-Al's Citadel.

Member of the Stone Raiders. Used to be an army medic, E-head without legs IRL. Going out with Esa. Works under Lucy as support, leads the healers of the Stone Raiders.

Joko

Dwarf

Shield bearer, member of Dwarven War Band under Lox's command, sent to guide people to Cliff-Hill. Friend and trainer of David Grahslagg.

Deceased.

Anna'Kal

Wolf Beast Kin/Administrator AI24681

Air mage. Originally a program meant to assist Lo'kal with the running of Emerilia. Anna was uploaded to a Player body and inserted into Emerilia. She became emotionally attached with her charges. When the Beast Kin people were wiped out from Emerilia she went into cold storage, waiting for her father to awake her when a chance came to fight against the prison they had created.

Member of the Stone Raiders and Party Zero. Daughter of Bob.

Lo'kal

Jukal

Scientist, created Emerilia. Awarded the position of the Gray God, maintains Emerilia, its people and Players. Other names: Bob, Bobby McMahnon, The Balancer, Gray God.

Kol

Dwarf

Dwarven Master Smith. Gurren's grandfather. Resides in Cliff-Hill. Taught Dave how to Smith. Runs his Smithies. Smithing art: Blind Man's Touch

Lady of Air

Goddess

Embodiment of the affinity Air. Known for causing mischief. Her Champions act as spies and information brokers, tilting the balance of Emerilia.

Lady of Fire

Goddess

Created Dragons, Mages Guild and College. Gave gift of 'knowledge' to the people of Emerilia. Mother to Deia, Lover of Oson'Mal and best friend with Bob.

Other Names: Ignil

Lady of Light

Goddess

Sent Players to kill/capture Dragons to make her own Creatures of Power. Created the race known as Angels. Large rivalry with the Dark Lord.

Lovan

Dwarf

Mithsia Mountain Warclan leader

Lox

Dwarf

Shield bearer. Was the commander of the War Band sent to guide people to Cliff-Hill. Friend of David Grahslagg. Member of the Stone Raiders.

Suzy Markell

Human (IRL)

High Elf (Emerilia)

Austin Zane's secretary and best friend. David Grahslagg's best friend and assistant with running Cliff Hill Smithy and Factory. Summoning Mage. Steven's contractor, member of Party Zero and the Stone Raiders.

Max

Dwarf

Shield bearer, member of Dwarven War Band under Lox's command, sent to guide people to Cliff-Hill. Friend of David Grahslagg.

Deceased.

Melhoun

Water snake made by the Water Lord.

Sealed away.

Mikal

Human

Rogue. Jules and Esa's party member. Member of the Stone Raiders. Friends with Party Zero.

Oson'Deia

Elf/Demi God Halfling

Elven Ranger and Fire Mage. Daughter of Oson'Mal and Lady Fire of the Affinity Pantheon. Resident of Cliff Hill and member of the Stone Raider's Guild, Leader of Party Zero.

Other names: Ouluv'Deia

Quino

Dwarf

Dwarven Master Smith, lives in Zolu Mountain. Trained the brothers Endur and Edmur. Smithing Art: Internal cutting.

Tounk

Dwarf

Shield bearer, member of Dwarven War Band under Lox's command, sent to guide people to Cliff-Hill. Friend of David Grahslagg.

Deceased.

Demon Prince Alkao/Alkao Travezar

Aerial Demon

Melee fighter. Commander of the Third Demon Horde and leader of Xerzit lands. Oldest of the five remaining Demon Prince's of Devil's Crater.

Dwayne Trebault

Human

Melee fighter. Lieutenant in Stone Raiders. Leads and trains the melee fighters in the Stone Raiders.

Lucy Vernia

Wood Elf/Human

Lieutenant in Stone Raiders. Spy master, deals with supporting the Stone Raiders and paperwork.

Water Lord

God

Embodiment of the Water Affinity. Created the Mer-People and water creatures. Created the Water Serpent Melhoun. Rival to the Lady of Fire.

Austin Zane

CEO of Rock Breaker's Corporation. Engineer specializing in space vehicles. Background in Astro physics. Other names: David Grahslagg

Wis'Zel

Wood Elf

Bard. Works for David Grahslagg, managing his Ceramics factories in Cliff Hill.

www.ingramcontent.com/pod-product-compliance
Lightning Source LLC
Chambersburg PA
CBHW070645310726
48982CB00001B/420